BINGE!

Other books by Richard Bryant-Jefferies

Counselling the Person Beyond the Alcohol Problem, Jessica Kingsley Publishers, London

The 'Living Therapy' series, published by Radcliffe Publishing:

Counselling for Problem Gambling
Counselling for Eating Disorders in Women
Counselling for Eating Disorders in Men
Counselling Young People
Relationship Counselling: Sons and their Mothers
Responding to a Serious Mental Health Problem
Counselling for Progressive Disability
Counselling a Recovering Drug User
Problem Drinking
Counselling a Survivor of Child Sexual Abuse
Counselling Victims of Warfare
Counselling for Obesity
Counselling Young Binge Drinkers
Counselling for Death and Dying
Time-limited Therapy in Primary Care
Person-centred Counselling Supervision
Workplace Counselling in the NHS

Also published by Radcliffe Publishing:

Models of Care for Drug Service Provision

A Little Book of Therapy, published by Pen Press Ltd, Brighton

BINGE!

Would therapy resolve what his alcohol use never could?

A Novel

Richard Bryant-Jefferies

iUniverse, Inc.
New York Lincoln Shanghai

Binge!
Would therapy resolve what his alcohol use never could?

Copyright © 2007 by Richard Bryant-Jefferies

All rights reserved. No part of this book may be used or reproduced by any means, graphic, electronic, or mechanical, including photocopying, recording, taping or by any information storage retrieval system without the written permission of the publisher except in the case of brief quotations embodied in critical articles and reviews.

iUniverse books may be ordered through booksellers or by contacting:

iUniverse
2021 Pine Lake Road, Suite 100
Lincoln, NE 68512
www.iuniverse.com
1-800-Authors (1-800-288-4677)

This is a work of fiction. All of the characters, names, incidents, organizations, and dialogue in this novel are either the products of the author's imagination or are used fictitiously.

ISBN: 978-0-595-44207-2 (pbk)
ISBN: 978-0-595-88538-1 (ebk)

Printed in the United States of America

And then the blood and ... oh god, the sight of her brain. He swallowed, his eyes clenched tight again, trying to drive the scene out of his head. But he couldn't. And he knew he had to talk, he had to say something. He couldn't keep it to himself any longer.

Chapter 1

'What the hell am I doing here?' This thought was very present for Andy as he sat watching the rain splattering on the windscreen. He shook his head, and then glanced over to the building on his right and read the sign above the door, blue lettering on a creamy coloured background: 'Therapy Centre'. He hadn't been here before, never noticed it. He'd made contact over the phone and had kind of expected something a little more, well, 'smarter' was the word in his mind. But there it was, an old, probably late Victorian house, three stories high in a suburban street. He looked at the wrought iron gate, which he noted to appear somewhat unhinged, and immediately wondered whether he was unhinged coming here. But there were lights on, he could see their glow through the curtains, and the light outside that illuminated the sign also lit up the bushes on either side of the path. They cast ominous-looking shadows.

This was another world for Andy. He had never done anything like this before, and, well, he wasn't really sure why he was doing it now, other than knowing that something didn't feel right for him. And, yes, it was all stereotypical—men talking about feeling—but the truth was that he didn't find it easy to talk about his feelings. Never had. Never really thought much about it. That was how he was, just how he was. He nodded to himself as he thought this. It had seemed OK to him. He'd got by. But now, well, now he felt different, on edge, finding it hard to contain his emotions on occasions.

His girlfriend, Julie, had 'persuaded' him that he should see a therapist. It was more of an ultimatum—do something or I leave. His first reaction had been a simple one, 'fuck off!', but he'd come round to realising that she was serious and actually she was important to him, the best thing in his life. So he had reluctantly agreed. He knew he was feeling more stressed, more uptight about things. Julie had had counselling herself in the past, at a time in her life when she just felt unable to cope. Through her counselling she realised that her difficulties linked back to her childhood, and in particular to her father's behaviour within the family. She had told him how counselling had helped her resolve her issues in relation to this. Andy wasn't totally convinced but he also knew there were aspects of his childhood that were difficult, things she didn't know about. Memories haunted him and when they really got to him the truth was that only alcohol brought him temporary relief. He knew that wasn't good. His drinking was also causing problems at home, and he needed to sort that out as well.

He thought about the guy he'd spoken to on the phone, Graham he had said his name was. His accent sounded as though he wasn't a Londoner. Though Andy had lived in Kent now for most of his life, it hadn't been where he was born. He'd originally come from the west of London, from Dagenham to be precise. But the family had moved when he was two. His father had lost his job, an incident at work. A fight with his boss. They'd moved to Dartford. Then he'd lived with his aunt and uncle in Luton before moving back south. Now he was near Sevenoaks, which was further south and in the Kent countryside. It was a nice area. The estate where he currently lived with his girlfriend was ex-council owned, now run by a housing association. It was handy for the motorways, and for getting down to Dover for booze-cruises over to France. He hadn't much of his own memory of Dagenham, but he went back now and then with his delivery work. He remembered much more about Dartford, but they were not good memories.

It was still raining and the clock on the dashboard was approaching half past six. Andy took a deep breath. Well, this was it. He'd give it a go, partly to please Julie, and partly to see what happened. Time to make his way in. He got out of the car and made his way up the path. He was already wet by the time he got to the door. 'Bloody weather,' he muttered under his breath as he pressed the bell. The door opened and he found himself looking at an older man. Andy thought he was probably in his early to mid fifties. He had short, greying hair and was clean shaven.

'Hi. I'm Andy, here for the counselling?' Andy could feel the hesitancy in his voice.

'Hi, yes, good to meet you. I'm Graham, we spoke on the phone, come on in. It's awful out there.'

Graham stepped back and Andy walked past him into the reception area. He felt awkward, not feeling too sure what to do or what to say. He was also surprised that Graham was shorter than he was. He didn't know why, just something he somehow hadn't expected. He wasn't particularly tall himself. He was grateful when Graham spoke again. 'Come on through, it's the room over here on the left we are using.' Graham lead the way, Andy followed.

'You found it OK?'

'Yes, no problem.' Andy looked around as he walked. It seemed to be quite well decorated on the inside, didn't really match how it looked from outside. The corridor was well lit, and it felt quite warm. Graham stopped by a white door and pushed it open. He stepped back and indicated for Andy to go through into the room. It seemed a pleasant enough room, two comfortable chairs arranged opposite each other, a table to one side. A dark blue curtain was drawn across the window behind the table. Andy noticed the box of tissues on the table and felt his jaw tighten. Well, he wasn't going to be using them, that was for sure. He turned to Graham who followed him into the room. 'Where do you want me to sit?'

Graham noticed the edge to Andy's voice. He didn't sound as though he was particularly enthusiastic about being there. 'Up to you,' was Graham's response. He preferred that his clients chose the seat. His initial impression of Andy was of a man in his late twenties, quite tall and broad across the shoulders. He was maybe a little overweight and wearing a short, black zipped jacket and light coloured jeans. To Graham, Andy looked quite tense and a bit pre-occupied, but that wasn't unusual. He knew that just the fact of coming to therapy could be quite stressful and anxiety-provoking, although generally this was additional to the anxiety that they were already experiencing in relation to something else in their lives. Graham's core model of counselling was person- or client-centred.[1] It was widely acknowledged within the approach that for constructive personality

---

1. Person-centred or client-centred therapy was founded by Carl Rogers. It is a way of working that emphasises certain relational factors as lying at the core of the therapeutic process. These have to be communicated to, and experienced by the client: genuineness or authenticity within the therapist, and their warm acceptance and empathy for the client. These were part of what have been termed as the 'necessary and sufficient conditions for constructive personality change' within the person-centred model of working. The main tenet of the approach lies in the recognition that many people who go to therapy do so as a result of difficulties linked to negative and conditional experiencing earlier (though not exclusively so) in their lives, in essence problematic relational experiences. By offering a relationship based on the therapeutic principles of the approach, the possibility is created for the client to explore themselves in an open and accepted climate, and to begin to genuinely confront incongruence within their self-concept and structure of self and start to redefine their sense of who they are and therefore what will best satisfy their needs as the person they are more fully and accurately realising themselves to be. The result is greater congruence and authenticity within the client and greater capacity for positive self-regard.

change to occur, the phrase used within the theory, the client would be helped to move from a state of anxiety and incongruence to a more congruent and authentic sense of self and way of being. For Graham, this lay at the core of therapy, helping people to find greater authenticity in themselves and in their lives, but what form this would take would vary from person-to-person. There were no set goals. The challenge and the discipline of the approach was in the establishing of a relational climate through which therapeutic process could occur.

Andy sat down on the chair nearest to where he was standing, which was also nearest to the door. Somehow that felt more comfortable to him. Graham walked over to the other chair. Andy was feeling strangely anxious. He was still looking around the room. His heart was pounding in his chest and he had a sort of tickly feeling in the pit of his stomach. But he wasn't going to show any of that. He met new people every day, and he felt he could get on with anyone, but this was different.

Graham began by checking Andy was OK with the confidentiality and length of sessions that they'd discussed on the phone. He seemed to Andy to be quite confident and matter-of-fact about what he was saying. In one way that felt reassuring, in another it made him more aware of his own anxiety.

He nodded in response to what Graham had been saying.

Graham accepted Andy's head movement as an indication of being OK with what they'd discussed. 'My approach to counselling is to let you take the lead. It is very much your time to talk about whatever you want. I see my role as being here to listen and to help you make sense of things, and help you to find a way forward that is right for you. I'm not the expert on your life, you are. So, where would you like to start?' Graham wanted to ensure that Andy was offered open space to say whatever he wanted, at his own pace and in his own way.

Andy was looking down at his feet, at a loss as to what to say or where to begin. He took a deep breath. He had a lot on his mind but there were things he didn't want to talk about, not here, not to a stranger. There were things he didn't talk to anyone about, not even to his girlfriend whom he had been living with now for a couple of years. There were memories from his past that would go round and round in his head, and which would also invade his dreams. They would also invade his daytime thoughts. Shouts, shrieks, thuds, feeling himself cowering, scared. Seeing his mother's bruises, and her having to wear dark glasses to hide her black eyes. Sometimes the images were indistinct, at other times crystal clear, like it was real, so real. But he didn't say anything. He didn't want to. It was family stuff. He didn't want to talk about it. He wanted Julie off his back and, yeah, he wanted some way of feeling less uptight all the time, but he didn't see that his past was to do with any of that. Just got to him sometimes. But it was the past. You got on with it. That's how he lived his life.

Graham knew just how difficult it could be for clients to speak, particularly men who felt awkward in talking about feelings or difficulties. He knew himself how difficult it was to admit to yourself, let alone someone else, that you were struggling with something, or feeling that some aspect of your life—or yourself—was out of control. He sat quietly and waited. He wasn't going to let the silence go on for ever, he knew that this could be oppressive. He wanted to form a therapeutic relationship with Andy but he also knew from experience that this process couldn't, and shouldn't, be forced. He sought to maintain his openness to his own experiencing as he sat with his attention on Andy.

Andy continued to sit, staring at his feet. No, he needed to say something. He looked up. 'It's like I said on the phone, I just feel so damned irritable these days. I don't know why, but I'm on edge, short tempered, waiting to explode.' He shook his head, tightening his lips as he did so, 'things get to me, you know? Didn't used to, but now they do'.

Graham nodded. He checked out that he was hearing Andy correctly, and that his understanding of what Andy was saying matched what Andy was seeking to convey. Empathy was such a vital component of effective therapy. 'Irritable, on edge, waiting to explode, not sure why, but things are getting to you in ways that they didn't in the past, yeah?'

Andy could feel the presence of that edginess within himself. He tightened his jaw. Thoughts were in his head. 'Like, I was in the pub the other day and this guy bumped into me when I was carrying my beer back to my seat. Yeah, OK, it was busy, and I'm sure in the past I'd have just let it go, accepted his apology and, you know, moved on. But no, I could feel myself flare up. Had to call him a dozy bastard, didn't I.' Andy shook his head. 'I really felt like I could have laid one on him, you know, but I didn't. He moved away, fortunately, and I went back to my seat. I was so pissed off? Fucking idiot. It really did take a while for me to settle down.' He shook his head. Just talking about it brought the feelings back. He thought about what had happened next, how he'd been calmed down by his girlfriend. 'Julie, my girlfriend, she helped, she's really good like that.' Andy snorted. 'Probably a good thing she was there.'

'If she hadn't been there …' Graham empathised with what Andy had just said, whilst inviting him to say more.

'I don't know.' Andy shrugged. 'I really don't know. And that's not like me, I mean, I'm usually much more laid back about things, but recently', Andy was shaking his head again, 'I just feel like I want to explode, you know, really, I don't know …'.

'Explode. Lash out?'

Andy could feel his fists clenching, and Graham had noticed his whitening knuckles. Graham responded to the body language, 'feeling it now?'.

Andy was momentarily lost in his own thoughts. He was back in the pub, thinking about that bastard who'd knocked into him. Hearing Graham's voice brought him back to the present. He could feel his fingers digging into his palms. He opened his hands. They felt tight. 'Yeah, back in the pub again.'

'Really gets into your body too, yeah.' Graham sought to empathise with the tension that was clearly visible as Andy sought to flex his hands to relax them.

'I just think about it and, yeah, there it is again. Winds me up.' He paused. 'I'm not like that, at least, I didn't used to be, but now, I don't know, it doesn't seem to take much these days.'

Graham was wondering how much it might be linked to Andy's drinking. Andy had mentioned this on the phone the previous week, and was one of the reasons he had said that he wanted counselling. Not easy for everyone to talk about and clearly Andy wasn't yet ready to make reference to it specifically today. That was OK. He didn't know how much Andy was consuming. He knew that whilst alcohol could relax you, and if you were a heavy, dependent drinker then when the alcohol was metabolised it could leave you feeling on edge, a bit more reactive to things. He set his thoughts aside and responded to what Andy had just said.

'Doesn't take much, yeah?'

Andy went silent for a moment, thinking about how tense he could feel sometimes. Afternoons could be a tense time, sometimes earlier as well. He could really feel on edge. By late afternoon he was more aware of it. In fact, the reality was, anytime up to that first pint or can of an evening could feel tense. Then he felt better. A beer made him feel more at ease, more relaxed, took the edge away, made him feel good. Yeah, that first one was always the best, and it did go down fast. He was smiling to himself as he thought about it.

Graham noticed the smile. He commented on it. 'Makes you smile?'

'Huh? Yeah. I was thinking about that first pint in the evenings, always tastes so good, makes me feel good too. Doesn't touch the sides but it hits the right spot?' Andy was still smiling.

'Good feeling?'

Andy nodded. 'Always did like my first pint. Used to take a bit more time over it. Not any more.'

Graham smiled back, yet his thoughts were that Andy was drinking very heavily, probably this was contributing to why that first one felt so good.

'So, you don't take so much time over it now.'

Andy appreciated Graham's smile, it sort of made him feel a little more relaxed. He felt as though Graham understood what he was talking about. Andy was still smiling, and now feeling thirsty as well. He shook his head, 'well, you don't, do you? Get it down and get the next one in.'

'Sounds like you're a fast drinker, Andy, I guess you get through a few pints in a session?' Graham sought to clarify the amount. He knew he was asking a direct question, but he wanted clarification, and the interaction felt easy at this point, almost conversational.

'Yeah, guess so, nine or ten most nights.' Andy felt good about what he drank. He could hold it, never got drunk. Well, got a bit rowdy sometimes, but that's what happens. He wasn't drunk, always in control.

'OK.' Graham didn't repeat back the quantity, he didn't want to labour the point, but he was aware that it was quite a lot, certainly a risk to health. Clearly Andy was oblivious of it, or so it seemed.

Andy wasn't sure what to say next. 'So, yeah.' He paused. 'Not sure what to say now.'

Graham nodded his head slowly, and waited.

Andy wondered just how helpful this all was. He wasn't particularly motivated for being there and it didn't seem to be going anywhere. 'This counselling business, I mean, it does help, doesn't it?'

'I believe so, but then I would say that, wouldn't I?' Graham smiled.

Andy smiled back. 'Guess so. But, I mean, well, Julie thought it would be helpful to talk about things, and, well, I don't know what to talk about.' Or even if I want to, were the words that were forming in Andy's head.

'Seems to me you have already been talking about things.' Graham knew that it wasn't necessarily what you talked about, but often the fact that you felt listened to and respected that was most important. He knew that so many people in their lives didn't really feel listened to. Conversations were often more of a competition, each person waiting their turn to get their comment in. Graham thought about how society these days seemed to place emphasis more and more on talking, and so little on listening.

'I guess so. Hmm.' Andy paused, even though he wasn't feeling it now, his thoughts went back to how he could feel ready to explode, of feeling so edgy so much of the time, not being able to feel as relaxed as he had been chatting a few minutes before. 'But I do want to sort out this edginess, you know?' He was clear that he wanted that sorted. He didn't like it.

'Yeah, that edgy feeling, it's a problem you want sorted.'

'It is. I mean ...', Andy shook his head. He didn't understand why he felt the way that he did. He enjoyed his work, that wasn't a problem. His work as a delivery driver brought him a certain amount of freedom and he loved driving and meeting with people. He'd been doing it for a few years now. But he knew that he got edgy and irritable as the day wore on, and he hadn't always felt that way.

Graham had not responded. He could see that Andy was thinking and he did not want to disturb his train of thought. He sat and waited, but maintained his attention and focus on Andy.

Andy was thinking about his past, about his childhood. Often particular events would come to mind, and then they'd go, and often he'd lose track of what he had been thinking about.

The silence continued for some while. Graham decided to comment, 'you look deep in thought, Andy?'

'Hmm? Oh, yes.' He'd drifted away from thinking about work, but now had lost touch with what it was he'd been thinking about. That was a bit weird. He must have been thinking about something. He frowned and tried to remember what, but it had faded, gone, he couldn't connect with it.

'You're frowning.'

'Yeah. That was odd. I was thinking about work, and then, I don't know, I must have been thinking about something, but it's gone. Can't recall it. Weird.' He felt puzzled. He knew he didn't have the best short-term memory in the world. The times he'd gone into a room to get something only to realise he couldn't remember what it was. It was something that had developed more recently. He put it down to getting older.

'You were thinking about something, and it seemed quite intense to me, you seemed really lost in whatever you were thinking about, and then', Graham shrugged his shoulders slightly, 'then it was gone.'

'Yeah, like I really was thinking about something but when you commented it was like I sort of jumped out of it in some weird kind of way.'

'Uh-hu.' Graham waited to see if Andy would explore it further, or reconnect with it. He didn't want to push or pressure him. He knew that in these situations memories were more likely to surface when the person relaxed a little. He had speculated for some while on how tension seemed to impair memory for some people, as though in stressful situations they are so overloaded by thoughts, feelings, anxieties, whatever is going on for them that they have no more memory capacity. He knew that in reality that wasn't the way it was, but it somehow seemed like that.

'I don't know.' Andy paused, 'Anyway, what I was thinking about previously was how I enjoy my job, but I get irritable towards the end of the day. Traffic jams and delays at the end of deliveries really wind me up, I mean, really get to me, you know? Sitting there, going nowhere, bloody frustrating.'

'Winds you up bad, yeah?'

Andy could feel himself tighten at the thought of it. 'Pity I can't just work in the mornings!'

'That would be a solution?'

'Be nice, but the money, you know. I mean, people like postmen, they start and finish early. That would suit me.'

'Has a certain appeal, yeah.'

'Be able to get down the pub earlier!'

'Early start in more ways than one.' Graham kept his response quite matter of fact.

'Yeah, that really does appeal, you know? Maybe …' He thought about it, but he also knew he enjoyed his job. Couldn't see himself on a pushbike. But then, not everyone delivered post on a bike. Hmm. Maybe.

'Has a certain attraction.' Graham was aware of feeling a wry smile wanting to break out on his face as he was aware of what effect it might have on Andy's drinking, which was already at a level that would mean he would very likely be over the drink-driving limit when he left for work in the mornings. Though it was in his mind, he was in two minds as to whether to introduce it into the dialogue. He wasn't there to tell Andy what to do, or to appear judgemental in any way. He was there to offer a therapeutic relationship in which Andy could explore himself more fully, enable him to be more in touch with himself, more realistic. Yet his thoughts were very much to the fore and he was aware they were making it difficult for him to focus on Andy. He knew that voicing troubling thoughts like this was sometimes the best way to clear them. He also knew the value of trusting this kind of inner prompting.

Andy had been thinking about the attraction of finding an early morning job. But he also knew that Julie wouldn't approve. She'd pick up pretty soon that it was giving him opportunity to start drinking sooner. She was pretty sharp. She'd be sure to have a few words about it. And whilst part of him wanted to say 'fuck her', the truth was that he really liked her, and didn't really want to make problems. He liked his job, being a bit of his own boss during the day. Yes, he had places to go, deadlines to meet, but the open road felt good. So it wasn't the most glamorous job in the world, but it had advantages. He liked being in his own space, having a laugh with the people he met, in a way feeling free to just be himself. He always got cups of tea when he wanted them at his more regular stops. He knew shortcuts to save him time, and give him the chance to stop for a while and read the paper. But if he could start and finish earlier, maybe that might be the answer ... except that the deliveries he made tended to be to offices and people tended only to be there to sign for their packages after 8am, and many of them it was only after 9am.

Graham was aware that his thoughts about drink-driving were becoming more present and he could feel that they were going to be a distraction to his being able to listen and be openly available to Andy. Yes, he could try and push the thoughts aside and take it to his own supervision (Graham met up with a supervisor to review his work twice a month), but that didn't feel right. He knew what he knew and it felt more respectful to Andy to tell him so he could be aware of the possible risk, rather than say nothing. Saying nothing did not feel right. 'Andy, there's something on my mind, and I want to say it because it is a concern I have. Are you aware that because of the amount you are drinking in the evening, and the time it takes for it to be metabolised in your body, it is quite likely leaving you at risk of being over the drink-driving limit in the mornings?'

Andy was taken aback. 'You're kidding me?'

'No, I'm not. And I guess by your reaction you hadn't thought about it.'

'I sleep well, get up, feel a bit worse for wear sometimes, but I feel good, ready for the day, you know?'

'Yeah, I do, and I know that the amount you are drinking is likely to take you over the limit.'

Andy frowned. He moved in the chair, feeling a little uncomfortable at what he was hearing. 'How can that be?'

Graham was aware that the focus was now on him and the information he had, and not on Andy and what he was experiencing. But he had raised the issue and clearly Andy wanted to know more. So he wasn't going to avoid a direct response to his question.

'Well, there are about two units of alcohol in a pint, unless it is a really strong beer or lager. So, nine to ten pints is around eighteen to twenty units. And it takes the body one hour to metabolise a unit of alcohol. So you're taking on board at least eighteen and maybe twenty hours worth of alcohol in the evening.' Graham decided not to continue, not to start talking about start times and how many units he'd then have in his body next morning. Rather, let Andy work that out for himself.

Andy was thinking. He started drinking around eight o'clock, sometimes a little earlier, depending on how soon he got in and they had their meal before heading out. He never ate too much, found it got in the way of his drinking. Eighteen units, eighteen hours. He left for work around seven o'clock, Seven units left. What did that mean? Ok, so he still had a bit of alcohol in his system, so what. He felt good, he could drive, what was the problem?

'OK, so I've a few units in me when I set off for work.'

'Equivalent to about three and a half pints in terms of alcohol content. And the risk is that just a few units can put you over the limit, though you would probably already be over anyway.'

'What do you mean?'

'Hard to be sure, depends on each person, how big they are and therefore how diluted or concentrated the alcohol is in the blood stream. But anything over four to five units and you're probably at risk.' Graham was looking at Andy thinking that he was quite big which would mean the alcohol would be more diluted in his blood stream. He never liked to be pinned down on how many units would take you over the limit, it depended on so much. And he knew as well that his two units per pint was a generalisation, some beers were stronger. He had worked in an agency in the past offering counselling to people with alcohol and drug problems in the past.

'I'd never thought. Are you sure?'

Graham was nodding. 'Well that's how it was explained to me.'

'I'm not the only one drinking like that in the pub. We all walk back home, most of us live close by. I don't think any of us give much thought to the next morning.' He shook his head. 'Shit!! You sure?'

Graham nodded. He didn't feel a need to add anything further.

Andy was taken aback. He just hadn't thought about it. He assumed you slept it off. He always felt OK in the mornings. He never felt brilliant, and even if that was the effect of the night before, he didn't think he was still affected by having alcohol in his blood. Well, he'd never thought about it and he was sure most of the people he drank with hadn't either, and probably most people too.

'Makes you think. And with licensing hours getting extended. How many people will then be over the limit the next day?' Andy asked the question with a sense of oh shit, how many other characters are on the road in the morning and in effect drink-driving.

'Precisely. Lots of people.'

'Shit, and you're sure about that?'

Graham nodded again.

Andy was aware of how important his job was to him. 'I need to cut back, don't I? Leave the heavier drinking to the weekends. I can't risk my license.'

'Reduce the risk by only drinking heavily at weekends.' Graham avoided saying yes, he didn't want to direct Andy to a particular course of action, rather he wanted to convey his empathic appreciation of what Andy was saying that he wanted to do about it.

'I've always taken pride in the fact that I don't drink and drive, but it sounds like I do, that I have been. Shit!' Andy was suddenly feeling very anxious, and a bit angry as well. It was going to mess up his evenings, and they were important to him. Could he get away with it? He always had? He obviously drove well, no-one had stopped him. But then, he only needed to be stopped once and then, shit. But he hadn't been.

'That's important to you, and it must feel difficult realising that maybe you do drink and drive.'

'Are you really sure, I mean, you know, we all drink that amount. I mean, no-one every worries about it.'

'I am sure, but if you want to contact a local alcohol counselling service, or call Alcohol Concern[2] in London, they have all the information about the effects of alcohol.'

Andy was shaking his head, it really had come as a shock. And he wanted to do something about it, and he didn't as well. He didn't want to have to change. He'd feel weird, his mates wouldn't understand. Or would they? He thought of Mick, the landlord, he wouldn't be best pleased if he started telling people to cut down.

Graham waited, aware that Andy was processing the new information and clearly wrestling with what to do about it. Whatever choice he made was up to him. It wasn't his, Graham's, responsibility. He would help Andy explore his options, and help him formulate whatever way of dealing with it that he chose, but the decision was Andy's. He waited.

Andy shifted in the chair. He realised his back had got stiff. It seemed stiffer these days. He stretched his shoulders back which felt good, and found himself unable to contain an urge to yawn. 'Oh. Got a bit stiff. How are we doing for time?'

Graham glanced at the clock and confirmed that there were fifteen minutes or so left.

---

2. Alcohol Concern, Waterbridge House, 32-36 Loman Street, London SE1 0EE www.alcoholconcern.org.uk

'I need to think about this. I mean, part of me wishes I hadn't come, you know, and another part of me knows that I should be grateful, that it could help me avoid a whole load of trouble.'

'Yeah, that's how it can be when you get information that's disturbing or challenging in some way. Partly grateful, partly not wishing you had been given it.'

'No, I am grateful. But I need to go and think about this, talk to Julie. I just hadn't thought. And you are sure?'

'I am, but please check it out if you wish.'

'Hmm. OK.' Andy was scratching his head. 'But I haven't got a problem, though, have I?'

Graham was struck by the sudden change of focus. Andy hadn't talked in terms of his drinking being a problem up until now. He was particularly aware of Andy's tone of voice. He clearly wanted reassurance that he didn't have a problem.

'That sounds like a really important question, yeah? Guess it would make a big difference to the way you see it if it was.'

Andy noted that Graham hadn't answered his question. 'You think I have, don't you?'

'Well, if you were to put me on the spot, I'd have to say that you're drinking an unhealthy amount, and that is has the potential of causing problems even if you may not be experiencing it like that at the moment.'

Andy didn't want to hear that. His drinking was OK. It didn't cause him problems, just liked a few beers with his mates, that was all. And yet ... There was something rather unsettling about all of this. He didn't want his drinking to be a problem. He knew how bad it could get. His thoughts were with his brother, Terry, who he knew did have a problem but didn't want to change. He rationalised that as it didn't feel like a problem it shouldn't be too difficult to cut back. That would prove it wasn't a problem. He didn't say this. He was also aware of the risk to his licence. What he did say was, 'I'll cut back a bit in the week, you know, I mean, I just hadn't realised how long it could be in the system. Shit. So 9 pints in the evening, starting around six o'clock, could leave me with, what ...' Andy wasn't sure what the amount left in his body would be.

'Well, nine pints of ordinary strength beer, you know, middle of the range stuff, be about two units a pints, so that's eighteen units, and therefore eighteen hours worth. So, eight o'clock and you've got four units in your body and you'll be over the limit, I reckon.'

Andy was aware that he sometimes was on the road before eight, often seven and sometimes six o'clock, taking driving to work into account. 'What if I eat something, you know, that'll help?'

When, in the morning or the evening?'

'Well, either?'

Graham shook his head. 'In the evening food in the stomach could slow down the absorption leaving you with more alcohol still in the system next morning. And food in the stomach next morning, that won't have much effect.'

'OK.' He blew out a breath. 'OK, I'll ease up a bit. My mates are gonna be surprised as well. And the landlord won't be too happy. But I need my licence, I can't take that risk. I never thought … I mean, no one ever talks about it like this. They all focus on the behaviour of some yobs in the evening, but not the amount of alcohol still in you the next day.'

The session continued, with a further exploration of Andy's reaction to this information and a bit more background information about himself and what his job was like. Eventually, the session drew to a close, but not before they discussed continuing with the counselling. Andy said 'yes', he was up for it. It had already given him something to think about, which wasn't what he had expected. He told Graham that whilst he was taken aback by what had been said, it had felt good chatting.

Andy left with the session on his mind. He was planning to head down to the pub, but he hesitated as he sat in the car. He wondered about giving Julie a call. He didn't need to make the decision, his mobile went off. She was calling him.

'So, what happened?'

'Shit, Julie, I've just been told I'm probably drink-driving in the mornings.'

'Really.' Somehow she wasn't surprised. She hadn't thought of it like that but she was very aware of just how much Andy drank. 'So it was useful.' She felt glad he'd been talking to someone.

'Yeah, but not what I expected. Not sure what I expected really. Anyway, yeah, he seems to think that it stays in the body for quite a while.'

'Yeah? You'd better take it easy then.' What about you being irritable all the time?'

Andy could feel himself reacting. 'Not all the time.'

'Well, whatever.'

'What's that supposed to mean?' Andy could feel himself reacting now. He didn't need this. He'd felt good during that counselling session. OK, so it had been a bit of a shock, but he could handle it. But he didn't need this kind of grief.

'Fuck's sake, I've been, I've talked, are you never going to be satisfied?' He muttered 'fuck's sake', under his breath.

'Look, let's leave it.' Julie didn't need Andy giving her grief either, but this was how he could be. Didn't take much and he was reacting angrily. 'Fancy going out for a curry? I've only been back home for a few minutes and haven't started cooking anything. I haven't eaten and I'm starving.'

Andy liked the idea of a curry but he could still feel himself tight inside, that familiar feeling of wanting to explode. 'Yeah, OK.' He wasn't sure whether it was really what he wanted, but he'd get a pint at the restaurant whilst they waited for the take-away. He liked that idea. 'Yeah, OK, pick you up in ten minutes or so.'.'

Andy pulled away. He felt pissed off. Not only with Julie, but now with Graham as well. He was back to thinking of what Graham had told him. He believed him although there was a nagging voice in his head questioning it. It wasn't something he wanted to know, and yet he did as well. It stayed in his mind as he headed home to pick up Julie.

* * * *

Andy was sitting in The Crown a couple of days later—his usual pub. He'd been going down there now for more years than he cared to remember. But it was a good laugh. Yes, there was Donna the barmaid, of course, and she was always good for a joke. But he had a number of drinking mates there as well, Gary, Alan, Steve, Matt. Gary and Alan were married—to Amanda and Trisha respectively. Steve was divorced and, well, had a string of girlfriends nowadays—the latest was Lorna. Gary's parents were Australian and he had a bit of an accent himself. Matt was gay. He'd been a friend for a long time. They'd been to school together and although it had been difficult at first when he 'came out', they'd accepted it and now it wasn't a problem. Matt wasn't in as much as the others, he tended to spend most of his time in the gay scene, but he'd drop in sometimes on his way out, or spend the evening with them.

It was a good pub. A bit old-fashioned in some ways. Lots of horse brasses and tankards hanging up. Not the modern city-centre pub you tended to get more of these days, or the kind of pub that had tried to turn itself into a restaurant, and lost all its atmosphere. Yes, they did food, but he didn't think of it so much as a place to eat, though they did do occasionally. It was a place to drink, have a few laughs. And a pub where you could sit down as well. So many new pubs wanted to keep you standing. He didn't want that. And you could sit at the bar as well, and that wasn't always the case in some of the more crowded ones. Funny really, in many ways he felt more at home in the pub than he did at home. It had been that way for a while. He'd had a friend at school whose parents ran a pub and he'd spent a lot of time there as a child. Just got used to the noise, the smell, the banter, and, yeah, he'd started to drink as well. Easy really in a pub. No one seemed to notice, or seemed to care. Really got a taste for it.

He was leaning against the bar. Alan and Steve were in, and Steve had his new girlfriend with him—Lorna.

'So, what's new then, Andy?'

'Not a lot. Same old strife, you know?'

'Yeah well. Work OK?'

'Yeah, the usual.'

'Wish I had your job. Out and about. On the road. You van drivers, bet you're always picking up hitchhikers, always got something on the go.'

'Oh yeah? In your dreams, mate. Nah. I've got deadlines. Not much chance for that. Anyway, I'm settled these days, you know. Julie and me, we get on really well. I'm settling down.' Andy knew they had problems, but they were also good together as well. But he wished it was a little easier with her at times.

Steve was smirking. 'Not worth it, mate. Glad I got away from it. Having me a really good time now.' He put his arm round Lorna and gave her a squeeze.

'Yeah, well, glad you two are happy. Me, I'm fine.'

The jukebox fired up in the corner. 'Blimey, that takes me back a few years. I was still at primary school when that was around. Remember my …' Andy went silent as an all too familiar and vivid memory came back to him. He reached over and took a few large gulps of beer. His friends didn't know about his childhood. He wasn't going to start saying anything now.

'What was that?' It was Alan that asked.

'Nothing, just thought I remembered that song, but maybe I'm mistaken.'

Alan didn't think any more of it, too busy reaching for his own glass. 'So, Julie coming down tonight?'

'No, she's working late. Promised I'd get a take-away on my way back. So better not forget that or I'll be in deep shit.'

'Yeah, and you won't get any tonight!'

'Oh yeah …' Andy drained the rest of his pint. He was often the first to finish a round. 'Come on you lot. You're so slow. Get it down you, I'm thirsty.'

They drank up and Andy collected the glasses and headed for the bar.

'He doesn't mess around, does he?' It was only the second time that Lorna had met Andy.

'He's always been a fast drinker, that one. We just do our best to keep up!'

They chatted about the local football team—they all agreed that they were crap, that they should sell the whole team and start again. It was a few minutes before Andy reappeared with the drinks. He put them down. His was already half empty.

'Well,' Andy announced, 'I'm cutting back on the booze a bit, but not tonight.'

Alan and Steve looked at him, not really taking what he had said with any seriousness. 'Oh yeah, since when ...?'

'No seriously, been to see a counsellor and he reckons I'm drinking enough to be over the limit sometimes.'

'Well, yeah, for sure, we all are when we go home, that's why we walk. So what's the problem?'

'The next morning.'

'Bullshit. You sleep it off.' It was Steve who was speaking. He didn't know what Andy was talking about. Sounded like a load of crap to him. 'Over the limit the next morning? Get a good nights sleep. You're fine. You drive OK, don't you?'

'Yeah, course I do.' Andy could feel himself getting a bit uncomfortable and he now wished he'd never mentioned it.

'Well then. Probably someone who never drinks and wants to ruin everyone's fun. Bloody counsellors. What the fuck do they know about anything. They're too bloody good at interfering, telling you what to do. He paused, 'but then they have their uses. My ex went to one. Bloody good job, I reckon. Caused us to break up. She started to want "something different from our relationship", or that's how she described it. I told her, if you don't like it, well you know what you can do. Fuck me, she did. Walked out. Just like that. Never came back. Probably still seeing her therapist. Hah! Did me a good turn, anyway.' Steve was raising his glass as he finished speaking.

'I don't know.' It was Lorna's turn. 'My sister had counselling. She was attacked on the way home and she saw someone for a long while. It really helped. I don't think you're being fair, Steve, I think they can help you, particularly if you haven't got anyone to talk to.'

'So why didn't she talk to you?'

'Don't know. We did talk, but I don't know, we were never that close I guess. She was depressed and anxious. Her GP sent her off to see the counsellor they had at the surgery. Saw her for a few months as I remember. Seemed to help. She used to keep thinking about what happened to her, kind of reliving it in her head, and it really got her down. She'd stopped going out, always afraid of what would happen. Now she says she doesn't really think about it at all. She's out and about, but she doesn't take risks. I think she's always aware of not taking risks now, I guess that's not surprising. But she's got herself together. No, I reckon you're being unfair. I reckon counselling can be good.'

Steve wasn't really listening. He was momentarily feeling a kind of sadness towards his broken marriage. Yeah, he talked a lot about how the break up had been the best thing that had happened to him, but there were still times when he missed Carrie, missed her a lot … He reached for his glass.

'Well, I'm giving it a go. And I'm going to try and cut back, but don't tell Mick, he'll ban me!!' Andy was looking over at the landlord, Mick, who was wiping down the top of the bar with his usual air of detachment. He never seemed rushed, just took it all in his stride. Now he was picking up some of the empty glasses. He moved in a way that suggested he'd been doing it all of his life. Truth was, he probably had.

'You won't do it. And anyway, you drink the same as us and we haven't got a problem with it, have we, Steve?' Alan looked over to Steve who was taking a deep draught, though still lost in his own thoughts. 'Steve?'

'Huh? What was that?'

'OK, well, maybe I haven't got a problem with it but it looks like you're well away, mate?'

Steve momentarily felt a flash of anger, but it passed as soon as it had appeared. 'What were you saying, you sad bastard?'

'About having a drink problem. I was saying, we're OK, so why's Andy suddenly think he's got a problem?'

Steve shrugged and he looked across at Andy who was sitting still feeling uncomfortable.

'It's not a problem, I just want to, you know …' Andy shrugged as well, 'anyway, can't we talk about something else?'

Steve had meanwhile drained his glass. He still felt sad, but the alcohol helped. 'It's my shout, same again?' Glasses were drained and Steve headed off for the bar. By the time he returned the conversation had moved on. He looked at Andy. He didn't have a problem, none of them did. Just enjoyed a few beers and get a bit pissed sometimes. He felt sure Andy would see sense. Yeah. He pushed the thought away.

The conversation didn't return to Andy's drinking, which Andy was grateful for. He felt somehow unsettled that they hadn't been a bit more supportive. It hadn't been easy saying something to them. It felt sort of strange how they'd reacted. They were his mates, he thought they'd understand, take him seriously. He now wished he hadn't said anything.

Chapter 2

Andy was sitting in the counselling room the following week. Graham was sitting opposite him and had just asked how he wanted to use the time that they had. Andy was aware of not being sure, but he did know he'd had a weird old week. He wasn't too sure what to make of it, and he was aware that it felt uncomfortable thinking about talking about it. In fact, he didn't want to. The truth was he hadn't been completely honest about how much he was drinking. Yes, he'd talked about the pints in the pub, but he generally had a scotch when he got back home, and sometimes more than one.

'Don't know, really. Been a typical week. Work's been OK some days and shit others. Those damned road works out on the ring road. Nightmare. I've been stuck in the queues so many times this week.'

Graham knew his empathy was tinged with sympathy, they'd caught him a couple of times too. 'Yeah, been a pain.' He paused. 'So, generally a typical week, up and down, OK and shit.'

'Yeah.' Andy sat in silence. He'd decided he wasn't going to bring up his drinking. Decided he'd talk about something else, about feeling uptight, what he'd really come about before they'd got sidetracked last time. 'Still getting uptight, you know?'

'Uh-hu.' Graham held his attention on Andy. It wasn't a surprise. No reason why anything should have changed. He was curious as to whether the conversation the previous week might have affected Andy's drinking, but he wasn't going to direct him towards that topic. If it was an issue for Andy, he felt sure he'd raise it.

'It's not just in the evenings. I mean, there are some arseholes about, you know? During the day as well I can feel, I don't know, kind of tense, yeah? And, I mean, that bloody traffic. One day, I don't know, when was it? Tuesday maybe, anyway, the traffic lights had failed, there was a guy with one of those stop-go swing things, you know?'

Graham nodded, he knew what Andy meant.

'Well, there I was, line of traffic, and he bloody well goes and changes it and the guy in front of me goes and hits his brakes. We could have got through, I was all ready to accelerate and the brake lights come on in front. Shit, I thought, and hit the brakes. Skidded but stopped in time. I was fucking furious. I got out the van and went over to the car and banged on the roof, and told him what I thought of his bloody driving. He just stared ahead and ignored me. I said a few more things before going back to my van—by now traffic was coming the other way. I sat there absolutely fired up. Never done that before.'

'Never got out in a situation like that?'

'And never felt like I did. I mean, I'd lost it, you know? I really had. If he'd opened the door, got out or something, I might have swung at him. I don't know. It didn't happen. But shit, I was close to it.' Andy was shaking his head.

'You look like you find your reaction hard to accept?' Graham sought to empathise with the experience that was present for him as he watched Andy sitting in front of him.

Andy blew out a breath. 'Maybe it was a bad week, maybe it was one time too many in the traffic, but I really did get out and have a go, and, yeah, I know I can blow, but I really did that time.' He continued to shake his head. 'I lost it, I was that close …' Andy's voice trailed off. He could feel the anger present inside him again and his jaw was set firm.

Graham had noticed this too. He responded to it. 'Yeah, I can see the anger's still with you, Andy, still with you.'

Andy looked up at the ceiling. 'Stupid bastard.' He was still feeling tense, like it was all happening again. Well, the man was an idiot so, yeah, why shouldn't he still feel like smacking him one?

Graham nodded. 'Really got to you, and still gets to you. Lots of anger, yeah?'

Andy was shaking his head. 'I don't usually react, but, well, more recently I guess I've been a bit more on edge, you know?'

'When you're driving?' Graham wasn't totally sure that Andy was only referring to when he was at the wheel. He suspected that maybe what Andy was feeling was a short fuse associated with alcohol withdrawal on some days, particularly if he hadn't drunk as much the night before, or maybe he regularly felt this way now during the day when the alcohol was washing out of his system.

'Yeah, sometimes.' Andy shrugged. He suddenly felt a bit uncomfortable, though he didn't know why. 'But I settle down again, you know?'

'Yeah, you have ways of settling back down when you're feeling like that?'

Andy nodded, yes, he thought, have a beer or two. Always feel better then. But he didn't say it. He didn't want to. He knew he'd talked about his drinking the previous week and it had surprised him about how long alcohol affected you. He had been trying to cut back but without much success, and he had convinced himself that Graham had got it wrong, that he was OK really. So he didn't want to get back into talking about his drinking. No, he thought, I'm OK. Deep inside himself there was a doubt about this, but Andy was learning to push that away and keep a lid on it.

'Yeah, I'm OK.'

'OK. That's great. You get wound up by things, particularly when you're driving, but you can handle it, you can wind yourself back down again.' Whilst Graham, was seeking to communicate his empathic appreciation of what Andy had been telling him, he also knew that he was trying to summarise it in a way that might enable Andy to say a little more. He added. 'It's not a problem.'

No, it isn't, Andy thought, although at the same time the uneasiness was there. He didn't like it. Made him feel like a beer …, or two. 'I'm OK.'

Graham nodded. 'Good.' Graham didn't say anything else. He kind of sensed that things weren't quite as Andy was saying, but he wasn't going to challenge him over it. It could be something in his own head, and not coming from Andy. He preferred to let the silences be, slow it all down and be open to whatever emerged from Andy. He knew that slowing down the pace of the session, in effect, empathically mirroring the silences and pauses, gave clients time to connect with what was happening for them. So often words could be spoken to avoid feelings. 'Just keep talking', he remembered a client saying to him when he was looking back over the counselling sessions that they had had. 'Just keep talking; thought it would stop me feeling. Didn't work, did it?'

No, it hadn't worked. Clients often spoke at great length about all kinds of things, describing their week as if they were reading from a diary, or talking endlessly about some event in the past, over and over again. It could all be part of avoidance, and necessarily so. No one likes or wants to engage with painful areas of themselves, especially if they have already spent a good part of their life avoiding them. Graham believed in giving clients time to find their own way. He trusted that the process, the relational process that was occurring between himself and the client, would enable the client to eventually begin to risk being more open to the difficult areas. Or maybe it was simply that rather than feeling able to connect with pain and hurt, or other forms of discomfort such as unease and anxiety, their own inner process simply pushed it all to the surface to make it visible within the counselling relationship.

Graham was a great believer that the secret of effective counselling was timing. He liked to think of as 'right-timing'. It had to be the right time for the client to engage in counselling, to feel ready or (as could be the case) desperate enough to have to talk to someone and share their painful feelings and experiences. The client was/is a human being. That very description—'human-being'—summed it up. It's process, the process of being human. It's not fixed. None of us is fixed. Essentially we are fluid, although people can adopt fixed attitudes. No, human beings are essentially individuals in process, a process that encompasses thinking, feeling, behaving, and perhaps more than that if you take into account some of the spiritual beliefs and experiences that people have.

So Graham continued to sit and wait for Andy to speak.

Andy was trying to feel good about things, but he remained unsettled and uneasy. His arms felt tight and his hands were trembling. He got the shakes a bit now and then—well, not really the shakes, just a little shaky, put it down to being a bit anxious. He made a point of pressing his palms down on his thighs, didn't want Graham to see he was shaking.

The silence felt uncomfortable. Andy wasn't used to silence. Most of his life he had sounds around him. In the van he always had the radio on, and at home, the TV was on most of the time. If he was out with mates they'd be talking. But just sitting and saying nothing, that felt weird. He didn't like it, but didn't want to give the impression that he couldn't handle it.

'I'll be OK. Things just get to me a bit sometimes.'

'That's clear. Things get to you but you think you'll be ok.' Graham simply kept with what Andy was telling him. He could see the tension in Andy's posture and he responded to it, 'and it can feel quite tense.' He didn't directly say that he could see Andy being tense, he felt that might be too strong, he wanted to acknowledge the presence of tension but without putting Andy on the spot, so to speak. He wanted to respect Andy's right to go at his own pace. He waited to see what His response would be.

Andy's shoulders dropped. 'Yeah, it does feel tense. Things get to me, you know.' Andy wasn't intending to describe what those things were, at least not those that most disturbed him: the memories, sounds, the fear and isolation he had felt as a child. Graham observed a slight tick in Andy's eye.

'Uh-hu.' He nodded in acknowledgement of what Andy had said. 'Things …' He left the word sort of trail off, inviting further clarification but without directly asking for it. Again, he wanted to offer the possibility of further exploration, but he didn't want to directly focus Andy on it in case it was not what Andy felt ready to do.

'Yeah.' He paused. 'Oh, I don't know, sometimes I just feel like I've had enough of it all. I just feel like it's all too much, and then, other days, I'm out there driving and feeling really good, really free.' He thought about what he had just said. Yes, feeling free really did sum it up and was what he wanted. He liked the open road, being in a way his own boss, although he wasn't really, but he could drive along at his own pace, be in his own world really, listen to the radio and, yes, it did feel good. He liked going to places. He knew he'd never cope with some kind of office job. It wasn't him. And he liked meeting people, when he got to his destination, bit of banter. Yes, he thought, life does feel good. And the thought came back to him that he had had before that first session. What the hell am I doing here? He didn't know. He felt he probably wouldn't come back.

'So, it really varies, day to day. Some days good, others not so good. Driving is really important to you, and being out there, on your own, making your own choices and stuff.'

'Pretty much.' Andy was thinking about how it could feel, driving along at his own pace. Yes, he had deadlines and he had places to go each day, but generally he had time, could take it easy. He'd cut corners, try to get it all done early, or have a quick morning and then a leisurely break at lunch-time. Read the paper, maybe, sometimes have a beer but he tried not to. His boss had made it clear customer's didn't want someone delivering stuff smelling of alcohol.

It seemed to Graham that Andy had drifted into his own thoughts. He responded to his assumption. 'Thinking about it?'

Andy nodded. 'Yeah, it is good sometimes. Just that some days I feel edgy, I can't relax and don't enjoy it so much, you know? Like I said, not every day, just some.'

'Some days you're so on edge you can't relax or settle down and it becomes a bad day. But that's not every day.'

'Yeah.' Andy shrugged. 'And that's life I guess, I have to get on with it, you know? Julie's good, mostly. She knows when I have a day like that and she doesn't tend get in my way? Gives me some space.'

'And that space is important?' Graham was acutely aware of wondering what Andy did with that space. But he wanted to leave Andy free to choose whether or not to elaborate on this, or whether he had said all he wanted to say.

'She can kind of pick up on when it's been a bad day. Let's me get on with it. Get home, have a few beers, you know, relax a bit, put my feet up. Yeah, it settles. Doesn't usually last into the evening, not unless something upsets me.'

'So if something upsets you then it stays with you, yeah?'

'Yeah, you know, like there's no beers in the fridge. I tell her, I don't know how many times, keep a few cans in, check it when you're going shopping. But she doesn't. Does my head in, you know?'

'Does your head when there's no beer in the fridge, when she hasn't bought some in.'

Andy was feeling tense. It really wound him up. He worked hard each day and he expected to have a few beers in the fridge. Not that he always drank them. They generally went down the pub of an evening. Sometimes he went on his own. But, when he got home from work he liked a couple of beers, it settled him down. That's how it was, how it had been for a while now. Too right it does my head in, he thought to himself. He was really in touch with feelings of frustration and anger. It did make him angry. He wasn't saying anything, but was nodding slightly.

Graham could see and feel the tension. Andy's jaw was set and it was clear he was in touch with some powerful feelings.

'Really gets to you, really winds you up.' Graham spoke slowly, holding the focus on the feelings.

Andy remained tense as he sat there. Strangely, he felt his attitude soften a little, and he wasn't sure what that was about. Just found himself wanting to defend Julie for some reason. Found himself speaking, not in any planned way. 'She's OK though, I mean, only happens sometimes, and it's when it's a bad day, you know, then it gets to me. That's all.'

'So most of the time it's OK, but on bad days it winds you up and bad days are when something's happened to upset you, yeah?' Graham could feel reactions within himself, and the strongest one was a feeling of sympathy for Julie. He just had a sense of her having to put up with Andy coming in and demanding that there be beer in the fridge. He could feel his concern flowing towards her and he realised it was taking him away from what Andy had been saying. He brought his focus back, but noted to himself that tendency to lose Andy in response to his feelings towards Julie. He would probably need to process those in supervision, or at least reflect on it later. And it might be that if it continued to block him he would need to voice it in the session.

Andy took a deep breath. Julie was OK. They'd been together for a while now, and they got on well, most of the time. They had their moments—didn't everyone, he thought to himself. No, they got on well. They had a routine (in truth it was mainly his routine) and he didn't like it upset.

'Yeah, most of the time it's fine, we really get on well. But like I said before, I just get so fucking irritable these days. Can't settle, just want to …' He thought for a moment. Just want to drink, that was what had come to his mind. He instinctively took a deep breath. He had been uncomfortable talking about his drinking before. He really didn't want to get back into that now.

'Just want to …?'

Andy heard Graham's response. He wasn't able to really stop himself, the words just came out, sort of without thinking, '… get pissed.'

"Just want to get pissed. That's what you feel like, can't settle, getting pissed helps, yeah?' Graham kept his tone ion a level, making sure his response was a simple, empathic statement of fact.

Andy nodded. 'Yeah.' He shook his head. 'shit, man, that sounds awful, and, it's not always like that but some days, you know.…' He suddenly felt very sad and lost. It was as though in saying what he just wanted to get pissed he'd let loose a lot of unsettling feelings. More than unsettling. He didn't feel good and hell he wanted a beer, or two. He looked up at the clock. Still a few more minutes to go. He was taking another deep breath. He felt wretched. His heart was thumping, he felt sweaty, a bit shaky all of a sudden. He hadn't had a beer all day. Last drink had been last night. He'd been busy, hadn't had a chance to have anything, and … he felt his hands shaking.

Graham had noticed it too. 'You're looking really shaky, Andy, is this something you often experience, this kind of reaction?'

Andy nodded. 'Yeah, sometimes. Beer or two settles me back down again.'

'Couple of beers, what, takes away the shakes? Anything else?'

'Dunno.' Andy shrugged. 'Just sort of settles me, you know? I mean, I've sometimes felt like this at other times, but usually in the afternoon. Can make it hard to drive sometimes, I have to really concentrate.'

'Because of the shaking?'

'Yeah, and I kind of can't concentrate too well. But a beer or two and I'm fine again. But I try not to, you know, not too much when I'm driving, but sometimes, well, sometimes I just have to.'

Andy hadn't intended saying any of this. He'd planned to keep it to himself. He didn't drink and drive, well, he didn't, not the way he saw it. A beer or two wasn't really drinking and driving. He knew what Graham had said the previous week, and yes, that had worried him, but a can or two, he felt sure that was OK. Deep down he knew it wasn't really OK, but he couldn't admit that to himself, not really admit it, and not to someone else either. He was coping, he was surviving. Yeah, so what, a bit shaky now and then and, OK, so he had a beer or two to calm down. But that was all. He could handle it. He knew he could. He had to … His hands were shaking again—well, they hadn't actually stopped, but he was suddenly more aware of it.

'Look, Andy, I am worried that you are getting a withdrawal reaction and, from what you've said it does seem clear that you are topping yourself up some days. And that's maybe how it is, but I am concerned that the alcohol is getting hold of you. Irritable, shaky, can't settle, finding a beer or two calms you down, you know these really are classic symptoms of alcohol withdrawal. I really am concerned.'

Andy didn't want to hear what Graham was saying. He hadn't liked what had been said the previous session. He took a deep breath. He was gritting his teeth. 'I'm OK.'

'You feel OK, but you don't look it. It's up to you, Andy. If you are struggling with the booze, it's one of the hardest things in the world to admit to. And I don't want to push you. I just want to convey my genuine concern. But I also recognise that you see it differently, and I also want to understand how you see it. Clearly, you don't think it's a problem, and you genuinely feel you're OK.'

'I do.' As he spoke Andy thought of the last time he and Julie had had an argument, a big row, more than that spat after the last counselling session on the phone—it had been over how much he had been drinking, and how much of a foul mood he had been in. He'd really felt angry and had nearly lost it. It had been a shock. He seemed to have forgotten about it, but now, it was vivid once again. He also felt strange, weird inside. Like he was a bit high, a bit spaced out. He'd felt this way before. 'Look, I think I need to go, Graham. I need to get away, settle myself back down. I really don't know if this is helping.'

'What do you want to be helped with, Andy?'

'With feeling irritable, just feeling, I don't know, wound up all the time, I guess.' He paused. What was he saying? He didn't need any help. He was OK. He could sort it. 'No, I can sort this out my own way.' He lapsed into silence.

'So you want to overcome feeling irritable, feeling wound up all the time. And you feel you can sort it out your own way—with a few beers, yes?'

Andy nodded. Yes, he thought, a few beers and I'll be fine. Nothing wrong with that. He wasn't the heaviest drinker in the pub. He didn't have a problem, despite what Graham seemed to think. He was OK and he was going to be OK. But he wished the shaking would stop. 'I'll be fine. I know you think I've got a problem, but I can handle it. I'll cut back, or maybe I'll just drink when I need to, you know?'

'Sounds good, give it a go. Cut back, but don't overdo it, your body is used to the alcohol in the system. It's dangerous to stop, just cut back. I probably sound like I'm giving advice and maybe that's not what I'm here to do as a counsellor, but I really am aware of the dangers of cutting back too quickly when your body is used to a lot of alcohol.' He didn't use the word dependent; he wasn't sure how useful that would be. But he knew that someone who was dependent on alcohol and suddenly stopped, could experience withdrawal reactions which could be life-threatening, in extreme cases. He knew he needed to check out what symptoms Andy may have had in the past. 'Ever cut back a lot before?'

'No, not really, I've had a drink every day now for years, I guess.'

'Take it easy, I really mean that, and if you do feel strange, call your GP, or have a beer to settle yourself back down, or both. I do mean that, Andy.' Graham felt very focused in what he was saying. He was concerned and he was genuine.

Andy was struck by how serious Graham, was looking. He really hadn't looked quite as serious as that before. It sort of took him aback slightly. It made an impression. He wanted to joke about it, lighten it up a bit. It felt uncomfortable. 'Can't be that bad. I mean, I never get hangovers or feel drunk.'

'Mean's nothing. Maybe you don't get so dehydrated to get a hangover, but not getting drunk, well, that isn't always a good sign. Can simply mean your body has developed tolerance to alcohol—adjusted to it in the system. Usually means someone's been drinking a lot for some length of time.'

Andy smiled. 'Come on. It's not that bad, is it?'

'I don't know, but I am concerned. I'm not pissing you about here.' Graham spoke deliberately and used language that he felt would communicate his genuineness more directly. 'Alcohol is a serious substance. Take it easy, but don't just try and stop.'

'Why? What can happen?'

Graham took a deep breath. 'People can fit and people can die. Or people experience delirium tremens, they start seeing things, or thinking things that aren't real. Scary stuff. You really don't need that. You do not want to go there.' Graham was aware that his voice had become more measured and he could feel the seriousness in his voice. He wasn't messing around. He felt a need, a responsibility, to say it as it was. He felt he had to be true to what he knew and communicate this to Andy. After all, he was there to offer unconditional positive regard, amongst other things. Offering information that could ensure Andy didn't just stop drinking and put his health, even his life, at risk, surely that was about offering this to clients. He cared about the people he worked with.

'You're serious, aren't you. I mean, really serious. You're not pissing me about this, are you?'

Graham shook his head. 'No, I'm not. Take it easy and let's look at it next time, yeah? I'm not going to tell you what to do, but let's just sit down and decide what's best; what you want to do.'

Andy was still feeling his sense of Graham's seriousness. It really had made an impression. He knew something was wrong, but he kind of thought alcoholics, well, that was for down and outs. He wasn't like that. Just enjoyed a few beers. That wasn't a problem, but suddenly it seemed like it was. What they'd discussed the previous week hadn't made the same impression as now. 'You know much about this?'

'I'm not an expert, Andy, but I've worked with people having problems with alcohol, did some training but don't look at me as some expert. I want to give you space here to talk things through, help you make sense of what you're experiencing—if that's what you want—and see what happens. These problems can be resolved, but they need a bit of time.'

Andy was suddenly feeling quite quiet. He still felt shaky, but somehow he felt as though he had a lot to think about. He still wanted a beer. That was the crazy thing. Here he was realising that he had a problem with alcohol, but he couldn't help wanting to get out and have a couple of beers. Didn't make sense. But the need was there.

'OK, next time.'

The session drew to a close and Andy handed over the fee and headed off. He drove slowly, thinking about the session. He was still feeling shaky, and he knew he needed a couple of beers when he got home. But he also felt determined to maybe cut back a bit. He'd see how he felt. The journey back home was uneventful. However, when he got indoors he discovered that there weren't any beers in the fridge. OK, he thought, feeling himself tense up at first, but then deciding that maybe it was an opportunity. He'd be OK. He'd not have anything. He'd get through and, yeah, prove to himself that he was OK, that he wasn't a bloody alcy. The more he thought about it, the more determined he was feeling. He hadn't had a drink since the previous evening and that hadn't been a very heavy session. Six or seven pints he thought, he wasn't too sure. Anyway, he'd be OK. He made himself a strong coffee and waited for Julie to get home from work. She was on late shift and wouldn't be back till after ten o'clock.

There was football on the TV. Andy settled himself down. Julie would bring in fish and chips later, he'd just get through until then and he'd feel better once he'd eaten. He'd be OK …

*   *   *   *

'My God you look bad. He glanced over to the landlord. 'Mick, get Andy a drink, he looks like he needs one.'

Andy nodded. 'Thanks, Gary. Yeah. Not feeling so bright. Didn't go to work today.'

'No, what happened?'

'Oh, long story.' Andy hadn't said anything to Gary about trying to cut back on his drinking. He hadn't been there the previous week when he'd mentioned it. And he hadn't really done much about it over the next few evenings when Gary had been in. This was the first time it was just the two of them.

'There you go.' Gary handed him a pint. 'Cheers.'

'Cheers.' Andy wasn't sure whether to say anything. He felt he wanted to. But he knew he didn't want to be ridiculed or put down about it. He had tried to stop—he thought he'd be OK. But it hadn't been. He'd felt bad. He'd had a few cans in the afternoon to settle himself down, and now here he was back in the pub again. Julie was working late again. She'd been reluctant to go in but he'd persuaded her that he'd be OK.

'Trying cut back on the booze a bit, mate. Started seeing a counsellor and he reckons I'm pushing it a bit, and maybe over the limit some mornings. And, well, I kind of think I need to do something. Mentioned it last week to Alan and Steve and they weren't too impressed. Anyway, yesterday evening I didn't have anything, and hadn't had anything since the previous evening, though that wasn't a heavy session. Anyway, bit shaky last evening and then in the middle of the night I really felt bad and ended up having some whisky. That was all there was. Drank about half a bottle. That settled me down, but I couldn't go in to work today. Shit did I feel bad. Julie couldn't get me up this morning. She phoned in. Got up at lunch-time. I still felt bad. Threw up the moment I tried to drink some tea. Spent the afternoon back in bed again, had a sandwich and then headed down here. I don't know. Didn't expect to react like that. The guy told me not to just stop but, well, you know, didn't think it would be a problem. Now I'm not so sure. I need to talk to him about it next week.'

'Sound like it's been rough. But you don't drink more than the rest of us?'

'I think I probably do sometimes. I do drink quicker. I know I often feel like my glass is empty first, and I need to do something about that.'

Gary thought about what Andy was saying and, yes, he was probably right. 'You may be right.'

'Anyway, I'm going to have to do something about it. Can't go on like this.' Andy was aware of feeling different with Gary. They didn't often get a chance to chat like this. 'You don't spend so much time with us these days, do you?'

Gary shook his head, 'no, well, partly work, but also I like to be at home as well, you know, with the kids and that. I mean, I realise how important that is for me. And I don't drink like I used to. So I can appreciate what you're saying, but I can also see that it isn't where Steve and Alan are, or Matt for that matter. Guess I don't come down so much because I just don't feel like it so much, you know?'

Andy nodded. 'I wish I felt like that. I feel really pulled between coming down here and staying at home. Maybe I'm getting old?' Andy smiled as he said it, but somewhere deep inside he felt a pang of regret. He wasn't old and he wasn't going to stop doing what he enjoyed. But he wasn't enjoying it as much, and that was part of the problem. The truth was that there was a lot he wasn't really enjoying about his life. He knew he needed something to change. He was in a rut. It had seemed good, but now he knew deep down things weren't good. He was irritable, argumentative, and he just seemed to spend time thinking about drinking.

'We're all getting old, mate, but not so old as we can't enjoy ourselves. Maybe we all need to take it easy.'

The conversation continued and Andy felt calmer as the conversation turned to the match on Saturday. It was early when they headed off home. It was unusual for Andy not to stay until closing time.

Chapter 3

'I've had a bad week, mate, really bad. You were right. I was worse than I thought. I tried to stop.' Andy saw the concern on Graham's face. 'I know, I thought I'd be OK. I was at first, but that night after I saw you last. I didn't have a drink. I was bad. Was sick, shaking again, sweating, couldn't settle. I really was bad and I didn't know what to do. I had a drink. Had some whisky. Not what I tend to drink, not in that quantity but, middle of the night I'd got up and, well, I had to have something. Ended up drinking half a bottle and didn't get in to work the next day.' He shook his head. 'Did I feel bad.' Another pause. 'And since then, same as ever really. Haven't been able to do much about it.'

'So, you tried to stop and got a bad reaction. Hit the whiskey and ended up not getting in to work.'

Andy was nodding. 'Wasn't the answer, but I didn't feel well. And Julie, she was really concerned. Said I needed to see the doctor but I didn't want to. I want to sort this out myself, not go there.'

Graham stepped away from the temptation to encourage him to see his GP, rather he wanted to allow Andy to explore what was happening for him. Whether or not he should see his GP could be discussed later if it felt necessary. 'So, you want to sort it out your own way, but just stopping clearly isn't the answer.'

Andy shook his head. 'I didn't think I'd be that bad. But I've been thinking. It really is years since I had a day without a drink. It's like it's what I do, you know?'

Graham nodded. 'Yeah, what you do.'

Andy was staring at the picture behind Graham's right shoulder. A boat in a kind of estuary, a few buildings in the background. He wasn't really taking it in, but it was like it gave him something outside of himself to focus on. He looked back at Graham. 'I can't carry on like this, I can't let it get hold of me.'

'Sounds desperate.'

'I can't go through what I went through that night.' Andy took a deep breath and shook his head as he thought back to it. It had shaken him. He really thought he could go without a drink.

'It was clearly a shock.' Graham, could see it in Andy's expression.

'Too right. Bloody scary too.'

'And it's scared you.'

'Yeah, and I want to do something about it, but I don't know what. If I can't just stop, I mean, what do I do?'

'What would you want to do, Andy?' Graham deliberately avoided coming up with answers. He wanted Andy to explore his options for himself, and maybe have ownership of any ideas that emerged. He was aware that he might not have any ideas and would end up more centred in his feelings about his drinking and his lack of ability to stop. Graham was aware that there were techniques and ways of working with people to help them formulate strategies, but he preferred to give his clients time and space to explore at their own pace and come up with their own ideas, if that was possible. Yes, he could suggest that Andy complete a diary to track his drinking—how much, who with, when, where, why, what effects etc. And maybe he would suggest that, but he'd rather Andy had the idea.

'I'd like to feel able to have a few beers when I want without it being a problem, without, I don't know, feeling the way that I do now.'

'OK, so a few beers and feel good about it?'

Andy was nodding. 'That was how it used to be.'

'So you used to feel good, not feel there were problems.'

'No, it's more recently that it's been a problem.'

'More recently?' Graham intoned his empathic response as a question. He was wondering how recent Andy was meaning.

'Last few months I guess.'

'OK, so it's become more of a problem over the last few months.'

'Yeah.'

Graham was wondering whether there had been a significant change to Andy's drinking pattern in that time, or what other factors might have contributed to it becoming a problem when before it hadn't been. Of course, he knew that simply the constant intake of alcohol could and generally did take people over a threshold, as if they had crossed some invisible line, after which alcohol never really seemed to be a solution but tended increasingly to be a problem. 'I'm kind of wondering what's changed? What's made it more of a problem? What's different?'

Andy thought about it. Nothing sprang to mind. Yeah, he had his past and his memories, but that hadn't changed. Work wasn't a problem, other than those bloody road works. 'Don't know. Just find myself thinking about drinking more these days. I guess there's nothing wrong in that, but …' He paused, thinking of what he had said. No, he thought, nothing wrong in thinking about it, but … He had felt bad and he was now really worried about what to do. He couldn't bring himself to go to his GP. He'd known Dr Shira for a while now, but he didn't feel he could talk to her. He didn't like the idea of admitting that he had a problem.

'So, more time thinking about it, about drinking generally, or your next drink in particular?'

Andy realised he was nodding. Yes, that was it precisely. 'The next drink. It's got worse over the last few weeks, I've been a bit more devious, I guess, and that's not helping. I mean, yeah, I do have the odd can at lunch-times. And I know I shouldn't, but I do. Steadies me down. I know I haven't said that before, but …' He paused and realised how desperate he felt about everything. 'Never thought I'd have a problem. Always vowed that I'd never have a problem.'

Graham was struck by what Andy had said. People didn't usually vow not to have a drink problem unless, somehow or somewhere in their lives, they had experienced something of the effects of someone close having a problem. He realised as the thought crossed his mind that Andy hadn't said much about his past, his family, his upbringing. Maybe that had been deliberate. Anyway, he wasn't going to push him. He wanted to let Andy take his time, tell him anything he wanted to say when he was ready. 'Sounds pretty determined, vowing that you would never have a problem with alcohol.'

Andy was shaking his head. Images from his past were flooding his brain. Difficult, painful memories of life as a child. His father had been a heavy drinker as long as he could remember. Always sitting in his chair in the corner, downing bottles of spirits, at least, that's how it had seemed. He used to get angry and violent and he could feel himself shrinking back as he remembered the shouting and how he hit his mother and sometimes turned on him as well, although his older brother, Terry, got it worse.

Terry. Andy took a deep breath. Terry was a mess. His drinking was way out of control. They met up now and then, usually drinking heavily together. And he phoned, usually in the night and usually very drunk. Sometimes quite abusive. He knew Terry was jealous of him, and of his being with Julie. It wouldn't come out in normal conversation but when Terry was in a certain frame of mind he could be really nasty. But he was still his brother, and he did understand why. Terry had had a tough time. He had to be there for him, however abusive Terry got. It made him sad and angry, sad for Terry and angry towards his father.

Graham sensed that Andy was deep in his own thoughts and he did not want to disturb him. He sat and waited. He could see that Andy was staring into space and he decided to wait until there was some movement, a sense that he had come back into the present. But the silence continued. Graham made the decision to verbally reach out to Andy. 'You look a long way away, Andy, just want to let you know that I'm here if you want to talk about it.' He spoke softly, wanting to communicate but without disturbing what was happening for his client. It was never an easy thing to do, and he was often unsure what time to speak when these situations arose. But experience had told him that often it was therapeutically helpful as it could encourage the client to begin to describe their experience, and sometimes whilst still within the thoughts or maybe memories that had become so powerfully present.

Andy took a deep breath and sighed. 'Yeah.' He paused. 'I was well away there.' He felt very emotional, not something that he was used to experiencing. He could see his brother's face as his father had gone for him on this one occasion, the last occasion. Shouting and cursing him, making ready to bring his hand down hard across his brother's face. He'd never forget his brother's eyes, wide with fear, pleading; his mother trying to pull his father away, also desperately trying to stop him. But no, he'd pushed her violently aside. He remembered the sound. It was an awful sound. The kind of sound you never forget. It was otherworldly and yet it wasn't. It was very much of this world. But not what you expected to hear. Or see. He felt suddenly cold and shivered. He hadn't spoken much about it. It was a secret he preferred to keep to himself. But it had come back at him these past few weeks, well, months. It had never really gone away, but recently, when it was in his head it just wouldn't go away so easily.

Graham could feel the tension in the room and he knew, instinctively, that whatever was happening was important. He had to be sharp, focused, empathic. He needed to be at his best. He'd often thought to himself how good therapists are like great tennis players—they're at their best on the big points. This felt like a big point in the therapeutic process. He had no idea what was happening for Andy, but he sensed hurt, pain, anguish. Andy's facial expression seemed to be a mixture of blankness and horror, a weird combination, and yet that was how it seemed.

Andy was taking another deep breath. He was pushing the feelings aside. He didn't want to break down. He didn't do that. He'd always coped with a drink or two, and maybe cried himself to sleep, but only when he was alone, or he was sure nobody could hear. He swallowed. His throat felt painful. He reached over for the glass of water on the table. It felt cool but he could feel his throat still burning and constricted. He put the glass back down and continued to stare ahead. He couldn't break out of the scene in his head. That noise, a kind of hollow crack, like a thick dry twig snapping, and yet nothing like that as well. Kah! Just that one sound. And then there had been silence, a horrible, shocking, murderous silence.

Graham was aware of how much Andy was locked into his thoughts and maybe would struggle to come back out. But they were present in the therapy session for a reason. He trusted this. He trusted that Andy's inner process needed this experience to happen now, and with him, Graham, there to bear witness. Bear witness, that was a concept that Graham had come to understand as having tremendous therapeutic importance. So often people carried memories and secrets which they were unable to share or make visible to another, and therefore unable to experience how another person reacts, unable to offer that other person an opportunity to respond, to care, to show love, and to reveal their own human side in response.

Andy blinked and looked across to Graham. He was back in the present. He didn't know quite what had brought him back, but he was aware of the room again and the scene in his head was a little less vivid. He looked deeply into Graham's eyes. Could he trust him? Could he? He hadn't talked about this, not as an adult. Could he cope with it? How would he react? What reaction did he want? He didn't know. He didn't know what he wanted but he knew he wanted something, and he needed it now. And it was then that the emotions hit him: hurt, pain, anguish, fear, loss. He closed his eyes and sought to bring himself back under control, but he couldn't. He wept as he had never done before. The pain in his cries cut through Graham like a knife, and he still did not know what lay behind it. That didn't matter, not for the present. Something was coming out, some major cathartic reaction was taking place and it was Graham's job to be present, to accept Andy with all the hurt that he was experiencing and to offer him, well, there was only one word for it, however much some therapists tried to dress it up in fancy terminology—love.

Andy had his head in his hands, his heart was thumping, he was hot, his eyes burned, his heart felt like it wanted to break out of his chest. And he felt so weak. His arms felt so heavy.

'I-just-stood … I couldn't do anything. I-I …' The crying continued, deep, guttural sobs that seemed to come from the depths of Andy's being. 'I-I …' He struggled to find the words.

Graham reached over and took Andy's left hand. Andy responded by clenching his own right hand to the back of Graham's. Graham, brought his left hand over, and they sat, holding hands, Andy's grip tight, Graham seeking to mirror the pressure. 'I-I can still hear it, in my head. It's horrible, horrible.'

'A horrible sound that just won't go away.'

Andy was shaking his head. He knew Graham didn't know what he was talking about, and he wasn't sure how to tell him. But it was horrible and it wouldn't go away. Kah! So sudden and sharp. And there she'd laid, still, totally still, a look of, well, almost surprise on her face. The blood trickling out from under her head where it had landed on the corner of the stone hearth. She'd gone over backwards, tried to brace herself but had fallen over the low coffee table. It had pivoted her backwards and her head had just gone right back and … Kah! And then the blood and … oh god, the sight of her brain. He swallowed, his eyes clenched tight again, trying to drive the scene out of his head. But he couldn't. And he knew he had to talk, he had to say something. He couldn't keep it to himself any longer.

'My father in a drunken rage killed my mother.'

The silence hit the room in a way that Graham had never experienced and could not describe.

'And you were there?'

Andy nodded. 'Yeah. I was there. I saw it happen. He'd gone out drinking, came back drunk—he always did. My brother had done something, I can't remember what, but my father had gone for him. He was like a fucking monster when he lost it, and he often did. My mother tried to stop him.' Andy paused, trying to quell the emotions so that he could continue. His voice was very wobbly as he spoke. 'But he pushed her away. I mean, really pushed her and she fell. I can see it happening, like it was in slow motion. She went over the coffee table backwards and landed … her head on the stone hearth.' He closed his eyes. 'I'll never forget the sound. It's the sound more than anything else. I can hear it, so clearly, so clearly.' He was breathing deeply, his jaw set tight as he sought to contain the anger that was now ripping into him. His grip on Graham's hands had tightened again—it was painful but Graham stayed with it.

'It's the sound that's really stayed with you.'

'And my life just fell apart.' He looked into Graham's eyes again, but no longer searching. Now there was a gentleness in them, and a huge watery sadness.

Graham nodded, his own lips tightened, he was only too aware that he did not know what to say. What was there to say? Andy had said it all. He had witnessed a horrible, tragic event and it was still replaying in his head. And now it had been made visible in the room and he, Graham, had been chosen to hear it. And he felt huge respect for Andy, aware that he had no idea of what had happened next and what had enabled Andy to re-experience this tragedy in such a vivid way within the therapy session.

'I don't know what to say. Maybe there is nothing to say. But I'm …' Graham shook his head, unable to find the words to convey what he was feeling. He wanted to say he was touched. Touched! Smashed into was more like it, thumped in the heart.

'Yeah. There isn't a lot you can say.' Andy had loosened his grip and he let go of Graham's hand. Graham also released his grip though he stayed sitting forward in the chair.

Graham felt a need for a kind of reverence. What had been shared was so personal, so intimate, so enormous. He felt he needed to be and to speak gently so as not to disturb what had been brought so forcefully into their therapeutic relationship.

'No. And it would be foolish to try and say something for the sake of it. But I feel for you, I feel so much, feel like I've been hit front on by a truck, and yet I know what I feel doesn't begin to approach what you have, and are, experiencing.' Graham was genuine in what he said. These were not words he had learned, not a textbook response. He was being himself, deeply affected and wanting to communicate it. Genuineness, authenticity—key aspects of quality therapy—and certainly at the core of his own practice as a person-centred therapist. That sense of being smashed into was there for him.

'Thanks.' Andy felt good about Graham's response. Not trying to make it better or make him feel better. Simply saying it as it was, as it is.

The two of them lapsed into silence, at least outwardly. Yet inwardly they both had their own thoughts and feelings. Andy felt suddenly calmer having said what he had said, and released so much emotion. And it had felt really important to have had someone there and to know and feel that Graham had been really affected. He was grateful for this.

Graham was in awe. He had no idea from his own experience how someone came to terms with an experience like that. And what damage could be done to a young person's development. He realised he had no idea how old Andy had been. It did not matter, not now. That would perhaps emerge later. He didn't need to know. His job was to listen, to be authentically present and to offer warm acceptance of Andy. He could certainly understand why Andy had started using alcohol, in spite of his vow. And it must have been so hard to come to therapy, given that to simply decide he needed to come was perhaps an acknowledgement that he had a problem. And, of course, he had come with feelings of being angry and reactive. All that with this tragic experience in his head—and in his heart.

Andy's emotional release and disclosure had come towards the end of the session, and Graham was very aware of that. Time was moving on and the session was now soon to finish. Graham indicated to Andy that he was likely to feel very sensitive given the emotional release, that feelings could still be close to the surface and that he probably needed to look after himself,. He also said that he could ring if he needed to during the week, that was OK. Graham sometimes offered this when a client was in a particularly fragile place and might be in need of some support or an opportunity to re-connect if things got difficult. Often people didn't call in these circumstances, but knowing that they had the option could be helpful.

Andy was grateful for that. When he did leave he was in a very quiet place within himself. The storm had raged, though it might never completely go away. But for now at least there was a calm. He knew he had to come to terms with his past. And he knew that there was so much more than what he had talked about in that last session. But there hadn't been time and, frankly, he was tired, worn out by it all. He'd no doubt talk more the next time. There was so much to try and resolve and make sense of; experiences to try and get away from to give himself a chance to move on within himself. And there was the drinking. Funny that, he hadn't really thought about a drink, but now that it had come to his mind, yes, he did feel he needed something. There were some cans at home, he hadn't finished them all the previous night.

Graham was shattered, completely wiped out by his experience of being there with Andy. He was so aware that what he had experienced was such a major event in Andy's life, yet he also knew that he had no idea what happened next. Was it murder? What had happened to his father? What had happened to Andy, or his brother? And were there other brothers or sisters that had not been mentioned yet? Whilst he wanted to know Graham knew that he didn't need to know. He didn't need to have all this information in order to form a therapeutic bond with his clients. He was there to relate to his clients as they were and to listen to what they wanted to tell him. Andy would tell him what he wanted him to hear when he was ready.

The power of the way Graham worked was in the relationship, and in not trying to be some kind of expert who knew best what Andy needed to talk about.

He respected Andy, and accepted that, like everyone else, he had an internal tendency towards making the best of things. He knew that within his model of working it was referred to as an 'actualising tendency', and that made sense to him. Create the relational climate and the individual's innate tendency to grow, or become more whole, more complete, to seek out a more satisfying set of experiences—there were many ways of describing it although each had a different emphasis—would move the person through a process of inner and outer change. He smiled as he thought about this, realising that the change might not always be visible; it could sometimes be a change towards acceptance of something. But how the hell do you come to terms with witnessing your father kill your mother? That left him cold.

He had no idea what lay ahead, for himself, Andy or the therapeutic relationship. He hoped that Andy would be able to talk through and resolve the effects of what he had experienced. Alcohol was no solution, he knew that. It might help short-term, but it wasn't a drug to be used long-term any more than any of the prescribed tranquilisers. Again he smiled. People didn't like to think of alcohol as a drug. It came in a bottle, in a can, or in a glass. Drugs were pills and powders. Well, drugs did come as liquid, and alcohol was a drug and the sooner society woke up to it and dealt with this most popular of drugs the better. But then, alcohol was such a good anaesthetic and people can have so much to forget—whether it is trauma from the past, or tedium and monotony in the present, or a sense of hopelessness towards the future. The universal anaesthetic—a good time in a glass—guaranteed. But when the glass is empty, the refill is needed to maintain the feelings. And people drink faster than the body can metabolise the alcohol so there is a build up, people get drunk, do daft things, hurt themselves and others. Not everyone, but a society that seems to have so much of its leisure time and recreational experiences centred around alcohol use has to be considered suspect.

Well, that was what Graham thought, anyway. Yes, he liked a pint himself. But he wasn't interested in the chemical effect. He'd learned not to chase that a long time back. The buzz in a bottle wasn't for him. But Andy hadn't been looking for a buzz, maybe just relief, a chance to get out of his head and away from the horrible memories that were replayed. He wondered if he'd used other drugs as well, but let the speculation go. He didn't know. He would wait to see Andy next time and be there with him, for him, offering a healthy and human relationship and allowing whatever needed to occur to take place.

* * * *

Andy was quiet that evening. He didn't say much to Julie, mainly because he was still very much absorbed with his own thoughts. They didn't go out for a drink, rather he had some cans at home watching the TV. They had an early night but Andy didn't sleep very much. He was up in the middle of the night. Memories in his head again. He had another can but that didn't make much difference. It was like he kept replaying events, but most of it was his mother's death that he couldn't seem to get away from. It was as though a tape was going round and around in his head. Sometimes the sounds sounded as though they were audible, not just a memory but real sounds. And the feelings that were present within him, they were vividly present.

He sat on the sofa with the can in his hand, shaking his head slightly. He tried watching TV—there was some sport on, Italian football, but he couldn't get into it. He just felt on edge. The thoughts, memories and feelings aroused in the counselling session with Graham were very much with him. It was now four o'clock in the morning, and he had to be up for six-thirty to get ready for a long drive. He got up and paced up and down, feeling as if he used some physical energy that might help to relax him. He tried some press ups to see if that would tire him. He wasn't too sure if it helped. It certainly made him hot and he decided to go outside to cool off a bit. It was a clear night, no clouds in the sky. The stars seemed so clear and sharp as his eyes adjusted to the darkness. The moon was really bright. It wasn't a full moon, but it was certainly very close to it. He thought about his own life in the midst of the vastness of space. It somehow seemed very small and maybe quite inconsequential in many ways. Here he was, one person on what was in effect a fairly small and probably quite insignificant planet in the scheme of things. Vast star systems, rushing away from each other, if the astronomers were to be believed. The scale of it was beyond his comprehension.

Andy realised he was getting quite cool and decided it was time to head back for bed. His thoughts had settled and he felt as though he was able to try and get back to sleep. Julie was fast asleep, quite oblivious to the fact that he had been up. He was glad he hadn't disturbed her. He got back into bed and must have eventually drifted off to sleep. He was woken by the alarm although he felt as if he had just been laying there, alone with his thoughts.

* * * *

The following evening Andy had gone to the pub with Julie. Alan and Trisha were there. They'd sat around drinking and talking—Alan and Andy mainly talked about football. Andy was drinking quickly. He wasn't aware that he was drinking quickly, he just knew he was feeling irritated because the rest of them were drinking so slowly. 'Come on, you three, you going to spend all night on those drinks?' Andy had stood up and was holding his empty glass. Alan responded by draining his. 'You're keen, mate, but yeah, go for it—and handed him his glass. Julie was only halfway through hers and said no, she was OK for this round. Trisha raised an eyebrow. 'Well I'm not turning a drink down.' She drained her lager and handed the glass over to Andy. 'Thanks.'

'Same again?'

Trisha nodded. 'Julie, you sure?'

Julie nodded. 'Yes, not this time.' She didn't often say no, but somehow tonight she didn't want to drink, not at this pace. She was concerned about how much Andy was drinking, and she felt she wanted to say something, but it seemed awkward with Alan and Trisha there, both seemingly happy to keep pace with Andy.

Andy shrugged and went up to the bar. The rest of the evening he just never seemed to let her forget. It became a big issue—Julie didn't know why. But it felt like from the moment she'd said no to that drink, Andy had got the hump. She knew he could be an irritable bastard at times. Maybe it had been a bad day. She knew he'd had a long drive. She wondered about the counselling he was going to. Was it helping? She hadn't really noticed any change, and Andy hadn't said much about it. As the evening wore on Andy seemed to be getting even more irritated with her. Even Alan and Trisha were looking a bit uncomfortable by the time closing time arrived and they went their separate ways.

'What was that all about, Andy?', she asked as they walked home. 'Why did you just keep going on at me?'

Andy denied it. 'What're you going on about. You weren't joining in, you didn't seem to want to say much.'

'Every time I did it felt like you bit my head off.' They walked on in silence.

Andy didn't know what she was talking about. He felt she wasn't really joining in. She'd gone on to non-alcohol drinks during the evening, and that sort of made him feel something though he hadn't really identified what it was. Well, he hadn't bothered, he wasn't that interested. He knew that it felt like she was making some kind of statement and he didn't like it. 'Just 'cos you can drink something else.' They were back home now.

'What do you mean?' Andy's comment had come out the blue. They'd both gone into the kitchen. Andy was rooting around in the fridge for a can.

'Well, fuck's sake, Julie, you know things are difficult after last week.'

'What do you mean?' Julie didn't know what he was talking about.

'Me, trying to cut back.'

'Well I'm not seeing much sign of it.' Julie was feeling her own irritation rise. She'd been the brunt of his comments all evening and she was fed up with it. 'Seems a bloody waste of time all this counselling. Obviously it doesn't work for you, just makes you even more of an irritable bastard.' With that she turned and strode out of the door, making sure she slammed it behind her.

It wasn't unusual for anger to break out between them. It was a bit of a pattern. It never became more than verbal. Sometimes she had thought Andy might hit her, but he never did. He'd always walk away. It was like he'd build up to a certain level and then stop. She didn't understand why, it was how he was.

Andy sat with his can in front of the TV. He felt pissed and he was glad. It stopped the thoughts in his head. He felt nicely blurred, thank you very much, and it was a good place to be. Sod the counsellor, he thought. But he wasn't only thinking that, he also felt he wanted to be a bit defensive as well. He didn't want Julie to be right. Anyway, it had been her idea. He could blame her another time. He took another mouthful of lager. It was cold in the back of his throat and felt good. He was aware of feeling hungry and decided to get up and make himself a sandwich. He was in the kitchen and was cutting up the bread when he suddenly felt a bit faint. He staggered slightly to the right, and steadied himself on the work top. He knocked something off the surface, he hadn't seen what it was. But he heard it land. It was a sickening sound and it was an all too familiar one. He realised he was sweating. He suddenly felt anxious, very anxious. He realised his hands were shaking. He looked over and saw that it had been a coconut, and it had split as it had hit the tiled floor. He was seeing his mother. The emotions hit him like they had done in the counselling session, only worse. He slumped down on the floor, propped up in the corner, his head in his hands. The tears kept coming. He felt like he wanted to die, so alone, so utterly, utterly alone.

Andy had no idea how long he had been sitting there. He heard the door open and Julie come in.

'What's happened to you?' She wasn't very sympathetic, seeing the coconut milk all over the floor. 'Can't you do anything right?'

Andy didn't move. He wanted to be angry. He wanted to lash out, shut her up, but he couldn't. All he could think of was his mother lying there. He couldn't move. He took a deep breath and slowly looked up and into Julie eyes.

Julie had never seen Andy looking like that. His look was so penetrating. It seemed full of hate and sadness. It was a terrible look and instinctively she knew something was wrong, something was terribly wrong. Her own irritation subsided.

'What is it? What's happened?'

Andy continued to look at her. What was the point, he thought to himself, what was the fucking point. He wanted to tell her to piss off back to bed, but that would leave him alone, and he couldn't face that. But he didn't feel he could get up. He sat and stared. The alcohol was also adding to his lethargy. His facial expression did not change, his jaw was tight, his stare continued to penetrate.

'Julie,' he spoke through clenched teeth, but he did not continue. Rather he shook his head as he lowered his face to look over to the coconut. As he did so another wave of emotion hit him and he burst into tears once again.

This wasn't Andy. Julie didn't know what to do. She went over to him. 'What's happened Andy, what is it? What's happened? Tell me, please, tell me? What is it?'

Andy shook his head. He wasn't sure how she'd react. He wanted—needed—to say something, but he couldn't. The words were stuck in his throat.

Julie had knelt down. Part of her wanted to just accuse him of being pissed, but this wasn't just being pissed. Andy didn't cry, not like this. He seemed utterly lost, his whole body convulsing with the sobs.

'What is it, love?' She had reached over to try to hold his hands, which he was holding over his face. She wanted to pull them away. They felt like a barrier between them. She had hold of his wrists and tried to pull them away. Andy resisted. He didn't want her to see his face. Julie loosened her grip. 'What's happened? I've never known you like this, what is it? What can I do?'

Andy's breathing was very disjointed. He suddenly felt very faint again. He dropped his hands and let his head loll back against the cupboard door. He misjudged it and cracked his head. But the alcohol had left him numb enough not to feel it. The couple of spirits—doubles—he'd had just before they'd left the pub were really kicking in. He wasn't thinking about them, though.

Julie reached over to rub his head. She had moved closer, balancing a little uncertainly on her right knee. Andy had closed his eyes, but he felt Julie close. He reached out to her—it was totally instinctive. But it wasn't Andy reaching out. It was a small boy who now needed a mummy to hug and be hugged by, to love and be loved by. It was the little boy that threw his arms, somewhat unsteadily, in Julie's direction. He held her around the waist, his head buried against her tummy. He was holding her tightly, it was uncomfortable. She moved a little to try and give herself a little more comfort. 'What is it, love, what is it?'

Andy was still holding her tightly, the tears still flowing, the sound, the awful sound, still filling his head, and the image, his mother, the cerebral fluid, the trickle of blood. He was holding his eyes closed so tight. But however tight they were closed, the image was still there, inside his head, inside his brain. It felt like he needed to crack his own head open to get it out. He could hear Julie talking, asking him what it was, what was happening.

Julie tried to reassure him. 'Hey, it's OK, it's really OK.' She felt suddenly very motherly and that wasn't how she usually felt towards Andy. She felt like she wanted to hold him forever, but it was a different kind of holding to that which she experienced when they were having sex or just fooling around. This was altogether different. She realised she was frowning, but didn't know why. Her own eyes were watering as well. She was feeling suddenly very emotional. She guessed the whole experience was getting to her.

'Please, Andy, tell me what it is? Maybe I can help. Please, tell me? I want to help. What is it?'

She felt Andy's head move against her tummy. It was a slight movement, a shake of the head.

'I know it must be difficult, but it can help to talk about it.' As she spoke she remembered what she had said earlier about the counselling. Shit, she thought, that hadn't been very helpful. She wanted to apologise but was this the right time. 'Look, I'm sorry what I said earlier. Whatever it is must have been building up all evening. I'm sorry, Andy, please, tell me what it is. Surely it can't be that bad?'

Not all evening, Andy thought, all my fucking life. And yes, it is that bad. He swallowed. He was feeling awkward, his body was twisted forward and he was aware now that his right leg was threatening to go numb on him, and his back felt tight. He took another deep breath and let go, slowly loosening his grip. He swallowed again.

Julie pulled back slightly, allowing a bit of distance between Andy's face and her tummy. 'What is it, Andy? What's happened? If you don't tell me, I can't help'

Andy took another breath, opening his mouth to speak, but he didn't know what to say. He knew he needed to say something, but he simply didn't know where to begin. He closed his eyes for a moment, trying to get a grip on himself, and trying to think what to say. But his head was stilly foggy. 'Memories …'

'Memories?' Julie didn't know what Andy was referring to. 'Memories of what?'

'Long time ago.' He paused. 'A long time ago …' He was speaking very slowly.

'Something happened a long time ago?' Julie remembered how she had felt a little while ago—wanting to mother Andy. She made a connection. 'Your mum?' She didn't know much about either of Andy's parents. He never spoke of them, he'd just said that his childhood had been tough and that they had both died when he was young.

Andy felt the emotion cut through him again. He screwed up his eyes and felt the hot tears once more dripping out and down his cheeks.

Julie drew Andy's head back to her and held him. She didn't know what to do, what to say. She was running on instinct.

He pulled away from her again. He nodded and looked up into her eyes, 'yeah'. He tightened his lips. He knew this was the moment to tell her what had happened. He'd kept it a secret, apart from telling Graham, but he had to tell her now, somehow. 'Yeah, mum. I've never told you, have I?'

Julie was shaking her head.

'Dad killed her.'

Julie closed her eyes as she felt her heart go out to Andy and the tears building up. What the hell had happened was the thought that was with her. 'Oh Andy, why, how, what …, what happened?' She had opened her eyes once again.

Andy sighed, it was a deep and heavy sigh. He again opened his mouth to speak but he was finding it hard to say the right words. 'He pushed her over.' He spoke quickly.

Julie was shaking her head and wanted to close her eyes again, but Andy was looking at her and she knew she needed to return his eye contact. 'What happened?'

'She was trying to protect Terry.'

Oh God, she thought, protect him—from what? She was aware of frowning again.

'He'd get drunk and take it out on us, and he went for Terry one evening after he got home. He'd been drinking.' Andy was speaking slowly now as the images filled his head, as he saw the scene rolling out once more, and seemingly in slow motion. 'He went for him and mum tried to pull him away. He turned and hit her, pushed her, I don't know, but she fell …'

His eyes had strayed over to the coconut. He nodded slightly. 'Just like that ...'

Julie wasn't sure what he meant, she turned to look at what he was staring at. She immediately looked back at Andy. 'What do you mean?'

'Just like that, cracked her head open as she fell. She died then and there, in front of us. Hearing the coconut just now, the sound, it took me back there. I'd talked about it in counselling, and I guess it's really close to me at the moment. But hearing it just now, took me back, took me right back ...'

Julie had now closed her eyes. She knew Andy had been taken into care, he'd mentioned that, and his aunt and uncle had brought him up, but she'd had no idea that any of this had happened. 'Oh Andy.' She reached out and drew him to her, as much for her own need as for his. They both cried.

Minutes passed. Neither spoke. They were in a place beyond words. But it was uncomfortable and it was Julie who spoke first. 'We'd better get up, Andy, it's uncomfortable down here.'

'Yeah, but it feels kind of safe down here as well, like I can hide in the corner.'

Julie nodded, 'yeah, but we still need to get up. Come on.' She stiffly got to her feet and pulled Andy up. He slowly got up, very stiffly. His right leg was numb but he could feel the pins and needles breaking out as the circulation improved. 'Shit.' He tried standing on it but it was too uncomfortable, so he tried shaking it. This helped a little.

'Let's clear up out here. What were you doing?'

'Making a sandwich.'

'Still want it?'

Andy nodded, he did. He still felt hungry, in fact more hungry now. 'Yes, and a mug of tea, yeah?'

'You go up and I'll bring it. What do you want?'

'Ham and mustard.'

'OK, I'll bring it up in a few minutes.'

Andy headed upstairs to the bathroom and eventually to bed, by which time Julie had appeared with the tea and sandwiches.

They sat in the bed, Julie holding Andy's left hand as he munched his way through the sandwiches. He still felt very raw and sensitive, but it somehow felt good that it was out in the open. He didn't have to carry it any more. Graham knew, Julie knew. Maybe it would help.

They sat and chatted for a while. Andy spoke more about the counselling and that he knew he had to do something about the drinking, that it was linked to the past, to how he felt, to the memories in his head. Julie said she'd be supportive in whatever way would be helpful. Eventually they settled down and fell asleep in each others arms. It turned out to be a good night's sleep for Andy, apart from having to get up for a pee. He felt tired the next morning, and was aware that he was still feeling hazy inside himself, but he also felt better for telling Julie.

Julie was reassuring him just before he left. 'You'll be OK, you'll see. We can work this out, together, and you're getting help as well. It'll be OK. I love you, Andy, I really do. And I think I love you even more now that I kind of understand things. I mean, well, I don't really, but, oh what am I trying to say?'

'It's OK, no need to say anything. No need to say anything. Thanks. I know. I love you to. Let's plan a weekend away, yeah?'

Julie was nodding. Her eyes were watering again. 'That'd be good.'

'We'll talk later.'

Julie nodded. 'Yeah. Take care, drive carefully.'

Andy nodded. He gave her a hug and a kiss, and headed for the door.

Chapter 4

Andy had arrived late for the counselling the following week, traffic problems again. It hadn't helped his mood. He'd been playing catch up all day from the moment he'd realised he had slept through the alarm. He was telling Graham about it. 'Too much to drink again. Hasn't been a good week. Feels like the memory has been closer, just kept thinking about it. I talked to Julie a lot. She knew that my mother had died in an accident, but hadn't appreciated what had really happened. Well, never really felt like telling her, you know? Anyway, now she knows.' Andy described what had happened. 'She was very good. We ended up crying together, Seems to have brought us closer. Not sure what that's about but it feels good. But I did drink too much again last night. Seems to have been a bit up and down. Some days I seem to drink a little less, others I drink more. I don't know why, it's just the way it is.'

'Like you feel it just happens?'

Andy nodded, aware of feeling that it was like he was watching himself going through the motions of life, and one part of that involved drinking and getting off his head. He had felt strangely distant from things since the last session. It was odd. He couldn't really describe it, and wasn't sure whether he could make much sense talking about it to Graham.

'Like I'm watching myself living my life, like I'm in a dream, a daze, you know? Going through the motions but not really … I don't know, not really in touch somehow? Does that make sense?'

'Sounds like it's hard for you to make sense of, Andy.'

'It is, I just sort of drift along and then, I don't know, it's not that the memories have gone. They haven't. And in a way they seem maybe more vivid. I don't try to stop thinking about them anymore. I can't. It happened. They happen. It's in my head.'

'Like you're in a state of shock, drifting along, unable to do anything about the vivid memories that are in your head.' Graham sought to sum up what Andy was saying. He was speaking gently, not wishing to disturb the focus that Andy had generated.

Andy looked distant. His voice sounded as though he hadn't quite got his brain in control of his vocal chords. The words came out, quite unemotional. 'Yeah. Like, that's how it is, just keep going.' He took a deep breath as he remembered how on two occasions during the week he'd narrowly avoided accidents in the car. 'And it's making me dangerous. Twice now I've nearly had accidents. Drifted off, in my own thoughts, not paying attention.' He shook his head. 'I'm usually a safe driver but I just feel so pre-occupied.'

Graham was nodding slightly as he responded, looking Andy in the eyes as he spoke. 'Can feel like all the action is in your head, it holds your attention, takes you away from what's going on around you, and that's bad news when you're driving, hence the two near misses.'

'Yeah.' Andy felt quite calm. He really felt like he was on automatic pilot. It was kind of like he was when he was drunk, but he was aware of himself as well, but in a different way. When he was drunk he couldn't sort of watch himself like he could now. It was weird. Wasn't sure what to make of it. And he didn't care either, couldn't really be bothered to try to make sense of it. Didn't have the energy. He felt heavy, tired, listless. He blew out a long breath with a heavy sigh.

The intensity of last week must have been such a shock, Graham's thoughts had returned to the previous counselling session. Completely wiped him out and he hasn't recovered yet. It would take time. He couldn't rush him, there was nowhere to rush him to anyway. His psychological system had to take its own time to heal, and he was aware as well that maybe there was more to come out before the healing could really begin. He still knew very little about Andy's past. He stayed silent. He wasn't sure whether to remain that way or to say something to reassure Andy that what he was feeling was a natural reaction. But Andy wasn't asking for reassurance. So he stayed silent although internally he was very alert to anything that Andy might communicate—verbally or through body language.

Andy was reliving in his head the two near misses. The second had been the worst, the car had stopped in front of him and he just hadn't seen the brake lights. He'd braked late and instinctively swung the wheel. The van had slewed, narrowly missing the car in front, and had ended up diagonally across the middle of the road. Fortunately nothing had been coming the other way. He'd felt really shaky afterwards and had pulled over and sat staring out of the windscreen for some while. Then he'd got out for some fresh air and a pee. Funny thing was, he didn't go and have a beer. Didn't even think about it. Instead he'd pulled over to a tea hut in a lay-by. Had a strong cup of sweet tea. He'd also bought a burger but hadn't finished it. He'd got himself together and finished the deliveries. He was still lost in his thoughts as Graham spoke.

'I'm here if there's anything you want to talk about, Andy.'

'Hmm? Oh, yeah, sorry, I was miles away. Thinking about driving and that near miss.' He closed his eyes and yawned. He suddenly felt very tired. He moved his head from side to side, his neck was feeling very stiff.

'Stays with you, still pretty vivid?'

Andy nodded. 'Yeah. I consider myself a safe driver, you know. Been driving a few years now without any really serious accidents. Cover a lot of miles. But it shocked me. I mean, I really was away with the fairies, you know?'

'That's how it feels how it felt, like you were away with the fairies?' Graham didn't know exactly what Andy meant, so he sought clarification. 'I guess I'm wondering what that means to you.'

'Like I'm in another place. I just can't seem to get a grip at the moment, can't seem to get hold of myself. I feel like I'm here but I'm not here. Like I'm stuck in the middle somewhere.' Andy stopped speaking. Yes, he thought, stuck, and its like a strange apathetic kind of stuckness. Can't move and can't be bothered to try to move.

'Stuck in a place of being here but not being here, just not able to get a hold of yourself.'

Andy shook his head and as he did so Graham noticed that he had lowered it. He sensed that this was so difficult for him and he knew there was no magical answer. He believed that Andy needed to allow what he was experiencing to be present—he didn't seem to have a lot of choice. His sense was that this was a natural reaction, not something to diagnose and treat. He was often dismayed at how often symptoms were 'treated' when in fact they were natural psychological and emotional reactions to process. He wondered at the increasing range of 'syndromes' that were being identified and defined within psychiatry, and yet so often they were merely psychological process that, whilst they may be more extreme than a society agreed as 'normal', they were often reaction to environmental factors and experiences rather than chemical imbalances requiring a chemical intervention. To put it simply, Andy needed to be how he was. It wasn't comfortable for him and yet maybe it was protective, protecting him from being overwhelmed by more feelings. He needed to be allowed his own time and space to move through this phase and not have it disrupted by a chemical intervention designed to make him feel better. It was an area that Graham had strong opinions on.

'And that's not really me, you know, not me at all. But since last week, since I …' He was shaking his head again as the sound of his mother's skull cracking open echoed in his brain. He closed his eyes. He could feel them watering and the hot, burning lump in his throat made him want to try and swallow. He couldn't stem the tears. They flowed once more. He sat with his face in his right hand, him arm propped on his elbow on the arm of the chair. His body shook every now and then as another deep sob was released. His breathing had become very disjointed. He could feel the tears on his cheeks. He took a deep breath and the sobbing took over once more. He'd loved his mother. She'd been so good to him, so good to both of them. She'd tried to protect them, and had died trying to. If only she was still alive, if only he could tell her how much he loved her, how much he had missed her and, if he was honest, still missed her. He often felt a pang of jealousy when people talked about their mothers. He'd had his aunt and uncle, but that hadn't really worked out. They never really got on. He'd left as soon as he could.

Graham sat and watched, full of his own feelings of sadness and heartfelt emotions as you do when you are sitting with another person who is hurting, upset and affected at a very human level. 'Yeah, since last week …' Graham, spoke with a sadness and a heaviness in his voice. It wasn't deliberate. It was how he felt.

Andy's feelings were changing. He was aware of his mother and how he felt at losing her, but now his thoughts had turned to his father, and his feelings had followed. 'It was all that bastards fault.' He was shaking his head, his jaw had tightened again. 'Drunken bastard. She didn't deserve him and I've got to think of him as my father. But he wasn't a father. Not to me, or Terry. He was just a drunken bastard, a fucking violent drunken bastard. And he had it coming and I'm glad.'

Graham was listening, registering the shift of mood and being left wondering quite what it was that had come to Andy's father. But rather than be tempted to ask him he stayed with Andy's own focus. 'No father to you or to Terry, just a fucking violent drunken bastard.'

'I'd have killed him, you know.' Andy had looked up and was looking Graham right in the eyes. 'I knew what he had done. If it happened now I would kill him. But, shit, I was only ten for Christ's sake. What could I do?'

'Nothing. You could do nothing.' Graham was very clear in his response. What could a ten year old do when his drunken father had just killed his mother? Nothing could be expected of him, nothing at all. And he certainly wanted to make sure he didn't say anything that might be interpreted by Andy as reinforcing any kind of self-blame for being helpless, for being only a child.

'I remember standing there and bursting into tears. It was Terry who reacted first, he ran over to mum, cursed my father and ran for the phone. My father just stood there. I don't know what he was thinking. He just stood there. Then he just turned and ran, just ran out of the door.' Andy was looking distant again. Graham sat and waited, not wanting to interrupt his train of thought with an empathic response to what he had just said.

'It was the last time we saw him.' He snorted and shook his head. 'Hung himself in prison awaiting trial.' He paused before continuing. 'No great loss.' He paused again. 'We were taken into care, into a home for a short while and then on to my aunt and uncle—mum's sister. They lived in Luton. We'd been living in Dartford. Drive past it sometimes, going round the M25, but don't go back. Can't. It's gone. Too many bad memories. Can't go back. So I just drive past.'

Graham was feeling an edge of concern as he listened to Andy's voice. It was very distant now. 'Yeah, so you drive past.' He was aware of not having responded to anything else that Andy had just said. Felt odd now to try and say something else. The moment had passed. At least he knew more of what had happened. But Andy was sounding so removed from it all. Maybe that was how he had coped. Maybe he had created a place in himself to escape to, to get away from the awfulness of it, of the feelings, the losses, the everything.

Andy looked up. 'I've told you more than I've told anyone before, apart from Julie. She knows. I told her last week. It seems strange telling you. It's like it didn't really happen, and yet I know it did? Does that make sense?'

'Like hearing yourself say it leaves you with a sense that it must have happened to someone else, but you know it didn't.'

'Something like that. Just ..., I don't now.' He took a long, slow breath. 'It's the kind of thing that happens to other people, and yet it happened to me, to us.' He was shaking his head. 'I know it happened and yet somehow it's hard to believe sometimes. Why us? Why did we have to go through that? Why?'

Graham shook his head, 'the kind of thing that it's so hard to make sense of and, as you say, "why?".'

Andy sniffed. 'I don't know and I never will. And it's something you kind of forget sometimes but you never really forget? You play at being like other people, you pretend to be normal, but you can't be, you know you can't because you're different, because this horrible something happened to you and you just know that you can never be like everyone else. And you start getting paranoid. And you think that they know. You know you're different but you don't want them to know why you're different. So you keep your guard up. You avoid people. You don't make friends. You don't feel you deserve friends. You're bad because something horrible happened and it happened to you.' He lifted his right hand to his mouth, and slowly drew it away. 'But you're not bad, not really, but you can't believe that. You're different, you must be different. This kind of thing didn't happen to people you knew. But it happened to you.' Andy was staring towards the curtains. No, he thought, it happened to me, it happened to us. He thought of Terry. Poor old Terry. How he'd struggled with it. In a way he'd reacted worse. It was him that mum had been trying to protect. It was his life that had perhaps been saved when hers was lost. He remembered what his father had shouted as he had run out the door. 'See what you've done, you ungrateful little shit, you've killed your mother.' Last words he heard his father say. He'd somehow forgotten that when he had described it to Graham. He instinctively took a deep breath.

'Yes, whilst you know you're not really bad, you can't really believe it.'

Andy shook his head. No, he thought, I can't believe it. He stayed silent, his own thoughts more real than the world outside of his skin. He found himself thinking about how, at times he just couldn't get the mess out of his head. Terry came to mind. He wasn't aware of it but he was nodding his head slightly. Terry ... He'd had his own problems, a lot of them, and most centred around his drinking. He still drank heavily, but more intensely, all or nothing drinking Andy called it—usually all—and he drifted a lot of the time. He never really settled, seemed like he couldn't settle. He'd never really got himself together and something in Andy felt that he probably never would. Terry'd had jobs but never held anything down for very long. He worked in the building trade and tended to move to where there was work. They still met up quite often, and it usually ended up in a heavy drinking session. They never talked much about the past but it was always there, in the room with them, unspoken memories that screamed out to be voiced.

Graham noticed how lost in his own thoughts Andy seemed to be once again. 'You're very much in your own thoughts, must be a lot of thoughts, memories, feelings ...' He didn't end the sentence, simply left it in the air and waited. He felt he was expressing empathy although he was being non-specific.

Andy nodded and tightened his jaw as he did so. 'Yeah., too many memories. Just thinking about Terry—my brother. He's messed up by it all, drinks more than me. I remember, he told me he tried going to AA[3] once, and started to talk about his past, but what he got was 'keep to the steps', 'stay sober, you'll be OK'. He couldn't hack it. Too much inside him. Too much shit in his head. We don't often talk about it but we did then. He felt so let down. He's never gone for counselling, and I'm thinking I should try and encourage him. Maybe it would help. I don't know. Still trying to make sense of it myself and work out if it's helping me.'

'And what I hear is that you want to help Terry, but you're still checking out counselling for yourself.' Graham also noted that he appreciated Terry's experience at AA, but he also knew that this was not what everyone experienced. He himself wouldn't hesitate in encouraging someone to attend AA meetings if that was what they felt they needed. He recognised that there were not any other organisations that could provide support groups daily, and lifts to meetings a little out of area.

He took a deep breath, breathing out slowly. 'And I know that this IS what I need, it's just so bloody difficult. I feel so raw at times, and it's been worse since coming, particularly since last week. Raw, like all my feelings are exposed and they kind of overwhelm me. And, yeah, I feel numb as well. And that seems crazy, but yeah, raw and numb.' He was shaking his head and looking down as he spoke. 'Oh I don't know. What do I do? I just feel so stuck at the moment. So fucking stuck. Sorry.'

'Say it as it is: raw, numb and fucking stuck.' Graham spoke with deliberation, wanting his words.

'Yeah.' His voice sounded heavy, weighed down by it all.

Graham sat quietly, allowing Andy the space to be with what he was experiencing. It meant that the sense of rawness, numbness and stuckness that had been mentioned could perhaps be more fully engaged with. Graham wasn't sure which of these three Andy was wanting to focus on specifically, and maybe he didn't want to focus on any of them, simply naming the experience might be enough for

---

3. Alcoholics Anonymous. Not everyone will have this experience. People should be encouraged to try AA which offers a lot of support for people who wish to approach their alcohol problem in line with their model of working. However, it is also true that it is not an approach that everyone feels able to engage with. And, of course, there are many other people who prefer it to a more psychotherapeutic approach.

him to bear at this moment. This was a tough session for Andy and Graham wanted to communicate that he was there for and with him. He wanted to be present as a companion to bear witness to effects of the horrible experience that had made such an impact on Andy's life, and continued to do so.

Andy felt stiff and heavy in his seat, and was aware that he felt sort of glad that he was where he was. He knew if he was on his own he'd be drinking. He knew he wanted to be away from it all. But he also knew what away from it all meant. It would be alcohol.

He shook his head again, still looking down. 'I don't know how to get out of this other than to drink. That's the only way I know, and I know that doesn't work. I have to cut back but if I try to then I just know the feelings are going to come back at me. And besides, I felt so awful when I tried to stop—I can't do that again. Somehow I've got to be able to come to terms with it all and bring the drinking down, and that feels huge.' He paused. Graham felt the atmosphere become more intense. He said nothing for the moment, sensing something was happening and he did not want to interrupt Andy. Andy continued, 'and I don't think I can do it.'

Graham was pleased that he hadn't interrupted with a verbal response. He well recognised the importance of empathy for the situation, for the process, for the atmosphere in the room. He'd been right to stay silent, it had offered Andy the opportunity to connect with and verbalise his self-doubt as to whether he could bring his drinking down.

'You know you have to come to terms with it and cut back. But, the tough realisation is not thinking you can do it.'

Andy replied thoughtfully. 'Yeah. I know.' He stopped and just sat thinking. He had to change. He had to. He was going to mess up his life. He wasn't as bad as Terry but he knew that he could end up that way if he wasn't careful. And with his work, he had to cut back on the alcohol in his system. He couldn't afford to lose his licence. It just all felt too big. Just too big.

'I really don't think I can do this on my own, I really don't.'

Graham nodded, and was aware he had to make a crucial decision: focus on the despair and self-doubt, or start to look at options. Maybe it could be both. He realised that momentarily he had slipped into an addictive way of thinking—this or that, black or white, never grey. He had to watch that, it was a powerful dynamic and it could get lived out in the counselling relationship. His role was to give Andy the time and space to explore and choose what he needed most.

'I'm wondering whether you want to focus on the feelings you have at this minute, or whether you want to discuss options, or both.'

Andy thought, he didn't know what he wanted. He knew he wanted to stop drinking and he knew he wanted to feel normal—not that he felt he really knew what that meant. 'I ...' He sighed. 'I guess I ..., at least, I mean, oh I don't know. I just don't know. Sitting here like this isn't fucking helping, is it?'

Graham heard the frustration and responded to it. 'Frustrating. You want to change, desperate to change, but really doubting whether you can.' Graham stayed with the frustration and the desperation—there was energy in this. Andy's frustration had a note of anger to it. 'And it leaves you fucking angry, yeah?'

Andy had felt the anger building up. 'Yeah.' He tightened his fists. 'Yeah.' His jaw was set firm, his teach clamped tightly together. 'I just wish I could blow it all away. The fucking, fucking bastard. Why did he do it? Because he was a fucking no good, idle fucking drunk, that's why. And he screwed up my life, he screwed up Terry's life, all just because he couldn't fucking hack it. Shit, I'm fucking glad he's dead but I hope he sees what he's done. I fucking hate him, you know?' Andy was looking into Graham's eyes, a penetrating, intense expression full of fire and anger, and somewhere behind it, Graham thought, an awful lot of pain and hurt.

'Yep, you *hate* him and you'd like him to see, and know, what he's done to you and Terry.' Graham was nodding and holding the eye contact. It felt so important to maintain this, to look into Andy's eyes and to seek to be with what they were communicating. A form of empathy—non-verbal but demonstrating sensitivity to the client's need. Andy needed to look deeply into someone eyes as he felt his anger. He needed it validated, perhaps. He needed it witnessed, maybe.

Andy wasn't moving, his eyes continuing to stare into Graham's. Graham held the gaze, his own face firm, ensuring that the seriousness in Andy's expression was matched and mirrored by his own. The two men sat holding the moment, maintaining their contact, separately and yet strangely together in acknowledging in their own ways the power of the contact.

It was Andy who moved first. He looked away. He actually felt stronger now, like he had a new energy. He felt hot. He pursed his lips. 'Fuck it I'm not going to let him bugger up my life. He's dead and buried and I want to bury him again.' As he said that a wave of sadness hit him, and took him totally by surprise. It followed a split second after a vivid memory returning—of them being taken out of the house, being taken away. He never saw his mother again. He only had that image of her, the blood, her skull cracked open, the fluid that had dripped out, the sight of her brain. He closed his eyes, they were watering. His throat burned hot, he swallowed. He buried his head in his hands as he wept, as he wept for what he had lost, for what could never be, for the mother he had never got a chance to know as a teenager or as an adult. He wept for Terry, for the way he had been affected. And he wept because that was all he could do.

Graham got up and squatted down next to him, and spoke softly. 'I'm going to put my arm round you, Andy, to offer you some comfort in your pain.'

Andy didn't hear him but was aware that he had moved over and he felt grateful for some contact. It felt lonely and empty inside. Graham had nudged the tissues closer to Andy as he had moved over, but he hadn't picked one up and handed it to him. He often felt reluctant to do that, certainly at the start of an emotional release like this. It could easily be interpreted as a signal to stop; dry your eyes, pull yourself together. There was no way that he wanted to risk communicating that. Andy needed to be as he was, he needed this release. He'd got behind the anger by allowing that anger and frustration to be present.

Andy lifted his head with another deep breath, his eyes closed. 'sweet Jesus!' Where did that come from?

Graham did not try to come up with an answer. 'Tears of pain, tears of loss.' Although Andy had not said this, that he had been expressing anger before the cathartic release of emotion, he sensed strongly that these were the feelings being conveyed through the tears. They were not angry tears. The tears were liquefied pain.

Another deep breath. Andy took a tissue. 'Yeah. Whooo.'

'You want me to stay here or move over there, or …?'

'I'm OK, thanks. Yeah, thanks.'

'OK.' Graham got up and moved back over to his seat. Andy was taking some water as he did so. 'Putting some liquid in the reservoir—may need some more before the day's out.' He forced a smile.

Graham had noticed the clock, the session was due to end soon, but he didn't want to hurry Andy.

'How're you feeling?'

'Shot, but better for it! I think I needed that, it wasn't nice, not nice at all, but, yeah, I needed it. Now I've got to get out of here and try to not have a drink.'

'You feel like one?'

'Funnily enough, no, but I think that as the evening goes on then I probably will. Not sure why I thought of it—habit, I guess.'

'Often is. And then you act on the thought. Getting over it is about learning to acknowledge the thought but then choosing not to act, or choosing some other response.'

'What, like going and drinking something else?'

'Yes, that's an option.'

'Wouldn't be the same.'

'No, wouldn't be, it wouldn't have alcohol in it …'

'Hmm, yeah. And that's what I'm drinking for, isn't it?'

Graham nodded. In a couple of sentences Andy had summed it up. Habitual thought—habitual action. People think they 'need a drink', but in reality they need a shot of alcohol. And often it is a feeling or set of feelings or memories that trigger the thinking that in turn triggers the urge to drink and the act of drinking.

'OK. Look, what can I do to try and limit what I drink? Is there anything I can take? Should I see my GP?'

Graham decided to respond directly to the question, this was a shift. First time Andy had suggested in a positive way seeing his GP.

'You would need to talk to your GP, but there isn't anything to take to limit your drinking. There's a medication people can take when they've stopped—you can't drink on it because you feel so bad—sort of aversion therapy. But to limit what you are drinking, well, I don't know. People start taking medication and end up with more problems. You're better off at the moment trying to bring it down slowly, and track what you're doing, keep a record maybe, a kind of diary of your drinking.'

'What, so do you mean like 'how much?''

'Yes, and maybe also when, who with, what triggered you drinking—feelings, thoughts, something upsetting you, and what made you stop and how you were left feeling. Look, I've got something here you might want to use, or you might want to design something yourself.' Graham, reached into his bag. He had intentionally brought some drinking diaries along—A4 sheets with a table on which to record each day the kind of things he had just described. He handed a couple to Andy. 'see how you go and we can look at it if you want to bring it next week and see what we can learn from it.'

'OK. I'll give that a go. Feels like I've got something I can try and do, you know?'

'Sure, that sounds important, and maybe gives you something to focus on.'

Andy nodded. He was getting up. The session closed and Andy left to drive back home. He'd folded the diary sheets and put them in his pocket to keep them dry. It was raining again. He wasn't sure whether he felt positive or not He was still feeling the effect of that emotional release, it had left him feeling rather frail, but he also felt a renewed determination as well, a determination to get himself together, to get his life on track. He didn't know where to start, but he knew he had to make changes. He drove off thoughtfully but with a certain amount of deliberation.

Graham heard him accelerate away. He was pleased that Andy had taken away the drinking diaries. It was such a simple and yet powerful tool for helping someone get a grip on their drinking pattern. It would give them both something to discuss next week—assuming Andy completed it or brought it with him. He knew not everyone did, and sometimes for good reasons. But he sensed that Andy had really taken to the idea. He looked at the clock, they'd overrun. He needed to quickly have a cold drink and clear his head. His next client would be due soon.

* * * *

Andy was in the pub later in the week with Gary. He'd been trying to cut back but had only managed one night at home. The nights he had been in the pub he had drunk quite heavily. They were also times when either Alan or Steve, or both of them, were in. They didn't help matters. He'd already decided to tell Gary what had happened in his past, which he did so that evening. He didn't want to tell the others, certainly not Steve and Alan that was for sure. Andy wanted to keep it to himself when they were around. It hadn't been easy talking to Gary. He'd felt uneasy inside as he did so, and strangely detached. It was different to how it had been talking to Graham. He wasn't sure why. Gary was a mate. Maybe that was different.

When Andy stopped talking there was a silence. He was aware that Gary hadn't said anything, but had just been listening. 'So that's what's been getting to me.'

Gary was aware of his own emotions, of a dryness in his throat and his eyes felt moist. 'Fuck.' He shook his head, not sure what to say next. 'That's a bugger, mate. Shit, how in hell do you cope with that?'

Andy looked at his glass in response.

'Yeah, not surprising. Shit, mate, so, yeah, I mean, what're you gonna do?' Gary's Australian accent somehow seemed a little stronger.

Andy told him about the counselling and the idea of keeping a track of what he was drinking to try and understand the pattern.

'Yeah, that's great, mate, but what about the past, I mean …?' Gary knew he didn't have a clue. Where do you begin? What do you do with memories like that?. What do you do? It felt overwhelming.

'I don't know. I think that maybe if I start with trying to control my drinking, well, maybe I'll handle the memories better. I've got to try something. I can't stop thinking about the past, but if I can control this, well, maybe. I don't know, I have to try—but not just stop, like last time, yeah?'

Gary nodded. 'Yeah, that was a bastard, phew, really was a bastard.' Gary's thoughts kept drifting to Andy's father. 'What happened to your father.'

Gary explained what happened to him.

'Shit, man, it gets worse. Anything else?'

Andy shook his head, 'no. that was the last time I saw him.'

'Bloody hell.' Gary took a deep breath and blew the air out, shaking his head as he did so. The sounds of the bar seemed distant. It was like he'd stepped out of that world into something else, listening to what Andy had been telling him.

Andy appreciated Gary's reaction. It was so genuine. It really brought home to him something of how significant it all was. He knew it was, but having someone react in the way Gary had, it sort of felt good, somehow. He doubted whether Alan or Steve would have responded quite the same. He guessed Matt would. Matt was pretty sensitive and he'd already decided that he might let Matt know, but he hadn't seen him for a while, and often he wasn't in on his own.

'Yeah, as you say "bloody hell" ...' Andy was staring into his glass, slightly spaced in his head. He sighed and shook his head.

Gary was stunned. He wanted to beat the shit out of Andy's father. How could he have done what he'd done, and then said what he'd said to Andy's brother? To a child? He was shaking his head as well. "I don't know how you've lived with that, mate, I really don't.'

Andy looked up and shrugged, and forced a smile, 'well, you do, don't you, just get on with things. Try and push it aside, forget it, but you can't really, it keeps coming back. That's why Terry drinks and, well, I've come round to see that it's one of the reasons I drink as well.'

'Yeah, but it's not just that, is it? I mean, you know, it's also about getting out, meeting up, having a few laughs with your mates ...'

'Yeah, I know, but I do drink fast, faster than all of you. And I can't carry on like that. I had such a bad time when I tried to just stop. It's got hold of me, Gary, and I've got to put the brakes on.'

Gary nodded. He was still full of his own feelings towards Andy's father. He couldn't really get his head around what Andy had been saying. His own experience had been very different. Yeah, there'd been difficult times, but his parents had stayed together and though he could remember arguments between them, he couldn't recall it ever getting physical. And as for the fact that he'd had to live with seeing his father kill his mother ... 'Well, he deserved to die, Andy. I hope I'm not speaking out of turn, but in my view he deserved it.'

'Yeah, I know ...,' Andy was aware of how he'd felt in that last counselling session, 'and yet, you know, he must have been troubled himself. He must have had his own demons to have been such a violent alcoholic. But what was in his past, I don't know and I guess I'll never know now. There had to be a reason.'

'I dunno, mate. Some people I think are just made bad, you know? You can't explain them, it's somehow how they are. They're just bastards; made that way I reckon.'

'Well, whatever, it's in the past, but it's still in the present and somehow I've got to stop it fucking up my future, you know?'

Gary nodded, 'yeah'. They lapsed into silence, each with their own thoughts.

'Ready for another drink?' It was Andy who spoke.

'Hmm? Oh, yeah, thanks. Hey, it's my shout. I'll get them.'

Gary picked up the glasses and headed over to the bar. Andy was left with his thoughts. He needed a drink again. He sighed. Shit, it was like whenever he got close to these feelings—or they got close to him—he just knew he had to have a drink. And he knew he had to find another way of coping. But he'd start that tomorrow. Right now he needed that drink, and he knew he'd be OK after it. For a while at least …

Chapter 5

'I've filled out the diary. Quite a shock. Tempted not to bring it. Part of me didn't want to have to talk about it, but I know I have to. So, here it is. See what you think.' He handed it to Graham.

'Thanks. He looked at it but rather than start to make any comment he wanted to draw out Andy's perception. 'So, what made the biggest impression on you filling it out?'

'How much it cost. It said about units but I wasn't sure what to say so I just put in how many pints or cans.'

'That's fine. We can look at that as well. But it was the cost and the quantity that, what, surprised you?'

Andy was nodding. 'I mean, yeah, Nearly a hundred and fifty quid, and more if I counted in what I buy for Julie when we're out. A lot of it is in the pub, that's where the cost is. OK, so I was buying rounds and stuff as well, but shit. There's no way I can keep that up.'

'Lot of money.' Graham was doing a silent calculation to get a yearly cost—he knew that often that figure could be even more shocking, particularly if it was converted into something else that was known to be important to the client. £7,800 pounds on alcohol in the year. A new car, a number of decent holidays. A lot of money.

'Yeah. No wonder I'm always a bit short, you know?'

'And not a lot to show for it either.' Graham knew he was stepping out of direct empathy, but he was taking a more motivational focus which he knew could help sharpen up Andy's perception of the impact of his drinking.

'Fuck all to show for it.'

'Pissed up against the wall, yeah.' Graham threw in the powerful comment, 'at that rate you pissed almost eight thousand pounds away last year.'

Andy hadn't thought of it quite like that and it did take him aback. 'What? Fuck's sake.' He thought about it and did the calculation himself. 'Shit—and last week wasn't as heavy as some weeks.' His expression was one of surprise and a sort of bewilderment.

'So maybe closer to ten thousand, whatever, it's a lot of dosh.' Graham was using his language carefully and intentionally, wanting the impact to be held.

'I can't … There's just no way I can carry on like that. I've got to find ways of cutting back.'

Graham nodded and felt sure that what had just been communicated had made a strong impression. But he was aware that Andy still looked astonished.

'That really has made an impression, hasn't it?'

'Yeah, shit, ten thousand quid—no, can't be right.'

'Think you made a mistake filling it out, then?' Graham handed it back. He felt sure that Andy wouldn't have done, but it all helped to consolidate the impact of what he had realised about the cost of his drinking.

Andy scanned down the diary, No, nothing seemed wrong. That was what he had been drinking, and what he'd spent. He knew he'd gone through at least a twenty pounds note each evening they'd been to the pub—which was every evening but one. No, that was what he'd drunk and what it had cost, even taking into account Julie's drinks when she had come with him.

He shook his head and handed it back. 'That's it. Ten grand.'

'Ten grand.'

Andy snorted. 'And I'd wondered if I had a problem. Well, that's a problem, isn't it?'

'It is if you don't want to spend ten grand a year on booze and have nothing to show for it other than a very large puddle of piss.'

'OK, I get the point. So, I need to change. But what do I do? I tried stopping a few weeks back and it was awful and, well, I can't do that, can I?'

Graham shook his head, 'No. We have to look at what you can cut out so that you gradually reduce, and then stabilise at that reduced level, and then reduce a little more. You have to adjust the pace of change in line with how you react. And you need some B vitamins as well—either from the GP, or from the chemist—thiamine in particular. Alcohol washes it out the system, you need to replace it, and particularly when you are reducing.'

'That's in corn flakes, isn't it? Seen it on the packet.'

'It is but you need to boost it up. They'll be cheaper to buy over the counter but you might want to talk to your GP. I'd advise seeing your GP because you might reduce to a level of alcohol at which you need medication to get you down the last bit, assuming you're aiming for abstinence. Takes out some of the physical reactions, calms things down, yeah?'

'Hmm. Haven't thought about that. Never really thought I'd stop completely, just cut back.'

'Well, it's an option. You could talk to your GP now about being given medication to help you stop—detoxify.'

'What, you mean I take something to stop me wanting to drink?'

'No, you take something that takes out some of the withdrawal reactions. It's not pleasant or easy, and you still have to say no to a drink, but it tranquilises you, staves off the kind of shakes and anxious reactions you experienced before.'

'Is it dangerous?'

'They have to get the medication level right so that withdrawal reactions don't break though.'

'Hmm, I imagine though they'd want me to stop if I did that.'

'Yes, probably, but you could discuss this. Some GPs appreciate that people want to stop their heavy use and then try and establish a lower level of drinking."

'I think I'll try it this way, try to make changes and bring it down slowly. But you say I may still need medication at some point?'

'We have to see how it goes. But take it carefully. Any uncertainty, see your GP.'

'I don't really want her to know about all of this. If I can get it under control myself, I'd prefer that. I've got ideas to try and I want to give it a go. I don't want to not drink, but I do want to drink less, you know, and feel I'm in control and can say "yes" to a drink when I want to, and "no" at other times.'

'Sure. It's up to you. People vary. Some people find they can reduce and stay reduced, others find it difficult and it kind of increases again or gets more of a binge pattern. We have to see how it goes.'

'AA says you have to stop, don't they?'

'Yeah, they do, and that seems to be what some people need, particularly heavy drinkers with long histories of alcohol use. And maybe where the issue is simply the alcohol use rather than the kind of experiences that you've had and which leave you wanting to drink to shut things out. We have to deal with those as well.'

'Yeah, guess you are right. So, I mean, I don't really want to go to AA.'

'Nobody's saying you have to. But it is an option. They can offer more support than anyone else in terms of groups being available every night if you are prepared to travel as there may not be a group every night locally.'

'The thought of sitting in a group—and Terry's experience …'

'Every group is different, Andy, ever meeting is different. From my experience, people seem to engage best when they feel in themselves a motivation to try it. But that's very subjective. It's up to you. I also know people who had vowed never to go but then did so out of utter desperation and it made all the difference. I'd always encourage people to try it because even if you do not work the steps—at least it gives you a place to go rather than the pub—and for many people, that is the first step.'

'Well, I've got Julie and we don't need to go down the pub so much.'

'So, maybe you can work something out between you on that one.'

Andy nodded. Julie wanted Andy to cut out his drinking, but he also knew she liked the pub atmosphere, and he wasn't sure how she would react. He couldn't see himself sitting there all night drinking orange juice. 'Hmm. Need to think about that.'

'You don't sound too sure.'

'Well, she does want me to cut back, but I'm not sure about whether she'd want to change her social life, I mean, she has said maybe I should drink something else.'

'So, you're not sure about going to the pub less. Are there areas of your drinking pattern that might be easier to change?' Graham was aware that there was never much point in tackling what was identified as the most difficult or ingrained part of a drinking pattern. Always look for the weakest link, the drinking that the client could realistically see themselves reducing or cutting out.

'The times I have a can or two, or a pint during the day, they feel important. I mean, I have them 'cos I really feel I need them.'

'OK. And you seem to regularly have cans when you get home, except for when you come here.'

'Yeah, well, I try to be clear when I come here. Don't think it would be helpful if I arrived with a can in my hand.' Andy smiled.

'I appreciate that. So it shows you can do it, but you need a reason and a distraction, like being here.'

'True. OK.' Andy was nodding, but unsure quite where to take this. He knew he couldn't come to counselling every night. He was about to think that he couldn't afford it, then realised that if he wasn't drinking he probably could, well four or five times a week. But that wasn't the answer. He must have smiled as he had the thought because he heard Graham say, 'I see you smiling.'

'Yeah, just found myself thinking about whether I could afford to come to counselling every evening! But that's not the way forward. I've got to do other things—we've got to do other things. Our lives are quite pub-centred.'

'That can be a problem. And everywhere you go there are bars. So it needs other things to focus on.' Graham was avoiding making suggestions. He wanted to see what came to Andy's mind, again feeling that they would be more likely to have meaning for him and be something that he could relate to and imagine himself doing. He had to ensure that any ideas were realistic. No point in setting someone up to fail, and see their motivation and self-doubt increase as a result.

'Hmm.' Andy was thinking. What could they do? Couldn't visit friends, they all drank. Cinema? He hadn't been to the cinema in years. But maybe. There was a newish complex that had recently been built in town ..., maybe. 'Cinema?'

'Sounds good. Do you go at the moment?'

'Haven't been in years—kind of get videos out, you know. But, well, guess that's an option. Once a week, maybe—if we can agree on what to go and see.'

'Think that could be a problem?'

'No, I'm sure we'd find something. I mean, we watch some crap on TV sometimes. No, it would be good. It must be years since I last went.'

'They've changed a bit—not just one screen and take it or leave it—lots of choice these days.'

'Yeah, I know. OK, So I need to find out about that. Be something to do one evening a week.'

'Fine. No need to change everything. Make a start. Try to chip away at it. Slowly introduce new things that you can enjoy and feel good about, you know?'

Graham looked back at the diary. 'You had a couple of evening in the pub when you don't seem to have drunk so much—you mention being with Gary those evenings. The other times you've written 'with friends'.

Andy explained how on a couple of occasions he'd been in with Gary, and described how he'd told him about the past as well, and how he felt Gary would be more supportive than the others.

'OK, so it seems like you drink less when you're with Gary than when you're with the others?'

'Yeah.' Andy was nodding.

'This'll sound simplistic, but can you spend more time with Gary?'

'Been thinking that myself. Probably. I have to break the heavy drinking pattern, and it does seem that I drink less with him. We talk more, doesn't get so, I don't know, so centred on the next pint, which is what I do, of course. Don't know why. That's how it is.'

'Do you meet up with Gary outside the pub?'

'How do you mean?'

'Well, do anything else together?'

'Like?'

'I don't know, snooker maybe, I don't know, meet up away from the pub and, well, maybe something like that might be an idea.'

'Yeah, maybe. Maybe. You're right, I do need to do other things. But I'm so used to the pub.'

Graham was nodding. 'I think you may have said that it feels like a second home.'

'At times more like a first home.'

'The pub really is such a familiar environment.'

'I feel at home there, you know?'

'The pub, the alcohol, or both?'

'The whole thing, really. Just feels good ..., but it's not the same now. I need other options, but I can't just stop drinking, can I?'

'Other options, maybe, but no, you can't just stop, not after that previous experience.'

'I know I need to take it slowly, and that I don't always have to drink so much. I need diversion and I need to spend time with Gary as well. And with Julie. I know I'm not sure how much she wants to change her social life, but I think she will. Well, we have to, don't we? She's said she wants to be supportive—it's what that means.'

'Yeah. That's right. You know you need to make changes and you have some options to still have a social life but with less alcohol intake, less pub-centred.'

'What about my past, though, I mean, how do I resolve that?'

'How has that been? We haven't focused much on it this week.'

'I don't know. Sometimes it feels worse, sometimes not so bad. I think it has helped getting out in the open but it was bad at first. It also helped telling Gary.' Andy told him about Gary's reaction. 'That was spot on. Sort of validated the awfulness of it all. Think I needed to hear that, and from a friend. But I still get overwhelmed and I'm aware now that it seems to be anxiety more than anything else.'

'So anxiety overwhelms you, what, when you think back?'

'Like I come over in a kind of cold sweat and just feel, I don't know, like wherever I am I need to get out.'

'Got to get out—sort of claustrophobia, or that too strong?'

'No, something like that. I need to watch that. It can really leave me wanting a drink.'

'Yeah, leaves you needing something to settle down.'

Andy nodded.

'Could be mild withdrawal reaction, but could be fallout from the past, leaving you particularly sensitive in some situations. Might be helpful to track that too, get a sense of what it's associated with, maybe?'

'Yeah. OK. So, I'm going to talk to Julie about some changes and I think it's going to be down the pub less, more time with Gary and different activities. To be honest, it's just too easy to drink in the pub. Daft thing to say, but that's how it is. I mean, at least it isn't a pub like some of the bars in town where there's nowhere to sit and you have to stand holding your pint. I know I'd drink more if it was like that.'

'Yes, they're a nightmare. Makes me think of Dodge City some of them, everything but the spittoon in the corner.'

'I imagine a few might even have that!' They both smiled. It was somehow a little bit of a relief to them both, it had become quite tense. Andy continued. 'OK, so take it slowly and not too much change at once. I've just got to try and reduce slowly, that the idea? And try and not swallow so many cans when I get home from work.'

Graham was glad Andy had something to work towards. Yes, he knew the past would not be resolved, and might never be. Andy might always carry with him particular sensitivities linked back to the death of his mother, and of his father as well. But he might be able to resolve any residual distorted self-beliefs that were rooted in that experience and how it had been with his violent father, and internalised to shape his self-concept.

'No, take it slowly, give yourself some variety and we'll see how it goes.'

Andy left the session feeling positive. It felt good having some realistic goals. Yes, it was strange, he didn't drink as much with Gary. But then in a way Gary had always been the quiet one in the group, more reflective, more likely to make his own choices. As he thought about it he realised that Gary never seemed so quite swept along by things, more his own person. Yes, made more sense to spend more time with him. He decided he'd mention this to Gary—maybe they could get together with Gary and his wife for a meal or something as well—Julie always got on well with Amanda. Yes, that felt good and realistic.

Graham sat back and contemplated the session and the journey so far. So much had happened in what seemed a relatively short period of therapeutic time.

It wasn't always like this, he knew that from experience. Sometimes it took many more sessions before things happened for clients, before past memories were loosened up or made visible within therapy. He believed in trusting the process. His role to create that therapeutic relationship within which the client could experience him or herself in a different way. Or maybe they would begin to feel more able to risk revealing or encountering aspects of their natures that previously they may have consciously or unconsciously denied to awareness, or shied away from, or just simply interpreted in a very different way.

Getting real was a phrase often used, and it sort of summed it up, but not in a really satisfying way. It was about openness and being able to experience yourself more accurately, without the subtle—and sometimes not so subtle—distortions that could occur during development. People being put down and ending up believing they are useless to the point of fulfilling that self-belief by pursuing unattainable goals, or simply not bothering to try to achieve anything; or the person who never really felt loved, who is left feeling that nobody could possible love them, or would more likely choose to love someone else. And then there were those who were significantly abused—wasn't all abuse significant? Normalising being brutalised and hurt, symbolising it within their awareness in such a way that they identify themselves as being the victim, and choosing partners and environments that perpetuate this primary identity.

Graham wrote his notes for the session and prepared to meet his next client. His thoughts went to Andy again. A lot of change to start to establish, he thought, but it can happen. However, Graham recognised Andy's ingrained need to drink as well, and it wouldn't be easy for him. Andy was dependent and would have to face the possibility that at some point he might need detoxification. But if he could bring it down slowly, prove to himself he could take control, establish a new pattern in his life, well maybe, just maybe, he could avoid this. Graham knew from experience that it was unlikely to be plain sailing.

* * * *

It was after they'd eaten and were sitting in the lounge that evening that Andy raised what he had discussed in the counselling that day. He explained what they were doing. He hadn't shown her the drinking diaries before, but now he did. He said how he knew he had to make changes, had to spend more time with people with whom he felt he was less likely to drink so heavily with, and make changes to his evening routine.

Julie wanted to help—but she liked going down the pub and meeting up with 'the girls' when they were in. She wanted Andy to change, but she really wasn't sure. She'd spent most of her social life in pubs and clubs, except as a younger teenager when they'd gone to the cinema, but that got dropped once they all started to go into pubs and could get served regularly.

'So, I need some other options, and one is to maybe have Gary and Amanda over for a meal sometime, and try and get out to do different things some evenings. I can't just stop. I can see that. And I can't cut back without replacing my drinking time with something else.' Andy sighed. 'The problem is, I'm still going to want a drink.' He looked at the can he'd opened a few minutes before which sat on the coffee table. 'It's instinctive. I reach for a can when I'm here, I reach for a pint in the pub.'

'I know, love, and I don't understand. Why can't you just say no to it sometimes? Why do you have to have it?' Julie knew that she wanted to help Andy but sometimes she just felt he didn't really help himself, and it irritated her. And she'd had a bad day at work and was tired, and really wasn't in the mood for this. She also remembered a relationship she'd had with someone before she met Andy—he'd been a drinker, and was such an insensitive bastard, or so it turned out. Though not to begin with. And she knew that her own father had been a heavy drinker as well, and had been warned to stop but hadn't, and had ended up dying a few years back, before she had met Andy—terminal liver cancer.

'Because of the shit in my head.'

'Alcohol just adds more shit, Andy.'

Andy could feel himself reacting. She wasn't being very sympathetic. 'Fucks sake, Julie, I'm trying. Don't you think I know that? If it was that easy, wouldn't I have got it sorted already?'

'I don't know, would you?' She was thinking of her father. How many times had he been told to stop. But he'd never really tried, not really. She never understood why, just how he was. She knew Andy was different. But sometimes …, sometimes she really wondered …

'What the hell is that supposed to mean.' Andy glared across to Julie and snatched up his can.

'Yeah, usual response. Pick up the can.' She shook her head, and was about so say something else when Andy got up. She knew she'd crossed a line and was sorry she'd said what she'd said. 'Look, I'm sorry …'

'Forget it. I thought you were on my side.' He headed for the door. 'I'm going up the Crown.' He slammed the door behind him, the ornaments on the shelf rattled and a china dog fell off. Julie closed her eyes. This was an all too common scenario. If he didn't like something, if you questioned him then, bang, off he'd go. She was sorry she'd said what she had said, but it had been said and now he'd come back drunk and be in a foul mood. What was she doing there? Why did she stay with him? Sometimes she knew, she could feel that love for him, but on other days, like now, she really felt like she'd had enough.

* * * *

Andy marched up to the bar. 'Pint of the usual, Mick.' He'd got his money down on the counter. He was feeling tense. The pub was quite busy, but then it was half past nine and it did tend to busy up as the evening wore on. He looked around.

'You look tense, Andy, what's got your goat?'

'Oh, don't ask, Mick, don't fucking ask. Who's in tonight?'

'Steve's around somewhere. Not sure where he is now, he was over there. Maybe he's gone for a pee or something.'

'OK, I'll keep an eye open. Cheers.' He took hold of his pint and gratefully downed half of it.' He lowered the glass. 'That's better. Thanks. Better get me another, I'm gonna be through this one pretty damn quick.'

'Sure, no problems, coming up.' By the time the second pint had appeared before him, Andy had just about finished the first. He waited at the bar until he had finished it, and then, with his second pint in his hand, turned to see if he could see Steve. He was just coming from the other side of the bar.

'Andy, you old fucker, we'd given up on you.'

'Yeah, well, trying not to come in so often but tonight I needed a beer or two.'

'Only two.' Come on over—I'm sitting over there. I see you've got one, I'll just get myself another.'

'I'll wait.' Steve got his beer and they headed over to a table in the corner.

'So, what do you mean, trying not to come in so often. What's pissed you off then?'

'No, nothing like that.' Andy wasn't sure about talking to Steve about his counselling and the idea that he needed to cut back, but it wasn't really that which was on his mind. It was Julie. Just felt he needed to sound off to someone about it. 'No, it's Julie really, she just ... oh I don't know. Never know with her. One minute she's great, and then she's having a go, you know? I don't know. Just wound me up tonight. Wasn't going to come out, but then I needed to get away.' He picked up his glass from where he had just placed it on the table, and took a couple of deep draughts. 'Anyway, enough about that. I'm feeling better already,' he lied. In truth, he was still feeling pissed off, and whilst he was glad to be down the pub, he was also feeling it wasn't where he'd planned to be that evening. He knew he shouldn't have come out, that he was trying to cut back, but … The first pint was beginning to get to his brain—not that he thought about it like that, he just felt a bit of the tension easing.

'Bit of a fight, huh? Better off being like me. Don't tie yourself down. Keep moving. That's my motto.'

'Yeah, well, most of the time it's great but it's been difficult recently and, well, I'm supposed to be cutting back on my drinking and spend less time in here.'

Steve choked on his beer. 'You're what?' His expression was one of incredulity as he lowered his glass and wiped the froth from his upper lip and nose.

'Seriously, I told you before I'm trying to cut back, and that means spending less time in here and doing other things.'

'Bullshit. You, not come in The Crown. What idiot put that idea in your head? That bloody counsellor, I'll bet.'

Andy was suddenly feeling uncomfortable. He didn't want to tell Steve any more about it. He felt suddenly quite defensive. 'No, it isn't that. I just feel like it isn't doing me much good, feel edgy a lot of the time. Tried to stop a little while back and got a really bad reaction. Julie thinks I'm irritable and argumentative.'

Steve made a somewhat derisory sound and shook his head. 'Ahh, Julie, is it, yeah, they like to do that, don't they.'

'What do you mean?'

'Blame it on the drink, bring you back into the house, get you under the thumb, you know? Yeah, I've seen it, I know the signs. Believe me, you're better off without it.' They both raised there glasses, they were both heading rapidly towards the bottom of their respective glasses.

'Yeah, well, maybe.' Andy paused. 'I don't know. Just pissed me off tonight and, well …'

'What you need is another. Come on, drink up. Telling us what we can and can't drink. Fuck's sake. Give me your glass.' Steve got up and marched over to the bar with the two now empty glasses. Andy sat and watched him depart. He didn't feel at all at ease with himself. Something was telling him this was not a good idea, but he didn't feel he could go back home. Steve was getting him a pint and he didn't want to be seen to be 'under the thumb', as Steve put it. He felt mixed up, and the alcohol in his brain wasn't helping matters. Not that he'd drunk much in the pub, but he'd already had a couple of cans at home before he had left. He took a deep breath and sighed. Why was life so bloody complicated?

'Hiya, you look pissed off, on your own?' It was Alan who had just come in and had noticed Andy sitting on his own seemingly without a drink.

'Hiya, I'm OK. Steve's getting a round in, he's over at the bar.'

Alan disappeared in the direction of the bar. They both returned a couple of minutes later.

'There you go.' Steve placed the pint in front of Andy.

'Cheers.'

'So, getting the grief, huh? Drinking too much, stay home, what, put up the shelves, wash the dishes, oh and just clear out that cupboard. That how it is?' Alan was grinning.

'What're you going on about?'

'Steve's told me.' He held his hand up, thumb down, gesturing in a downwards motion.

'It's not like that. Why do you think I'm here? I wouldn't be if it was like that, would I?'

'You tell me?' It was Steve now who was talking. 'Sounded like you were pretty keen to not be here just now—trying to cut back on your drinking. What's your problem?' Steve shook his head and grinned at Alan. 'Maybe it's all too much for him.' He winked. 'Maybe he's going to become do-me-sti-ca-ted.' They both burst into laughter.

Andy wasn't laughing. He was staring at his pint and wishing he hadn't said anything or come out that evening.

'Fuck's sake, gimme a break here. Jesus.'

'Yeah,' Alan was smirking from behind his glass. He took a mouthful and swallowed. 'You'll be in a …, what do you call those things …?'

Steve looked at him, 'what do you mean, what things?'

'You know, you wear at the sink, when you do the dishes.'

'Oh, what, an apron?'

'No, there's another word for it, you know?'

Mick, the landlord happened to pick this moment to be walking by having collected up some empties. 'Hey, Mick, what do you wear when you do the washing up?'

'What the fuck are you talking about?'

'Andy here's getting domesticated and we may need to have a whip round for some of the tools of the trade.'

'What, like marigolds, you mean?'

'What?'

'Rubber gloves. The wife always uses them.'

'Oh yeah, bit of rubber. You'd like that, Andy …'

'… so would Julie.'

They were all at it now, and Andy was feeling thoroughly pissed off with them. He wasn't in the mood to laugh and joke about it. At other times, maybe he would have been, but not tonight. It just irritated him the hell out of him. 'You bastards.' He felt suddenly angry. What did they know. Fuck all! But he also felt very uncomfortable. He really struggled when he was picked on, a link back to the past.

'You could always use the *rubber* glove yourself …,' Alan had a wicked look on his face, and the others waited for the punch line which was inevitably coming. 'Come in handy that, real kinky hand job! Probably get 'em in different colours too.'

'And flavours'. It was Steve that time, whose mind had gone off on one. 'Yeah, maybe matching marigold and condom sets, just what you need, handy for, well, almost anything! His n' hers sets.'

They all roared with laughter, except Andy, although he did allow himself a smile, as much to try and hide his feelings of insecurity. At least the focus had moved away from him. Maybe it was funny. Mind you, most things could be funny after a few beers. He shook his head. 'You fucking bastards, fucking crazy, the lot of you.'

'Ooh.' They all laughed again.

'Yeah, OK, have your fun. Jesus, once you lot get going.' Andy was shaking his head hoping they'd all start talking about something else.

Mick was moving away, still smiling. It hadn't been that funny, but he was the landlord, and if the punters wanted to laugh, you laughed with them. It's what they expected. They didn't want some miserable old fart behind the bar. Give 'em what they want, and they'll keep buying. He smiled to himself. That was what mattered. Keep 'em drinking and the cash register would keep registering. He thought of the two weeks he had planned in Greece coming up soon. Every pint sold would put a few more drachmas in his pocket.

'Well, come on, you asked for that. Now, forget all this crap about not drinking and let's have another round. Whose shout?' Steve was looking at Andy.

'Yeah, OK. Why the hell I'm buying you two a pint beats me though, after you give me such a hard time.' But it was his round and, well, you paid your way. That's how it was.

'Ooh, get you, it's Donna over there who wants the hard time. Bet she uses, what were they, marigolds!' Alan laughed at his own joke and they all joined in, the alcohol had loosened them all up and, well, anything was likely to seem funny now.

By the time he left the pub he'd had five pints in all, Alan had got a round in before closing, and they'd all had a large whisky for the road. He'd kind of put the ribbing behind him, but not completely. It still pissed him off. Alan and Steve had gone their separate ways.

Andy got home and was unlocking the door. The place was dark except for their bedroom light. Julie must have gone to bed but was probably still awake. He wondered what mood she'd be in. he guessed she wouldn't be happy. He went off to the bathroom—he needed a pee badly. He didn't feel drunk, but he was a bit unsteady. He decided to have a shower and then headed for the bedroom. The light was still on.

'Hi love.' He swayed slightly as he came into the bedroom.

'Pissed, huh?' Julie shook her head. 'What are you about? I thought you were trying to give up?'

'Yeah, well, you shouldn't have pissed me off.'

'Me? So it's my fault that you chose to go out and get pissed?'

'Yeah.' Andy had sat down on the bed, slightly more heavily than he had intended.

'Watch out!'

'Sorry, misjudged it a bit.'

'You've misjudged a lot of things.'

'Meaning?'

'Andy, I've had enough. I want to help but you've got to help yourself.'

Andy had got into bed. 'You're no bloody help. And I get crap from the lads as well. What's the point, what is the fucking point?'

Julie frowned, 'what do you mean, crap from the lads?'

'Oh, they just spent the evening winding me up about trying to cut back on the drinking, said I was under the thumb—your thumb.'

'Oh, so you blamed me.'

'Yeah, well, no, I mean, no, but, well … Oh, I don't know. Here give me a kiss.'

'What, you blame me for trying to help you and now you want a kiss?'

'Just a little one.'

'I am not interested.' With that Julie turned off the light.

Andy sighed and rolled over. 'Have it your way.' He sighed again as he closed his eyes. He felt suddenly strange as he did so. He thought it must be the beer. A bit dizzy. He didn't usually feel quite like this after a few beers. He opened his eyes again. 'I don't feel to good.'

'I'm not surprised.'

Andy tightened his jaw. It was a strange feeling, like he was retreating inside himself, getting smaller. He couldn't really describe it, it was just a sensation. It felt like the room was suddenly much bigger, and he was much smaller. There were sounds in his head. It was his father, hitting his mother. It was so clear, so, so clear. He tightened his eyes, trying to make it go away. It was like he was back in his room as a child, listening. It was terrible. He could hear her pleading with him to stop and then the sound of ... He could feel the tears hot in his eyes. He felt awful, terrible. Nowhere to hide from it. Nowhere. They didn't understand down the pub, Julie didn't care, and what good was Graham? In his alcohol-affected mind it just seemed that no-one really cared about him any more. What was the point of living? The thought kept going round and around in his head. What was the point? He'd never get away, never. He'd always be bullied. Images came at him from his school days. He had been bullied then, it had been a tough time. Sometimes he wished he'd never had a childhood.

It suddenly felt as though his whole world was collapsing in on him, and there was no-one, nobody to turn to. His head was spinning and he felt so spaced out. 'I'd be better off dead.' He hadn't realised he had actually said the words out loud. He thought he had only thought them. Julie heard him.

'Don't be stupid.'

'I'm not. I really think I'd be better off dead.'

Julie had put the light on, 'what, because I wouldn't kiss you?'

Andy sighed. 'You haven't got a clue.' He paused. 'No, because of all the stuff in fucking my head.'

He sounded so pathetic and Julie felt her attitude changing. She knew what the stuff in his head was, though she still didn't understand why the hell he had to drink to deal with it.

'Yeah, but you're dealing with that.'

'Am I? I don't know. I just don't know.'

'There's got to be an answer. People do cope with things like that. They must do?'

'Do they? Who do you know?'

Julie didn't have an answer. 'I don't know. But you don't really want to die. Not really.'

'I really think I do. Lying here now, with what's in my head, I really think it's what I want.'

'No.' Julie was shaking her head. She had propped herself and was looking down at Andy who was still lying with his face away from her. 'Come on, look, there's always something to live for.' She reached out to him and touched the back of his head.

The touch felt good. 'I really don't know. Maybe it's just been a bad day, but I just do not know.'

'Something happen in the counselling today?'

Andy thought about it. 'No, we were looking at my drinking pattern and what I could do to change it. Nothing really heavy.'

'Work OK today?'

'Normal kind of day.'

'So what is it? What's got to you?'

'I don't know. I felt like I was in the wrong place in the pub. And I hate arguing with you. Just feel unsettled, like I don't belong anywhere. And I guess I have had too much to drink and I guess it just all feels hopeless at the moment.'

'It's not hopeless, come on.' Julie felt a surge of love in her heart and a wave of sadness as well. 'It's just that, I find it hard to accept how you are. And what with my own father dying, and I'm scared it'll happen to you as well. And I don't want that. I want a better life for you, for me—for us. I couldn't bear it to see that happening to you. I really couldn't. And I don't know that I could face that if I really knew that was what the future was going to be.'

Andy swallowed. 'Yeah.' He paused and thought about what Julie had said about her own background and her father, how he had been with his drinking. 'Yeah, I forget about what you've been through.' He tightened his lips. 'Selfish bastard, aren't I?'

Julie didn't know what to say, so she said nothing. She simply slipped back down and put her arms around Andy.

Feeling that contact felt so good. Andy pushed himself back so there was more contact. He felt Julie's breast against his back, and her thighs against the backs of his legs. He wanted her, Oh God how he wanted her. He wanted to lose himself in her, bury himself in the warmth and acceptance of her body. He rolled over and pulled her to him, holding her tightly as he searched for her mouth in the darkness.

Their lips met. It wasn't what Julie had expected, she wasn't planning to make love, but the way he was holding her aroused something deep inside her and she knew that she wanted him too. She felt his erection, hard and pressing against her. She continued to kiss him deeply, her tongue pushing against his. She was feeling suddenly very hot and pushed the duvet down a little, to feel some cool air.

Andy had unbuttoned Julie's top and was sucking playfully yet quite intensely on her left nipple, slowly drawing it into his mouth before releasing it. Each time he did this it sent a spasm of delicious sensation. She was rapidly becoming moist, very moist.

'Oh God, Andy, Oh God, I want you, I want you now. Please.'

Andy manoeuvred himself quite deftly considering what he had drunk earlier, on top of Julie and opened her lips before sliding deep inside her, feeling her tummy arch up against him as he fully entered her. He placed his hands under her buttocks and pulled her towards him, enabling every millimetre of his penis to enter her. For some minutes they moved against each other. It was not long before they both came, and then all was quiet as they lay together. It was as though some unknown passion had unleashed itself and now they had nothing left to give.

They lay in the dark stillness, both lost in their own silent worlds of thoughts and feelings. Julie feeling warm and satisfied, holding the man she loved and wanted, but who so infuriated her at times, and scared her when she thought about her own past and what their future might become. Andy, his eyes tightly closed, wanting their lovers embrace to last forever. It felt like it was filling a huge hole inside himself, but he'd need to stay holding and being held forever to feel that it had been filled.

Chapter 6

The counselling session had begun. 'Well, it wasn't an easy start but the week settled down and Julie and I are now establishing a different kind of routine. I've put a brake on going down the pub. Still drinking more than I should, but we've made some changes.' Andy went on to describe what had happened after the last session. How he'd argued with Julie, gone down the pub, got pissed and fed up, how it had been when he'd got home. 'Something changed, Graham, but I can't describe it. It was being with Julie, holding her and being held. I'd felt so small just a short time before, hearing voices from childhood, and it's like it was sort of healing in some way. I can't explain it.'

'Healing, making love, holding, being held?'

'It's been better between us. I've filled out the diary. Yeah, bad that first day when I was here, few cans when I got home, four pints in the pub, I think that's what it was anyway, and a whisky before we left. But that was the heaviest day of the week.' Andy handed Graham the diary.

'And you've not really been down the pub much since?'

Andy shook his head. 'No. We went to the cinema on the Thursday. Tuesday we'd stayed in. Guess the memory from the night before was still with us. I was a bit edgy but took it carefully. Still had a few cans, but I was OK. Had a few drinks on the Wednesday. Julie drove. We realised I probably needed to let her drive as I'm likely to get over the limit. And, well, I don't want a bad reaction to it again. Friday we went out for a walk, yeah, and Julie drove and we went to a different pub in the country. Saturday we met up with Gary and Amanda for a meal. That went well. Didn't drink too much, but still drinking, you know, probably more than I should be.'

Graham totted up the units. 'About ninety, maybe one hundred units, how were you feeling because this is less than your last diary.'

'OK. Not sleeping too good. That seems to have got worse as the week went on. Edgy. Can't settle. I sweat. Bit shaky sometimes.'

'Yeah, you sound like you are just on that edge, just drinking enough to get through.' This wasn't unusual and it was an experience that Graham had heard other clients talk about too.

'Some evenings I really wanted more. I did sneak an extra couple of cans when Gary and Amanda were around. I had to.' He paused as another recognition came to mind. 'And I seem to drink more at the weekends. I suppose I always have, really. Lunch-time, you know?'

'Hmm, yeah, more at weekends, and something to do with lunch-time.'

Andy tightened his lips as he thought about his pattern of drinking. 'But I need to change. I've got to keep on with this.'

'Keep on with making changes, you mean?'

Andy nodded. 'I'd like to cut back more, but at the moment, I don't know. I want to try.'

'So, apart from the weekends, no cans during the day. That's also a change.' Graham felt it was important to acknowledge this.

'Yeah, it is. Wasn't easy though. But I'm managing. Getting through lots of coffee and cola. Taking a big bottle of cola with me on the van each day, and a flask of strong coffee.'

'Cola and coffee.' Graham wasn't surprised by this, heavy drinkers often needed to maintain liquid intake, and sugary drinks and/or caffeine were often popular choices, though not necessarily healthy ones, and certainly not long term. He found himself wondering about what Andy was eating. 'And how are you eating?'

'Yeah, well, not to bad. Didn't tend to eat so much when I was drinking really heavily, but now, yes, I'm eating better. Never been one for breakfasts but I have been having something at lunch time. Used to duck lunches.'

'Sorry?' For some reason best known to himself. Graham had heard it as meaning Andy was used to eating duck for lunch.'

'Used to missing lunch.'

'Oh right, yes, it happens.' Graham did not mention his misunderstanding, wouldn't have served any therapeutic purpose. 'Alcohol takes away the feeling of wanting to eat. I think it shrinks the stomach, plus when people drink a lot they can simply find it hard to keep it down. Thankfully you're not there.'

'All in all, maybe not a bad week as far as the drinking is concerned.'

Graham was struck by the sense that whilst the drinking had been OK, there was something else. 'so, OK with the drinking.'

'Yeah.' Andy shook his head and bit his lip. 'But I'm not doing well with the memories.'

'How do you mean?'

'They seem to be with me more of the time, and really intense. So real, like they're almost happening.'

'Like you are reliving them but they are really in the present?'

Andy was thinking of the memories of his mother being beaten by his father, as well as his brother—and of course, himself. But it was the sounds of him hitting his mother, of her pleading with him to stop. And of Terry crying, and the sound of that leather belt. Thwack!, it would go, a really stinging sound matched only by the sharp stinging pain that his own body had become accustomed to. He could relive it now, on his back and on his chest, and his arms as he had tried to fend it off. He was always careful to keep his body covered at school. They had long sleeve shirts for sports. He'd felt ashamed, didn't want anyone to know. Nobody ever did. His father had rarely hit him across the legs and so wearing shorts for sports and PE wasn't an issue. The occasional marks were put down to the rough and tumble of being a boy. He just said he'd been kicked or knocked into playing football. He always seemed to be believed.

Graham watched Andy as he sat with his own thoughts. Graham was not going to disrupt him. Things came up that needed attention. Sometimes this involved talking, sometimes it was the client having time to reconnect with some experience which might—then or later—lead to a re-evaluation of the experience and a shift in the way that experience affected them. He saw many clients who blamed themselves for things that had been done to them in childhood. Gradually, as the experience was revisited from an adult perspective, and the client was accompanied by their therapeutic companion in a relationship that was experienced as being trustworthy, honest and supportive, they would begin to challenge the meaning that they had attributed to that early experience or set of experiences.

He would often hear someone suddenly say, 'It wasn't my fault, was it?'. For Graham, this was always such a significant shift. Responsibility had to be apportioned to where it rightly belonged—in the hands of the one who had abused or damaged in some way the client that was now seeking help through therapy. 'No,' he would say, 'it was not your fault.' And there would then follow a lengthy period in which the client wrestled with this new idea, and their inner structure of self struggled to adjust to this new information, having to re-adjust their sense of identity in order to take account of what had changed. It was a wonderful process—painful, so painful, but the emergence of a person who was freer from their traumatised experience was so rewarding, and for Graham a huge part of why he was a therapist.

Andy was speaking. 'It was awful, a nightmare that seemed like it would never end. And it feels like I am closer to it at the moment. I guess the alcohol held it back to a degree, and now it comes through—at night when I can't sleep, during the day. Sometimes I can forget about it, when I am focused on something else, but sometimes it's just suddenly there.'

'Alcohol keeps it at bay but now you find that the memories are more present, and it sounds like it can happen at any time?'

'Pretty much.' Andy took a deep breath. 'This will get better, won't it?' And felt and looked concerned.

'Yes, and I can hear your concern as well. You really don't want to stay with things the way they are at the moment.' Graham felt for Andy, he felt struck by the humanness of his struggle.

'No, I couldn't bear it. I have to let it all go, at least find a way of not so much forgetting—I've used the alcohol to try and do that. I don't suppose I'll ever forget. It's about being able to get on with my life. I'm sure I've said that before …'

Graham nodded, he thought so too.

'… but I cannot let this get in the way. I want a life with Julie. I want us to settle down. I want kids, you know? I want to love them in ways that I never was. Well I was, my mum, you know, but …' At this he closed his eyes, feeling a surge of emotion. 'Sorry.'

'Take your time, these are painful needs …'

Andy nodded and drew a deep breath into his lungs. 'Yes, I know. I know …' He lapsed into silence as he struggled to regain his composure. 'I want it to be different, and that scares me, Graham. But what if I can't? I did feel love from my mother, she tried, God knows how she tried. She was there for us, and yet she never left him. She could have left and took us with her, but she never did. And …,' Andy paused, very much with his thoughts and with a feeling of tightness in his stomach, 'I find myself thinking about this. I guess she had reasons. It wouldn't have been easy, but it would have been better. Why did she stay?' Andy felt a little light headed. He was very concentrated in his thinking, in his inner struggle to make sense of it all. It wasn't new, he'd thought like this many times over the years. He didn't have an answer, and he sort of knew he never would have one, and yet he also felt as though he needed to know, as if it would make some kind of difference.

'That's hard for you to understand. Why did she stay? She could have left and taken you both with her, but she didn't, for whatever reason she stayed and that meant you stayed.'

Andy didn't really hear Graham's response. His inability to find an answer, and the not knowing that it left him with was giving way to another feeling. 'And I'm angry about that, but how can I be angry. She tried, and she died trying to protect us.' Andy had closed his eyes and was feeling hot, burning emotion in his eyes and throat, and a huge pressure in his chest ...

'Yeah, you feel angry and yet how can you be angry ...?'

'My whole life has been messed up by that ... It's like I carry the legacy, not him. He goes and kills himself, but me, we, Terry and I.' His voice was raised. 'How do I get it out of my head? *How* do I get ...?' Andy lifted his hands to his face and began to cry. His shoulders shook as he sobbed. His breathing came in short bursts, otherwise he did not move. The tears flowed. Graham reached over to place his hand on Andy's shoulder. There was nothing to say. So much emotion still locked up inside. Was this release the answer? What really happened in these moments of cathartic release? Did something really get released, or was it all down to brain chemistry? What are emotions? Do we have a body of emotions as some believe, or are they chemically produced within the body, triggering a range of sensations to which we attribute the descriptor—emotion?

Graham had witnessed many times this process of release. It often did seem helpful, and as though something was let out of the person. He didn't believe it was simply brain chemistry. He reckoned human-beings began forming their sense of self from their first breath, although he knew therapists who claimed they could work with pre-natal memories. He did not know. He had not experienced this. And, of course, others claimed to work with people through recovered past life memories. Again, he was unsure about this. Did we carry memories from a previous life? Could they be accessed? Could certain physical or psychological conditions that seem difficult to explain in this life have their origin in some unexplained way in a previous life? Graham had pondered these questions and had come to the conclusion that people had enough pain and trauma from their current life to resolve before worrying too much about what might have gone on before. But it did intrigue him, none the less.

He looked at Andy, a man who had experienced more in his young life than many would have to face in a whole life time. And he had spent more than the last fifteen to twenty years—in fact the majority of his life, and certainly all of his adult life—trying to forget something that was unforgettable, trying to escape from thoughts and feelings that were inescapable These were thoughts and feelings that were in a sense bound to him as if by strong ropes. Yes, Graham thought, we carry ourselves around with us, our demons, our joys, all that contributes to the person that we have become. Some of it we try to avoid, or we deny. Some of it we embrace. The reasons for choosing which may not always be clear. We are conditioned into thinking in particular ways about ourselves by the influence of significant others. We symbolise meaning within our self-structure and generate a sense of self as we try to achieve satisfaction from our encounters. Encounters with what? Ourselves, other people, life, experience, everything that occurs on this journey through a lifetime.

Life can mess us up, distort our sense of who we are, of what is right, of how we should be as we seek approval and the satisfying sense of belonging and of feeling loved. Graham did not dwell on these thoughts as he sat with his hand on Andy's shoulder. These had been some of the many thoughts that had contributed to his feeling that somehow there was something about the way you related to people that could create a healing process. He was no healer in the sense of being someone different, or special, as if he had some gift. But he did believe that everyone who could relate from the heart was a healer.

What caused the kind of deep sadness and pain that he witnessed daily? Screwed up relationships. He knew at some deep fundamental level that if he could create what he termed 'right relationship' with people—and he didn't need to be a therapist to do that—he could create or contribute to a healing environment.

Andy continued to cry. Was he crying as the young boy who had seen his mother die violently at the hands of his father? Or was he crying for the void of never having known a loving father, or experienced a happy family life in those early formative years? Or was it the loss and separation of being taken into care for that brief period before going to his aunt and uncle, and of having to live with them whilst knowing that both his parents were dead and will never be seen again? Do we really understand what this kind of experience does to a young heart and mind? To know the certainty of death before life has hardly started? Or maybe it puts life in perspective, shattering the grand illusion that somehow death is distant and something not to think about. What is probably a fact is that the child is left with a knowing that terrible things do happen, and that they can happen to you. If young enough, the child might develop dissociative processes to find freedom from the pain, hurt and utter bewilderment as to what is happening to them. Perhaps when they are younger this is more likely. It is a time when the structure of self is less developed and resilient. Or they may carry it with them like a wound that never heals, constantly hurting, leaving the child in need of finding other ways to block out the pain, or to distract attention from it in some way.

Graham took a deep breath as he watched Andy and instinctively felt his hand gently squeeze his shoulder. He wanted to simply communicate, 'I'm here, you're not alone'. How many times must Andy have felt alone? His heart went out to him, silently, no words to carry the desire to reach out. What was that feeling? Caring? Compassion? Love? What did love mean in a therapeutic sense? A sense of common humanity, the heartfelt response of a human being to another in pain? As he looked across at Andy he found a simple question forming in his mind. Where are you now, Andy? So many years you have carried so much pain and hurt in your being, desperately trying to anaesthetise it. And now the anaesthetic is being withdrawn.

'Oh God.' Andy was rubbing his face with his hands. He felt very still. He could feel the contact from Graham's hand, and he was grateful for that link into the outer world. Not that his inner world wasn't real, but he could so easily get lost in it, overwhelmed by the swirling storms of emotional upheaval that seemed to form such a large part of who he was. He glanced over to Graham. 'Thanks.' He took a deep breathe and blew the air out. 'That was for mum, Terry and me, for what we never had, for what was taken from us, for how we have been left. That was for us.' He paused. 'I've made up my mind—I need to talk to Terry about all of this. I don't know if it will do any good, or whether he'll be interested, but I feel I need to talk. It's like we share a common heritage and somehow it feels right to try and get ourselves back on track—and in some way in memory of our mother.'

Graham had drawn back into his seat. 'Something about the three of you and now the two of you sharing that heritage, that …' Graham did not finish the sentence. He was unclear what to add.

'It's something we went through together and we must come through it. It's like if we don't, well, he's won, hasn't he?'

'He's won? You mean your father?'

Andy nodded. 'And you know, not just him, but everyone who abuses and hurts children. If I don't, we don't, make something of our lives then the damage lives on and …' Andy paused. '… and then the damage gets passed on to the next generation.' As he spoke he looked into Graham's eyes.

Graham returned his gaze. The thought that struck him was whether Andy felt he might carry it into the next generation. Or was that his own thought? He saw the look of concern in Andy's eyes.

'That's frightening, yeah?'

'It's another reason to sort myself out. I'd like kids, but not while I'm like this. I wouldn't want to risk it, just in case. I mean, I'd never want to hurt a child, but I worry about how my past has affected me. What would I be like as a parent? I don't know. I just don't know.'

Graham had a split second to decide on his response. 'That's an awful thing not to know.' He paused before adding the thought that had come to him, 'and I want to say, yeah, you'd be a great parent, and I'm sure that's what you'd want to be able to say, but you don't know, you just can't be sure.'

'That's why I have to do this, I have to keep coming here, I have to get the alcohol out of my life and the memories out of my head.' Andy smiled, but it wasn't an easy smile. 'I guess I need a detox in every sense of the word.'

'Mind and body, as it were.'

'Hmm.' Andy sighed and looked down, dropping his shoulders. He hadn't realised how tense he had become. His back was stiff and he sought to free it up by moving his shoulders. 'Ooh ... my back seems to get so stiff these days.'

'Toxins in the muscles—can be alcohol-related.'

'Damn stuff gets everywhere, doesn't it?'

Graham nodded, but he remained alert to the fact that he had perhaps contributed to moving Andy's focus away from the idea of detoxing his life as well as his body. The conversation had become body-centred. 'So, a detox in every sense of the word.' Graham brought the focus back and waited to see if Andy wanted to pick up on this.

He nodded. 'I need to make changes, a lot of changes. I've made a start I know, but it isn't easy. I feel edgy but I know I've got to keep on trying. Part of me still wants to say, 'sod it, you're OK, don't worry about it', but I know that's not right. I feel like I'm trying to change direction but if I don't sort of keep the pressure on I'll just drift back into the old ways.' He paused.

'That's a real fear, that you'll drift back into the old pattern?'

'It's like I know what I need to do, but there are times when I just need a drink.'

'That felt need can be really powerful.'

'Incredibly powerful. I just lock into thinking about a drink, it's all I think about. It's there, in my head. I can taste it, feel the sensation. The urge is so strong.'

Graham stayed with the struggle and the power of the urge to drink that Andy experienced. 'Powerful urge, like it takes over—you have to have a drink.'

'And sometimes I do, and sometimes I can hold on. But it isn't easy. Mostly I have a drink when it's like that unless I'm doing something. I got the feeling really strongly in the cinema. There was a scene and people were drinking—well, seems like most films these days involve people drinking—and it set me off. I had to close my eyes for a while to try to get a grip. I really wanted to get out but I knew I couldn't. Thank goodness we were in seats in the middle and not at the end. I really might have got up and gone out for a drink if we'd been at the end.'

'That close.' Graham was tempted to highlight that at least he now had a strategy, but he didn't want to divert him from exploring the intensity of the experience and what it meant to him.

'Yeah.' He shook his head. 'I never really thought it was this difficult, I mean, I never thought I had a problem, but I do now. I can see how my life has become alcohol-centred. Without thinking I just drifted into it.'

'Big part of your life for a long while.'

'Since teens, since I discovered that alcohol helped me to blot things out. Funny really, never felt tempted much into drugs—guess I'd already found alcohol and it worked for me.'

'Horses for courses. Alcohol did what you wanted it to do, it was reliable, so why use something else?'

'I guess I didn't have a reason. And yet, you know, although I drink heavily, I've never really gone for it like Terry. I mean, he binges himself till he keels over. My pattern's different.'

'So, Terry's drinks himself to a standstill?'

'Into oblivion. I kind of drink steadily but he has intense periods of drinking, then he stops for a while—not for long, mind you, and then he goes for it again—all or nothing, that's how it is with Terry, and usually it's all.' He took a deep breath and shook his head—'what a mess, what a tragedy. If only … things could have been so different. Why did we have such a crap childhood? I mean, I know it got better later, well, sort of, though neither of us really settled. I guess we'd both been too badly affected. Terry didn't do much at school—well, he wasn't there most of the time. He's never really settled, not with anything. It's like he just can't rest, he just can't. He can't put the demons to rest.' He sighed. 'I wish I could help him. Maybe I will, maybe what I'm learning here I can use to try and help him.'

'You'd really like to help Terry.' Graham spoke softly.

Andy nodded. Then he shook his head and sighed once more, 'but he's so much more down the line.'

'There's always hope—people do change and sometimes when we think it's too late. He's got time to change, but he's got a lot to come to terms with.'

'He's got a lot to get out. He just drinks. Been in trouble a few times—usually violence. I wonder if that's because of what he experienced himself. He's usually drunk when it happens, gets into fights. Been arrested a few times. Nothing really serious, thank goodness. But sometimes I feel it's only a matter of time before something really bad happens and then he'll really be in trouble.' Andy raised his head back to look up at the ceiling. 'I don't know. What a mess. What a fucking mess.'

'Yeah, what a mess.'

Andy sat in silence. So many thoughts and feelings. Last time he'd seen Terry they'd drunk too much. They'd got back really late. It hadn't helped his relationship with Julie much. Terry didn't like Julie. Andy thought he was jealous. He'd often say some pretty nasty things when he was drunk. 'I need to talk to him.'

'Seems important to you to do that.'

'But if I see him it'll be difficult not to drink, or at least, not go over the top.'

'So, you want to see him, but if you do then the risk is your drinking will go over the top.'

'And that's not much help to me, is it?'

'No.' Graham felt the best response was a direct and honest one. He felt strongly that this would not be a good time for him to see Terry in terms of the impact it might have on Andy's alcohol use, but then maybe Andy needed to talk to Terry, and it might be more important and outweigh the drinking risk. How was he to know? It was so simple to say, 'don't see Terry, it'll make it worse'. But what could be worse? And here were two brothers, connected not only by blood but also through a tragic shared experience that somehow they needed to come to terms with. In what way would that be achieved? How was he, Graham, supposed to know what was best? He didn't know. He couldn't know, and in a sense it wasn't for him to try and know. He was there to trust Andy's process, his own inner experiencing and adjustments, changes, whatever you called them, that occurred in response to experiencing this something called therapy. His role was clear—to offer Andy the consistent warmth and acceptance, empathy and genuineness that he knew lay at the heart of therapeutic relationship and process.

'No, you're right. But maybe in a while I'll feel ready to talk to him … Maybe.' He felt very reflective as he sat pondering on what he was saying. It didn't feel right. Terry was his brother, he couldn't not try and reach out to him. He wanted to share what he was learning, what he was doing. He wanted Terry to know and he wanted to try and help him change in the way that he was trying to change. 'Maybe we should try and help each other?'

'You'd like to feel that you could change together?'

'Yeah, but it won't happen, will it? I mean, he's not there, is he?'

'Probably not, not just now, anyway. But, neither were you a few weeks back.'

Andy nodded. 'Yeah, that's true, but Julie was pushing me. It wasn't me deciding. And Terry hasn't got anyone to push him—at least he didn't when we last spoke, a few weeks back. No, he's not there yet. But maybe one day.'

Graham had noticed that the clock was against them and the session was soon due to end. He mentioned it to Andy.

'Yeah, time to head off. Let me have another drinking diary. I think they're helping.'

'Sure. Anything planned for this week?'

'Cinema again on Friday. We've decided to go out Saturday, get down the coast if the weather's good. Gonna try and stay in during the evenings. Need to do something, though. Can't just look at the box every night. Need to keep busy, particularly when Julie works late. They're tough evenings.'

'Sounds like you need some company.'

'Yeah. Match on TV on Wednesday—European game—maybe Gary's free, help me watch it without downing too many beers.'

'Sounds like a good idea.'

'Maybe get a pizza or two in. I'll give him a call.' He looked at the clock. 'Shit, time to go. Got to pick Julie up from the hairdressers.'

The counselling ended with Andy heading out the door into the rain which had started during the session. Graham watched him dash down the path and slowly closed the door. He was aware of still feeling for Andy and his brother—what a nightmare experience for them in childhood. Whilst he knew the theory around psychological processes and how people could move on, he still wondered at the way human beings survived, although sometimes that survival perversely involved acts of self harm. He was pleased to be having his own supervision the next day. He went to see Stuart, his supervisor, twice a month to talk about his clients. He'd spoken to him about Andy before, but was aware that he was feeling affected by the image of those two boys and what they had witnessed. He shook his head as he returned to the counselling room.

Last time he'd talked to Stuart it had been after Andy had talked about the death of his mother. It still felt shocking to him. In a way, he was grateful for that. It was shocking and he should feel shocked. It was appropriate and Andy needed someone to be genuinely present and in touch with realistic feelings, thoughts and reactions as he revealed his inner world, his past and his present. The cost of being a therapist, Graham thought to himself. Being a therapist wasn't always comfortable, in fact, often it was distinctly uncomfortable. He needed to feel the effects of what his client's experienced and described. He needed to be in touch with that edge of connection. He knew he sometimes drifted from it, but he tried to be there.

The thought that kept coming back to him as he remembered how Andy was in the sessions when he was distressed, he kept coming back to wondering about Terry. So much pain for Andy, so much hurt, so much loss, but what about Terry? What about the brother who was blamed for his mother's death, even though he wasn't to blame? The brother who, at some level within himself, probably still carries a belief that he was to blame. And now Terry drinks, binges to a standstill, trying to drown out the horrible feelings and thoughts that assault his senses, and probably, as well, now has to drink to stave off withdrawal reactions as well. The double dependence—psychological/emotional and physical/chemical. Graham felt himself taking a deep breath as he let the immensity of it sink in, and the human tragedy that it represented. What must it be like for Terry? He had no idea. He simply knew that the thought hurt, and that his heart felt full of compassion, not only for Terry but for the thousands, no, millions of people all over the world who struggle to survive tragedy and trauma during their early lives, and who find their own solutions even if that cause more problems. For Graham, it all put life into a rather different perspective.

Chapter 7

Stuart lived about fifteen miles away in the country and Graham enjoyed the drive over. It was good to have that bit of space to reflect and prepare his thoughts. He had a number of clients to talk about but he was aware that Andy was very much present for him. He was troubled. He had already discussed Andy but somehow he was feeling more affected now, more touched by his story and about the struggle that he, and his brother, had faced and still faced in coming to terms with it. As he drove along—it was mid-afternoon—he thought about his own circumstances. Married with three children, a further son by his first wife, a nice house just on the edge of town, a steady job with the freedom that came from being self-employed. He felt pretty much in control of his life and his choices. He felt clear as to why he made decisions. He'd been in therapy and had resolved a number of issues from his own past. Nothing particularly traumatic although the upbringing he had experienced had left him with a number of beliefs about himself that he had generated in order to please those around him—particularly his parents.

They were now on good terms but there had been a phase, in his late thirties, when he had rebelled. He'd been married for fourteen years but realised he wasn't happy, that he was going through the motions in many ways. Corrine had, he realised, been someone he had got into a relationship with not because he wanted to but because it fitted his view of himself as someone who wanted a routine life, everything fairly predictable. But during the counselling training, as he went through his own process of getting greater clarity as to how much of himself was adaptive and conditioned into being, he realised he wanted something else. The next couple of years were difficult and he really did not know what to do, but gradually it became clearer and clearer that he needed something else, and that he really wasn't experiencing the kind of feelings for Corinne that he knew he should do for them to have a really good relationship.

In fact, the process of their marriage breaking down was a mutual one. Corinne, too, was seeking something else. She had gone back to work a few years earlier and had begun to develop her own social life. She had married young and was soon pregnant and now she wanted to live a little. One thing had led to another and they finally agreed to break it up. Toby, their son, lived with Corinne initially—he was becoming more independent himself by then and was now living his own independent life away from home.

It was during the break up that Graham had met Melissa, and they had just clicked right from the start. They moved in together and Melissa fell pregnant with Tim, their eldest. They decided to marry once the divorce was through and were now settled down together. Melissa also worked as a therapist and she had a business offering training to companies: team-building, relationship and communications skills, that kind of thing. They now had two more children, twin girls.

Yes, Graham thought, as he turned into Stuart's road, life was good. Nothing like Andy, or Terry, was experiencing. He was fortunate and it felt important to acknowledge that to himself. They were in such a different place. He knew he'd heard what Andy had to say, felt deeply affected by his story and the release of emotion that had taken place in the sessions. He did feel like he could relate to him, and yet ... Somehow there was a gap, a gulf even. No, not as large as that, but a sense of not being able to really connect and get inside the inner world that was Andy's daily reality. It seemed like something was blocking him, which was unusual in his experience, and he felt he needed to discover what it was. Although he felt present during the sessions, and whilst he didn't dwell on it at the time, he often found himself reflecting between sessions on how the world must seem for a person whose history included witnessing the death of his mother as a result of the actions of his father, and the then suicide of the father. And as he thought this his mind wandered further afield—the people in war-torn countries where children witnessed horrendous atrocities. He could feel himself going cold at the thought if it.

He'd pulled up and took a moment to bring his thoughts back into himself and to run through, in his mind, the clients he planned to talk about. He thoughtfully got out of the car, locked the door and headed along the path.

They had sat themselves down in Stuart's front room—where he held his supervision sessions. He lived alone and wasn't disturbed by anyone intruding on the space. It was quite a modern design with spots lights set into the ceiling. The walls were painted a pale green and the room contained a dark green sofa and two chairs. He was sitting in one of the chairs, Stuart was in the other. Stuart had a couple of paintings on the walls, both landscapes. There was an open fireplace with a coal-effect gas fire. The room felt warm. Graham shook his head and took a deep breath. 'Andy's getting to me, at least, I find myself thinking about him and his brother. You remember I told you about the death of his mother?'

Stuart nodded. He remembered it well. He had found it quite shocking as well and had talked it through with his own supervisor. He now felt clear in himself to be present for Graham and to help him explore what it was that was troubling him.

'I keep trying to imagine what it must be like to go through that experience. How does it leave you feeling?' He shook his head again. 'How do you cope? What kind of person does it make you become?'

'Big questions, Graham. Their story has really made a deep impression on you and it is demanding of you that you find answers to a whole range of questions.'

'I do feel I need answers.'

'Where do you want to start?' Stuart trusted the wisdom of his clients' and his supervisees' psychological processes to prompt them into exploring what was most pressing. Graham had given a number of questions and it was for Graham to decide which he wanted to explore.

Graham had closed his eyes. 'You know, in a funny kind of way, it isn't Andy. I mean it is, but it isn't. I don't feel I am connecting as much as I could, or maybe I'm giving myself a hard time—but it's his brother, Terry.'

'What is it about Terry. What exactly?'

'Being blamed by his father for his mother's death. Seeing it happen in a moment when he would have been full of his own fear, and probably hatred towards his father. He must have been so full of difficult feelings in that moment and then it happens, she falls, and that's it. And he has to live with it. But there is something about the intensity of the feelings that must have been around. The trauma must have been buried in the midst of so many sharp feelings. And now he drinks, binges to oblivion.' He shook his head and pursed his lips. 'What a life.' He was still shaking his head.

'Yes, what a life. And so many questions and thoughts and feelings …'

'I just can't get my head round it.'

Stuart was struck by a powerful urge to say something and he had learned to trust these urges, particularly in moments of deeper contact, when there was a genuine seriousness present in the relationship. 'Your head … or your heart?'

Graham's response was wholly instinctive. He just felt himself taking a huge deep breathe and holding it for a second or two, before letting it back out. 'Hmm.' He sat and pondered not just what had just been said but what it had left him feeling. 'Shit. I'm in my head and that's why I'm not feeling connected. It's all about getting my head round it, but it isn't, not really. You're right. It's about getting my heart open to it. I know I have been affected but the truth is I want to cry with him, Stuart. I want to share my own tears for the horror of what he has had to face, and Terry.' Graham swallowed, his throat had gone dry. 'I want to cry for both of them.'

'Tears for them both, bottled up inside you, unable to get out.'

'Yes.' A pause and another deep breath. 'Yes.' He lifted his hands up to his face. 'Oh God.' Another deep breath and this time he could feel his eyes watering. 'Poor kids.'

'Yeah, and in particular something about Terry.'

'Yes. He'd be about the age of my eldest now …' Graham went silent. He looked across at Stuart. He had tightened his lips as he nodded slightly. 'Yes. I guess that's it. We're actually very close. The twins—the girls—are both younger. It's Tim.'

'Can you say a little more?'

Graham thought about it, he wanted to find the right words. This felt so important. 'Yes, I guess at some level I am contrasting Terry with Tim.' He sat back and cupped his chin in his right hand, supporting it with his elbow. Another deep breath. 'Tim's got a good life, lots of friends, doing well at school. I think he feels loved—I sure hope he does. We do stuff together as a family, and he and I. And the thought that's with me now is how would Tim change if he was faced with the experience that Terry, and Andy, had to face? What would he become? What of his potential would be lost or buried under the intensity of the experience?'

'Mmm, how much would get lost.'

'And I guess for Andy, and Terry, they probably never really knew the kind of experience that my son has, they may not have known what they were losing, or had lost, because they'd never had it. They'd already been robbed of it.'

'So, yes, the sense of loss for them, but was it loss or something else?'

'I don't know. But it makes me angry, Stuart, I am really aware of it. How the hell could he have been like that, and yet he would have had his reasons. He was messed up by something as well as the drinking probably. I want to blame the father, get angry with him, and yet, somehow, somewhere, I know that it's not that simple, that perhaps he was trapped in his own nightmare as well.'

'So you're left wanting to be angry, feeling angry, but you don't know who to direct it at.'

Graham nodded. 'Yes. Anger towards the father, and yet he hanged himself. What torment must *he* have gone through? I mean, he probably dried out after being arrested and who knows what he then went through.' He paused, he hadn't quite thought about it like this before. 'Can you imagine it, you come out of the alcoholic haze maybe for the first time in a long time—I don't know if he was a dependent drinker—and you realise, without the blurring effect of the alcohol, the reality of what has happened, of what you have done. Or maybe he did it in blackout!' He sat quietly after having had this thought and Stuart maintained the silence, it felt appropriate.

'Two sons, now men, each with nightmares locked up inside of themselves. One drinking and out of control, driven to try and blot out the feelings, thoughts, memories that keep trying to bubble through, the other at least now learning to release the feelings without using alcohol so much to bury it, and not drinking with the same all-or-nothing intensity.' He paused again and looked up at Stuart. 'It's a bugger, isn't it?'

'Yes,' he nodded, 'it sure is. And there's you.' He said nothing more, again allowing Graham to be with his own inner experience, enabling him to maintain connection with his own process.

'Yeah, and there's me, trying to help.' He shook his head.

'And at some level and to some degree you really are in there, Graham, or else we wouldn't be having this conversation now.'

'Hmm. I guess not.'

'You're living with the reactions inside yourself, Graham, you're affected by it all, but I hear you wanting to be more affected.'

Graham knew what was present for him as he listened to Stuart. 'A man did those things, Stuart, and I'm a man, and men do awful things. I know that it isn't just a gender thing, but most of the atrocities, the horrors in our world, are down to men. A man, for whatever reason, drinks, is violent, attacks his wife and children time and time again. He scars their lives. They carry those scars. Maybe they're open wounds. That seems a better metaphor. Andy has now recognised the wounds, he is no longer trying to anaesthetise them to the same degree that he has done in the past, and is seeking to find a way to heal and to move on. Terry, though, can only drink to try to take away the pain and in so doing keeps the wounds open and painful. He anaesthetises, perhaps, but keeps them open.'

'And Andy has come to you and he is seeking to heal in part through his relationship to you. You can't heal Terry. Andy is your client and you are there for him—big time.'

Graham nodded. 'Yes, thanks, I-I think I needed to hear that. I can't help Terry, can I? Maybe I can indirectly, but I have to keep my focus on Andy. As you say, he's my client.'

Stuart nodded. 'Yes, he's the one you have the primary relationship with.'

'Andy wants to help Terry and, well, I'm not so sure. I'm glad I didn't encourage him—I could have done so easily and got him to live out my needs. Thankfully that didn't happen.'

'But they are bound together as well, and maybe each can only heal to the degree that they both heal, or something like that, it's just that Andy is the first to seek another way to be in this world, another way to handle the effects of his traumatic childhood.'

'Hmm. Maybe.'

'What do you need, Graham, and specifically what do you need from me, here, now?'

'I think I needed your reassurance and support, and I feel I have got that. I think I needed you to remind me that Andy is my client—dwelling on Terry takes me away from Andy. I need to be clear about any reactions in me that are tied up with my own son, and my gender identity as a man as well. I think realising more acutely the probable torment that perhaps Andy's father went through has opened me to a greater sense of compassion towards him. Perhaps I can more easily set aside anger towards him now which might also have been obstructing me from hearing Andy or feeling for Andy in a way and at a depth that I want to.'

'I think you are feeling for and with Andy, Graham, but maybe there is more to feel, more to be open to—both for Andy and you. In a sense—and this is my image so it may not have relevance, but it feels quite vivid—in a way Andy is taking you by the hand and leading you into his nightmare. He is familiar with it. But for you, it is a new experience and perhaps more intensely frightening and disorientating. Hold his hand and let him show it to you, let him lead you to where he needs to go, and where he needs your presence. Be the companion that I know you are, and that he needs and wants. Then you will stay in and with his world, and it won't be pleasant, it'll be horrible, and it'll mess you up and you'll need ways of separating yourself back out and washing it away because you can't stay in there between sessions. But you will go back in each week as long as he wants or needs you. And he will become the stronger for it, and so will you. And I will be here for you to help you process the whole experience and the effect it has on you. This is the living edge of therapy, Graham, take courage. Whatever you experience will never be as bad as what Andy experienced. And he's surviving albeit with problematic aspects to it.'

Stuart could feel the tears in his eyes as he was speaking. It was coming from his heart, from a deep knowing that he needed to communicate to Graham. It was emanating from the core of his being, a place where he knew that what he was saying was right. Some might call it a spiritual place. He preferred to think of it as a place in which accumulated wisdom was present and could be drawn on in times of need. He had learned to trust it's presence and it had not failed him, and he believed—it was, in truth more than a belief—he knew that in essence therapy was about helping the person who is the client to get closer to that inner source of wisdom.

Graham felt silent, and very still. It was a powerful moment. Stuart's words resonated strongly, echoing in and around him, seemingly reverberating in his very soul. 'Thank you.' He nodded. 'Thank you.' There was nothing else to say. Something passed between them that was intensely restorative for Graham, self-affirming, vitalising. He needed nothing further from Stuart insofar as Andy was concerned, or Terry. He stayed with the very powerful and poignant stillness that had descended.

Graham took a deep breath. 'Wish I'd recorded that, and yet it wouldn't be the same because what you said was right for that moment and something deep inside me needed to hear it. I'd like to dwell on it but I have to talk about other clients.'

Whilst they did then move on to talk about other clients, the moment stayed with Graham. Something profound had occurred. He had touched something deep inside himself and he left the supervision session later experiencing a stillness and a calmness that carried a quality of assurance. He was in another place, a strong place, and he needed to carry that focus into his sessions with Andy and yet be ready to enter into Andy's place at his request.

*   *   *   *

The phone rang and Andy picked it up. The voice at the other end was familiar.

'I'm pissed and I don't give a fuck anymore. Just wanted you to know.' Terry's voice was slurring terribly, he sounded well out of it.

'Why? What's happened? Where are you?'

'Questions. Questions. Questions.' As he repeated himself his voice got slower and slower.

'Yes, because I want to know.'

'Well, I don't want to tell you.'

This was bad. Terry had phoned before when he was drunk, but something in Andy made him sense that all was really not well.

'What the hell's going on, Terry. It's three o'clock.'

'Can't find the time to talk to your big brother then? Bastard.'

'Terry, what's happening, where are you?'

'What do you care? You're OK, with your house and job and little miss Julie. You don't give a shit about me.' He was raising his voice.

'That's not true, Terry.'

'Fuck you.'

The phone slammed down.

'What is it, love?' Julie had stirred and was rubbing her eyes.

'Terry, he sounded in a bad way, never heard him quite like that before. I mean, I know he can be abusive, but he isn't usually that way to me. Never heard him talking quite like that. I need to call him back.' He redialled but there was no connection. If it had been his mobile he must have switched it off. He called Terry's phone at home but there was no response, it switched to the automated answer message so he left a message and hung up.

Andy was feeling rising anxiety. It didn't sound good and somehow hearing Terry speak left him feeling really unsettled. He found himself thinking about a drink. It was crazy to anyone looking on, but that was what he felt he needed. He got up and went downstairs.

'Where are you going?'

'Need some air.' He wasn't going to say he was heading off for a can or two.

Julie said nothing. She turned over and tried to go back to sleep.

Andy went to the fridge—only a couple of cans, but that would do. He drank them both. He still felt anxious, but he didn't know why—not that he was trying to figure it out. He simply felt anxious and wanted a drink to get rid of it. He went to the drinks cabinet and poured some whisky. He slumped down in the chair with it. The first glass made no difference, he poured another. He wasn't really thinking, just felt on edge. He wasn't even thinking about Terry, rather he was locked into his own inner world. It was like he was submerged in some kind of region within himself that just filled him with anxiety. The truth was it was more the reverse. Not so much he was full of anxiety but somehow this pit of anxiety was full of him. He wasn't trying to rationalise it though, just trying to get rid of it or get away from it.

It was half an hour later that Julie came down and saw him still slumped in the armchair, the bottle next to him, an almost empty glass in his hand.

'It's not going to solve anything.'

Andy heard her but it was as if it was through some kind of haze, like she was strangely distant, almost in another world. There was a kind of phase-shift between them. He was locked into his own world, she stood out there in the world outside, and there was some kind of gap. He didn't try to bridge it, he wasn't bothered to try. Just remained fixed in his own pit of anxiety.

Julie tried to encourage him back to bed but he wasn't listening and eventually she gave up. By the time she came back down Andy was asleep. He'd dropped the glass and had clearly consumed more of the alcohol. He wasn't going to get in to work today. She phoned in for him, said he'd been sick all night and was now still asleep and she didn't want to disturb him. Apologised and said she'd get Andy to call later once he was awake to let them know how he was feeling and whether he expected to be in the next day. His boss wasn't too pleased. It wasn't the first time and he was getting fed up with it. Meanwhile Andy continued to sleep. He was dreaming. He had a smile on his face. He looked so relaxed. Julie went out to the kitchen to put the kettle on and waited to see if Andy would rouse himself. She decided she'd give him a bit longer but she needed to get herself ready to head of for work and needed to wake him up before she went.

Andy did stir, about twenty minutes later. He felt rough. He was still very alcohol affected. 'shit, look at the time, why didn't you wake me?' He was struggling to get up but misjudged it and fell back into the chair.

'It's OK, I phoned work, said you'd been sick and were still asleep, that you'd call them when you woke up.'

Andy was rubbing his face in his hands and trying to wake up. He felt bad. Is head ached, his back was stiff and his mouth felt like he'd been eating a mixture of garlic and glue, with a bit of sand and sawdust thrown in.

'Want a coffee?'

'Yeah. What happened?'

'You don't remember?'

'Yeah, I do, Terry phoned and then I just remember needing a drink.'

'You came down here and you can see what's left in the bottle.'

'It got to me, I don't know, couldn't have been thinking straight.'

'You looked in another world. Why do you have to drink?'

'I don't know. I'd better call him. Shit. He sounded really bad, Julie, worse than I've heard him before. I mean I know he drinks heavily but there was something in his voice—I don't know what it was, something that sounded hopeless in some way. Can you get me the phone?'

'Yes, but don't let it upset you again. It's not doing you any good—it's not doing us any good.'

'Look, I need to talk to him, he's my brother for Pete's sake.'

'I know, but he gets to you.'

'He'd get to you if you'd gone through what we did.' He was becoming increasingly angry.

'Ok, OK. Do what you need to do. I'm going upstairs to wash and get ready for work.'

Andy dialled Terry's number. Still no reply. Still the answer machine. He was tired, he couldn't stop yawning. He decided he needed to go back to bed. He'd drunk too much and he wasn't going to be able to drive over to Terry's, and the buses were a nightmare. He dragged himself up the stairs, still yawning, went to the bathroom for a pee and brushed his teeth to try and freshen his mouth up a bit. Gave his face a quick douse with water, dried himself and headed into the bedroom. Julie was putting on her make up, pouting into the mirror as she inspected her lip stick.

'Right, I've got to go. You get some sleep and don't worry about Terry. He always gets by, you know what he's like. He's probably drunk himself into a stupor and he'll be back in touch when he comes out of it.'

Andy nodded, but he wasn't sure. There was something about the way Terry had spoken. He had sounded different. But Andy couldn't really define to himself what that difference was. He knew it left him feeling unsettled and that he felt more concerned than he had at other times over Terry's drinking. Within himself he was aware of a need to keep trying to make contact.

* * * *

It was in the afternoon that he finally got through to Terry. He'd been asleep and clearly hadn't heard, or hadn't felt inclined, to get up and answer the phone when Andy had called first thing. But he had been awake when he had called the last time and had heard the telephone message. He'd picked up the phone because the message didn't make much sense.

'What do you mean, I called you in the night. No I didn't. I was asleep.'

'You called, Terry, you may not remember it, but you called.' Andy recounted what Terry had said and how he had sounded.

'I didn't call. I was asleep. What the hell are you playing at?'

'Terry, do you think I'd make something like that up? You can talk to Julie when she gets back, she was woken up by the call. It really troubled me, you sounded in a really bad way.'

'Well, she's obviously in on it as well. It didn't happen, so don't wind me up. You think I'm an idiot?'

'No, but I'm telling you it happened, Terry. Why the hell would I lie about it?'

'Wind up, that's why.'

"Well it isn't. You phoned. I've been trying to get in touch with you today to see what was going on. Do you think I'd be spending time doing that? You were obviously pissed and you've forgotten.'

'Well I don't remember it, I really don't.'

'Maybe it was the drink, had you been on a bender?'

'Well, yeah, I had, but I usually have an idea of what's been happening, you know, but I don't remember calling you, I really don't.'

'OK, well, look, you did but there's not much to be gained from arguing about it. But you really did sound fed up, in fact I'd say desperate.'

'Yeah, well, haven't been feeling too good, but, look, I didn't call you. I really didn't. Why are you telling me that I did?'

'Drop it, Terry, we're not going to agree on this.'

'But I want to know why you're making this up. Shit, it's doing my head in. I need a drink.' Andy heard the sound of a ring pull—Terry must have opened a can holding the phone close to it.

'So did I, last night. I'm off work today 'cos I overdid it. It really got to me. You really sounded in a bad way, pissed off with me and with everything, you know?'

'Yeah, well, I do feel like that sometimes, but I didn't call you.'

'Drop it, Terry. But I'll let you know if it happens again.'

'It didn't happen last night. You're crazy. I don't need this.' He slammed the phone down.

Andy looked at the phone in his own hand, trying to decide what to do. Terry clearly didn't want to know. But he had phoned, he'd heard him. He was here at home now because of it. But why didn't Terry remember. Had he simply been that pissed? But he had sounded different, more desperate. He didn't know what to make of it. He was still tired. He lay back on the bed and must have drifted off. He was woken up by Julie who was back home.

'So, get to talk to Terry?'

'Yes, but he flatly denies it happened, ended up putting the phone down on me. Accused me of making it up. I said he could talk to you, but he didn't want to know, said you were in on it as well.' Andy shook his head, 'but he did call. I didn't dream it. It woke you up too.'

'You didn't dream it and it disturbed you enough to set you off as well, I know that.'

'Yeah, I know, sorry about that. But he really sounded desperate. It got to me. Just felt so anxious. It was a kind of familiar anxiety although I wasn't exactly sure what it was about, but there was something about the way he spoke. So helpless, so pissed off about everything.'

'That how you feel sometimes?'

Andy felt tears in his eyes. He blinked a couple of times, trying to clear them, but he knew that Julie had touched a sensitive spot. He was more sensitive these days since the counselling and since trying to address his alcohol use. Seemed like he wore his feelings on the outside, they were so easily touched and affected. And yet last night it had felt much more inside himself. But he didn't know what it was all about and couldn't make sense of it. He knew he'd talk to Graham about it next time, but that was next week. He just had to hold it together. They had things planned for the week and he had to stick to that. Last night was a blip, and he had to make sure it stayed that way. He felt like a drink now, but he knew it wasn't the answer. Julie had made him a coffee and had brought it up with her. Andy knew he had to try and settle himself back down.

'Yeah, I do, about the past, about what happened and about feeling stuck in a rut, and realising I've got a problem with the booze that I didn't know I had. Somehow it was easier when I didn't know, now I do and it's like another pressure. And there are times when I don't want to bother, and I guess last night was like that. Just felt weird and needed a drink so that's what I did. And I overdid it. And that's not good. It's a nightmare, and when I don't drink, I feel edgy and can so easily dwell on things. It's like everything blowing up inside me and the one thing I want to do to contain it I can't do. Yeah, I do feel pissed off.' He paused, hesitatingly slightly, 'but not about you, about us. I want this to work, Julie, but I'm a mess at the moment. I know that. I need you, I really do.' The tears were in his eyes again. They ended up in each other's arms and in fact made love. It was much later that they got up and ate together. It was 9.00pm and Andy hadn't had a drink since early in the morning. He was feeling a bit on edge but actually a lot calmer than he had been. It seemed that having something good to feel took out some of the discomfort. But he had a couple of cans—one before, one after the meal. He didn't sleep well that night, but went off to work next day, determined to get his alcohol under control but still carrying a concern for Terry and wondering how he was and what was happening. He hadn't phoned back, he'd decided there wasn't much point, he'd leave it to the weekend and maybe try and get round to see him.

Chapter 8

'It was an up and down week, as you can see on the diary I had a heavy session Wednesday night well, more Thursday morning. I'd been doing well. Hadn't gone to the pub at all, and had contained the drinking at home.' Andy felt generally pleased at what he had achieved over the last 7 days as he sat in Graham's counselling room.

Graham looked at the diary—four cans Monday and Tuesday, four more on Wednesday, plus the whisky in the night—he'd written half a bottle. Two cans Thursday. Then back up to a six cans Friday, two on Saturday plus a couple of pints at lunch-time, and then six on Sunday. Andy had written as well 'plus spirits' on the Sunday but without giving an amount. At least as far as drinking during the day was concerned there were only the two pints on the Saturday but obviously the earlier start to drinking on the Sunday had got out of control. At least he hadn't drunk during the day during the week but it was a lot and that whisky hadn't helped the overall total. Andy had written down the strength of the cans—5% most of the time, a few occasions with something stronger. Graham knew that to convert this into units per can you multiplied the strength by the quantity in millilitres and then divided by a thousand. Five times 500 (mils) divided by 1000 meant 2.5 units per can, and that meant fifteen units for a six-can evening, with a bit more when he had the stronger cans. And half a bottle of whisky (70 cls) was fifteen units on its own. Yet what was just as important for Graham was his sense that Andy was now more able to be open and honest about his drinking.

'So, that felt good, yes? Staying in, trying to contain the drinking and keeping away from the pub.'

'Yeah, though I had to fight the urge to go down to the pub, particularly by nine o'clock. Something about the atmosphere, I mean, wasn't so much that I wanted a drink 'cos I'd been having the cans, but there's something different about a pint pulled, you know? But, yeah, I felt good that I'd kind of kept it to four cans most nights, and only two cans there, on Thursday. But, overall, still quite a lot, isn't it?'

'It is, yes, three to four units a day is the government recommendation for safe drinking levels[4].'

For Andy it seemed a million miles away. The night he'd just had two cans he hadn't slept well although he had slept a lot of the day. But the thought of drinking just two cans a night—and even then it would be five units, still more than that recommended amount. He couldn't believe how low it was. 'That's a long way off still.'

'I guess it is but at the moment you are trying to change the drinking pattern more in terms of where you drink, and what else you do with your time. But the whisky apart, it must reflect a reduction on some nights. Four cans is ten units—that's only about five pints.'

'Yeah, four cans is a reduction, and that feels good to achieve, except, as you can see, it wasn't every night, and it got bad again later in the week.'

'Yes, what was happening?'

'Terry.'

'Terry?' Graham was reminded in his head of his last supervision session. Andy is my client, he thought to himself, it's Andy's world, how Andy feels that I need to keep with.

'He phoned me up on Wednesday, well, early Thursday, it was three in the morning. He was drunk, but he sounded really desperate. He was angry as well, gave me a lot of verbal. Then he hung up on me. When I called him later he totally denied having made the call. I don't know what that was about. I talked to him at the weekend and he still denies it. I know alcohol can make you forget things a bit, but I usually have a general idea of what I've done.'

Graham was immediately thinking of alcohol blackout and was tempted to explain this to Andy, but decided to stay with Andy's experience—at least for the moment.

'So he calls you in the middle of the night, drunk, abusive, and then denies it when you talk to him.'

---

4. This is the figure for the UK, it varies from this in other countries.

'Yes, and really sure of himself that he hadn't called. But he had. Julie was there and she'd vouch for it. I wasn't dreaming it. And it left me, well, as you can see, I drank a fair bit and didn't get into work the next day.'

'So, something about the way Terry was on the phone triggered you into drinking?'

'It was his voice, he was angry, yes, but there was something else, something … I don't know, I've been trying to make sense of it. He sounded desperate, and it was like he'd just had enough.'

'Enough?'

Andy hesitated before speaking. 'Well, of life, really. Like he'd had enough of everything, and he went on about how lucky I was but he was really quite sarcastic. He sounded, well, I don't want to say it about him, he's the only family I have, but he sounded horrible, I mean really horrible. And I've not experienced him like that before.'

'So, a sense he'd had enough of life and something horrible about how Terry was, and that was new.'

'Yeah. We've got drunk together and had difference in the past and stuff, but this was different.'

'What were the differences, Andy?' Graham was immediately aware of the fact that Andy was not drunk—although he would still have had alcohol in his system from the evening before—and he wondered if his more sober state was enabling him to be more aware of how Terry could be. He awaited Andy's responses.

'Well, I guess I wasn't drunk. Yes, I'd had a few cans that evening, but I was feeling OK. But then, when he put the phone down' Andy shrugged.

'So Terry put the phone down and …?'

'Not so much put down as slammed down and cut me off. But I kind of reacted.'

'Reacted?'

'Just knew I needed a drink.'

'You *knew* you needed a drink?' Graham didn't ask questions about how Andy felt, it was not his style of counselling. Graham believed very much in the power of working in this more non-directive way. He knew he didn't always manage to maintain this, but he tried to.

Andy was nodding. 'Stupid, really, I'd already had those cans and I must have still had alcohol in me, but I needed a drink.'

'Something about the way Terry spoke and the way it left you feeling or thinking, and you *knew* you needed a drink.' Graham was aware of keeping an emphasis on the knowing that he needed a drink. It felt emphasised in the way Andy was speaking.

Andy nodded again. He was thinking back to the experience. He'd felt really edgy, anxious, disturbed. But he shouldn't have needed to drink, not like he did. He felt a bit ashamed about the whole episode now, that he should have been able to handle it without heading off for the whisky. But he could still feel that sensation, an unease. It hadn't gone away, not really, not when he thought about it.

They sat in silence for a few moments. Andy wrestling with whether to say how he felt about it; Graham keeping his focus on what Andy had told him and his sense of how it must have been to Andy, though he found his attention being pulled towards speculating upon what must have been happening for Terry. Yet he knew he had to step away from that and keep his focus on his client.

Andy took a deep breath. 'Went round to see him at the weekend.' Graham noted the shift of focus away from what presumably was still uncomfortable. He went with Andy on this shift, trusting that for Andy this was a necessary shift and that he, as his therapist, needed to convey acceptance of this.

'Was that pre-planned or because of what had happened?'

'Because of what had happened. Dropped over on our way to the coast on Saturday but he wasn't there. Wasn't as good a day as I'd hoped. I guess I was still too pre-occupied with him. Shouldn't have gone round on the way, should have left it to the Sunday, but that's what we did.'

'So Saturday wasn't such a good experience, having found he was out.'

'I don't know, I couldn't settle, I mean, he's my older brother, we've been through a lot together and I was worried about him. Still am.'

'Yeah, you have been through a lot together and yes, as you say, he's your older brother and you are worried about him, about how he is.' Graham reflected back what Andy had said, it felt important to acknowledge and affirm Andy's position. He spoke slowly, and deliberately, to give time for the words and their meaning to be very present for Andy.

'Anyway, where was I?'

'Worried on Saturday.'

'I went round on the Sunday. He was in but he'd had a few again. He let me in and he gave me a can. I drank it with him, thought it would help to try and get him to talk a bit, you know? Didn't think it would help if I'd refused, but I knew I had to limit it—I'd driven over and didn't want it to get into a drinking session.'

'So, you were quite clear on that. Was that unusual?'

'Well, now you say that, yes it was. We usually get drunk, but this was different. I didn't want that. But I did have a few cans but over a period of time, not so intense and heavy as in the past. But I still ended up having to stay over, I couldn't drive back. Came home early this morning. Julie gave me grief, and well, can't blame her but I thought she'd understand, you know?'

'You thought she should understand?'

'Yes, well, I mean, he's been drinking heavily for years and we've always drunk together when we've met up, she should be used to that.'

'Maybe she has other expectations now?'

Andy nodded, 'yeah, she made that clear, and I know she's right. I know that I really shouldn't have drunk so much like that on the Sunday. Another day being pissed. And what did I achieve?'

'What did you achieve, Andy?'

'God knows. What kind of sense do you get with two drunks talking? Not a lot.' And sat back in the chair, his face in his hands, and yawned. He'd felt tired all day. He'd not slept well on Terry's sofa, still stiff. He yawned again.

'Tired?'

'Yeah, didn't sleep good last night and then a long drive today, and being here. It's been a long day.' He yawned as if to confirm the fact.

'So, let me recap on what you've told me, Andy, check I've got it right. You went round to see Terry on the Saturday as a result of the phone call, he wasn't there and it left you uneasy for your trip to the coast. You went back on Sunday and whilst you didn't feel *you* drank in the same way as you have done in the past when you've been together, you still ended up drinking too much and had to stay over?'

'Yes, got over there mid afternoon—thank goodness I hadn't gone round in the morning, but I'd guessed if he had come back he'd be likely to be sleeping in the morning.'

'So, my wonder now is where this leaves you.' Graham wanted the focus on his client, the discussion in his supervision session was still with him. He didn't want to get into a speculative conversation about what was happening for Terry.

Andy sat and thought about it, whilst he struggled to stay awake. He really felt tired. His thoughts drifted back to the conversation with Julie on the Thursday. Yes, he did feel fed up, and he was suddenly feeling quite emotional again as he thought about it, but he was determined not to let his emotions get the better of him again. 'You know, it actually leaves me just wanting to go to sleep, get away from it all.'

'That's the first thing that comes into your mind?' Graham was wondering whether Andy might acknowledge that at least he wasn't thinking of needing a drink, though he might be and just hadn't said it.

'Yeah. I tried to tell Terry about coming here. He didn't want to know. Said it was family business, he wasn't going to talk to some counsellor about it. He'd handle it his own way, like he'd always done.'

'So he's not interested and I'm wondering how that was for you to hear his reaction?'

'Frustrated, I guess. I mean, I didn't think he'd be interested although I kind of hoped that he would. He sounded so bad when he phoned, and I just couldn't seem to get him to understand or believe me. As the evening wore on he seemed to be more accepting, but we were both a bit pissed by then.'

'So after a few drinks he seemed more accepting that maybe he did phone you?'

'Sort of, didn't react to it so strongly, seemed more ready to laugh about it. But I'm still not feeling good about it. I mean, can you do things when you're drunk and not remember them, I mean really not remember them? We all get a bit drunk and end up hazy about what happened the night before, but this was different.'

'You sound like you want an answer?' Graham felt that the question deserved something other than an empathic acknowledgement of what had been said. Andy sounded desperate, sounded like her really wanted to know, really wanted to make sense of what had happened.

'I do. He was so adamant, so absolutely dismissive of the idea, and really angry with me that I was suggesting it.'

'There is a condition called 'alcohol blackout' when people live a period of their lives whilst alcohol-affected but it is as though the memory of this period—and it can be hours, can be days—doesn't get stored in the brain in the normal way, at least that's how it appears.'

'How do you mean?' Andy thought it sounded strange. Surely your brain knows where it puts memories?'

'Well, let's say someone finds themselves in bed with someone one morning. They have woken up, haven't a clue how they got there or who they are with. They remember going out the previous morning with the intention of drinking. That is all they have in their heads. They've lived a period of time but have gone into this state of 'alcohol blackout'. They don't know what they've done or who they've been with, but they have been conscious. It's not a passing out kind of blackout.'

'I've drunk a bit but never experienced that. Usually if I forget something it eventually comes back to me when people tell me. But that's not what you're saying. People who have this experience, you call it "alcohol blackout", they really can't remember?'

'No, and it can be scary because the person affected doesn't know what they have done. They could have upset someone, borrowed money, all kinds of things, yet have no knowledge.' Graham remembered a client who told him how drinking buddies would try and convince him he'd leant them money when in alcohol blackout.

'And it's a reaction to the alcohol?' Graham nodded. He had his own thoughts on this but did not want to go into them with Andy. He was convinced that people who had been traumatised to the point of entering into a 'dissociative state' (a state of mind that has been created in reaction to trauma in which memories of an experience are held, but which may not be accessible in normal waking consciousness) could later in life be triggered back into those states through excess alcohol. He felt sure that some people might re-engage with very difficult memories in blackout and yet have no recollection of having done so afterwards. He had the theory that in those states people could be at heightened risk of suicide, but he didn't want to start talking about any of that to Andy. He simply needed to stay with what Andy wanted to know and then focus on the thoughts and feelings that Andy experienced to what was discussed.

Andy took a deep breath as he thought about what Graham had said. It made sense. Terry had been clearly awake when it had happened, and yet he vehemently denied it ever having occurred.

'Is it dangerous, I mean, is it harmful?'

'Well, apart from the fact that the person may have put themselves at risk during blackout—bearing in mind they will have been alcohol-affected, and have no idea what they may have done—then there is that potential harm. But the main harm is that they have become so affected by heavy alcohol use that they can have this kind of experience. It means they must have been drinking a lot over a significant period of time with all the health risks that are associated with that. And, of course, alcohol impairs memory anyway. Lot's of people who drink heavily struggle with memory problems.'

Andy didn't like the sound of that. He knew his memory wasn't the sharpest. He didn't like the idea that he might have one of these blackout experiences one day. It felt to him like another reason to cut back on his own drinking.

'And anyone could have them?'

'Sure, and in my experience of working with people who have histories of heavy drinking, it is not uncommon.'

'Shit.' Andy let it sink in. He didn't want to ever get to that state. At the same time, part of him was saying to himself that he was OK, he was in control, he wouldn't allow himself to lose it like that. Terry was different, wasn't he? Drank much more and had done for longer. He didn't drink like Terry ...

'You look quite shocked?' Graham decided to pick up on Andy's facial expression as he wasn't saying anything specific about how he was feeling or what he was thinking.

'I am' He shook his head. 'And this really happens?'

'Oh yes.' Graham said nothing more, leaving Andy to assimilate his own thoughts.

Andy hadn't come across this idea before, but it did make sense. Terry really had been so clear that he had not phoned. It was like the memory just wasn't there or, if it was, he couldn't find it.

'I'm going to talk to him about it. I don't think he appreciates any of this. In fact, I'm sure he doesn't. I mean, I hadn't been aware until talking to you.' He paused and thought for a moment. 'OK.' He paused again. He was still feeling somewhat shocked by how alcohol could affect you and seemed to be affecting Terry. He glanced down at his drinking diary on the table. He tightened his lips. It didn't look good. He may have cut back a bit some nights by staying in, and he was keeping out of the pub, but he was still drinking consistently, and he knew it wasn't going to get him anywhere. It wasn't an answer to anything.

'I've got to cut back more. I mean, it's still too much.'

'Feels like you're drinking too much and that's something you want to change.' Graham stayed with being empathic, allowing Andy to be with what he had said a little longer. He waited for him to continue.

"I've got to cut back. But what to, I mean, you say three or four units a day—that's not much, is it?'

'Between a can or two of 5% beer or lager.'

Andy took a deep breath as he contemplated the idea. 'I can't see it, there are sure to be times when I drink more, even if I get it down.'

'That troubles you?'

Andy nodded. 'Yeah. Just seems like, well, I've never done it, you know?'

'Never drank that little—consistently?'

'No. And I know you're right. I know it's what I have to aim for, but it seems out of reach.'

'You don't have to try and get there in a week, or even in a month. It's about taking it slowly, making realistic changes, taking small steps, establishing different levels of drinking and routines in your life, and then slowly, slowly bringing it down.' Graham emphasised the *slowly, slowly*. He did not believe in people rushing into change, although that could work. But he preferred that people took their time and really owned what they were doing, understanding the choices they were making and giving the change the best possible chance of becoming sustainable. He added, 'people can change but the trick is about maintaining the change, making sure it is sustainable. That's what's important.' Graham paused. 'Of course, the detoxification with medication is still an option to talk to your GP about.'

Andy shook his head. He didn't want that. He felt he could bring it down himself, even though in a sense he struggled with this idea as well.

The session continued and Andy went back to the diaries again. He wanted to try to get some idea as to how he would make the changes he wanted the next week. He came up with the idea of setting himself the goal of not going over six cans of 5% but aiming to hold it at four. 'That'll be how many units over the week—I think I need to aim for a weekly total. I'm going to roll with it each day. But a weekly total, gives me something to work at, and to bring here.'

'Ok, well four cans a night would be seventy units in the week, six cans would be one hundred and five.'

'Right, that's clear, mustn't go over a hundred units again. That's something I can go for and I know it's high, but that has to be my first rule now. Keep the units to double figures in the week, but if I can get down to close to seventy units, that would be good. But how will I feel? I mean, will I get a reaction?'

'Well, you've had some four can days and a two can evening although you would still have had the alcohol in the whisky in your system throughout the day. So, how were the four can evenings?'

'OK, but it's the next day I'm worse, you know.'

'That's to be expected, the alcohol is coming out of your system. When does it get tough?'

'Most of the next day. On edge, sweating, bit shaky at times. But not enough to cause me to get a can.'

'Right, well, don't push it. You could try and bring the strength down a bit, go for a 4.5% but with the same quantity. That can sometimes work for people. Dropping down .5% is actually a 10% reduction. And reducing the strength of the alcohol also reduces the level of inflammation that the alcohol causes on its way down—that warm, burning sensation?'

Andy sat and thought about that. Somehow that seemed like an easier way to tackle it. .5% didn't seem a lot of difference, and he was sure that the pints in the pub were a bit weaker than the cans, but it would mean he could drink the same quantity. That appealed to him. 'I like that. So, you reckon if I go for a 4.5% then that would get me down by ten per cent. Yes, it would, wouldn't it?'

'And ten per cent reduction on a hundred units brings you down to ninety. And if you keep pushing the strength down, I mean, in theory then the next week is eighty-one and then seventy-three.'

Andy was nodding as he thought about it. He liked the idea although he also knew he felt uneasy as well. He really didn't want to get a bad reaction. And he knew how easy it was to drink—he only had to think about last week and his reaction to Terry phoning and then visiting him. He was still struggling to control it, and he knew it, but he also knew he had to keep trying.

'I'll go for it. OK. Now, yes, I can get 4.5% cans and aim for four most nights, but if I need six?'

'It's OK, don't put yourself under pressure, Andy, take it slowly, but plan around it. And try and keep spirits off the agenda. Distract yourself, drink other liquids as well, but keep away from too much of the sugary stuff. People often do find a sugar craving begin to kick in, but watch it. Another addiction!' Graham smiled.

'Probably a safer one though.'

'But watch out for it. Having said that, some people find carrying a bag of sweets around can help—but generally that's after people stop and they're looking to boost their sugar level. Anyway, just feel your way along, as you say, plan ahead, plenty of liquid. Eating OK?'

Andy nodded. 'A bit better some days.'

'Should improve as the alcohol comes down.' Graham felt an urge to really encourage Andy. He knew he wanted him to succeed and he knew he could. He'd helped too many people change to feel daunted. It took time and it could be like going to hell and back for some people, but he knew it could happen, people could change and adjust to a reduced drinking pattern, or end up stopping altogether and maintain abstinence. And he believed that his genuine encouragement and confidence was important, whilst also being sensitively empathic to the self-doubt that was often present within a client.

Andy was nodding thoughtfully as he looked ahead to the evening before him. Julie was working late again. He'd got six cans in the fridge and he knew he wanted to try and only drink four. He heard Graham saying, 'you can do it,

Andy, don't buy into this sense that people are helpless when it comes to changing their drinking. People *do* change and *you* can.'

'Hmm? Yeah, I know. Just thinking about whether I should keep less booze in the house, you know?'

Graham nodded. 'Worth thinking about.' Graham wanted to encourage Andy to explore his own ideas—they were likely to be more realistic and also more likely to be owned by him, rather than feeling he was doing something because he was being told to do it. Graham was mindful of Andy's difficult childhood—somewhere in him was likely to be a part of himself that had had years of being told what to do, and being told off when he got it wrong—or worse. He didn't want to set Andy up by triggering this part to emerge and in some way sabotage the process. 'What do you have in mind?'

'Well, I think I may need to get the spirits out the house. It was too easy last week after talking to Terry. If it hadn't been there I couldn't have drunk it.' He thought about it, aware that there were a couple of bottles of spirits. 'Suppose I could give them away.'

'Sure, anyone in mind?'

'Gary comes to mind. Can't give them to Terry that's for sure.' Andy smiled weakly, but it wasn't a humorous smile. There was a lot of sadness. 'We're really messed up, aren't we. The two of us.' He shook his head. 'But I'm going to crack this, Graham, for mum and for Terry. I want to help him.'

Graham nodded and also felt the alarm bells for he knew from his experience that the most powerful and sustainable motivation seemed to be when people undertook change for themselves. But he understood where Andy was coming from. He kept empathically in touch with what Andy was saying.

'Yeah, I can see how important that is. You must be close?'

Andy breathed deeply and his eyes moistened. 'Yeah. We were and I guess we still are. Blood thicker than water, you know? He can irritate the hell out of me but, well ... he's my big brother, stupid idiot that he is at times.'

Graham nodded.

Andy's eyes had watered and he sniffed and closed his eyes. 'silly bugger.'

Graham wondered if he was referring to himself or to Terry. He decided to ask, it felt right somehow.

'You or Terry?'

'Huh, both of us ... both of us.' The atmosphere changed. Graham could feel a sudden stillness descend into the room, and he felt goose bumps. Something important was about to be said, he instinctively knew it. He stayed alert.

'I love the soft bastard.'

Graham did not reply but nodded his head and held eye contact with Andy who had looked at him after speaking. There was no need to say anything. He'd heard Andy, he respected the silence that followed and allowed what Andy had acknowledged and shared to kind of echo into the silence. Graham swallowed, it was getting to him as well. He was flipping back to the image he had in his own head of those two brothers and he got that Rolf Harris song in his head—*two little boys had two little toys …*

Graham trusted these moments and what could emerge when he was feeling deeply connected to a client who, themselves, were touching into and being touched by deep emotional content. He spoke softly, 'two little boys …' And he felt the tears in his own eyes and realised he couldn't stop them escaping down his own cheeks.

Andy saw the reaction on Graham's face and it seemed to hold him in his own experience. It felt as though someone was feeling his pain. He knew he couldn't be, not really, and yet … Graham had tears on his cheeks, and Andy felt the tears escaping over his own eyelids as well. They sat looking at each other.

Graham spoke from the heart when he said, 'I hope, I sincerely hope, that one day you and Terry can sit together like this, sober and supportive, united by what you have gone through and both able to look ahead. I wish I could make it happen for you both …'

Andy nodded. It was one of the most powerful things he had ever heard anyone say to him. He couldn't have put it better himself. Yes, he wanted to be able to sit with Terry and yet he knew that he probably never would. There was something different about Graham. He had a calmness, an assurance that he did not know in Terry. He looked down and swallowed. He wiped his eyes with the back of his hands.

'I wish you could, but only we can do that, and I've got to make the first moves. I've got to start changing to give it a chance, Graham, I know that and in some way this evening has confirmed that for me. I've got to give Terry a chance by giving myself a chance. We have been close and we still are, but alcohol has become too much part of how we are together. I have to find a way of being with him without getting drawn into the drinking. I don't know how I'm going to do that. I really don't know.'

'And that's a goal, a big goal, to be able to make that difference for him, in his life.'

'I can't change the past. I'd love to. Sometimes I lay awake at night and wonder how it might have been, how I might have been, how we might have turned out if it had been different. And what's really sad is that I don't know. I can't imagine myself different to how I am, and I can't imagine Terry different either. And that's scary. It's so ingrained, we are so fucking damaged.' Andy's tone of voice suddenly got harsher. 'So fucking damaged.' He breathed out with a heavy sigh as he spoke those last three words.

'Yeah, so fucking damaged …'

Andy's thoughts moved to his father. 'I'm sure he had his reasons to be like he was but we'd all have been better off if he hadn't stayed around.' He looked up into the top corner of the room. 'But that wasn't to be.' Another deep breath. 'Oh well.' His jaw tightened. 'Bastard. Fucking, fucking bastard.' He spat the words out and had clenched both his fists which he slammed down on the arms of the chair. It was an explosive movement.

Graham responded to the body language as well as what was being said, 'looks like you want to punch his fucking lights out'.

Andy was nodding. Then he was shaking his head. He was staring ahead of himself at the wall to the right of Graham. He wasn't really seeing anything though. Just sitting staring into space. He didn't feel at ease. So many feelings inside himself but he couldn't describe them. He just knew that he needed a drink, God he needed a drink. He could hear the can opening, the sound of the ring pull. Oh yeah, he thought as he took a really deep breath, a cool beer flowing down his throat. Oh yeah, that's what he needed now. He brought his focus back into the room. What was he doing? He had to stop thinking that way.

'Thinking about him?' Graham had made an assumption, but was wrong.

'No, actually I was thinking about a cold beer. Felt so real. You know, I can taste it. There are six cans in the fridge at home and I'm trying to drink only four of them, and Julie's not back till ten. Not gonna be easy.'

'Sounds like you're expecting a tough time avoiding drinking all six.'

'I probably will, but I'd like to think I won't.'

'Sometimes giving yourself permission to have all six takes the tension out and you find yourself not drinking them all. Sometimes it works.'

'No, if I give myself permission to drink all six, then that's what I'll do.'

'And is that what you want to do?'

'Yes … and no.'

'And that's the trouble, isn't it?'

'Like a devil on one shoulder and some kind of angel on the other shoulder, or something like that.' Andy tightened his lips and shook his head. The clock caught his eye, time was just about up. Graham had also noticed and was commenting having seen Andy glance at the clock. 'Yes, only a few minutes left. Caught between the devil on one shoulder and an angel on the other.'

'Yeah. I've got to go for it. I'm going to try and hold it down to four cans. I'm going to go for a drive, it's light out there. Take a bit of time out and then head back, and pick up a take-away for later. I think I need a bit of time. I'm feeling a little more settled just at the moment. It's helped talking. Maybe it'll help to just not rush back home.'

* * * *

Andy sat in the car outside and felt quite strange in many ways. He felt slightly spaced out after the session. He still knew he wanted that cold beer, but he also knew he needed to prove something to himself. He was determined not to go straight home. He turned the ignition and as the car started he pressed the accelerator. The sound touched him in some strange way. Yes, I need some power. He turned on the CD. U2. The guitar riff filled the car—the start to … he couldn't remember the name, just those lines, *in the name of love* … He turned it up and pulled away. He allowed himself to lose himself in the music. He let it rip through him, felt like it was cleansing in some way, blasting away all the crap that had built up in him over his life, *in the name of love* … What the hell did love mean? He thought of Julie. He thought of Terry. He thought of his mother, but he had no memory of her other than photo's—and the last time he saw her she was lying there dead, with her skull cracked open. He heard the CD change to another song. *I can't believe the news today, Oh I can't close my eyes and make it go away, How long, how long must we sing this song, how long, how lo-o-o-o-ong'* It felt like the words were echoing in his head, speaking to him. 'Sunday Bloody Sunday', wonderful song with such a powerful message. *And the battles just begun …* Yes, it has just begun, my battle has just begun. He tightened his jaw. He turned the CD down, suddenly he needed quiet, he just wanted it in the background as he drove away from the city and into the country side. He knew he needed to get away from people, from the busy-ness of it all. He needed some space. Needed to get away. He didn't really think about where he was going, he just knew he had to keep driving. He turned off the main road and continued down a lane out into the countryside. He knew where he was, but he wasn't thinking of going anywhere in particular.

Another song came on, the guitar rhythm caught his attention and he turned it up. It was a fast rhythm and it picked him up and he felt himself nodding to it. Again it seemed to speak to him, seemed to be words that were for him, and for him alone. He couldn't pick out all the words but what he heard was. *I want to run, I want to hide I want to tear down the walls that hold me inside … I want to reach out and touch the flame, where the streets have no name ...* Something in him wanted to break out, break free. The music lifted him, transported him. He nodded his head to the rhythm as he drove along. The song seemed too short so he ran it again.

He had reached a pull-in by a gap in the hedge. The sun was going down and he could see across the fields. He needed to stop and just look. The CD continued, He tapped his foot to the rhythm, *I want to feel some light on my face, I see the dust cloud disappear without a trace ... where the streets have no name.* He let the track run through again before turning it off. He got out and walked around the car to a gate and leaned on it, looking over towards the sunset. *I want to feel some light on my face ...* Yes, he thought, I need this, and as he stood and thought about it he could also feel that other sensation building up inside himself, telling him that what he could really do with was a drink.

He pushed the thought aside and looked at the clouds, the wonderful peachy-pink that glistened as the sunlight caught the them. He wasn't one to watch sunsets, and yet somehow it seemed compelling. He just leaned on the gate and allowed himself to drift. His mind went back to the cans in the fridge and the thought of how he would feel if he drank them, of the sensation, but it was hazy. He had a kind of feeling that he wasn't doing what he should be doing, that his place was to be back at home enjoying those cans. He felt a little unsure and uneasy. What was he doing here? And yet ... the unease grew. A deep breath and he decided to head back home.

He stopped off at the Indian take away, had a beer whilst he waited for his order—it felt good, just like the one he had been daydreaming about earlier. The beer was cold in his throat and he could feel it swirling all the way down into his stomach. He had another. He hadn't planned to but they seemed to be taking a while to get his order together.

Half an hour later and he was back home and starting in on his curry. He'd left some for Julie in the trays in the oven on a very low heat for when she came in later. He'd already opened one of the cans. He knew he should be trying to not drink them, but they tasted good and he felt more at ease. That weird sensation he had felt earlier and during the session had passed. He'd get it back in control tomorrow. He deserved a reward. It had been a long day and he needed to relax and unwind.

By the time Julie came in he had got through two more of the cans, and was about to have the fourth.

'You go to counselling and you come back drinking. Andy, when are you going to change?'

Andy felt himself react. 'Just a couple of cans. Been a heavy session, you know, and I just needed a couple of cans.' He didn't say anything about the two beers at the take-away.

'Well, six this morning and only two now—given two of them to the cat?'

'Yeah, well, OK, maybe I had a couple more. Look, I'm trying. I needed to relax. Don't go on at me, I'm fucking trying, you know, it's not fucking easy. Shit, it's only a few cans.'

Julie was aware that she had had a heavy day as well, but she hadn't had to have a drink. And she really didn't need Andy going off on one. He'd followed her out into the kitchen, can in his hand. 'Just get out of my space, Andy, I just want to eat and go to bed. I've had a long day too, and I'm tired and I really don't need you like this.'

'Like what?'

'You know what. Now, out of my way, I'm hungry.'

'No, what do you mean, like what?'

'Andy, get out of the way.'

'No.' Andy was getting more belligerent. 'No, like what. Like fucking what?' He was a little unsteady and spilled some of the beer from the can he was holding in his right hand.

'Andy, just …' she shook her head. She went to push past him but he blocked her way and pushed her back forcefully. He'd had enough, all she did was nag at him. She didn't give a fuck. He wanted to hit her. He felt his jaw tightening and his fist was clenching. She needed to understand what it was like. Yeah, then she'd know. His head was full of sounds from his past. Shouts, thumps, cries of pain. That's what he knew. That was what he was used to. That's what she needed to understand. He shifted the can into his left hand.

'I'll fucking show you.'

Julie cowered away. Andy had never been quite like this before. Suddenly, for the first time in her life, Julie felt scared. There was something different about Andy tonight, something menacing. It wasn't the Andy she knew, even when he got drunk. She looked to the door. He was in the way. There was no way out. She wouldn't be able to push him, she'd only anger him more if she got physical. She had to protect herself, she looked around quickly, but there was nothing to get hold of, and anyway that might only escalate things. She had to keep him talking, try and calm him down.

'Andy, what's the matter with you.'

'Nothing's the matter with me, nothing's the matter with me. Got that?' He was really in her space, glaring down at her. Suddenly she saw real ugliness in his face. She'd never seen that before. It was awful. She wanted to cry but she couldn't let herself do that.

'OK, nothing's the matter with you. You're OK, Andy, you're really OK, yeah?' She didn't say anything else although she knew her words were somehow totally unreal to the situation.

He could hear is mother shrieking in his head. The image of Julie before him began to blur. There were tears in his eyes. But he wasn't going to back down.

'I just want to eat, love. That's all.' Julie's heart was pounding. The adrenaline was kicking in. Her senses were on high alert. 'Is that OK?' She tried to keep her voice steady but soft. She knew instinctively that any kind of edge to her voice might make things worse.

Andy stood very still, he wanted to lash out, show her what it was like. That was what you did. He knew that. He'd learned it long ago. But something was stopping him, something deep inside him was holding him back. He wasn't thinking about it or experiencing it in that way, but somewhere deep inside was a part of himself that was terrified that he could become like his father. On the surface Andy still felt utter contempt for Julie. His head was spinning a little, a mixture of the alcohol and the adrenaline that was now very much in his own system. He had to focus at keeping his balance. Maybe another time, he thought. He relaxed his fist. He relaxed his jaw.

'Huh', was all that he said.

Julie sensed a shift in Andy's tone of voice. 'Come on,' she spoke softly, 'I am hungry and the curry smells good. I do just want to eat.'

The intensity with Andy was subsiding a little. He returned the can to his right hand. 'OK, yeah, guess so, OK.' He moved aside and took a deep draught from the can, draining it completely before throwing it towards the swing bin in the corner of the kitchen. It didn't go in but bounced of the top of the lid with a clank and clattered off the cupboard door beside it before skidding across the kitchen floor, ending up against the cooker. He didn't bother to pick it up. He glared at it before turning and going back to the front room where he sat down heavily on the sofa.

Julie didn't move for a few moments. She was shaking, She hadn't realised she was shaking until now. She burst into tears. It was only after some minutes that she felt able to compose herself and take the curry out of the oven. She was hungry but her stomach was churning. She didn't feel as if she had much appetite. She picked at it from the carton. Every mouthful was a struggle, and she had to force herself to swallow. The tears were still very close. In the end she gave up and went to the lounge. Andy was asleep and snoring. She didn't say anything, but turned and went up to the bedroom where she stayed for the rest of the evening, trying to read a magazine, but not really taking anything much in.

Downstairs Andy remained asleep He'd drunk most of the cans. The TV was still on. He woke up a couple of times, drank some more each time and fell asleep again. He felt so many things as he sat there when he was awake. But all of them affected by the alcohol in his blood and in his brain. Most of all he felt sorry for himself. Nobody cared. Nobody ever cared. He fell asleep again with that thought on his mind.

* * * *

It was the next morning. Andy hadn't been concentrating when the car in front of him braked. He saw the lights come on but he hadn't completely registered. By the time he hit the brake himself he had no chance of pulling up in time. Bang! The metallic thud resonated around the van and he could hear stuff falling about in the back. The car in front seemed to crumple under impact, the back stove right in. He heard the screech of brakes behind and he waited for the impact but none occurred. He looked in the mirror, the car behind had managed to steer to the right and fortunately nothing had been coming the other way. Andy felt the adrenalin rush. His heart was thumping. 'Fuck,' he muttered under his breath.

He felt angry and got out. The occupant of the car in front was also getting out. Andy was straight into giving him the verbal. 'What the fuck are you doing stopping like that.'

'What the hell do you mean. The light was red, I pulled up, and then you come thundering into the back of me, you dozy bastard. Look at the back of my car, look at it.'

'Yeah, well, insurance will sort it out.'

'Your insurance will. So you'd better give me your details.'

Andy was still feeling angry. 'Maybe you should have seen the lights earlier.'

'Maybe you should have been looking where you were going.'

It was at this moment that a police car pulled up. A police officer got out and strolled over. 'So, this is a bit of a mess. Who's car is it.'

'Mine.'

'And you?'

Andy replied, 'I was driving the van.'

'You don't believe in using breaks then?'

Andy felt himself fire up and but managed to control himself.

'Didn't see his lights.'

'Oh, right. Well, now we're here we're going to breathalyse you both. Just in case. Just stay here.' He turned and called to his colleague who was also strolling over. 'Jim, get the breathalyser.'

Andy suddenly felt panic set in. Oh shit, what had Graham said about units, one an hour. He tried to work it out, but he couldn't think straight. Started at half past seven, or was it later? He wasn't sure. Two bottles, four cans, how strong were the bottles? He didn't know. Shit. No, it was six cans, fifteen units—fifteen hours. Seven-thirty, that meant fifteen hours. It was now ten o'clock in the morning, only twelve, no fourteen hours since he had started drinking. He'd only have a unit of alcohol plus the two bottles in the take away, so a unit plus whatever was still in his system from the two bottles. Oh shit. How strong were the bottles. They weren't big, but they weren't small either. He knew he needed to get out of this somehow, but he couldn't think. Should he run away? What was the point. Oh hell. Now what. He'd lose his license, lose his job. Oh fuck no, no, he couldn't. It wasn't fair. It wasn't fair. He hadn't caused the accident, the idiot in front had, pulling up like that. Maybe he'd be OK. Maybe, think again, started at half past seven, no, it must have been nearer eight o'clock. Six cans, fifteen hours. He'd have one unit plus the bottles, yes, so maybe he should play for time, give his body a little longer. He didn't know what the limit was, he'd heard people say two or three pints—he was surely less than that.

Andy decided to play for time and went around to the back of his van to see if there had been any damage, he knew he hadn't been hit but he thought he'd just spend a few minutes inspecting the back of the van. The other car owner had got out. The other policeman was talking to him. He could hear him explaining how he saw the van lights come on, heard it skidding, heard the thump and had managed to turn out to miss the van. By now, traffic was building up—it was a busy road and it was now well into the rush hour. What the hell was his boss going to say? Andy didn't want to go round the front of the van, so he sort of hung around on the side by the kerb.

The policeman appeared. I need you to blow into this. He explained what it meant. 'Just a moment, let me just see what the damage is at the front.' Andy went and had a look. Yes, the van being higher up didn't have so much damage. The bumper had taken the main impact from the back of the hatchback. But it had been enough to damage the radiator, there was a pool of water under the front of the van. 'I need to call my boss, let him know what's happened, arrange to get the van collected.'

'All in good time, we may not want the vehicles moved just yet. Now, breathe into this here.'

'Now?'

'Yes, now.'

'But I haven't had anything to drink this morning. He's the one you should breathalyse, he was the one who just stopped suddenly.'

'Maybe, but I need you to blow in this now.'

'Look ...'

'Now!' The policeman was getting suspicious. 'Come on, a few minutes won't make much difference.'

They bloody well might was the thought in Andy's head as he blew.

Chapter 9

Julie got home that afternoon to find Andy already there. She wasn't best pleased to see him, not after the incident the night before. She had been on an early start and she was tired. 'You're home early. What happened?' She was tempted to say something about him being able to start in on the cans earlier but after his reaction the previous night she thought the better of it. She didn't know what to do, but she didn't want to set him off again if she could avoid it.

'Had an accident.'

'What? Are you OK? What happened?' Julie was a little concerned though not as much as she might usually have been. Now she thought about it, Andy did look a bit pale.

'This idiot braked in front of me. Went into the back of him.' Andy went on to explain what had happened.

'Was anyone hurt?'

'Don't think so. Anyway, I had to go to the police station. They talked to me. But they breathalysed me at the scene.'

'Were you over the limit?'

Andy shook his head. 'No, fortunately, but it did register me having alcohol in my blood. I explained that it was from the night before, that I didn't drink before driving, that we always walked to the pub in the evenings. They didn't seem too impressed though.'

'So what are they going to do?'

'Seems that although I had some alcohol showing up, because I was under the limit, and there was no proof I was driving carelessly, they're not going to charge me. But it must have been close. If it had happened a couple of hours earlier, I mean, if I'd had an early start....' He shook his head.

'Well, maybe it'll teach you a lesson.' Julie turned to walk towards the kitchen.

Andy felt himself reacting, whilst another part of him knew she was right. He didn't want to hear it, but maybe he did need to hear it. The shock of the day reduced the anger he was feeling and he stayed in control. He was feeling sorry for himself.

'I've got to stop, I can't go on like this.'

'So, had anything tonight?'

Andy shook his head. 'I felt like a drink but no. Didn't tell Derek about the breathalyser. He had to know about the van, not much damage but the radiator was split so it had to be towed away. He's getting it fixed and reckons I can use another van tomorrow. He was pissed off with me. Had a go, but then, well, I came over strange, some kind of a reaction I suppose. Anyway, he said to take the day off. So here I am.'

'And you haven't had a drink?'

Andy shook his head. 'No, no I thought about it but I also feel sort of weird still, like I just want to sit.' He looked over to where she was standing. 'It was close, Julie, too close. I can't risk losing my licence. I've got to stop.'

'So, what are you going to do?' Julie was speaking with an edge in her voice. She wanted to know what he was going to do.

Andy turned his head away and looked down. 'I don't know, I really don't know. I tried stopping before and reacted. I don't want that again although I feel I'm drinking a little less now.'

'Go and see Dr Shira, see what she says. Maybe she'll give you something? Give her a ring, the surgery is still open. Maybe get an appointment tomorrow morning or something.'

Andy shook his head. He didn't want to go and talk to her about his drinking. He didn't feel good about it. He wanted to cut back in his own way.

'You'll have to see her eventually, you can't go on like this. You've tried to cut back but it isn't working.'

'It has sometimes. I've had evenings when I've drunk less.'

'And when you've drunk more.'

'Yeah, I know.' Andy felt deflated. He was still looking down. 'I just can't seem to keep it under control. But it'll be different this time. It really has shocked me, Julie, I really do know I have to stop, or cut back. Look maybe if I just have a couple of cans tonight, maybe I can get through. To be honest I'm not sure that I feel like a drink at the moment.'

'Hmm, so, what do you want to do this evening.'

'Let's eat and see how it goes. I'm not feeling too hungry, a sandwich or something will do me.'

Julie went off to the kitchen, leaving Andy to sit and reflect on the day. He was sitting in the sofa, his hands up to his face. It had been close, too close. He wasn't sure how many units had been in those bottles, but it must have been low, or maybe what Graham had said hadn't been right. He'd check it out when he saw him next time.

He thought back to the last counselling session. He hadn't said anything to Julie about getting rid of the booze in the house, but he knew he had to. He went out to the kitchen to tell her.

* * * *

After they'd eaten, Andy gave Gary a call. 'Look, mate, I need a favour. Crazy thing really, but I need to get the booze out of the house.' He paused as Gary responded. 'Yes, yes, I know, but I really am struggling and I can't have it here. It's too tempting. I had a shock today and I can't have it around, I've got to cut back, mate.' He explained to Gary what had happened and Gary agreed to come over. It was about half an hour later when he appeared. Julie had put the bottles in a box. There weren't many, but it turned out that there were more than Andy had realised.

'This seems weird. What do you want me to do with them? Just keep them?'

'I don't know. I just need them out of here.'

'Well, look, I could buy them off you?'

Andy shook his head, 'don't be daft. Just take them away, stick them in the loft or something unless you want to drink them. I don't mind if you do, honest. I just need them away from here. I don't want to be tempted. I know I don't often drink spirits, but if I'm trying to stop there are going to be times when I'll really want a drink and the thought of hitting the spirits … Well, it's not a good idea.'

They sat and chatted for a while, discussed the weekend's football, and set up an evening for Gary to come over again with Amanda.

'Well, it seems kind of odd me taking these with me, I must say,' Gary was getting up to go, 'but I'm not going to drink from them. I'll put the box away somewhere and you can have 'em back when you want them.'

'Yeah, OK. Thanks. Look I appreciate it. But don't let me have them. Wait for Julie to ask for them. Must seem strange to you, but it feels even stranger to me. I have to do it. Talked about it at my counselling on Monday. Probably would have called you then but the drinking got a bit heavy last night. And then with what happened today. No, I have to do this. I hate the idea of admitting to myself that I can't trust myself, but that's how it is. So, thanks. And we'll see you Saturday around, what, seven o'clock or so?'

'Yeah, look forward to that. We'll bring a ... Well, maybe not.'

'No, I don't want to stop you having wine, and I'm not planning to stop, I just need to keep it under control. So, please do. I've got to learn to stay in control.'

Gary nodded and walked over to the box and picked it up before turning and heading for the door. 'Bye Julie,' she was in the kitchen.

'Bye Gary, see you Saturday.'

"Yeah, just saying, we'll look forward to it.'

Julie came in, 'well, you're loaded up,' as she looked at the box of bottles.

'You OK with this.'

She nodded. 'Yeah, we don't need it. Take it away. We'll be OK. Thanks for doing this.'

'No need to thank me. Glad to help out. I'm not often asked to take booze home like this!' He smiled as he spoke, but he also felt sorry that it had come to this for Andy. Yet he was glad Andy had made the decision. Couldn't have been easy for him. He respected him for it. He headed towards the door. Andy opened it for him and came out with him to the car.

'Thanks. Be in touch.'

'Yeah. Take care of yourself, mate, and drive carefully!'

'That's for sure.'

Gary left and Andy came back in. 'so, that's gone. Still haven't had anything but I'm feeling a bit edgy, and a bit shaky.'

'OK, well, look, I put the cans I bought today in the fridge. What're you going to do?'

'Try to get by with a couple. See how it goes.' He went out to the kitchen and opened one. He tried to sip it but he was halfway through the can before he stopped. He came back into the living room and sat down.

'We need to plan the week, Andy. We need to try and keep you drinking less these next few days, see if you can do it.'

'I've got to do it, but I felt so awful last time. Maybe if I have these two and an early night, maybe that'll help.' Andy wasn't convinced, his sleep pattern was pretty bad. He'd either have real trouble getting to sleep or he'd wake up early and not get back to sleep. He yawned and glanced up at the clock. It was a quarter past ten. He hadn't held off having a drink that late for a while, well, apart from when he'd tried to stop. Maybe that was the answer, maybe if he started later? If he could just have a couple of cans last thing, that would help. What else had Graham said? Oh yes, reduce the strength. He looked at the can in his hand—5%.

'There was something else Graham suggested—try to switch to 4.5% cans. Can you have a look next time. Something similar but a bit weaker. See if that helps.'

'Try anything if it gets you drinking less, love. Sorry I had a go earlier but, after last night, you know, you scared me in the kitchen. You really …, I don't know, I just felt scared.'

'I'm sorry too, but it doesn't help you having a go, it really doesn't.' He shook his head, feeling a mixture of shame and sadness, and quite vulnerable too. 'Makes me want to drink. And that sounds like an excuse, and I don't mean it to be, but feeling wound up does make me just want a drink. I know I shouldn't drink like I do, like I have been. I need you to understand. Try not to have a go at me. Please?'

'I know, but some days it gets to me. I had a long day Monday, I was tired and I come in and there you are, pissed again. And you hadn't even waited for me before you started on the curry. It can't carry on like that, Andy, it really can't.'

'I know, and I'm trying. I really am trying, Julie. It's not easy. You must realise that.'

'I do, but I think of my father sometimes, you know, and he never got it under control and it killed him in the end. I don't want that to happen to you, but I can see it happening if you don't change.' There were tears in her eyes. Yes, Andy made her angry, irritated, frustrated, but she loved him and wanted to be with him. 'I don't want those cans,' she looked at the can on the table, 'to come between us, but it's threatening to. I don't want that. I want to know an Andy who hasn't always got a can in his hand.'

Andy looked down and shook his head. A thought had come to mind. 'Andy, the man with a can—never mind man with a van. Sums it up, doesn't it?'

'Come on, let's have an early night. Bring the can with you if you must. Let's go and have a bath and …' Julie moved over and gave Andy a squeeze. 'We can eat something later.'

* * * *

The telephone was ringing. Andy's eyes were still shut as he reached out for the phone.

'Hello.'

Silence.

'Hello, who is it?' He could now hear the sound of breathing. 'Terry, is that you?'

Still silence except for the sound of breathing.

'Come on you daft bugger, don't mess around.' He opened his eyes to look at the clock. 'Shit, it's three o'clock in the morning.'

He heard the sound of the phone hanging up.

Julie had stirred. 'What is it?'

'Someone called. He dialled 1471. The voice gave him Terry's number, called at 02.59.'

'It's Terry. I'd better call him back.' He rang the number, the phone was engaged. He was either making a phone call or maybe he'd rung off but not put the phone down properly. He tried again. Still engaged. He put the phone back down. 'The idiot's probably not put the phone down.' As soon as he had finished speaking the phone rang again.

'Terry, that you? I know you just phoned. What's up?'

Terry was sitting on the edge of his bed having just thrown up. He'd been drinking all day and was in blackout. His head was spinning and he was feeling desperate. Somehow his drinking was taking him into more of a state. It used to make him feel better, helped him forget, helped him block out the memories and the hurt. Now he just seemed to be more lost in it. He felt like shit. He felt like he wanted to die.

'I've had enough. I need help. I'm going to fucking kill myself. I can't handle it any more.'

Andy could hear the sound of Terry crying.

'Oh shit, Julie, he's crying, says he wants to kill himself. What do I do?'

'I don't know, keep talking to him. Keep him on the phone.'

'I know it's bad, Terry, it's crap, but come on, you'll pull through. It's just the booze getting hold of you, making you think crazy things.'

Terry wasn't listening. He could hear Andy's voice but he wasn't taking it in. 'I can't go on any more. I can't handle it. I can't hold it together any more.'

'I know it's tough, I've got memories and I'm trying to control the booze as well. I know it's hard and horrible. But, hey, come on bruv, we've come through a lot, we've got to find a way to come through this.' He paused, hesitating on what he wanted to say. He said it, 'for mum's sake.'

He heard the sound of the phone being dropped. 'Terry, Terry? Pick the phone up. Come on, pick it up.'

Nothing. 'Terry.' Andy was raising his voice. He was now very anxious. He looked across at Julie, 'he's dropped the phone, can't get him to pick it up. What do I do?'

'I don't know. What was he saying?'

'Said he wanted to kill himself, couldn't handle it any more. Oh shit, I'm going to have to go over, see if he's OK.'

'Look, I'd better have the phone then. He sounded that bad?'

'Yeah, really bad. Crying and…. I hope I said the right thing, mentioning mum. She wouldn't want him to give up.' Andy handed Julie the phone. He got up and started pulling on some clothes. 'Don't know what I'll do when I get there, or what I'll find.'

'Look, should I come?'

'No, better you stay on the phone in case he picks it up again. Don't know how he'll react if we've hung up. Keep the line open in case. Shit. Where's my fucking sock?' Andy was hunting around at the foot of the bed. 'Oh, here it is. He pulled it on then looked round for his trainers. He found them eventually, one was under the bed the other under a pullover he'd been wearing the day before. 'OK, I'm off, gonna be about half an hour before I get there.'

'What if you can't get in?'

'God, yeah, he's never given me a key. I don't know. I'll take the mobile, give you a call. Shit, I can't if you've got the phone open. Oh Christ.'

'Look, I'll call your mobile in about half an hour, give you time to get there and then we'll decide what to do. I'm sure he'll be OK. He's probably passed out with the booze and dropped the phone.'

'Yeah, but, shit, he said he wanted to die. I mean, you don't think he's done something stupid?'

'No, no he never has before, why should he now. No, he's probably fallen asleep.' Julie wanted to reassure Andy. Try and calm him a little before he headed off.

'Maybe, but he really didn't sound good.' He paused again. 'Shit, I wish you were coming with me. I just don't know what's best.'

'I can come if you want.' Julie made to get up.

'No, no, you stay here in case he wants to talk again. I'll head off.' He leaned over to give Julie a kiss. 'I'll see you later, but, yes, call me in half an hour, or before if he says anything and hangs up, or whatever. Yeah?'

'Check you've got the mobile on so I can call you.'

'Yeah, OK.' Andy had it in his hand and pressed the on button. He generally left it off overnight. 'Thank God I hardly drank anything last night.'

'Well, if you had, I'd have had to have driven, wouldn't I?'

'Yeah. OK, look, I'm off.' He leaned over to give her a kiss.

'Ok. Drive carefully, love, please drive carefully. No sense in you taking risks as well.'

Andy nodded and turned, heading out of the bedroom.

He drove fast but tried to keep within the speed limit. There was no-one much around, the roads were quiet. He had so many thoughts going through his head, and memories of Terry and situations they'd had to face together. He remembered their first day at the new school after they'd gone to his aunt and uncle to live. Both of them had found it hard to adjust. Terry had looked out for him. He'd often done that. He seemed to have taken on his mother's role as a kind of protector. But then later, as he got into his early twenties, he had begun to drink more and more and become something of an isolated figure. He had never really had any relationships, nothing more than a few months anyway. He'd drifted further apart from Terry since he'd met Julie. He had the CD on as he drove, the same songs as from the evening before. *Oh I can't close my eyes and make it go away.* He turned the CD off. He wasn't in the mood. He needed silence.

He pulled up outside Terry's house. A light was on. Julie hadn't called. He phoned her. Engaged. He looked at his watch. He'd made it in twenty five minutes. She probably hadn't hung up yet to call him. He went up to the door and knocked. No reply. He knocked harder. Still no reply. He opened the letter box and called out. 'Terry. Can you hear me? Come on, come and let me in.' Silence. He could feel the anxiety increasing inside himself again. Come on, Terry, let me in, he thought to himself.' His mobile rang and he started, it seemed so loud in the silence and the darkness. 'Hello? Julie?'

'Hi, yes, I held the line open but nothing. What's happening?'

'I can't get any response. What should I do? Break in?'

'I don't know. Any windows open?'

'I haven't looked. I'll go around the side.' But there were no windows open. 'shit, they're all closed. I'll have to break in. There's a glass panel in the door, or maybe I should break a window. What do you think?'

'Look, why don't you call the police, see if they could send someone round to break in without doing so much damage?'

'No, with my luck it would be the same copper that I saw this morning. No, I'll try and break the glass quietly.' He looked around for a largish stone, noticing a large one by the step. He picked it up and wrapped it in the sleeve of his jacket. The glass broke easily, he reached in—the key was in the door. He turned it and opened the door. It was dark and Andy couldn't remember where the light switch was. The smell was horrible. He caught himself on something—must be the edge of the table, he thought. 'Shit!', he muttered under his breath. He moved more carefully and found the light switch. As the light came on he saw that the kitchen was a mess. Empty bottles, takeaway cartons, unwashed plates. He went through into the hallway and put the light on. He headed into the lounge. Terry was flat out on the sofa. He'd been sick, vomit down the side of the sofa. He was lying with his face to one side, snoring gently, the phone hanging by the side of the sofa. Andy picked up the phone and put it back in its holder.

'Terry, wake up bruv.' He pushed him. 'Terry stirred and groaned slightly but didn't wake up. 'Terry, wake up. He shoved him a little more.'

'Huh, what is it, who's there?'

'Me, Andy, you phoned.'

'Yeah, so why are you here. What's going on?'

'You remember phoning, said you were going to kill yourself. Remember?'

'Yeah, I do, But I guess I fell asleep.'

'Yeah well, shit you're in a state.'

'Yeah, well, leave me alone, I want to go back to sleep. Piss off and let me sleep.'

'Look, you've thrown up all over the sofa, you're pissed, I've had to break in to get in here. And you tell me to piss off because you want to sleep. For fuck's sake, Terry, get a grip here.

'Just bugger off and leave me alone.'

'I can't. I had to break the glass in the door to get in. It'll be unlocked if I go.'

Terry was snoring again. He'd gone back to sleep. 'Shit, thought Andy, now what? He decided to get a bowl and wash some of the vomit off the sofa and floor, but he couldn't do much more than that. Terry was flat out again. After he'd finished he tried to rouse him again but without much success. He called Julie and explained the situation.

'What're you going to do?'

'I guess I'd better stay here while he sleeps it off.'

'What about you going to work tomorrow, I mean, today?'

'I'll have to go in. I'll go in from here. I'll stay here, try and get some sleep in the chair. Maybe he'll wake up before I go, but I don't hold out much hope. I'll have to …' Andy heard someone calling out and he moved over to the window. He noticed lights in the front garden. 'There's someone outside, I'd better go and see.' He went back towards the kitchen. He heard a scrunch, someone must have stood on the glass. 'Hello, who's there?'

'Police. Don't move.'

'It's OK, I'm his brother, I had to break the glass to get in.'

Two policemen in uniform had stepped into the kitchen. 'We had a call, someone heard glass breaking and saw a light come on.'

'It's my brother, Terry, he phoned me earlier, said he was going to kill himself. He's got a drink problem. I came round but had to break in—I hadn't got a key. He's asleep. Tried to wake him up but he sort of woke up but then went back to sleep again.'

'Someone been sick?' One of the police officers was wrinkling up his nose.

'Yeah, been trying to clear it up. He's in a real mess.'

'Where is he?'

'In the lounge.' They went in. 'Yeah, he doesn't look too good, does he. You're his brother, you say?'

Andy nodded.

'You look like you could be. Got any identity?'

Andy handed over his driving licence. 'You can call my girlfriend, she knows I've come over.'

They phoned her and she confirmed what had happened.

'So, what are you going to do?'

'Stay here, I guess, hope he wakes up before I have to head off for work.'

'You say he was suicidal.'

'Said he was going to kill himself.'

'Any idea why?'

Andy nodded. 'It's a long story.' He told them about what had happened in the past. The older of the policeman nodded knowingly. 'You know, I remember it. I remember it happening. I wasn't long in the force, it was in my patch. It was Dartford way, somewhere around there, wasn't it?. And your father, he died, didn't he?'

'Killed himself.'

'And you say it all happened because your mother was trying to protect your brother. Bloody hell. What a mess.' He shook his head. 'What a thing to have to live with. Messed him up, yeah?'

Andy nodded. 'Hasn't done me a lot of good either. But I seem to have coped better than Terry.'

'OK, look, we'll need to report back. But we'd better roll him into the recovery position, less likely to choke on his own vomit if he throws up again.'

'Don't think there's much left for him to throw up.'

'Of course, we don't know what state of mind he'll be in when he wakes up. You may need to leave him a note or something if you have to leave. What time have you got to go?'

'About 7.00am.'

'OK, we'll try and arrange for someone to drop over to see if he's OK. Give us his phone number as well.'

Andy gave them the number. 'There you go. I'm worried about the door. I guess I'd better fix something to that panel for now, and if I have to go before he's awake, lock it and put the key back through the letter box.'

The police left and Andy went back into the lounge. Terry was still out of it. Andy decided to patch up the door. He found some cardboard, picked out the glass from the panel and jammed the card into the hole. At least it had been a smallish glass panel in the door. It would have been better to have taped it up but he couldn't find any tape. He went back into the front room, deciding to leave the light on, and laid down. He called Julie, told her what had happened and asked her to phone the mobile at six-thirty wake him up so he didn't oversleep, and to keep calling in case he didn't hear it the first time. He must have drifted off eventually because he was woken by the sound of the phone. He was initially disorientated, but then he remembered where he was. He answered the phone.

Terry was still asleep. He tried to rouse him again, but Terry was still out. Andy went into the kitchen and made a coffee. No milk anywhere, but that was OK, he needed it strong. He found the sugar. He went into the bathroom and had a quick wash, and wrote a note for Terry which he put on the floor next to him. He left another note on the kitchen door. It was nearly 7.00am and he needed to head off. He took one last look at Terry who was continuing to snore.

*   *   *   *

It was as he left Terry's place that Andy realised that with his pre-occupation with everything he hadn't had a drink, and hadn't really thought about it that much. He decided he'd not head back after work, but leave it and call Terry in the evening now. He'd left him a clear note about what had happened. He felt concerned, but he felt he had done all that he could. And the police had said they'd get someone to make contact or call round.

*   *   *   *

Andy was describing what had happened to Graham the following Monday. The accident, the police, going over to Terry's house, and how he had then decided to go back over to see Terry the following evening and explain what had happened. Terry couldn't remember but was still drinking heavily. Andy had tried to encourage him to think about stopping but he wasn't interested. In the end Andy had left. He knew he couldn't spend another night there. He was tired. He also explained how he hadn't had a drink there, but that he'd had some when he'd got back home.

'I took your advice and am on the 4.5% cans, and haven't gone above four this week. I'm trying to keep myself busy. We ended up at Terry's again at the weekend. He'd stopped the binge but still didn't want to admit to the phone calls. I took Julie with me this time—decided that would make it less likely that we'd end up drinking together. I suggested he speak to someone himself. There's an alcohol advice service he can call that's actually not far from where he lives, but he didn't want to know. I don't know what more I can do.'

'What would you like to do?'

'Take him to see someone, but that won't happen.'

'Yeah, you want him to get some help and advice. What about you as well, would it help if you had a chat with them about the situation? See if they have any ideas as to what you can do?' Graham was aware that Andy was sounding desperate and wanting to do something constructive, but clearly was unsure what direction to take, or what his options were.

'What would they say?'

'I don't know, but it's probably worth your while talking to them. See what they say. They may be able to offer advice as to how you can handle the situation.'

'Hmm, well I can try, but I don't know what they can do if he doesn't want to see anyone.'

Graham was very conscious of how much of the session was being taken up with handling Terry and whilst that was clearly important for Andy, it wasn't focusing much on Andy's own drinking and issues.

'It's a lot for you have to carry and try to find answers for, particularly as you are also trying to make your own changes and deal with things differently.'

Andy nodded. 'I know. It's not easy, but I am making changes at home. We have been out more, and I'm doing more around the house, keeping myself busy. Worked a bit later a couple of times—took on a couple of longer deliveries. I figured that if I did that on evenings when Julie worked late that would reduce the drinking time. I'm also having a bath when I get home instead of a shower—takes a bit of time, helps me relax a bit. That's helping. But I'm still drinking every evening.'

'Drinking every evening, but you are making changes and you are bringing the quantity down, yes? What's the total for last week?'

'Well, Monday I drank too much, about eighteen units I suppose. The rest of the week has been pretty good. Two cans Tuesday, four Wednesday—had a couple but couldn't sleep and had a couple more. Thursday again had four. Friday we went out—I had a couple of bottles and then a couple of cans when we got back. Saturday, had a couple of beers at lunch time and again in the evening, not too bad. Then a couple of beers Sunday lunch time and four cans in the evening.'

'Well, I reckon that comes out around 70 units or so, that's good, a real reduction, particularly with the amount you drank on Monday because it means the rest of the week you were at a level that would have brought meant a lot less that 70, probably neared 60. You've really made a significant change, Andy. You look surprised?'

'Somehow I thought it would be more. I mean, I knew I'd been drinking less, and yet still around four cans, but, well, the weaker strength may have helped.'

'Yes, and if you can stabilise at this and really adjust to it, that'll be a great achievement. How are you feeling with drinking less?'

'Bit shaky at times. Very tired, but then I can't seem to sleep too good. It didn't help having to be over at Terry's that night. And not sleeping well the following night either. But I can live with that, though I have to be careful driving. I mean, driving extra is good, but I guess I just need to be really careful, you know?'

'Sure. Tiring time for you and yes, that need to take care when you're at the wheel.'

'Particularly after having had that accident, you know? These things happen and I need to be careful. But I'm pleased with reducing, it has come down and I haven't had a really bad reaction.'

'No, that's great and with the amount you are currently drinking, well, over half of each day you are not alcohol affected, so it is enabling your body to acclimatise to not having alcohol in the system.'

'So, should I stay as I am, or reduce further?'

'That's really up to you. What do you feel?'

'I need to really hold this four can maximum, or, what are we saying in units, about 9 units a day?'

'That's about it. Still more than double safe drinking, but better than it was.'

Andy felt this was realistic. And he knew he had to put evenings like last Monday behind him. 'Yeah, last Monday wasn't good.'

'No, and those days may still happen, but hopefully not as often or with so much being consumed.'

Andy nodded thoughtfully. 'It's not easy. I really have to work at it. I can't seem to not think about it.'

'Well, no, and that may take a while to change. And in a way, the fact that you are still drinking can make that more difficult. It's not that alcohol is out of the picture and you are learning to think about different things. You are continuing to drink, albeit less, but it means the idea of drinking is still alive to you. Does that make sense?'

'I guess so, but that sounds like you think I need to stop completely.'

'I really don't know. We have to find a way that works for you and that ensures your reduced alcohol use is sustained. Sometimes a period completely dry can help this, help people to begin to think differently and to establish a genuinely alcohol-free lifestyle. But that isn't your current goal, though it may be one day.'

'You're probably right but I know I don't really want to face that. The thought of not drinking feels a long way away.'

'No, you're not there, and it is about helping you where you are. That's reality. There's no other place to work from otherwise you end up being set up with unrealistic goals, and that's no good for you or for anyone.'

'This is so different to what I've always thought, that when you had an alcohol problem you had to stop and that was that. But this way it makes so much sense. Does to me, anyway. But I guess it doesn't work for everyone—and I still have to prove it can work for me.'

That, thought Graham, was the crux of it. They spent a little longer discussing how helpful it was to take this slowly, slowly approach and Andy identified how it was making him adapt slowly, forcing him to make changes which he hoped would see him through in the future.

They also looked again at his drinking pattern and discussed how he might give himself targets for the following weeks, trying to identify days when he might aim to reduce a little more. The idea that emerged was to try and tie that in with any days when he worked late and there was less drinking time in the evening, and less time on his own. There was also the acknowledgement of the uncertainty over Terry, and Andy was aware that it really troubled him. Andy described how he had been back over since that last call and Terry had got his act together and ended the binge, as he could do. Also that he had actually got himself back to work by the end of the week and had held things together over the weekend. But Andy knew the pattern. He'd tried to encourage him to seek help, but Terry wasn't interested. Said he'd get by. Said that he realised the last binge was a bit of a rough one, but that he wouldn't let it happen like that again, that he could control it. Andy explained that Terry still had no recollection of the phone calls and of the degree of desperation he had been feeling. Those memories were locked away somewhere in Terry's head, the effect of the blackout phase of his binge.

Graham knew that this was not an uncommon reaction, complete denial of the scale of the problem and a false belief as to just how much control the individual had. He felt for Andy, watching his brother perhaps slide slowly further downhill. He thought back to his own supervision and was aware that he was feeling different, he did have a stronger sense of Andy as his client and that it was Andy with whom he was working although Terry was obviously a factor in the therapeutic process. Yes, he felt for Terry, but Andy was more present to him. He was glad to feel a stronger sense of connection to his client.

Chapter 10

Andy was spending much less time now in the pub. In fact, the past couple of weeks had seen him keep away, although a few of times he had thought about it and been tempted—the pull of the atmosphere as much as anything else. He had not managed to dip under the four cans. He didn't really know why, but whatever time he started drinking of an evening there was something in him that seemed to make him believe he needed—or had earned—the right to have those four cans. They seemed to mean more than simply being four cans of lager.

It was now Thursday and he hadn't had any further contact with Terry since the weekend. Andy had decided he needed to focus on getting himself together. He had called Terry a couple of times on the phone, but he hadn't been in, and hadn't returned his calls. He anticipated the worst though he liked to think that maybe he had some work on that was taking him out in the evenings. He knew Terry did occasionally do smaller jobs of an evening, or if he was working on a site out of area and being driven over he could get back late. But in truth he suspected he had started drinking again. Not that it always stopped him working. But that did seem to be happening now more often.

Andy was getting ready to watch a European football match on television. Gary was round with Amanda. The women were talking in the kitchen and had left Andy and Gary to get on with it. Andy was just opening his first can of the evening.

'So, you really are keeping away from the pub these days. Alan and Steve were asking about you when I dropped in there earlier. Said I was coming over. They didn't seem too bothered that you weren't there. They made a joke about it. Said you weren't being allowed out. I told them it wasn't like that, and you really were making some changes and cutting back on the booze. They didn't seem too impressed. They're in another place, aren't they?'

Andy nodded. He rather liked Gary's Australian accent. It wasn't strong, but it had a certain lilt to it. 'I really can't be too bothered about them. I'm sorry, it seems hard, I've known them for a long time, but I've got to move on. Its not easy, but I have to make a different life for myself and for Julie, and put my past behind me.' He had got up to draw the curtains; the football hadn't started. 'I really have got to do this, Gary. I see Terry, what alcohol's doing to him, what the past is doing to him, eating him up from the inside, and I can't go there. I can see that my drinking may not have felt like a problem, but in effect it has been. It's the same for Steve and Alan. They don't see their drinking as a problem, but it is. It's damaging them and setting them up for a problematic future. You just can't keep boozing it like that without something giving—your health or your mind.'

'Not everyone has problems with it, mate, you know people who have lived for years and drunk heavily without any seeming damage.'

'True, but I can see that the risk is there and I'm not going to take that risk any more. My drinking has been driven by my past, and then because it became a habit. I'm breaking that habit and trying to deal with my past. And with Terry I can see what happens when you don't do this. He's a living reminder to me. Not that I want him to stay like that. God knows I want him to change, but he's not there He just does not see it as a problem. But at least now that he's off the booze again we're not getting the phone calls.'

'Yeah, I remember you told me about that. Weird, phoning someone but not knowing you've done it. Real spooky.'

'Anyway, looks like the teams are about to come out. Where's that pizza. I'd better go and see what those two are up to. This is serious business, this match, we need to keep our strength up.' He looked towards the kitchen, 'Julie? Where's the pizza you promised us, there's two starving men in here …'

* * * *

Terry was sitting at home, he'd stayed dry for a few days again, that was his normal pattern, and then he'd binge once more. He didn't remember much about the binges any more, and his memory generally wasn't too good. Always going into rooms and not knowing why, forgetting to buy things, or pay bills. He could get by at work, his labouring jobs were pretty routine on the building sites, though he was finding it hard. He didn't have the energy and he ached so as well.

Like some of the other guys he worked with, he skived off for a beer or two. He could drink sometimes between binges without it getting out of control, but he had a definite weekend bingeing pattern and some weeks, well, it just carried on.

He was sitting, feeling bored. He could sense the familiar feelings inside him, urging him to have a drink. He felt unsettled, disturbed, a kind of strange inner hurt that would rise up at him. And he felt the cravings, that gut-wrenching need to have alcohol in his body. He hadn't eaten much. He was tired and pissed off. It had been a hard day and he was slumped on the sofa flicking TV channels but not really taking anything in. The images were in his head, not on the screen. As usual he was thinking about his past. He had never been able to lose that feeling of self-blame for what had happened all those years ago. Deep inside himself he knew he was to blame for his mother's death. However illogical it might seem from the outside, inside himself that was what he believed. As an adult in more lucid periods he could rationalise that away, but it didn't remove that core belief.

What was the point, he thought to himself. He knew he needed a drink and he knew he'd go and get one. The off-licence was down the road. It was still daylight—just. As he became closer to acting on his need for a drink his thinking narrowed. This was the usual pattern although he didn't think of it in those terms. It was part of the psychological preparation, the mechanism through which his internal processes set him up to take alcohol in order to bring relief to a psyche under strain. Like everyone else, he made choices in order to feel better. Everyone like's to feel better when they are not feeling good. But the meaning of 'better' varies from person to person. For Terry it was clear—alcohol eased the hurt, the psychological fragmentation, the experience of being a human being whose core identity had been bruised and battered by a set of childhood experiences that he could not forget.

The truth was that he had been traumatised and he'd never really dealt with it. He'd tried to put it aside, in his own way, and get on with his life, but it never really worked. Nothing really worked, except a drink. He had flashbacks, incredibly clear ones, and they took him to a very dark and violent place in himself. He drank to get away from them but it didn't really make any difference, just knocked him out. They continued and in fact they made him more depressed when he was drinking. He could see it all now and he could feel this strange but all too familiar sensation inside himself, but he'd never been able to describe it or put it into his words. Some might describe it as a knife in the heart, an arrow through his soul, there was something about it being a very deep and crucial part of himself that had been pierced by an unwanted experience, that had in effect … No, it wasn't just a hole or a cut, it was a poison as well. Like something had been forced into him that rotted him away, ate into his very being, like acid. Like acid. A cold yet fiery burning that devoured all that came it's way.

Of course, and Terry wasn't making this connection, but that was precisely what alcohol gave him—a cold burning sensation. He was using something to take something away that actually carried a similar kind of effect—though with alcohol the cold burning sensation was physical. For Terry it was his emotions and his heart that were being burned by this cold intrusion from his past.

He got up and headed for the door, checking he had his wallet as he did so. He wasn't thinking now, not in his usual way. He was a man driven, possessed by an urge and seemingly powerless to make another choice. He jumped in his car and drove the short distance to the off-licence. He'd never really thought about why he drank whisky, he just did. It was what his father's drank. That was part of the tragedy, but he was beyond dwelling on that. He did drink other spirits sometimes, but he'd come back to the whisky. That was what he was used to, what his body expected. That was what he was wanting now.

Terry had never been able to make sense of his drinking. He knew he'd vowed never to be like his father. Well, he wasn't violent, but he did drink the same drink as him. What did that make him? He wasn't thinking of it quite this way but in effect his drinking could be seen as an act of self-punishment. He had internalised what his father had said at the end, and believed it. He had killed his mother simply because she had been trying to protect *him*. He was to blame. It was his fault. These beliefs built on the earlier years of traumatic violence in the home, leaving him believing there was something wrong with him, and that was why he had been punished so often.

Going into the off-licence was a blur, he just did it, mumbled some thanks to the girl behind the till, and returned home. He got a couple of bottles. He didn't have a specific intention, just bought them, just knew he needed them and that was how it was. He wanted that sensation in his body, that beautiful taste in his mouth and the sensation as it warmed his throat and stomach. Warmed! That was how he experienced it but of course there was no real warmth. It fooled him, inflaming the lining to give the sensation of a burning warmth. But these were not Terry's thoughts.

He drove home, almost in a kind of daze. It was going to be OK. The bottles were in a carrier bag on the seat beside him. He felt good, they gave him reassurance. He knew he'd soon feel better. He pulled up outside his house and went in. He paused in the kitchen only long enough to pick up his favourite glass from the draining board. He sat down, the bottle in front of him, and clicked on the TV. His attention turned to the whiskey and he reached over, his hand a little unsteady, and poured the golden liquid into the glass. Carefully, and with a certain unsteady yet purposeful action, he put the bottle back on to the table. As he raised his glass it was as if he was offering a toast, and then brought it to his lips. He poured it into his mouth, swilled it around to get the full sensation on the inside of his cheeks and his tongue before swallowing it in a large gulp. 'Ahh. Fuckin' magic. That's what I needed.' He could feel the liquid passing down towards his stomach. It felt good. He'd had a few stomach pains at times, but he got through them with a few pain killers, and taking it easy a bit now and then. He'd never bothered the doctor. He refilled the glass, settled back and had soon drained that as well. It did not take long for the effect of the alcohol to reach his head. That buzzy, numb-like feeling felt so good. It took him away a little from the psychological hurt that was his seemingly twenty-four/seven companion.

As he continued his way down the first bottle, he became increasingly morose. At some point—and he didn't know when—he switched into alcohol blackout. He was now in that place in himself where the memories of what he was experiencing were being lost, or at least not being captured in the usual or normal way. It brought him closer, as well, to the traumatised memories of his past although he could also feel strangely detached from them due to the alcohol in his system. He was unaware in his normal waking consciousness just how much he dwelt on the past when in blackout. He felt heavy and must have drifted off to sleep.

When he woke it was dark. He felt sad and angry, everyone was a bastard, nobody gave a fuck about him. He didn't care. (In truth he did, but he wasn't close to those feelings now.) Life was pointless. What had he achieved? He looked around the room. The stained walls; they'd been white once, now they were a kind of brown-grey colour. He started to roll a cigarette, somewhat unsteadily. He took a deep breath, drawing it fully into his lungs. His head flopped to one side. His eyes were staring at a photo on the shelf. It was of himself and Andy as children. He didn't have any photos of his mother. No images to replace the one that had stayed in his head for so many years. The few he had had he'd burned some months back during a binge. He felt tears in his eyes. He loved his brother, but he dare not let himself feel those feelings. To feel love for Andy would open him to feeling love for others, for his mother. And he couldn't allow himself to feel that, it hurt too much. It would be like taking hold of a scar and forcing it open, tearing it apart. It would tear him apart. He kept feelings of love at bay, or at least, his inner process kept them away from him—and, of course, the alcohol helped.

He reached over and picked up the phone, pressing one for the memorised numbers. It was Andy who answered.

Terry heard his voice. He hadn't really planned to call him, just felt like pressing a number and telling someone they were a bastard.

'No-one gives shit,' his voice was slurring heavily, 'no-one.' He pressed the button on the top of the phone to break the connection, and then pressed number two. Another voice, one of his mates from work that he drank with sometimes.

'Hello. Who is it?'

Terry didn't respond. He just sat holding the phone, staring at it. His arm was unsteady, the phone moved around.

'That you Terry?'

'What if it is?'

'What the fuck are you calling me for, don't you know the time?'

'Fuck off.' He slammed the phone back down. Bastard, he thought. The phone rang, he looked at it. No-one really wants to talk to me. No-one cares about me. He threw the phone across the room, the handset parting from the holder and spinning under the table.

The image of his mother trying to protect him all those years back came powerfully to mind. It wasn't that it was a forgotten memory but somehow, in this particular moment, it seemed more vivid, more real, almost like it was happening now, like it was being replayed and he was in the midst of it.

'No, no, keep away. No, I'll take it. I'll take it.' The tears were hot in his eyes. He could see his father's face, angry, twisted, reeking of alcohol. He hated that face. He wanted to pound it into jelly. Oh how he hated him. If he could meet him now he would kick the shit out of him for what he did, smash him into pulp.

He reached for the bottle, albeit rather unsteadily. Empty. He lifted it up and held it upside down, looking at it with an air of curiosity, as if he didn't know quite how it had managed to empty itself. He dropped his arms and let the bottle fall. It rolled across the carpet. He reached for the other bottle. He was shaky, his body was moving quite unsteadily, his hand had a slight tremor as he poured another glass. He raised it. 'Fuck them all!'

He drifted back into the past, to the fights he'd been in at school. Life had never been easy. He couldn't remember a time when it had felt easy—except when he was drinking and out of it. Those blank times.... He took another mouthful from the glass. He choked as he swallowed it. He coughed a few times, and spat out some phlegm into his stained handkerchief.

'Bastard!', he shouted at the image of his father that was in his head, 'you fucked off, left us, you fucking bastard.' He took another gulp from the glass. 'You weren't good enough to be *our* father, we deserved fucking better than you.'

Terry hated his father. Just images of pain, violence, shouting, and that face staring at him, sneering. Yeah, he wanted to get him back. He'd escaped. He'd escaped. Well he was going after him. He'd had enough, he didn't want the pain any more. 'I'm going to fucking come for you.'

He pushed himself up off the sofa, he was very unsteady on his feet, and he picked up the bottle and staggered out into the hall. He took another mouthful this time from the bottle and started to climb up the stairs. He made slow progress, tripping a couple of times but quite oblivious to the bruising to his shins.

It wasn't that he so much planned to kill himself, although that was in his mind. It was more that he wanted to get away. He had no particular method in mind as he staggered up the stairs, but he was thinking of how he needed to get after his father, and he was thinking that if he died he might be able to find him in some after-life. He'd not got any particular beliefs about what happens when you die, but in his thinking was the idea that maybe he could track him down. His head was full of a mixture of thoughts, all jumbled up into a confused and bewildering cocktail, with alcohol to add to the tangle of thoughts and feelings. The hurt from the past, the anger, the wanting to inflict revenge on his father; his sadness, his feelings of isolation Terry was depressed. He'd had enough. The alcohol in his system was dragging his mood down. His thought processes were slowing, his central nervous system dulling.

He moved into the bedroom as if in a trance. There were tears running down his cheeks, and he continued to move very unsteadily. No, what was the point. He'd had enough. He was going to end it. He drank like his father, he'd end it like his father and then track him down. He dragged the sheets off the bed. Whilst he was thinking of ending it, his main thought was really about getting his father. 'I'm fuckin' comin' after you, you fuckin' bastard.' He had some hazy notion that he'd be able to track him down.

He turned with the sheet in his hand and went back out to the landing. He'd tie the sheet round the banisters, make a noose of some kind. He'd seen it on the TV, seemed quick. Twitch a bit and he'd be gone. And fuck them all. And then he'd right a few wrongs. It was like he was running two parallel trains of thought. Wanting to end it all, and wanting revenge. He set about tying the sheet to the bottom of one of the wooden supports. He pulled on it and it seemed pretty secure. He took another swig from the bottle.

He stood up, but a little too quickly and felt himself losing his balance. He felt dizzy. He stepped to the side to try to regain it but his foot had got tangled in the sheet. He made to move it but it stayed firm and he felt himself falling. Everything seemed to be happening in slow motion. He watched the wall going past his face. The bottle he had let go of as he reached out to try and steady himself seemed to be travelling next to him through the air. The stairway loomed before him. He could feel himself falling, falling, it felt like an eternity. His foot pulled free from the sheet, had it remained there it might have saved him. But Terry fell heavily on to the stairs, his body twisting as he continued to fall, bouncing off the steps. He landed heavily, crashing on to the table that stood by the wall. He didn't feel it. The first impact had broken his neck, his head had been jammed into the corner of one of the steps and with his body weight pressing down the stress was released through the weakest point. Then his body had twisted free as it had fallen further down the stairs. Now he lay there, his eyes open, staring blankly up at the ceiling, his lifeless body twisted, a small pool of blood seeping out from his fractured skull.

The bottle landed in the hall, shattering to spread it's connects across the wooden floor. It had broken with a crack. Had Terry been conscious he would have recognised that sound as being not dissimilar to that of his mother's skull fracturing on the hearth.

All was now silent, utterly still. No-one had heard the sound. The people next door were fast asleep. Terry had gone. His twisted body remained as a testament to his damaged existence.

*   *   *   *

Andy looked across at Julie. 'Can't get through. Line's engaged. Must be pestering some other poor bugger. At least he's OK if he's on the phone to someone. What the hell are we going to do about him, Julie? Can't go on like this.'

Julie was still half asleep. She'd heard the phone ring and the bit of the brief conversation from that end. 'I know he's your brother, but what can we do. He's trying to handle things I suppose in his own way.'

'Yeah, and messing other people about as well. I mean, it's one thing getting drunk and trying to forget, but phoning people up, and then not knowing. He's a bloody liability. I mean, shit, he's my brother, I don't want anything to happen to him.' In truth, he couldn't imagine life without Terry, without knowing he was around even if he could be such a pain in the arse.

'I know. Look, come back down and give me a hug.' Julie reached over and stroked his left nipple. Andy responded. 'Feeling like you want something?'

Julie moved closer and felt Andy pulling her to him. It wasn't long before he was inside her and momentarily they had both forgotten about Terry and the phone calls.

* * * *

Andy tried to call Terry again the next morning and later in the day, but could not get a connection. He called to get the line checked and was told that it seemed that the phone was off the hook. Andy was uneasy. If it had been off the hook this long, well, maybe he'd made a mistake and just not put it down properly. He'd been drinking, he could tell by the way Terry had been speaking. He was working late that night but he had a delivery that would take him past Terry's. He'd drop over, check that he was OK and try and talk some sense into him. He had to make his realise that he needed help, that he was out of control and that he had to find a way to get himself free of the alcohol.

* * * *

It was still light later that day that Andy pulled up outside Terry's house. He turned off the engine and opened the car door. He felt a bit irritated. Maybe it was nothing. He'd tried phoning a number of times during the day and each time got the same engaged tone. Why did Terry always seem to cause difficulties? He was predictably unpredictable. He always seemed to struggle in so many ways. Nothing had been easy for him, and lately Andy knew that Terry had seemed to have got worse. He had closed the car door and was walking up the path. There were lights on. That seemed odd, it was only six o'clock and quite a sunny evening. All was quiet. Terry's car was there, so he was probably in. Andy rung the bell on the front door. No answer. He rang again. After a minute of waiting he headed around the side of the house. He found that the back door was closed but unlocked. He turned the handle and pushed it open. The kitchen was, as usual, a mess. Terry didn't seem to do washing up, and often ate out of takeaway cartons. There were a few on the kitchen table. There was a staleness in the air. He called out.

'Terry? Are you there?' He felt like adding 'you dozy bugger', but something stopped him. He walked into the hall and noticed a sheet hanging down from the banisters above him. He felt himself frown. What the hell was that doing there? He didn't come to any conclusion, but it somehow made him feel more apprehensive. 'Terry? You there? You OK?' He remembered how he had found him that previous time, passed out and having vomited. And then police turning up. He shook his head. That had somehow been typical. He turned into the lounge. Strange that the light was on. But no sign of his brother. He looked around the room, nothing seemed unusual or out of place, well, not that you could tell. There was an empty whiskey bottle and an overflowing ashtray. The curtains were drawn which seemed odd. He turned and walked back towards the door. He turned left and turned his head towards the foot of the stairs. He stopped, 'Terry? Terry!'. There was urgency and alarm in his voice. He had seen his brother's twisted body lying at the foot of the stairs. He felt frozen to the spot, an icy sensation ran down his back and he felt his stomach churning. His heart was thumping. 'Oh God, no, no.' He ran the few steps to where his brother lay. His eyes were staring up, and it seemed that they were somehow staring straight at him. 'Terry!' He knew he was dead, but it didn't stop him from continuing to call his name. He felt tears on his cheeks. 'Terry, oh fuck bruv, what the hell have you gone and done to yourself.' He reached out and touched the side of his brother's face. He was cold, stone cold. Andy swallowed. What should he do? He didn't know. He needed to sit. He felt dizzy. He sat at the foot of the stairs next to his brothers body. He reached over and took his hand. He couldn't take it in. Terry was his brother, Mr indestructible, but there he was, laying there, all twisted. The silence was unbearable. He sat for a while longer. He somehow needed to be with him. He knew he had to phone Julie, she'd be able to cope. He didn't know what to do. He felt numb, he couldn't move, he just continued to sit beside Terry, staring at him, feeling yet not feeling, thinking and not thinking. He couldn't take it in.

He was brought of it by the sound of his mobile phone ringing. He reached and took it out of his pocket. It was a semi-automatic movement. He wasn't really thinking about what he was doing. It was Julie.

'Hi love, are your there yet? What happened? How is he?'

Andy didn't say anything. He could hear Julie's voice but he couldn't respond immediately. He was still taking it all in, trying to collect himself together.

'Andy, can you hear me?' Julie was concerned, she thought she had a connection but there was silence from the other end of the phone.

'Terry's dead.' Andy spoke very softly, almost a mumble.

Julie heard him even though it was indistinct. 'What! Oh God no. What happened?'

'He's lying here.'

'You found him?' Julie felt awful. Oh God what a terrible thing, to find your brother dead. She'd had her differences with Terry but she wouldn't have wished this on him, and certainly not on Andy. 'Oh my love. I'll come over.'

'Yeah, I think so. I guess I need to tell someone.' His voice seemed flat.

'Call the police. Do you want me to?'

'Can you?'

Julie could hear the flat tone to Andy's voice. She knew he wasn't really functioning too well.

'Sure, I'll call from here and then head over. What happened?'

'Looks like he fell down the stairs, must have broken his neck. Lights are on, must have been in the night, maybe. Don't know. Sometimes he left lights on. He hated the dark. We used to leave the light on in our room. It seemed less awful than listening in the dark to dad beating mum up.' Andy could see the room so vividly. It was as though he had stepped back there again. The sounds, the voices, his mother pleading with his dad to stop. He rarely took any notice of her. The thumps, the cries, occasionally the sound of something being thrown or of furniture breaking.

'Oh love, I'm so sorry.' Julie didn't know what else to say. 'I'll be with you as soon as I can.' She paused. 'Are you OK, do you need to go to a neighbour or anything?'

'No, no, I just need to be with him, on my own, you know?'

'Sure love, whatever you need to do. I'll hang up and make the call.'

'Yeah, yeah thanks.' Andy was in shock. He took the phone from his ear and switched the connection off. He continued to stare at his brother. 'I know it was shit, bruv, but we could always face things together. You were always there for me.' He felt his eyes welling up with tears. He knew he had not been there yesterday when his brother needed him most. It was painful to think about. Why hadn't he come straight away? He could have probably saved him. He could have maybe stopped it even happening. If they hadn't made love, Terry might still be alive. The thought haunted him. Why had they done it? He continued to stare at his brother. He couldn't take his eyes off of his face. 'Oh what am I going to do?.' He hurt like hell inside. He needed a drink. He knew there must be something in the house. He wasn't thinking about whether or not it was a good thing or the right thing to do, it was simply the only thing to do. He got up and walked into the lounge. He looked around, but couldn't see anything. An empty spirits bottle was under the sideboard, another by the TV. The cabinet where Terry kept drinks was open. He noticed a bottle there and walked over to it. He picked it up. Rum. He didn't often drink rum. But he knew he needed it now. He turned the top and took a mouthful straight from the bottle. It burned. He didn't like the taste but it was alcohol. It would help, make him feel better. His mobile phone rang again. He put down the bottle and raised the phone to his ear.

'Yeah?'

'Police are on their way, and so am I. They will be there in a few minutes.'

'Sure, OK, thanks.'

'Oh love, look I'm heading out to the car now so I'll be there very soon. Make yourself a cup of tea or something, get a brew on the go. It can't be easy. Oh love, I'm just so sorry.'

'I know.' Andy was taking a deep breath. He knew it wasn't her fault, not really. It was just a tragic turn of events. And yet there was still that wonder about whether he could have saved his brother if he'd come over straight away. 'I should have been here.'

'You weren't to know.'

'He's my brother.'

Julie had no answer to that. She thought back to the call, how Andy had reacted to Terry, and how they had made love afterwards. The thought then struck her that Terry might have died when they were making love. She felt herself go cold. It had been so lovely, but Oh God, had Terry been dying? She took a deep breath and pushed aside the thought as she reached for her jacket and hurried towards the front door.

Chapter 11

The phone rang at the counselling centre. It was Monday afternoon the following week. Graham took the call. It was Julie on the line. She explained who she was.

'Look, I don't know if Andy is going to come tonight. He's in a hell of a state. Terry's dead.'

'What?' Graham felt the urge to ask what happened, but pushed it aside and instead asked about Andy. 'How is he? What a shock.'

'In shock. I just needed you to know because I don't know if he'll make it tonight. He's off work and he's drinking, and he's not going to be able to drive over, and to be honest, I'm not sure how fit a state he'd be in even if he made it.'

'Is he really out of it?'

'No, not as bad as that, but he's drinking more again. If he did want to come, would you see him?'

'If you could drive him over I'd be fine about seeing him. I'm not going to stop him coming if he wants to, or I'm happy to talk to him over the phone if he would prefer that. I'll be here at the usual time.'

'OK. Look, I have to go. I'll try and encourage him to come over, he needs to talk to someone other than me. One of his mates has been really good, been spending time with him, but the end of last week was hectic with everything and now he's got time to think I guess and it's beginning to sink in.'

Graham had put the shock to one side and was clear he would not ask what had happened but wait for Andy to tell him. He didn't want Andy to be robbed of the opportunity to tell the story as it was for him by thinking someone else had already told him.

'Yeah, OK. Well, as I say, I'll be here. Thanks for calling.'

'OK. Bye.'

'Bye, take care and if you let him know you've spoken to me, pass on my condolences. But I really am OK with seeing him if he wants to come over, or talk on the phone if he would prefer that.'

'Thanks again.' Julie rang off.

Graham sat back in the chair. That was not a conversation he had been expecting to have. What had happened? He knew the rest of the day he'd be pushing his speculation aside, but he felt strongly that he wanted to witness Andy telling him what had happened from himself. He was there to be a companion with Andy in his inner world and sometimes it meant not getting information that might affect that process. Sometimes, of course, such information was unavoidable and then that had to be worked with too.

* * * *

Julie was glad to know that Graham would see Andy. She had told Andy that she would phone. Andy had mumbled that that was OK. He was still in shock, and the alcohol wasn't really helping him be very clear about things. He'd had a couple of cans at lunch-time. The weekend had been worse. He really had had a tough time on the Friday night and it had run into Saturday. Terry lying there was now another ghastly image in his head that he couldn't seem to get rid of.

There was going to have to be a Coroner's report. Seemed pretty clear what had happened. He'd obviously tripped and fallen. The sheet tied in the way it was indicated that he may well have had suicidal intent. Andy told the police that Terry had talked of wanting to kill himself recently, but that he hadn't thought he was being serious.

Julie had come back in to tell Andy of her conversation, and that Graham was happy to see him if he wanted to come over for the session, that he sent his condolences and if he preferred to talk on the phone instead that would be OK too.

'Hmm. OK. See how I feel. Not sure what good it'll do at the moment.'

Julie went over to him and held his head against her chest. 'I know, love, I know.' She paused. 'He sounded really nice, really concerned. I'm sure you'd benefit from seeing him, but I understand that maybe not tonight. Perhaps you could see him later in the week?'

'I'll see how I feel later.'

* * * *

Andy took the option of phoning Graham. He didn't feel like going out, and he had had a couple more cans during the afternoon and knew he'd have to get Julie to drive and whilst she was OK with that, he wasn't so sure. Seemed simpler to talk on the phone. He dialled the number, it rang twice and he heard the received being picked up.

'Hello, Graham? Andy here.'

'Hi Andy. What can I say. Sorry, so, so sorry. Julie didn't give me the details. Just so sorry.'

'Thanks.' Andy was taking a deep breath. 'To say it was a shock, well, understatement.'

'Yes, I can imagine, well, I can try to imagine.' Graham had decided not to approach the call as a therapy session as such, but rather more as a supportive conversation and to see how it developed. He would take his cue from Andy, from what he wanted to say and how he needed to be. Telephone work was different to face-to-face contact. In some ways Graham felt it was more intense, you had to concentrate far more on the limited means of communication, and yet there wasn't the same ambience as when someone was in front of you in the room, in that shared space, so to speak.

Andy had lapsed into silence. Graham spoke first. 'I'm glad you called, Andy. How do you want to use the time? You probably don't know.'

'No, I don't. But I felt I needed to talk to you. I mean, I don't know how much I want to get into it all of this on the phone, I think I may need to save that for when I see you next.' He paused as he thought about that.

'Sure, that's find, whatever you need.'

'Don't suppose you have a free time another evening this week. Maybe I'll get myself together to come over. It's just that, well, I've had a few cans today. The drinking's gone pear-shaped.'

'Sure, I could see you tomorrow, I've had a cancellation. Little later though, half past seven. Would that be OK?'

'Sure, look, maybe I'll leave it until then. I'm going in to work tomorrow. I know I can't sit around here. I'll have to take time off for the funeral arrangements ...'

Graham heard him go silent.

'Yeah, a lot to do, I guess, and that's not easy to face.' Graham was thinking of the funeral as he spoke.

Andy shook his head and had his eyes closed tight, the tears forcing themselves between his eyelids. 'No, no it isn't. He's my ... Oh God, I can't say he is, can I? I mean ...'

'Take your time, Andy, there's a lot to adjust to. Say it as you want to say it.'

Andy was taking another deep breath as Graham finished speaking. 'He was trying to kill himself, Graham, he was trying to kill himself.'

Oh, thought Graham, so that was what happened, trying to kill himself but clearly didn't succeed and yet he is dead. He knew he had to put any questions aside and stay with Andy.

'That's so hard to get your head around.'

Andy was silent, he sniffed, 'oh dear, sorry 'bout that.'

'No need, you have every reason in the world to feel what you are feeling, Andy. Every reason in the world.'

'Thanks.' Andy swallowed. 'They've said it was '"misadventure". What a bloody awful word. You hear it said but when it's your own ...'

'Yeah, makes it different.'

'I found him, lying there, foot of the stairs, all twisted and, oh that awful stare. A mixture of shock and surprise, just staring up. And everything so still. Like it seemed unreal and yet so real, so horribly real.'

Graham stayed silent, listening. Andy was clearly in flow and there was nothing to be gained from interrupting to show empathy. It seemed in this moment Andy needed to talk, and the best empathic response to his need was to give him full and undivided attention, to really listen and be present.

'I just stood there, I heard myself saying, 'Terry? Terry?' I knew he was dead but I still called his name. Crazy. But I did. He just lay there staring up. I remember looking up and seeing the sheet and wondering what the hell was going on. I saw it had been tied at the top of the stairs. Funny how you notice things. I went over to him, he was cold, it was a horrible sensation. I sat there with him, and then I had to go into the other room. I kept seeing his eyes. And the blood. And it took me back and it was like, "oh no, not again".'

Graham was nodding, wishing that he could convey his physical responding down the phone. 'That must have been an awful moment.'

Andy didn't want to dwell on that. 'Julie called. She phoned the police and then came over. I phoned my boss—he's been really good. Everyone's been good. People have come over to see me. But I can't take it in.'

'Too much, too close, yeah?'

Andy was nodding. 'Yeah.' He sighed. 'What a state he must have been in. He'd phoned again, but we thought he was OK, the phone seemed engaged so we thought he was talking to someone else. It was only after I got the telephone people to check the line that we realised the phone was probably off the hook. We didn't know then how he was so I dropped over late afternoon—on Friday. That was when I found him.' The tears welled up and the raw emotion which Andy had fought to hold down surfaced. 'I can't believe it's happened, not Terry, not Terry. I know he's had his problems, we've both had, but no, not Terry, not like this.'

'Not something that seems possible …'

'… not to Terry, not to my brother. And that's what he is …, yes, he still is, to me. I can't believe he's gone, not really. Keep thinking the phone will go, but I know it won't. Even if he phoned to say "fuck off!", that would be fine … That would be great, hear his voice.' Andy lapsed back into silence as he realised he'd never hear Terry's voice again. And thinking about what he'd said. The words that somehow Terry would be remembered for. It got to him, pulled on his emotions a bit more. The huge waves of sadness and distress seemed to rise up a little more inside him.' Another silence. Graham heard Andy taking a deep breath. 'But he has gone.' He spoke quietly, more to himself than to Graham. 'He has gone.'

'Yes.'

'Maybe he's free of the torment now. I want to think so. Maybe he is, I don't know, never thought about it much. Well, no that's not true, but, I mean, you know, what happens? I guess in a way I've always thought that when you die, well, that's it, you know? But somehow I can't seem to accept that. And I'm not sure I really think that because part of me still hopes I'll meet up with mum some day, and maybe Terry. It's like I need to believe that even though I know I don't.'

'Yeah, hard to know what to believe. What you want to believe doesn't fit with what you think you believe.'

Graham heard the doorbell coming from the phone.

'Sorry, someone's at the door. Look, I'd better go. Julie has gone round to the shop, so I'd better see who it is. I'll see you tomorrow at, when was it?'

'Seven thirty.'

'OK. Look, thanks for giving me this time. I'm glad I phoned' The bell sounded again. 'Look must go. Till tomorrow.'

OK, take care, Andy, take care of yourself.'

* * * *

Andy had driven himself over to see Graham. He'd managed to limit himself with the drinking. He'd had a beer at lunch-time—he and Julie had been out in the town making arrangements. He hadn't gone in to work. They had stopped off in a pub for lunch.

He was finding it very difficult, life suddenly felt very bleak and empty. It wasn't that he spent a lot of time with Terry, it was something else, something deeper. He was simply aware that he felt strange, and he couldn't get the image of Terry's stare out of his head.

'I'm really sorry, Andy.' They were sitting in the counselling room. Some minutes had already passed, much of them in silence.

'Thanks.' Andy tightened his lips as he stared down at the carpet. 'I can't believe it and yet ..., I mean, I saw it, I still see it, and yet ...'

'Mmm, hard to believe,' he paused, 'hard to believe'. He spoke slowly. Graham's heart went out to Andy. Mother, father and brother all dying tragically. How do you live with that? What impact does it have on the way you see life, see yourself, think about things, feel about the world? And all in the midst of a personal battle with alcohol.

'He told me he wanted to kill himself. I knew something was wrong, he sounded different. I should have done something.'

'Leaves you feeling that there was something else you could have done?'

'I keep thinking that I should have gone over again I could have done, but I thought he'd be OK. I thought he was on the phone. Never thought that he'd left the phone off the hook like that.'

'How could you know, Andy?'

'I don't know, but I should have known. I should have done something.' The tears were welling up in his eyes and the hot gritty lump in his throat had returned. He closed his eyes and tightened his fists as he sat trying to contain his feelings. 'He was just lying there, staring up, and as I walked over I moved into his line of vision. It was like we stood staring at each other. His eyes are so clear to me. Blank yet staring. A kind of surprised look. No fear. But his eyes were blank, and they're still there in my head.'

'It must feel like a frozen moment in time, his eyes looking at you.'

'It's with me so much at the moment, and I want it to go away. It's been really hectic the last few days, people visiting. I did drink heavily Friday night and into Saturday, and in truth it's only today that I've got some control back ...' His voice trailed off. He lost his train of thought as the image of Terry became clearer once more in his mind. 'Oh God.' He shook his head. Within the loss, hurt and disbelief he was feeling there was something else, not strongly present but a realisation that was starting to take root. It was to do with the part that alcohol had played in Terry's death. He felt hatred for his father, but now he also felt something similar towards alcohol. Deep inside himself was the dawning of an angry intention not to let alcohol destroy his own life as well. But it was dimly present, on the edge if not over the horizon of his awareness. He just felt angry.

Graham did not try and respond. Rather he reached forward and touched Terry on his shoulder, a firm touch seeking to convey support and understanding where there were no words to use. Andy brought his own hand up and held Graham's. His grip was strong. He continued to stare down, breathing heavily. He swallowed. A couple of minutes passed. The anger was diminishing, replaced by other feelings. He could feel a kind of creeping numbness all over his body, his arms felt heavy, his back was stiff, his stomach felt empty and churning.

'He was going to hang himself. He'd tied that sheet up ready to hang himself. He must have been in a hell of a state.' Andy had closed his eyes and was shaking his head. 'He'd said he wanted to kill himself. I didn't take it seriously enough.'

'That's a terrible thing to know. Yes, he must have been in a hell of a state, and it's left you feeling that you didn't take it seriously?'

'I should have been there. I should have known, sensed something, done something. He wouldn't have done it if I'd been there. He'd be alive. He'd have a chance to live his life …' Andy lapsed into silence. If only he'd gone over, if only … The feelings of guilt were very present now. He'd let Terry down, in the moment when he most needed him, he'd let him down.

'That's how it feels, like you should have somehow known.' Graham sought to keep his response simple. It was an awful thing to contemplate—whether realistic or not—that he might have saved his brother. He could be offering Andy alternate views, trying to make him feel easier about it, but that would not be therapeutic in the sense that Andy needed to allow how he was feeling to be present and for it to feel accepted. Andy felt responsible, he was no doubt feeling guilty. In reality, he probably had no reason to feel guilty, how could he have known and what could he have done given that if the event had not happened now, it could have happened at any time. But Andy was not thinking like that. His reality was simple. His brother told him he wanted to kill himself, and Andy was left thinking he could have saved him.

Andy had lapsed back into silence again. He knew it wasn't just him, he *knew* that. He knew he hadn't caused Terry to die, but he also felt that he could have done something different, responded differently, acted because of the way Terry had been speaking. The thoughts were going around and around in his head. His eyes were moist and his throat once more felt dry and tight. He could have saved him. He could still be alive … He could be. If only …

The session continued with Andy exploring further his feelings of guilt and responsibility. It was a slow process, with many silences, with Graham taking care to acknowledge how Andy felt. Yet Graham also knew there were other perspectives that would probably emerge as time passed, and that Andy would need to embrace those for himself when the time was right for him. That time wasn't now and it could be some while ahead, probably not until after the funeral at least. He didn't know and there was no point in speculating. Andy was how he needed to be now, he was making sense of everything in the best way he could, and he was blaming himself, feeling responsible, and feeling guilty.

There was about ten minutes to go. Andy had looked up again and was looking into Graham's eyes. 'Thanks for listening. I feel like I'm rambling here, but it's good to get out of the house and talk and know I can walk away at the end of the session.'

'I'm glad it feels helpful. I appreciate the effort it has taken to come over tonight. I respect how important this is for you, and I want to say it is important for me, too. I want to help you through this terrible tragedy. And yes, if it helps for you to bring what's happening for you here and leave some of it behind, unburden yourself a little, then so be it.' Graham realised he had said more than he had intended. It was like he was getting himself into a bit of a monologue which had not been his intention, but it had happened that way. Probably his focus and concentration had built up an energy within himself and it was a way of letting that out. He was aware of feeling for Andy. Although what must have been happening for Terry would have been awful, somehow Terry was not so present for Graham. In a sense he'd gone, and it had made Andy more present, more real. He made a note to talk about this in supervision later in the week. He was glad it was soon, he felt he needed to talk all this through, not necessarily to get answers, but to get support and to process what had happened and how it was affecting him. He knew he wasn't always aware of the impact that such traumatic events had on himself when he heard about them from clients, he was too busy staying with them and their own need to communicate what was happening for them. He needed that supervision space to allow himself to connect with his own process.

'Life has to go on, and maybe something in me knew that something like this might happen. I think it's something I've pushed away, but it's like death is no stranger to me, and suicide isn't either. It isn't that I've witnessed suicide, but I suppose my father's death—I didn't really understand at the time—but later on it was sort of something that you knew didn't only happen to other people, it could and did happen within your own family.'

'I guess you see things differently, they are more real, more possible, as you say.'

'Maybe knowing it can happen can make you not want to believe it will happen.'

'Like knowing suicide happened in your family made it harder to want to really accept it was possible it might happen for Terry?'

'Maybe, maybe something like that.' Andy thought about it. 'It's like you know it can happen but you don't want it to happen, so you push it away.'

Graham nodded. 'Push it away, don't think about it.'

'A way of coping, I guess.'

'Could be.'

They both lapsed back into silence, Graham aware that there really wasn't much to say, and Andy just being very aware of how close death seemed to him at the moment.

It was a few minutes before either of them spoke. It was Graham who highlighted the time, and that the session was coming towards a close. He checked out how Andy was and what else he may have wanted to say or discuss.

'No, there isn't anything else to say just at the moment. It's been good to talk. I feel a little calmer than I did earlier. It's like the upset builds up and then once released things ease back down again, for a while at least. I've got to find a way of getting through it.'

'And you will, and there will be times when you feel overwhelmed and times when you feel a little clearer and on top of things. It'll take time.' He paused, 'and I hope coming here will help.'

'I think I need to continue. It's not easy to talk about all of this, but I have to, don't I?'

'Well, it's up to you, and I do appreciate that it is painful and can make you feel worse in the short term, as you connect more fully with feelings. What has happened is uppermost at the moment and yet nothing can really be separated out—the past, the drinking, and now Terry's death.'

'It's all horrible.' He paused as Julie came to mind 'No, not everything. There's Julie. She's been wonderful for me. God, if we can come through all of this together, well I hope we can. I mustn't lean too heavily on the booze in all of this.'

'Julie's clearly been good for you. Alcohol just adds a complication and yet it is perfectly understandable as a kind of "get me away from this" anaesthetic.'

'I'll come through. I have to adjust. But it's too soon, too early, too much in my head.'

'People can try and move on too quickly and they can regret it later. You need to take things at your own pace, and I'll certainly respect that. There's no fixed timescale on this kind of thing.'

'Hmm. OK, well, till next Monday then. Thanks again, it's been really helpful, and thanks for last night as well, I think it helped to get me here this evening. Gave me a focus. Now I must get on with things as best I can. In a strange way I'll be glad when the funeral is over now.'

'Yes, it's a difficult time this, between his death and the funeral, being in limbo, unable to really, well, end I guess.'

After Andy had left, Graham was pondering on the situation as Andy had described it. Can we save another? When someone is suicidal like that, Graham could see how we might stop them acting in a particular way but unless the person's inner motivation is changed, it was likely that the action would take place another time. He knew that some people do make the change and do not pursue a course of continued suicidal intent, but many did. So often a failed suicide attempt was a pre-cursor to achieving that end at the next attempt. Once a person had attempted suicide it was no longer something new, something unthinkable. Once suicide was thinkable, the risk increased. And once a person knew what had stopped it working before, they probably then knew how to make certain the next time. It was never easy to help someone want to live when they felt there was nothing to live for, or they felt that it was the only way to get away from inner hurt and anguish.

* * * *

Andy left the session, feeling a little easier than when he had arrived. He drove back home thoughtfully. Julie was there when he arrived. She had just got in and was cooking. She gave him a kiss and asked him how it had gone.

'Fine, it really does help but it's quite painful as well. I'm sure I'll get through it. It's going to be a tough few weeks—for both of us.'

'I know. Anyway, I hope you're hungry. It'll be ready in about twenty minutes.'

'Great, yes I am. Feel like I haven't eaten in days.'

'I don't think you have.'

Andy thought back. No, he'd drank a fair bit at the start of the weekend, and just hadn't really had any appetite for food. It felt like his stomach was empty, a kind of gnawing sensation. Yes, he felt hungry, but in a sense it was more of a kind of empty feeling. 'I'm going to have a cup of tea. Funny, I was thinking about a couple of cans but somehow I don't think I want them just at the moment. During the session, when I was feeling bad, I really did think about that first can when I got back, but that seems to have passed now I'm here. And that cooking smells good. What is it?'

'Oh just frying a few things, you know, something to get some strength back into you.'

Andy busied himself putting the kettle on. It felt strange. He wouldn't normally drink tea at this time, not after just coming in from work, or from the counselling. But it somehow felt the right thing to do. He wasn't sure why. There was so much happening for him, and yet he felt a little bit numb again. It was almost as though there was a kind of relief, though he wasn't sure that it was very comfortable; a momentarily feeling that something was over. It didn't last long. By the time they had finished eating and were settled down on the sofa watching TV, Andy was beginning to feel uneasy again. They decided to have an early night. It didn't prove successful. Andy couldn't understand why, but he just could not get an erection. Julie was good about it, but he just was not responding. He wanted to, but it just wasn't happening. Too many thoughts. His inner world was much more present than the outer one.

They tried again the following evening, and the next, but still no response. It was like something had switched off. It wasn't that Andy didn't feel aroused, but it simply wasn't reaching the parts that mattered. He'd never had this problem before and he didn't know what to do. He felt ashamed, angry, frustrated. He became more tense each time they tried. He didn't know what to do, and he didn't know who to talk to about it either. Julie told him it was probably linked to the stress of the situation and that it be OK later. They agreed not to try for a while. They hadn't made love since the night that, unbeknown to them at the time, Terry had died trying to kill himself.

*   *   *   *

Graham, was sitting in Stuart's lounge, His supervision session had only just started. 'I need to spend time talking about Andy. Terry, his brother, has killed himself. Well, that's not quite right. He died while it appears he was trying to hang himself, but fell down the stairs. Andy found him.'

Stuart noted his own reaction of horror and immediately brought his focus to Graham. He could ask about Andy later, but Graham was his supervisee and he would have been affected by this.

'Must have been a shock to you, how is it leaving you?'

Graham thought for a moment. 'Well, one strange thing is that Terry suddenly seems very distant. I guess he was more on my mind when it was uncertain what he was doing. So, in a strange way I feel more connected with Andy. And that earlier supervision session helped with that, I had already begun to feel much more connected to Andy, but I've noted a shift since it happened. It's not that I've seen him much, it happened last week and I had a telephone session—well part of one—on the phone with Andy on Monday and he came round for a proper session on Tuesday evening.'

'So you feel more connected to Andy, and Terry is more remote, would that be fair?'

'Yes, but it's not that he's gone away. He's a presence, yes, but Andy is now so much more centre-stage, if you like.'

'Mhmm, feeling more connected.'

'Yes, at least to his pain and struggle to come to terms with it all. I realise it's an experience far removed from anything I have faced. He mentioned on Tuesday how he has had a different experience of death in his life than many other people, how close it is to him, particularly at the moment. I found myself pondering on what effect it must have on someone, given what he has experienced: mother killed in front of him by his father, his father hanging himself, and now his brother dying whilst it would seem attempting the same but falling down the stairs. And Andy found him. He talked a lot of the expression on Terry's face, of his staring eyes. I can't pretend to understand what all that must feel like, but I can hear his pain, his anguish, his self-doubt. He's really blaming himself for not being there.'

Graham went on to explain what had happened as far as he understood it from what Andy had told him. Stuart listened, aware that he himself was struck by a sense of the tragedy of it all. It felt almost Shakespearian in some awful way. A tragedy being played out before them. He voiced his reaction.

'It makes me think of it as a kind of Shakespearian tragedy, except that it's for real, not fiction.'

'Yes, it is a bit like that.'

'I wonder, taking the metaphor and extending it, where you fit in to all of this?'

'I guess I feel like I'm standing in the wings, watching the story unfold. And it's like I've not seen it before, as though it is my first time. I've seen other plays with tragic circumstances, but not this one, and not with the actors in the characters that I am observing.' Graham paused and pondered on a thought that had struck him. 'Funny, isn't it, metaphors can really develop once you start to try and link them to what you have been experiencing.'

'How do you mean?'

'Well, it's like I see Andy, but not actually on the stage. I'm backstage, as it were. I see Andy, when he comes off stage and tells me what is going on and then departs. So, yes, it's like he's now told me that a really important character has died. And yet somehow it feels remote, it's happening and yet there's a curtain between me and what is actually happening. And I can only see what happens through Andy's eyes, and after it has happened.' Graham was intrigued by this process and had no idea where it was going to lead.

Stuart nodded thoughtfully, and at the same time was holding an awareness that the metaphor could take them both too much into their heads and away from the feelings that must be represent in response to what was occurring. He didn't want the metaphor to become a barrier.

'But your reactions are real, and what he is experiencing is real for him, and for those around him?'

Graham took a deep breath, 'yes'.

'And those reactions are very present for you.'

Graham nodded, aware that it was like the metaphor had suddenly ceased to be something in his head and had become something far more intimately present and part of himself. 'A sense of horror, and a feeling of wanting to push it away.'

'You want to push the horror of it all away?'

Graham was nodding again. 'I don't want to know about it and yet I am compelled to listen.'

'Compelled?'

'By my professional role, but more than that, by something inside me that is somehow, well, I guess like watching something frightening, some horror film, and you don't want to know what's going to happen next but you can't take your eyes away from the screen.'

'That sounds very powerful, like there is a sense of horror for you and you can't stop looking at it.'

'It's not been like that all along, but, you know, talking about the idea of it being a kind of theatrical tragedy makes me feel like I'm kind of, I don't know, I don't like the word that's come to mind …'

'Something that disturbs you?'

'Well, it's sort of fascinating, and yet…. I'm sure I wasn't thinking like this during the sessions, it's only now, on reflection, and particularly after the last session, that I can sense this wanting to know what happens next—and part of me not wanting to know as well. I realise I haven't been fully in touch with myself in the sessions and I need to explore this now, re-connect in some way so that I can be more connected again when I'm with Andy.'

Stuart was genuinely surprised at what Graham had said. He did not sense disconnection. He sensed that Graham was very affected by what had happened and whilst he appreciated the metaphor had taken them into their heads, did that mean there wasn't emotional and heartfelt contact between Graham and his client? 'I'm curious what makes you think you were disconnected with Andy. Having a different perspective now doesn't mean you were not connected at the time. Are you sure you're not giving yourself a hard time here for some reason? Seems to me that wanting to know what happens next is a sign of involvement. But clearly that is my experience, and not yours.'

Graham had to stop and think about this. The metaphor had felt right. It did seem sort of voyeuristic somehow. And yet, counselling was about looking into another person's world. So what was he getting caught up on now? 'I …, hmm, I'm not sure what it is. Yes, it is fascinating, yet horribly so. The events in Andy's life are somehow compelling, the stuff of novels that you read and think, "no, that doesn't happen in real life". But it does, has, is happening, and in front of me. I'm having this story brought to me and it has been unfolding week by week. And now it's like a sudden shocking development has taken place that in a way everything has been leading up to, wasn't really expected.' Graham thought about it. 'Yes, it's as though maybe at some level I had a sense that this was where it was heading, but perhaps I was denying it, or pushing it away, or it as over the edge of my awareness. Maybe it was too disturbing for me to fully acknowledge. But now it has happened and I'm left, well, yes, I guess I'm wondering "what next?". And I have to wait for next week's instalment. And that sounds awful, but it feels like how it is.'

'I think I'm getting a hold on what you are saying. It is as though you are watching something unfold. You kind of knew the story line, and yet how it has developed is both shocking and is having the effect of leaving you wondering what next.'

'It's as though I've now been given the whole process, the complete scene and it's like, OK, what now? Where is it going to go from here? How're you going to help that man come to terms with what has happened? It's as though I've been given this huge, tragic process and am now expected to solve it in some way.'

'That sounds like a lot to ask of you, to solve what has happened, and been happening in the past up to the present.'

'It's huge. It feels enormous. It feels utterly overwhelming. As I sit here now I am aware of feeling like it's too big to come to terms with. And whilst I was shocked in the session, the enormity of it hadn't really hit me, not like it is now.' Graham could feel himself becoming anxious and numb at the same time. It was as though he was transfixed psychologically, unable to move his thoughts or his feelings. 'Yes, and the fascination—I think that's the wrong word—but the whole thing is compelling, riveting, and I come back to a sense of it being voyeuristic as well.'

'And that's distinctly uncomfortable for you?' Stuart was concerned for Graham and yet felt assured in himself that he would find a way to resolve his reaction and discover a place in himself from which he could work with Andy.

'It's like looking at some awful, unbelievable horror through a window. Part of me feels I shouldn't be looking, it's somebody else's world I'm looking at, but I can't take my eyes away. I have to know what happens next.'

'Yes, you have to see the next instalment, as you say, and that doesn't feel like the right focus for you as a counsellor?'

'That's right.'

'But it is how you are feelings?'

'Yes, I think so. But it's not right, is it?'

'Well, like I say, it is what you feel. It is your reaction. I'm not sure of a right or wrong about this, it is simply what is, for you, in response to what is happening for Andy.'

Graham frowned. That sort of sounded profound but he knew he needed to absorb it. 'so you're saying it is OK for me to feel like this?'

'Do you have to judge it? Can you simply accept it?'

Graham felt himself smiling. 'No, no, I can't accept it. What happened to Terry and to Andy in their childhood should not have happened, and shouldn't happen to children. But it does happen. And, no, everything that occurred since perhaps should not have happened.' He stopped, thinking again. 'I don't want to accept what happened to Andy and Terry, and to their mother. I don't want to accept it. That's what's happening. I don't won't accept it. But I have to, it happened.'

Stuart nodded.

'Hmm, It's like I don't want to look this tragedy in the eye, and yet I can't take my eyes away from it. That's the dilemma, you see?'

Stuart nodded again. 'Hence you have to look but you don't want to look.'

'Part of me wants to look, and part of me wants to turn away and doesn't want to accept it is happening, or it happened.' Graham breathed out heavily. 'This isn't easy.'

'No, but you need to clear this. It's something about tragedy, of seeing things happen and feeling you can't stop watching although you know it is making you uncomfortable and you want to look away, but you can't.'

Graham nodded. 'OK, so something in me is causing this reaction. I'm not simply being a kind of clear mirror into which Andy can reflect himself and see or experience himself through what I reflect back. I'm contributing to what he gets back, perhaps, or maybe it hasn't happened like that in the sessions but is in danger of becoming like that given what has now happened. Maybe that's a more accurate way of looking at it?'

'So I wonder what that would mean, then, how would it get played out?'

'I might try and hold Andy on the detail that I want to experience, or I might try and move him away from something that I am finding uncomfortable. Either way, I am at risk of directing him, and that's not how I want to work. As a person-centred counsellor I need to be able to experience my acceptance of him as he is, and to allow him a non-judgemental relationship in which to explore what is happening for him without my agenda disturbing his process and causing waves, so to speak.'

'So the risk is that your reactions, what is happening within you, will cause waves?'

'Yes, and if you think of the mirror as a surface like still water, then waves will scramble it. And I can't allow that to happen. I have to be able to accurately reflect back what he is telling me; my empathy has to be clear and reflective of what he is communicating.'

'Sure, that's the theory, now, where are your waves coming from?'

'Just thinking that myself. It's not merely a reaction to Andy. There's something already within me that is being triggered by this, I'm sure of it.'

'OK, what comes to mind when I say 'tragedy'.'

'Something terrible that did not need to happen, that could have been avoided. Something where a mistake is made, something isn't realised until it is too late.'

'Can you be specific?'

Well, at first I was back to Shakespeare, but then I find myself looking at the world. There are tragedies everywhere that could be avoided, things happening in places. There are wars and conflict between ethnic groups, say, and the world watches but doesn't do anything. I mean, yes, I watched TV recently and it's the human side of things, isn't it, the Iraqi man who has had his whole family killed because a bomb was mistakenly directed at his home. I watch but feel powerless to help. It's so enormous and overwhelming and yet the world watches and he remains alone. Who is reaching out to help him?'

'Who is reaching out to help him, to help the victim of tragedy?' Stuart repeated back slowly the essence of what Graham was saying.

'It hurts, Stuart, it hurts.' Graham could feel the emotion welling up inside himself. 'It's like I've learned not to respond. Yes, I can feel, but what can I do? We're being made into observers of tragedy, every day, in the news, on TV, in the papers, everywhere, tragedy, tragedy, tragedy, and much of it caused needlessly. And yet we watch, I watch. People starving, people working in sweat shops, people being poisoned by chemical plants, people having the water drained out of their wells by multi-nationals who want it for their own production processes, people everywhere experiencing unnecessary tragedies, people being badly affected by the actions of others.' He closed his eyes as he felt the tears begin to escape. 'We live in shit-awful world where people die so needlessly. Here we are, the 21st century and people do not have fresh water or enough food to eat. And I'm in the rich west, rich because in part we continue to exploit. And I hate it, Stuart, I absolutely hate it. It sickens me. I recycle what I can, I buy fair-trade food, I try to avoid clothes that may have been made in exploitative industries, I try to keep away from products that are developed through processes which have a bad impact on the environment, but I can't do enough. I can't make a big enough difference. It hurts, Stuart, it hurts.'

Stuart was so touched by the power, the desperation in what Graham was saying. He knew Graham was right. The more we open our hearts to the plight of others, the more we hurt, and if we don't do anything, or don't feel we're doing enough, it hurts even more. Yes, he thought, and we are either hurt into action, or hurt into submission. But he didn't say this, he stayed with what Graham was feeling. 'It hurts you.'

'And perhaps if we allowed ourselves to feel that hurt more, rather than allow ourselves to be distracted by the "entertainment industry"' or the '"fashion industry" or all the other "consumer-centred" means for keeping people away from feeling the pain, well maybe things could be different.'

Graham briefly acknowledged to himself how he regarded person-centred therapy as being a process that could lead people to questioning values that society and others put on them, and how it could help them think and feel for themselves. Become more congruent to their own experiencing. He felt that the world needed that.

'I've gone off on one, but I'm glad I did. I need to connect with these feelings. They make me feel alive. Yes, it hurts, but I want to hurt. I want to be affected. I want to, I don't know, be hurt into action, hurt into caring. I don't believe in compassion fatigue. In truth I think people get tired of hurting and of feeling helpless and that's sad. I'm sure if we were more able to really experience our feelings as witnesses to human tragedy and suffering, without the distractions', Graham was thinking of the cult of celebrity as he had said that, 'then maybe we wouldn't tolerate what is done in our name by Governments, or by multinationals and the dictators of the world.'

Stuart had been listening and accepted Graham's need to connect with his thoughts and feelings in the way that he had. It was tempting to get into a philosophical exploration on the state of the world, but Andy was being lost sight of, and he felt he needed to connect back to him. 'OK, so, where does this leave you, us, with regard to Andy?'

'I've got to get in there where it hurts and believe that I can make a difference, that I can stand with him as that companion in his tragic world and offer support, caring, warmth, but most of all some kind of companionship, a readiness to stand with him in his pain and despair.' He shook his head. 'I feel different having said my piece just now. It's like I feel as though I've risen above the urge to watch and the urge to turn away. They're like opposites but I've risen above them. It's about compassion and being prepared to stand with that other person, get in there, be affected …, hmm, be affected.' A line from a book came to his mind, but he could not remember where he had read it. 'How can they feel our love if we cannot feel their pain?' Graham looked at Stuart. I read that somewhere, can't remember where. But that's it, isn't it? I have to stand with Andy in the counselling sessions. I have to feel his pain and anguish that he might feel my warm acceptance and unconditional positive regard, the qualities that I believe are so crucial for effective therapeutic counselling.'

Stuart nodded. He could feel the shift in Graham. He was suddenly focused, centred, more in touch with himself, clearer as to who he was and what he was about. He just seemed more solid and distinct in some way. He voiced it. 'You seem more present, more whole.'

'I feel it. I really needed this session. I know I've taken up a lot of time on Andy, well, actually on me, but it's been worth it, not just for Andy but maybe for how I am with all my clients. I think I've owned something that is important to me and I need to work that out in my life with some renewed impetus.'

'It seems like you've connected to something very important to you and a shift has occurred, giving you a renewed sense of purpose.'

'Maybe I've become more congruent?' Graham smiled.

'Maybe you have. Maybe you are more accurately connected to your true feelings, more able to hold them in awareness and, therefore, more able to act on them.'

The exploration drew to a close and the supervision session moved on to focus on other clients. It was a significant session for Graham. He left knowing that he had made some kind of inner commitment and he knew, as well, that he was more connected with what he wanted to do and how he wanted to be. As he drove back through the country lanes that he knew so well, he let his mind rove across the supervision session. He thought of Andy, and how he now felt towards him and the working he was doing with him. He realised he was experiencing a mixture of compassion and a certain calm and purposeful assurance that he was going to be a damn good counsellor for him, not because he was going to try to be a good counsellor, but because he knew, in his heart, that he could feel what he needed to feel in order to connect with Andy at that most healing of levels, the heart. He smiled. The idea for a new approach to counselling and therapy came to mind—'open-heart therapy'. Yes, he thought to himself, yes, that is exactly what it is all about. He pondered on whether it would be that much different to person-centred therapy. He thought not. Perhaps it was more a matter of emphasis, and of making visible the significance of the heart and of heartfelt responses within the therapeutic process. He didn't think that there was enough understanding of the role of the heart in psychological and emotional processes, and particularly in relation to the healing aspect. Something more for him to think about. He was always grateful for supervision putting him in that more reflective space within himself. It felt good. He realised his attention was not so sharply on the road ahead as it should be and he refocused himself on his driving.

Chapter 12

'How do you want to use our time this evening, Andy?' Graham was sitting feeling quite calm as he waited to hear Andy's response. The previous supervision session had made a difference, it had left him more connected with himself and somehow feeling more complete. He felt that he was ready for the evening's inner journey with Andy, if that was what he wanted. But if he wanted to reflect on his alcohol use, or the events of the week, or something else, that was fine by him. He felt no sense of an agenda, just wanted Andy to feel he had a supportive place in which to be as he needed to be, a place where he could feel heard by someone who accepted him as he was and who sought to be genuine and open in his responses.

'I don't know. I seem to find everything's an effort. Getting here wasn't easy, I nearly called and cancelled, and then I nearly just didn't come. Life seems meaningless at the moment. Just feels like I'm drifting, not sure where I'm heading. I just don't know.' He shrugged his shoulders and tightened his jaw as he finished what he was saying.

'A sense of not knowing and of drifting.' Graham responded to the end of what Andy had been saying so as not to disturb the flow.

Andy took a deep breath, 'yeah, that's how it is.'

Graham waited to see what Andy might say next. He wanted him to find his own focus and to develop it in his own way. He continued to wait, maintaining his attention on Andy's face but trying not to be too intense.

'You know, I was thinking on the way over that I suppose I should be grateful, somehow. I mean, I could have been Terry, it could have been the other way around.'

'A sense that Terry's life could have been yours, is that what you mean?'

Andy nodded. He tightened his lips and sighed. 'I don't know.'

'Yeah, a real sense of just not knowing.' Graham was aware that he had repeated himself but it felt OK. It really did capture what he felt Andy was communicating. It seemed heavy and he wasn't surprised Andy had trouble getting to the session. Often clients could take a while to settle down into the not knowing or the stuckness, but Andy was straight there.

'So I don't know what to talk about and I don't know what to do. I'm drinking more, I guess I'm taking risks with my driving and, to be honest, the way I feel at the moment, I just don't give a shit.'

'Don't care about what you're doing and what the effects might be?'

'Just don't care. Life's a shit, fucks you up. I don't know. I'm not sure why I came, but I guess I had to do something.'

'Sounds like you're in a bad place and don't feel you've been doing much.'

'I haven't. I mean, I've been into work, but I'm not really focused. I know that. I'm sort of being careful but I also know part of me really doesn't give a damn. It's like, what matters, what really matters? Nothing really matters. You struggle on but for what? Terry struggled on, tried to survive but look where it got him? Is that where I'll be in a few years time?' He shook his head. 'What's the point?'

Graham nodded and noted the concern he was feeling at Andy's depressed state of mind. The thought crossed his mind that maybe he should check out the level of Andy's depression, but then he would simply focus Andy on something that Andy might not want to talk about. He wasn't sure that was therapeutically justifiable. Trust him, he needs to be like this. Accept his low mood, it's a realistic reaction. He's in shock. Don't start getting anxious.

'So everything seems kind of pointless at the moment.'

'Yes, well, maybe not everything, I mean, people have been good, been supportive, you know. Gary and Amanda have been great, and Matt's been round a few times as well. Hadn't seen him for a while. But he just turned up, bought me a bunch of flowers!' Andy smiled. 'Crazy idiot.'

'Made you smile though!'

Andy nodded. He could see him standing in the doorway with this bouquet and hear his voice: "Life's a bitch. Here. Brighten things up a bit." 'I've never had flowers bought for me before. I just didn't know what to do. I must have looked stupid, just stood there, but it did make me smile. He just wasn't going to let it get him, or me, down, and he came in and bubbled away about the latest man in his life and the colour scheme he was having in his new flat. I don't know, he's just so typically gay—whatever that means, and I don't want to stereotype him, I know it's his personality. But he is like a breath of fresh air.' Andy took a deep breath as he thought back to yesterday when he had visited. 'And the clothes he wears, I mean, he's just so outrageous, but wonderfully so. You just have to smile.'

'Seems like he's really important for you at the moment.'

'Yeah, funny isn't it, last person I kind of expected to suddenly appear, but, well, there you are.'

'So there's a bit of a positive in this. Matt's around a bit more and you're appreciating him for who and how he is.'

'Yes. I think the flowers were a deliberate ploy to kind of throw me. I had no response. I guess I could have retreated more into myself, but I didn't do that. I just had to laugh.'

'So he really helped you to connect with experiences that were otherwise somewhat distant from you.'

Yes, Andy thought, Matt was good for him. He lifted his hands, rubbed his face and yawned. He was feeling very tired. He wasn't sleeping well, more alcohol induced than anything else. It had been a particularly heavy weekend. 'Ohhh,' He rubbed his eyes which were feeling gritty and heavy. 'so, what now?'

'What do you want now, Andy?'

'To go to sleep and not wake up for a very long time.'

'That why you're drinking, putting yourself to sleep?'

'Probably. And to try and not feel. Doesn't work, I mean, it does, but then it kind of doesn't.' He yawned again. 'I've got to do something about it but at the moment, I don't know, I really don't feel like trying, you know?'

'So in a way you're leaning on the alcohol a bit at the moment, using it to kind of get by.'

'That's a positive way of looking at it. Actually I think you're being a bit generous. I just feel I need to get away and that's what I'm doing.'

'Back up to how it was?'

'Pretty much, at least, it was over the weekend. Just started Friday night and I suppose not having to go to work I just continued. No reason not to.' Another yawn.

'So there doesn't seem like any reason not to drink, and it's leaving you tired and not feeling like trying to do anything about it.' Graham paused as a sentence came to mind. It felt as though it summed things up though wasn't words that Andy had said. He voiced them. 'It's like "what's the point?"'

'Yeah, I keep thinking that. Terry couldn't crack it, you know, and maybe that's my destiny. Maybe I'm heading the same way and what's the point in fighting it.'

'You make it sound all very inevitable, that how Terry was is how you're going to become. No choice, no alternative, that's how it'll be, yeah?'

'Yeah, well,' Andy hesitated, it sort of felt right when he had said it but hearing it coming back at him from Graham he wasn't so sure. 'I just think that it's inevitable. I don't want to think that way, you know, I really don't, but …'

Graham nodded, 'it's like you can see something inevitable about it but you don't want to see it as well?'

'Yeah, just don't want to think about it, so I have a few cans, well, more than a few cans at the weekend. Hit the whisky. Did I feel bad on Sunday. Just spent Friday night and Saturday drinking at home. Julie tried to encourage me not to, but, I wasn't listening. I wasn't there, man, and we argued and, well …' He shook his head. 'Things are not good at the moment. I guess Julie can see something of her father in me, and she's backing away, protecting herself a bit. We feel distant all of a sudden.' He shook his head again and felt the emotion rising inside himself. 'I don't want that, I really don't want that.' He brought his hand up to his face and covered his eyes as the tears began to flow. He felt awful, absolutely wretched. He desperately wanted to be with Julie, but he couldn't face the pain. He needed a drink, but it was destroying them. 'Maybe I'm just not good enough for her, maybe she's better off without me.'

'You really feel that, I mean, *really* feel that?'

Andy took a deep breath. 'sometimes, yes, but no, not deep down, not really. But, oh I don't know, somehow I need to get a hold of myself. But at the moment …'

'One day at a time, yeah?'

'That's what the AA say, isn't it?'

Graham nodded. 'Yeah. One day at a time. Don't think too far ahead, deal with now, don't think about tomorrow.'

'I can understand that now. It's too much, you know? I can't take it all in, I get overwhelmed. I can't think ahead, I don't want to think ahead, but I do. I wonder what the future will hold. And I hate it.'

'Hate it?'

'No, not hate it, fear it, so I drink to escape.'

'It's important to have somewhere to escape to.'

'Yeah, it's too much otherwise. Too much to deal with.' Andy was shaking his head slightly and looking down.

'Too much to deal with, hence one day at a time.' Graham decided to repeat the AA mantra. It was such an insightful idea.

'You're right, I know. I'm sure it'll somehow be better after the funeral. It's being arranged for next Monday. Bit of a delay—we hadn't really started making arrangements and it seems like it's really busy. Anyway, oh yes, that means, well, I mean, I'm not sure, whether I should come.'

'Well, that's up to you. In the circumstances I'm happy to hold the slot open. I can't offer you Tuesday as I'm currently committed that evening.'

'It'll be in the afternoon and people will be round into the evening, and I guess I can't not be there. Terry had a number of drinking pals and I guess they'll come along. It's likely to be a boozy send off.'

Graham nodded. 'Hmm, brings it's own problems, yes?'

'Yeah. I really don't need any encouragement at the moment. I just want to get it over and try and get on, though I have to say I wonder why.'

'Wonder why you want to get on?'

'But I have to. I can't stay like this all the time. I have moments when I seem to feel a bit lighter but then I lose it.'

'Yeah, the lightness fades and it all feels very heavy again.'

'I can't see myself getting here, I think I'd better make it the following week, unless there are any other options for later in the week?'

Graham reached over for his diary. He did have a space on the Thursday but it was in the afternoon. He mentioned this to Andy.

'I'll take it. Work has been good, I'll tell them I need a bit of time for some support, and then I'll come the next Monday as well.' He paused. 'I've got to get myself out of this, Graham. Do you think I need anti-depressants or something?'

'I think that's a really difficult question to answer, but clearly you are wondering about it.'

'Well, just something to give me a boost, maybe.' Andy wasn't sure. It sort of appealed, the idea of something in a sense making it easier. Not that he wanted to start taking loads of pills. He didn't think of himself as a person that needed to rely on drugs. He didn't do drugs—and like so many people, he didn't see alcohol as being a drug in liquid form.

'Well, you could see your GP but they may not prescribe anything because you are drinking. Something to lift your mood may get wiped out by the effect of the alcohol. And in a way, what you are experiencing is really a kind of normal human reaction, but that doesn't mean that there aren't times when we need something to give us that artificial lift to get us through.' Graham didn't say more, though he knew that he could easily give a monologue expressing his thoughts and feelings about how medicalised (he hated that word) so much that is normal uncomfortable human experience and reaction had become. There were now so many syndromes and diagnoses and treatments being established. Yes, something to give you a lift, to alleviate symptoms, when someone's mood was very low and putting them at risk to themselves, but only as a means to an end, not an end in itself. How many times had he read statistics about how many people would be depressed at some times in their lives, implying that mental illness was far more widespread than often thought. But often depression was a normal human response to events, circumstances, difficulties, not something to be made into an illness. And anyway, maybe the mental health of the nation was more to do with the values, attitudes and priorities of society, and it was society, the cause, that needed diagnosis and treatment as much as the individuals that carried the symptoms and psychological effects of that unwell society. He brought his thoughts back to Andy who had begun to speak after a few moments of thinking about what he felt about seeing his GP.

'Yeah, I'll see how I go. If I stay low I may need to consider it.'

'I can only say discuss it with your GP, and trust your own sense of what you feel you need.'

Andy yawned again and he felt the tiredness sweeping over him. 'It's no good, I think I'm going to have to head off and try and get some sleep.'

'Sure.'

'I'll try and keep on top of the drinking. I can't keep having weekends like the last one. That's no good to me, or to Julie. I've got to get a hold on myself, it's just so difficult, so hard. Just so easy to have another drink, but you don't need me to tell you that. You must have heard it many times.'

'It is so easy, that's the problem, so easy and so available. And somehow you have to have reasons to say no.'

'Well, Julie's one reason. She doesn't need me like this. But I don't either. I've got to bring it back down again, got to.'

'First thing is get the spirits back out of the frame, yeah?'

Andy nodded. He realised that.

'And try to aim to get the cans back to what it had become, what, four a day?'

'Yes, I have to. And I crept up to stronger cans, and occasionally had the really super strong lagers. Tasted horrible but I needed it. Didn't tell Julie. She'd go mad. Had the odd one during the day last week.'

'They're strong …'

'Four and a half units in a can.'

'… it has to stop,'

'Give yourself permission to have the normal strength cans in the evening. Get it out of the day first then tackle the evenings, but don't push it. Take your time. Let's get next Monday over with and then, well, there's no magic wand, but at least it will mark an ending and perhaps some kind of new beginning.'

'I hope so, but not because I want to forget Terry. I won't ever do that.'

'I'm sure you won't. He's your brother, part of your life.'

The emotions were rising again, 'I just can't believe that he's gone, that he won't phone up again, that he's just not there to banter with, get drunk with, anything with.' Andy closed his eyes and swallowed back the lump in his throat. 'Ohhh, got to move on.' He paused as he got up. 'Thanks Graham, and I'll see you Thursday.'

'Sure, and if you change your mind about Monday, let me know, Yeah?'

Andy nodded. He shook Graham by the hand. It wasn't something Graham could recall him having down before at the end of the session. He appreciated it.

Andy left in silence, aware that his emotions had subsided a bit once more. He still felt wiped out but at the same time a little lighter, as if he had unburdened himself a little. It was going to be a tough week now. Arrangements to finalise. He wasn't working the long days this week, but keeping to shorter runs. He was grateful for that. He wasn't sure how safe he would be on longer journeys just at the moment. He liked the idea of getting away, but was it to escape? And how could he escape? Only drinking seemed to help, but it didn't really, he just ended up feeling worse.

* * * *

The following evening Andy was driving back from work. It was a bit later than usual, beginning to get dark. Julie would be back later. He suddenly felt extremely alone, actually the sensation was more one of feeling abandoned. It was a feeling that was familiar but it came upon him with a sudden intensity. He'd been listening to the radio and there had been a kind of phone-in. Someone had written a book about how people as adults are affected when they lose both their parents. The kind of feelings that were being described were those that he knew and they simply became more present to him. He had to turn the radio off, he couldn't listen to it any more. He felt very small and the feeling seemed overwhelming, as though he was nothing but the feelings. He wasn't able to rationalise in any way what the feelings were. He just knew he felt awful, abandoned and very alone. It had been the part where the chap being interviewed had talked about how he had wished he had had brothers and sisters, but he had been an only child. No-one in the generation above him, and no-one in his own generation.

Andy pulled up at the parade of shops and got out. He had one intention and that was to drink. He went straight into the off-licence, he wasn't thinking about trying to control himself in any way. He wanted a drink. He needed a drink. He was going to have a drink. He came out with a bottle of whisky and headed home.

When he arrived he walked in, threw his jacket on to the chair in the hallway and went into the lounge. He collected a glass from the cabinet and sat down heavily on the sofa He opened the bottle and poured it into the glass and began to drink. He felt so alone and so overwhelmed by everything. He felt so small, so …, he didn't know what he felt like he just knew that everything was too big for him to cope with. He needed to escape, to get away. He needed it all to stop. He took another gulp of the whisky. He needed that sensation, the burning, the warmth, the wonderful invasive comfort of that golden elixir. But it wasn't stopping what was in his head. He was into the second glass before the alcohol got to his brain. He could feel himself going a bit fuzzy and it felt good. Beer, lager (except for the strong cans) didn't quite have this effect. It was more gradual. He continued to drink. He looked around the room. It felt bare. The wallpaper was old and peeling in places, he found himself tracing the patterns with his eyes. He used to do that as a child in the bedroom, following the shapes of the flowers on the wallpaper. Looking at how the patterns linked together, counting the number of flowers and the times the pattern repeated itself. He was doing that now, but not really thinking about what he was doing.

He liked the impact of the whisky. Memories of the past were with him but they seemed a little distant. He felt sad, lonely, with only the effects of the whisky to comfort him. It was as though his past and his present had come together. There he was, in one sense feeling like a terrified and sad little boy with no-one to care for him, and the next moment a sad and lonely man feeling as though no-one understood him or could help him take away the memories in his head and the feeling of loss and hopelessness. He poured his third glass.

Yes, he liked the feeling of the whisky kicking in. It brought relief. He continued to drink, experiencing himself as sliding away from the feeling of being alone. It wasn't that it had gone away, rather that he had retreated from it, like he knew it was there but he was in a different place and it didn't touch or affect him in quite the same way. But he remained sad.

He didn't think very much about it, though. In fact, the more he drank, the more he began to just stare ahead of himself. The effect of the alcohol was building up all the time. His head was heavy, as if it was held down to the sofa by some invisible force. He wanted out, wanted to get away from everything. He wanted to just lose himself in the warm buzzy, fuzzy sensations that had now spread all over his body. He pressed the remote and the TV came on. Wasn't anything he really wanted to watch, just wanted some sound, something to fill the silence of the empty room. He was finishing the third glass when he suddenly burst into tears. And once they started they wouldn't stop. He felt pain as he had never felt pain before, not physical pain but emotional pain, as though his very heart was being burned in hell. So small, he felt so small. But it was the sensations inside that were the most distressing.

He missed his mum. The feelings emerged in a sudden rush. It wasn't just her death, it was the continual violence that he had been witness to over the years, And yet intermingled with this was the sense of horror of what had happened in front of him when she had died. The absolute horror. It was as if he was experiencing it through the eyes of a child, yet a child that in some way also had the understanding of an adult. Why? Why had it happened? Why his mum? And a deep longing for her, for the sensation of her being close, her smile, feeling her body pressed close to his as she gave him a hug, her smell. It was all so vivid. And it was gone, never again to happen. And he was so alone, so, so alone. And now there was no Terry either. Just him. He took another mouthful of whiskey and swallowed it although his throat felt swollen.

The tears burned in his eyes. He felt as though the burning extended right down to the pit of his stomach. But it was more than that. He couldn't have really described what was happening. He so wanted someone to be there, his mum, Julie. It was like two parts of himself each wanting the person they most wanted, but at the same time. He couldn't face this on his own, he wanted to die, he wanted to be free. His thinking was still a confusion of past and present, the two were intertwined, as if the alcohol had opened some invisible door that otherwise kept them apart. As though his demons—if that was the right way of thinking about them—were rushing in on him from both sides, feeling as though he was surrounded, coming at him from both past and present.

The TV continued in the background. But Andy wasn't taking it in. He closed his eyes. His head was spinning. He felt very ill. He needed to lie down. He shifted awkwardly on the sofa, barely aware that he was spilling some of the whiskey on his trousers as he did so. He felt the cushion beneath his head. He was already feeling heavy and numb, but now he felt as though he was sinking into the sofa. He was holding the glass in his right hand lying on his left side and facing the TV. His arm seemed so heavy but he made himself lift the glass and bring it to his lips. He drank a little, but not the large gulps that had he had taken before. He could feel himself drifting, sinking away. His hand relaxed and the glass fell to the floor, spilling the rest of its contents on to the carpet. Andy did not hear it land. He was asleep, passed out. He did not feel his stomach cramping or the burning in his throat as he vomited the contents of his stomach.

* * * *

Julie found Andy when she came home. He was lying on his side on the sofa. There was vomit on his face and chest and neck, and it had run down either side of him on to the sofa. He was out cold.

'Andy, Andy, you OK?' She noticed the almost empty whisky bottle on the floor beside him. 'Oh Andy, what have you done.' The smell was awful, but she went over to him and shook him. No response. He felt like a dead weight to push. She began to panic. 'Andy? Andy! Oh God, Andy, wake up!' She shook him more violently. Still no response. She tried to feel if he was breathing, he was. She closed her eyes and took a breath herself. She didn't know what to do. Should she let him sleep it off? She didn't know. She'd never experienced him being out cold like this. She was frightened. She knew how her father sometimes went comatose, and how they'd had to have him taken to hospital on a number of occasions. She picked up the phone and dialled 999.

'Look, it's my partner, he's out cold. Yes, he's been drinking, but he's really hit the bottle. His brother died recently, and, well, he's not doing well coming to terms with it and he's been sick but I think he's breathing, but, Oh God, I don't know what to do. I can't wake him up.'

'Does he often drink till he passes out?'

'No, and he looks like he's drunk almost a bottle of whisky, and he's been mainly off the spirits now for a while. What do I do? I can't wake him and I don't know what to do.'

'OK, where are you, we'll send a crew out to you.'

Julie gave them the address.'

'Keep him on his side in case he is sick again, then it will come out and won't go back into his lungs. We'll have someone with you soon.'

'Please hurry, he looks awful. I'll try and clean him up a bit.' Suddenly it seemed the most important thing in the world to clean him up.

'OK, look, as I say, a crew will be with you soon, just keep him on his side. Is the room cold? Put a blanket over him to keep him warm.' It gave her something to do.

'OK, right, OK, thanks, I'll do that. A few minutes, you say?'

'Yes, but please call us back if you need to, yes?'

'Sure, thanks, and, er, yes, OK.' Julie put the phone down. She didn't want to leave Andy to get a blanket, but she knew she should, and she wanted to get a flannel to wipe away some of the vomit that had begun to congeal around him.

It was about eight minutes later that the ambulance arrived and the paramedics came in to assess the situation. 'Has he been like this long?'

'I don't think so. He would have been back from his work about an hour or so.' Julie thought for a moment, 'That's if he went. Oh dear, maybe I should check, he might have started drinking earlier.'

One of the paramedics radioed through to the hospital and explained the situation. 'Not sure how serious it is, but he's out and his pulse is weak. He's drunk most of a bottle of whisky, been sick, maybe at risk of being sick again.'

They continued the conversation. 'OK, we're taking him in for observation. May need to stomach pump him to get the alcohol out of his stomach, stop any more being absorbed and making it worse. He's passed out quite quickly if he only recently started drinking and we're not sure what that's about.' They lifted him on to the trolley that had been brought in and proceeded to wheel him out to the ambulance.

One of the paramedics turned to Julie. 'Suggest you come along—don't know if you want to drive or come in the ambulance?'

'I'll come in the ambulance. I don't want to be separated from him.'

'Anyone you need to let know. Any family?'

Julie shook her head. No, she thought, and sighed heavily, that was the problem. 'No, parents died when he was a child and his only brother has just died.'

'Oh, so he hasn't anyone then, apart from you?'

'I guess not. I don't know of any other family, well, only his aunt and uncle who brought him and his brother up. I'd better let them know. It's his brothers funeral on Monday. They're coming over for that.' She paused, looking at Andy, 'He-he's going to be alright, isn't he?' Julie suddenly had a vision of a double funeral.

'Sure, we'll get him going. So don't you worry, he's in good hands.' The paramedic who had been talking, Ed, looked over to Andy. 'Poor bugger.' He turned to Julie. 'We see a lot of people turning to alcohol, it's a real ...' He stopped himself short of saying what had been in his mind to say. 'It's a real problem.'

'Yes, I know, killed my father.'

Ed shook his head. He had strapped Andy in. His colleague, Dave, had climbed into the drivers seat and they were soon on their way. They had the light flashing and the siren running—first time Julie had experienced that. They arrived at the hospital fifteen minutes later and Andy was immediately transferred into Accident and Emergency to be assessed by the duty team. A nurse took Julie aside. 'They'll need to do some tests, come and sit down and have a cup of tea.' Julie didn't want to leave Andy, but the nurse persuaded her that it was best, and they'd let her know what they were doing and how he was as soon as they knew.

They did pump out the contents of his stomach and then transferred him and kept him under observation. They weren't sure exactly what had happened. Maybe it was alcohol poisoning, or perhaps for some reason he had fitted, they weren't sure. Julie told him that he had been bad when he'd stopped drinking a while back, but hadn't fitted and didn't think he'd ever had that happen.

The doctor came to speak to her and said that he seemed stable. They had run a blood test and would do some other investigations, but he was still unconscious. It was more than just falling asleep drunk. She could stay if she wanted—it was now close to midnight, or they could order a taxi. Had she anyone to be with?

She thought about it and Amanda and Gary came to mind. She probably should have called them before. They had become closer these past few weeks. She called their number, the phone rang a couple of times before she heard Gary's voice.

'Hi, Gary here.'

'Gary, oh, look, sorry to call, but, well, I'm at the hospital and …'

'What's happened?'

'It's Andy, we don't know. He drank some whisky—quite a lot it seems, and we don't know what happened, I found him out cold, and he'd been sick and I called 999 and, well, here we are.'

'Is he OK?'

'Well they seem to think he's stable but he's still unconscious.'

'What about you? He'll be OK, Julie, he's tough and he'll come through.' Julie heard Gary's voice, he must be talking to Amanda. 'It's Julie, she's at the hospital. She found Andy unconscious—he'd hit the whiskey.'

'Let me speak to her.'

'I'm handing you over to Amanda.'

'Julie, oh what can I say, oh you didn't need this, poor Andy, what happened? Are you OK.'

'I think so. It's all been a bit of a shock.' Julie suddenly realised she was hungry, that she hadn't eaten anything since that sandwich at lunchtime.

'Look, can we do anything? What's happening?'

'Well, they've suggested that I might head home, they'll let me know if anything changes. I don't know what to do. If I do that, well I want to see him first, and then I haven't got the car here.'

'Look, don't worry, we'll come over. We're close by, don't forget. Where are you?'

'At the Accident and Emergency Department but they've taken him on to a ward.' She looked over to the nurse, 'some friends are coming to see me and pick me up. Should they come here or …?'

'Yes, that'll be fine. They can wait for you and I can phone up and let you know when they're here.'

Julie explained to Amanda and then called off. 'Can I go and see him?'

'Sure. I'll take you, I just need to make sure they know where I've gone.'

The nurse took Julie up to the room where Andy was lying, attached to various monitors. The nurse said she'd leave her for a few minutes and left Julie in the doorway. She shook her head. He had a breathing tube and looked a ghastly colour. 'Oh Andy, what have you done to yourself.' She closed her eyes as she felt tears forming in them. She opened them, blinking. 'Oh God, please don't let him die, please get him through this.' She wasn't religious but the words came out quite spontaneously. She went and sat next to him and touched his wrist, stroking it gently. She wondered whether he could hear her. She spoke again. 'Andy, I want you. Please come back, please wake up. I need you, Andy, everyone's so worried. Please wake up.' She looked at him, but there was no movement other than his chest moving rhythmically up and down. She had placed her hand over his wrist and was giving it a squeeze. She felt suddenly very alone with him. She so wanted to communicate but he just lay there. It was a few minutes later when there was a sound behind her. The nurse had brought Amanda up.

'Oh Julie, I don't know what to say.'

'Nothing to say, Mand. He's still unconscious. They've pumped him out and now all we can do is wait and pray that he comes out of it soon.'

'We came as soon as we can. Gary was quite shocked. He's parking the car.'

'Thanks for coming. I appreciate it, I really do.'

Amanda had come over to where Julie was sitting and had placed her hands on her shoulders, giving them a gentle massage. Julie stretched her back. 'Oh Mand, what's going to happen?' She burst into tears. As she turned, Mandy drew her head towards and held her as she sobbed. Julie felt so wretched, so helpless and suddenly so very vulnerable. She clung on to Amanda who stroked her head gently, trying to offer something to soothe her a bit. 'There, there, it'll be OK. He's in the best place. He'll come round and be his old self again soon, you'll see.'

Julie continued to cry but the sobs were less frequent. 'Yes, I have to believe that, but I know what alcohol can do to people. It killed my father, Mand, I've seen what it can do. I love him, I do so love him and I couldn't bear the thought of losing him, not like this, not to alcohol.'

'You won't lose him, he'll be awake soon, you'll see.' She continued to hold Julie's head and was gently rocking her.

'I hope you're right.'

'The nurse asked me to encourage you to head back home, that they would call you immediately if he became conscious. What do you say? Gary and I have discussed it and we've agreed I can stay with you, or you can come back to our place for the night.'

'I don't know, I mean, I think I'd prefer to be at home, but I'm not sure I want to go. What if he …' She burst into tears again.

'They say he's stable now, it is a matter of waiting.'

'I want to ask them how long.'

'Sure, we can do that.'

'Oh Julie …' It was Gary's voice. He was standing in the doorway. It made him feel very uncomfortable. He didn't like hospitals and seeing Andy lying there left him feeling quite cold and suddenly anxious. 'What's he done to himself?'

Amanda glanced over to him and gestured him to be quiet.

'Thanks for coming, Gary.' It was Julie who spoke. 'Is the nurse still there?'

Gary nodded, turned and beckoned her over.

'Yes, what can I do for you?'

'I don't know, should I stay, I mean, will it help him if I stay?'

'It's really up to you, but he is stable now and there's no more alcohol that can be absorbed, we've pumped it all out. So we can only wait for him to regain consciousness. We can call you as soon as that happens if you like?'

Julie suddenly felt sleepy, maybe the adrenalin had begun to wear off. She did feel the need to sleep, but she didn't want to leave.

'Stay with us, Julie, we can get you back here quicker than if you go back home. We've got the spare bed.' It was Gary's voice.

'I don't know …'

'At least you won't be on your own and it is closer than your place. The bed's made up.'

'Are you sure?'

'Course we are.'

'OK. Look can I just have a couple more minutes here on my own with him, and then I'll come out.'

Amanda and Gary left, saying they'd wait outside in the corridor if that was OK with the nurse. She said it was.

After they had all left, Julie turned back to Andy. 'Come on love, we can beat this. Come back to me, wake up soon. Everything will be OK, you'll see.' She squeezed his wrist again and with tears in her eyes leant over and kissed him on the forehead.

It was so difficult for her to pull away and leave him. It tugged at her heart, it felt like it tore at her very soul, but she was feeling so tired and she knew she needed to rest. She slowly got up. She didn't want to stop touching him, but eventually she took her hand away. 'I'll be back soon, darling. I'm just going back with Amanda and Gary. They'll look after me. Don't worry about me. I'll be OK. You get yourself awake and I'll see you soon.'

She edged towards the door, still looking at him, willing him to wake up, willing his eyes to open, but they didn't stir. She had reached the door. She blew him a kiss and turned, but continued to look at him through the window as she walked slowly along the corridor to where Gary and Amanda were waiting for her. It had been a long day. Her eyes were full of tears and her throat burned. She felt tired, and yet strangely alert at the same time. It was going to feel like a long night …

*   *   *   *

The phone sounded at five-thirty. Julie heard it and lay there wondering what was being said. Gary had picked it up. Julie got up and headed to their room.

She arrived just as Amanda was opening the door.

'It's OK, it's the hospital, Andy's regained consciousness, but he is asleep again now. They say there is no need to rush over, that he needs the rest, but to come in sometime during the morning.'

Julie closed her eyes and gave a sigh of relief, and promptly burst into tears. It was a spontaneous release of the emotions that had been building up, as fear turned to relief. Amanda gave her a hug. Gary had by now appeared. 'It's all OK, he's woken up and asked where he was and what had happened. He asked for you, and they explained where you were and what had happened. He's since gone back to sleep again and …'

Amanda interjected. 'I've told Julie that she can go in during the morning.'

Julie yawned. She was still very tired. She went back to bed and soon drifted back off to sleep once again.

* * * *

Julie was sitting next to Andy in the hospital the next day, trying to understand what had happened. Andy was piecing the events together. He could remember the radio programme and then things had begin to get rather hazy. 'I'm sorry, love, something happened to me, something got to me. That radio programme, one of the speakers, just got to me and, I don't know, something happened. I don't understand.'

'Sounds too close to your own experience, Andy, must have been awful, but I so wish you didn't keep turning to alcohol to cope.'

Andy was shaking his head and took a deep breath and sighed. 'I know. I don't want to. I hadn't planned it, but suddenly there I was, in the off-licence. It was like I had no control. I just had to get a drink. Nothing else mattered. Nothing else mattered, and then, well I really don't remember what happened at home. That's gone.' He shook his head and looked into Julie's eyes. 'I'm so sorry for the chaos I've caused. You've been so good, and Gary and Amanda, coming over and everything. I really have to get my act together.'

'It's not been easy, but, well, at least it's over.'

'Is it? What about the next time?'

'Well, we'll have to deal with that. But there must be ways of stopping it happening.'

'I need to talk to the doctor here and see what he says. He's been around but was more interested in what happened than what happens next.'

'What did he say?'

'Explained what they'd done, said they wanted to keep me in overnight tonight, keep an eye on me, and then probably discharge me tomorrow.'

'What then?'

'I don't know. I want to talk about whether I can take something. I was thinking about it before you came in. I've got to do something radical. I've got to stop, and I need to know how to go about it. Graham talked to me about detoxing, but I said no. But now, well, now it's different. They've got me on something now, to calm me down. Didn't catch what it was. Maybe I need to keep taking that, I don't know. I need to ask him.'

'So how are you feeling now that you've been awake a few hours?'

'My stomach feels awful, my throat feels raw and I still feel sort of spaced out, a little bit floaty.'

'A bit high, you mean?'

'Just floating, like I'm sort of not really solid. It's weird, I mean, you can feel like this with a few drinks and it's similar but not quite the same.' He paused before continuing. 'I guess it's the effects of what they did and maybe the tablets, I don't know. I feel tired, hard to really move, just want to lie here.'

They sat for a little longer and Andy drifted back off to sleep. Julie sat for a while before going off to find the nurse and see what was being planned. The doctor was with her so he responded to her. 'Hello. I'm Dr Finch.' He explained what they had done and why. 'Well, we think it was alcohol poisoning. It doesn't seem that he took anything else, but we pumped him out because we really weren't too sure. Has he been like this before? He said he hadn't but, well, people do deny things.'

'No, nothing quite like this. He's drunk heavily for many years. You know about his past?'

The doctor shook his head.

'Well, his father killed his mother and he was a child and, well, he's never really got over it. He's having counselling at the moment, trying to talk it out and put it behind him, but it's not easy.'

Dr Finch shook his head. 'That's terrible. He'd said about his brother dying recently. So he's been drinking for some while. Hmm. Has he had specialist help?'

'Well, no, but it seems as though his counsellor has experience of working with people with alcohol problems.'

'OK, but we may need to have him reviewed by the local alcohol team. He is probably going to need to stop. When people establish heavy drinking patterns early in life, well, it's not good news long-term.'

'I know, my father died from the effects of alcohol.'

'I'm sorry, but you'll understand what I mean. It would probably be in his best interests to stop drinking. He's obviously dangerously susceptible to it and we need to reduce the risk of further problems like this, or other problems if he carries on.'

Julie sighed. 'I know. I'd wondered about him seeing his GP first?'

'Yes, he could, and we will write to her anyway, but maybe we should refer him directly in to the community alcohol team for an assessment as well.'

'Well, you may want to discuss that with Andy.' She wasn't sure how he might react to that, though he seemed adamant that he wanted to change. 'He knows he has to change, we were just talking about it before he drifted back off to sleep.'

'We have him on medication, we weren't sure if he might react to not drinking.'

'He tried stopping a few weeks back but was unwell, very shaky and had to drink again. Up until last week, when his brother died, he'd been reducing and it seemed more under control for most of the time. But then it all got out of control again.'

'I think he needs a specialist assessment and then see what they recommend. I can have him referred but they like people to call them to confirm they want to be seen—it is part of ensuring people have some motivation. I'm not sure that that's always the best way, I think we have a role in getting people to appointments to persuade them to think differently and to encourage motivation. But anyway, that's the process. So, I'll have a talk with Andy later about this, and maybe you can support me in this when you next talk to him?'

'Yes, I will. I'll be back later. I'm working a shorter day today because of the situation so I'll be back this evening.'

'Can he get home OK tomorrow?'

'If it's in the morning I can come and collect him—I'm on a late shift. And I'll arrange for someone to be with him during the evening. I guess it won't be easy for him to start with.'

'Well, no, but he's off the alcohol now and he should see the GP as soon as possible. He's still on medication to help him relax, and to stave off a withdrawal reaction. He'll need to carry on with that for a few days and then gradually reduce it. He needs to see his GP about that and hopefully he'll be seen then by the alcohol service and, well, we'll see what can be offered. Perhaps you could make an appointment to see her as soon as possible. We'll be sending her a discharge summary—I'll make sure it is faxed over so she has it as soon as possible.'

'Thanks. I'll do that. What about the counselling he's been having?'

'If that's helpful for him—and it seems like he has a lot he needs to talk through and find ways of dealing with other than drinking—I think he should continue.' Dr Finch was a firm believer in talking therapies. He didn't himself encourage people to take medication unless it was absolutely necessary. With Andy it was, they didn't want him to go into alcohol withdrawal. Now they wanted to maximise the opportunity given as by the time Andy went home he would have had a couple of days not drinking. Not very long, but a start and could lead to the detoxification he needed if everyone co-operated. But he would need support. 'He might also want to consider Alcoholics Anonymous—they can give him support and a place to go to be with people who will appreciate something of what he is going through.'

'I don't think he'd be too keen on that. He knows what his problems are—too many painful experiences in his life and discovering alcohol as a way of coping. And now he has to find another way.'

Dr Finch nodded. 'Yes, it can sound so easy but alcohol is such a hard habit to break. It's just so available.'

'I know. Turn on the TV and the programme is either sponsored by an alcohol producer or the programme is either centred in a pub or seems to involve people drinking all the time. When do you ever see any movies that involve people drinking tea or coffee? It seems to always be alcohol. Anyway, my problems are closer to home. Thanks for all you've done and are doing. Now it's up to us and up to Andy.'

Dr Finch nodded. 'If I don't see you tomorrow, good luck. I will be talking to Andy and encouraging him, and we'll discuss ways that he can reduce the risk of lapsing back into drinking. We want him to use this as an opportunity to detoxify himself.'

'Is there anything I could read about alcohol and how to help someone?'

'There are a few titles around. *Dying for a Drink* and *Counselling the Person Beyond the Alcohol Problem* are two that come to mind. There are others.[5] And there's *Alcohol Concern* who have lots of information sheets. They're based in London.'

Julie left feeling somewhat encouraged by Dr Finch's tone. She accepted that it wasn't going to be easy, but there was an opportunity. So much depended on how Andy reacted longer term to what had happened to Terry. Only time would tell on that, she thought to herself, aware that she was feeling quite emotional at the thought of not really knowing what would happen, and still having the image in her mind of her father, looking so old and yellow as his liver slowly gave up its battle against alcohol's toxic onslaught.

---

5. Please see suggested reading list at the back of the book for details of these and other titles.

CHAPTER 13

▼

They got back from the hospital just a little after midday the following day, giving Julie time to turn around and head off to work. Andy was still feeling quite tired. He was continuing to take the tranquilisers he had been prescribed, they certainly helped although he couldn't say he didn't want a drink. It was certainly on his mind a lot of the time, but he had made a decision that he had to stop—at least for a while. He knew he had to deal with his past, and he had agreed with Dr Finch that he would seek further help. In fact, the ward had phoned through to the local NHS Community Alcohol Team and they had offered him an assessment appointment, although not for over a week. Friday after next was the earliest they could offer.

He had got an appointment with his doctor that evening, so he planned to go to that. It would give him something to do. Five 'clock. And then Gary was coming round. Julie had phoned him and asked if he could be there given it was Andy's first evening home—and she'd asked him to try to keep encouraging him to keep off the alcohol.

The afternoon felt a bit strange. From the noise of the hospital it suddenly felt too quiet. Andy had the TV on just to fill the silence. He phoned work and explained the situation. He was going to see his doctor and would call them as soon as he knew whether she was signing him off for next week. He agreed to call his boss at home to let him know when he got back from the doctor's if the office was closed.

Andy still hadn't really taken in what had happened. In some ways he had, but essentially he hadn't, not really. It did all still seem a little distant. He knew what had happened, and he had been able to recall most of it now, although it remained a mystery as to exactly why he went for the whisky in the way that he did. He'd been upset before and wasn't sure why that radio programme had got to him in such an intense way. However, it had happened and he knew he had to be on his guard. The problem was he had clearly been so out of control. He had no recollection of fighting the urge to drink, he was concerned that he seemed to not be able to resist it.

The afternoon wore on. He felt tired and decided to go to bed for an hour or two. He set the alarm to be sure he was awake and had time to get to the doctors. He slept for a while but then woke up and decided he needed to get up. He did one or two things around the house. He still felt quite weak. He thought about drinking. There was nothing in the house, though, Julie had made sure that there were no cans there once she appreciated that this was an opportunity for Andy to try and stay dry—at least for a while. He did feel a bit of craving but it wasn't so bad that it pushed him to go in search of a drink. He was able to acknowledge it for what it was, as doctor Finch had advised him, and focus on something else. He also had a good supply of strongly flavoured fruit juice—that was something else he'd recommended. 'Always have something with bite to it—more likely to give you a good taste sensation. That can help. Alcoholic drinks generate intense oral stimulation and if you're going to substitute it with something else then you've got to satisfy that to some degree.' That was what he'd advised. So on the way home from the hospital they had picked up cartons of cranberry juice, pineapple juice, and some exotic fruit juices.

Andy was glad it was a short walk to the doctors. He still didn't feel like facing a great deal. The thought of going to the doctors wasn't one that excited him terribly. But he knew he had to go. The phone rang and it was Julie, checking how he was, and encouraging him. He promised he would go to see Dr Shira. He got himself ready to go. He took it steadily. The urge to drink had thankfully passed again.

*   *   *   *

Dr Shira was running late—she had had an emergency earlier at the start of her evening surgery and so everyone was now having to wait about fifteen minutes longer to be seen. Andy went outside. The bustle of the waiting room seemed too much for him, left him feeling on edge. He came back in and sat down and waited for his name to be called. In fact, she had caught up a bit and the wait wasn't as long as the receptionist had suggested. He heard his name. 'Mr Davis, please go to room three.'

He headed off. It was a compact and busy surgery with a constant queue of people at the desk checking. He noticed the notice boards overflowing with posters. He went along the corridor the short distance to room three and knocked on the door.

'Come in.'

'Hello doctor.'

'Hello Andy. Haven't seen you for a while, not since that wrist injury last year.'

'No, that's right.' Andy had sprained his wrist when he had fallen awkwardly when he was lifting some boxes off the back of the van. But it was well mended now and never gave him any problem. They'd had to do X rays to check he hadn't broken anything.

'So, we have a summary from Dr Finch. I'm sorry to hear about Terry, of course, I never met him, he's not one of our patients, but it must have been a terrible shock.'

Andy nodded, closing his eyes briefly as he did so. 'Yes, I found him, and it wasn't very pleasant.'

'No. No, a tragic loss.' Dr Shira had found people dead herself, but not a family member and not in those circumstances.

Andy nodded again having tightened his jaw. Yes, he still found it hard to believe what had happened, still hoped he'd wake up and find it had all been some awful dream. He knew it wasn't but somewhere inside himself part of him was still hanging on to the hope.

'Yeah, it's not been easy.'

'No, and, well, you've clearly been overdoing it with the alcohol, yes?'

Andy nodded again. 'I never thought I'd ever find myself having to admit to having an alcohol problem, but I have, haven't I?'

'Well, I look at it this way. People often ask me if I think they have an alcohol problem after I've raised concern. I always ask them if their alcohol use is in any way causing them some kind of a problem which, if they were not drinking, would resolve itself. Most say yes, and then I say that if your drinking is causing you problems that would otherwise not be there, then the drinking has to be regarded as problematic.'

'Yes, well, I've realised this. Not just as a result of what has happened, I've been having counselling and that helped me realise I needed to make changes, and I had been I thought doing quite well, bringing it down slowly, and then it all went pear-shaped.'

'Maybe it going pear-shaped—as you describe it—was symptomatic of the fact that things have actually been pear-shaped for a while.'

Andy hadn't quite thought of it like that but, yes, it made sense. Things hadn't been right in his life for a long while, but now he had to deal with it. 'You're probably right. I'm learning a lot about myself through the counselling, but Terry's death just floored me. I suppose I knew it could happen but never thought that it would, I mean, you know, you don't, do you?'

'One generally tries not to, however likely it might seem. Anyway, I understand Dr Finch has put you on some medication to quieten things down a bit and whilst we don't want you on it for too long, it has got a part to play in helping you through all of this.'

'It does help, seems to calm me a bit, but I do want a drink, doesn't stop me wanting a drink, you know.'

'Yes, well, we can't really take away the cravings. There is something else we could try you on that seems to take out some of the urge to drink, but, well, I'm loathe to use medication unless it is necessary.'

'I had wondered whether I might have anti-depressant. I've been feeling really low and, well, must have been something to do with why I drank so heavily. I still feel low and it seems that everything is a bit of an effort.'

Dr Shira nodded. 'Yes, I can well imagine. Look, let me be honest. What you've experienced would cause anyone's mood to lower. What you are experiencing is probably a normal human reaction to a tragic event. Sometimes anti-depressants are helpful in lifting mood and stabilising it for a period. But sometimes it can create a false experience. I'm also aware that you've had to stop drinking—at least, whilst you were in hospital.'

'I plan to stay stopped, at least for a while. I have an appointment to see someone about it.'

'Yes, I have a copy of the referral to the Community Alcohol Team. But what you also need to remember is that people's mood can drop once they stop drinking as part of the loss and feeling lost without alcohol. So you have a lot of psychological reasons for feeling low at the moment, but at least you are free of the alcohol which itself lowers mood. So I don't want to rush into prescribing anti-depressants. I'd prefer to give the talking therapy a chance, but we'll keep it under review, and I'll take opinion from the Community Alcohol Team as they will write to me. Do you know who you are seeing?'

'No, I can't remember, it was done over the phone.'

'OK, and when's that for again?'

'Next Friday.'

'Right, so we need to keep you dry till then if possible. Does that seem a reasonable goal?'

'I can try, but it feels a long time.'

'OK, well, first of all, we'll keep you on the tranquilisers for a little longer. Come and see me say Tuesday and we'll begin to reduce it down if you feel ready for that. We don't want to rush anything but we don't want you to develop a dependency on them either.'

'OK, but no anti-depressants?'

'No. Again, we keep it under review. Now, what you need is to be able to occupy yourself for the next few days.'

'Well, that won't be too hard with Terry's funeral on Monday.'

'Oh yes, of course, I somehow hadn't thought about that. Right, OK. But you need to plan things to keep yourself focused on other things if you can, and drink plenty of fluids.'

'I am, I had a tremendous thirst in hospital and I still have. I got through so much orange squash. Now I'm on strongly flavoured fruit juice, and lots of water, and coffee. My coffee intake has gone up.'

'OK, but try to switch to the purer fruit juices. Less additives. And also plenty of plain old-fashioned water, which you are doing—keep flushing the system out, as it were. But watch the coffee. Gives you a boost, all the caffeine, but it won't help your sleep pattern which I imagine is probably not too good, it's usually problematic in these situations.'

'It isn't good. No chance of any sleeping tablets?'

'No. We need to try and let your body settle back down naturally, but we'll keep it under review. So, how much medication did the hospital leave you with? Their letter suggested that you would have enough for today only?'

'Yes. I will run out this evening.'

'OK, so I will prescribe the same amount for you through to Tuesday and then see how you are then.'

They discussed time off work—Andy confirmed he would self-certificate until he saw her on Tuesday and then decide whether he needed more time or whether getting back to work would be better for him. Dr Shira also prescribed him thiamine as this was something people with alcohol problems were often deficient in and it was important to boost this during detoxification.

The conversation came back around to alcohol. 'Andy, I must encourage you to keep off the alcohol. You will experience urges to drink, but keep yourself occupied. Monday will be difficult, and not a good time to try and stay dry I imagine.'

'Lot of Terry's friends were drinkers and, well, it won't be easy, will it?'

'No, but think ahead, plan it as best you can. Have reasons for saying no to alcohol in your head, and have other options available—and not all the same thing. Have variety. People will get bored with the same soft drink but strangely rarely get bored with a particular alcoholic drink.'

'OK, I'll take that on board. You really think it's best to stop for a while?'

'I do. You've put your body under a lot of strain with the alcohol and it needs time to recuperate. So take it easy. Give it a break. Give your liver a break. Alcohol is toxic. Treat it with respect and with a certain degree of caution.'

'But it isn't that I can never drink again?'

Dr Shira smiled. 'Who knows? Don't worry about the future. Make healthy choices in the present, that's all we have, the present. No point in dwelling on drinking in the future. What does it give you? Let the future take care of itself. Today, tomorrow, the next day, that's the focus. Get through them making healthy choices. And so on. They say 'one day at a time in AA' and it's very wise. One day at a time. You've chosen not to drink today?'

'Ye-es.'

'Well then, good, feel good about it, you're taking control. Now you have to do the same tomorrow, and, well, worry about the day after when you get there. Remember, one day at a time and then you'll be here on Tuesday, not having had a drink and we can plan the next step.'

'You make it sound simple.' Andy was struck by Dr Shira's somewhat matter-of-fact tone which actually felt quite encouraging, though he did wonder whether she said this to everyone and wondered how everyone else got on.

'It isn't, I know that, I'm just telling you the steps to take. Give yourself a chance. And I'll see you Tuesday and we'll review how things are going.'

Andy got up and moved towards the door. Dr Shira thought about mentioning Monday but decided not to. Andy didn't need reminding. He actually seemed a little more positive, let him be with that feeling for a little while longer. Why bring his attention back to the funeral? He will have time enough to dwell on that.

Andy left feeling positive. Somehow there was something about the way the doctor spoke that just made so much sense. Maybe it was her Indian accent, but she made it sound so simple and logical. Yes, of course it wasn't going to be that easy, but why not 'one day at a time' and, yes, he'd get through today without a drink and then worry about tomorrow, well, tomorrow.

* * * *

Gary came around about half an hour after Andy had got back. Andy was sitting eating his way through a bag of fish and chips he had picked up on the way home. He'd suddenly realised just how hungry he was. He hadn't expected Gary quite so early. He gave him some of his chips and a piece of the fish—fortunately he'd ordered large portions of everything.

'So, good to get to the end of the week I should think?'

'I don't need another one like this, believe me.'

'No.' Gary was feeling a little awkward. It seemed like somehow he didn't know what to talk about. He sort of felt he should be different somehow, and wasn't sure whether he needed to avoid talking about alcohol or not. Not that he felt he had anything to say on the topic, but, well, it's like when you're told not to think about something it's immediately the first thing on your mind.

They sat in silence munching their respective fish and chips.

'Thanks for coming round. I still feel quite wobbly. It's weird. I sort of feel calm but guess that's the tablets and yet at the same time I feel like I'm on edge all the time. And behind all of that I can hear that little voice—not literally—but the idea that if I had a drink I'd feel OK.'

'Must be strange, I mean, I guess I can't really guess what it's like. Do you want to drink after what happened?'

'Yes, I really do. And yet I know I mustn't. But the urge is there. It comes and goes but it's close. But then I spent time thinking about drinking before all this happened.'

'Yeah, but you weren't trying not to have any then.'

'Yeah, but because I'm trying not to it's like I'm more aware of it. It's a real pain. I wish something would take it away and just leave me feeling, I don't know, normal I suppose.'

'Like being able to have a drink?' Gary smiled although he wondered how helpful that was to say.

'Yeah, that's pretty much how it is. I'm damn sure, you know, if it wasn't for these tablets I'd have gone straight out and got something.'

'You've got it bad, haven't you?'

'I just really hadn't appreciated how much it was affecting me, I really didn't, but I do now. You know this is the longest I've gone without a drink for, well, I reckon it must be years. I've drunk every day for as long as I can remember. Not always heavily, but pretty steadily. Now, well, what is this, third day dry. But there are people who hardly ever drink, just occasionally. That's how I want to be.'

'Sort of take it or leave it?'

'Yeah, I mean, you don't go down the pub as much as I did, and, well, do you drink every night?'

'No, never have, never really got into it quite like that. Yes, you know I like a few beers, but.... I don't know. Maybe I just react differently to it.'

'Maybe you didn't have the crap childhood I had which gave you a reason to drink like I did.'

'Maybe. May have something to do with it.' Gary thought back to his own childhood and yes it had been happy. Parents had been there for him and his sister. They'd not got into trouble really, did fairly well at school. 'I didn't start drinking until I was seventeen and then I never really got into it that much, not until I left school when I was eighteen and had a bit of money. But even then, it wasn't every night.'

'Yeah, well, that's where I was different. Started much younger and, well, always seemed to be ready to have a drink if I could and by sixteen I was drinking regularly. Got served OK in the local so I just carried on.' Andy took a few mouthfuls of the can of diet cola he'd just opened as Gary had been speaking.

'It's weird stuff, isn't it?'

'It's made me see it differently. And I know that not everyone maybe sees it like I do now.'

'Well Steve and Alan certainly don't. Have they been round to see you?'

Andy shook his head. 'No, that may be a good thing, actually.'

'They ask after you sometimes in the pub when I've dropped in. But they don't seem to take what's happened to you that seriously.'

'Well, I guess you find out who your friends are, who'll stick by you. Seems as though they're only interested in their next pint.' He paused. 'No, that's maybe not fair. Perhaps I'm just pissed off that they haven't bothered to come round or give me a call.'

'You know I think you could be right. Maybe so long as they're in the pub with a pint in their hand, well, they're happy. But anything that disturbs that, they just don't want to know.'

Andy looked down at the now empty paper that the fish and chips had been in. 'I don't know about you but I'm still hungry. Guess my stomach's settled down now and I'm catching up for the meals I lost.'

'Fancy some more?'

'Yeah, why not?' They got up to head out to the fish and chip shop. Gary drove. Andy didn't feel like walking again.

As they were driving Andy was aware of wanting a drink. 'You know, I could just do with a pint, just the one. I know I shouldn't but …'

'I'm under strict instructions, no alcohol, though I have to say, I can't see how one would hurt.'

'Doctor said I shouldn't drink on the tablets.'

'Well, don't have any when you get back!'

'You trying to encourage me?' Andy suddenly felt uncertain. The thought of a pint really pulled, he could taste it, feel the froth on his upper lip, feel the coolness in his mouth and throat. He was salivating at the thought of it and the craving was suddenly very strong. 'Come on, just the one.'

'You sure?'

'Yes, I'll be OK. Come on, I'll buy. No rounds, just the one, in and out and no more.'

Gary was the one feeling hesitant now. 'I'm not sure it's a good idea. You've only been off it three days.'

'Well, if you don't want to come, then fine. Stop the car, I'll go on my own.'

'Andy, just stop and think for a moment. You haven't been in the pub now for ages. Why's it so important now? What the hell will you gain? One pint! It's not worth it.'

'That's true, one pint was never enough. Just the one for me was more like just the one gallon! Oh hell, I don't know what to do. Shit I want a drink. Look, let's get the fish and chips and get back home. You're right. Shouldn't have come out. Too tempting. It's too damn easy, isn't it? Everywhere you look, pubs, off-licenses, supermarkets—can't get away from it. No, come on, you're right, I've got my sensible head back on again. Keep driving, let's get the food and get back.' Andy was suddenly very aware of just how easy it would have been to have dropped of for that pint. Exactly what made him not act on the urge he wasn't sure. But he knew it was close. He wasn't going to be so confident another time. The doctor had encouraged him to stay dry for a while. Three days! Was that all he was going to manage? No, he needed to prove something to himself.

They had pulled up outside the fish and chip shop. Gary looked across at Andy. 'You've gone quiet.'

A sentence had formed in Andy's head and it had shocked him once he realised what it was that he had been thinking. 'Hmm, yeah, sorry, miles away for a moment.'

'Going to share them?'

'Stupid thing to think.' He went silent again.

'And?'

'Well, just thinking, you know, how easy it would be to have drink and what if I could only manage three days dry. And then the thought just came to me that I needed to prove something to myself—that I'm not like Terry.' As he said that he felt his throat fill with a lump. He closed his eyes. 'Sorry.'

'No, no, it must still be such a shock.'

Andy was back seeing Terry's face staring up to the ceiling, his body twisted and his neck turned at that far too unnatural an angle. 'Some images just don't go away. I've lived all these years with seeing my mother lying there when she died, and now I've got Terry's face in my head as well.' He closed his eyes. 'And I just know a drink would make it go away, but I also know it wouldn't last.'

'Yeah. Hasn't the counselling helped?'

'I thought it had, I mean, I haven't dwelt on my mother so much recently. Talking about that, letting go of the secret has helped. Felt lighter somehow although at first it was horrible—just brought it all back, like I was reliving it. But now, no, I feel less overwhelmed by that. I mean, it still makes me sad, but it doesn't sort of get to me the same. So, yeah, it has helped' He shook his head. 'But now there's Terry …'

'Yeah, and no alcohol to blot it out.'

'No, not this time. Been there, done that, didn't work. Got me by but long term, no, messed me up. Now I've got to find another way.'

'I'll never really be able to understand what you've been through, can't pretend to. Just don't know what to say, not too good with words sometimes …'

'It's OK. I'm glad you're around.' He glanced across at Gary. 'Come on, let's see what they've got.'

*　　*　　*　　*

Monday was the day of the funeral. It was fortunately dry and sunny, although quite cold. Andy had thought about how to handle it. They were going back to a local hotel afterwards for a buffet meal. Andy had decided that he didn't want alcohol in the house, that it would be better if they went somewhere although his experience that evening with Gary had unsettled him. He and Julie decided they would stay together throughout the buffet meal. He didn't want to find himself tempted.

The ceremony went off quite well, there was quite a small number of people gathered there at the local crematorium. Some of Terry's drinking friends came back to the hotel and established themselves in the bar. Andy decided to let them get on with it. He was still feeling tired. Somehow, ever since that episode with the whisky he had found himself really struggling as the day went on. Steve and Alan were also there but they had attached themselves to the group at the bar.

By the time they got home Andy was ready to go to sleep, even though it was only six-thirty. He suddenly thought of Graham. He'd completely forgotten that Graham had agreed to put the time aside for the counselling session. But he was too tired. He just felt he needed to relax. He had the appointment Thursday.

"I've just remembered the counselling, Julie. Graham said he'd hold the slot open for me. Said I'd call him—completely forgot with everything. I'd better give him a call.'

'Sure you don't want to go over?'

'I feel really tired. No, I think I'll give it a miss.' He yawned. 'Oh dear.' He reached over for the phone but could not remember the number. He had it written down on a card in his wallet. He went to get it and made the call.

'Hi Graham, look, I'm sorry for not calling. I just forgot. It's been a hell of a week, it really has, and with the funeral today, well, I just clean forgot. And I'm feeling so tired, I just feel like I need to try and get some sleep.'

'Sure, Thursday still OK?'

'Yes, that'll be fine. And, look, I'll pay for today. I should have let you know. A lot's happened but I'll tell you about it on Thursday.'

'OK, but it went off OK today?'

'Yes, yes it did actually. Better than I expected. Still hard to believe what has happened even after the cremation but, well, I guess I'll get used to it eventually. But it still doesn't feel like it's happened, and yet …' Andy shook his head. 'Anyway, I don't want to get into that just now.'

Graham respected his choice in this. 'Sure, so I'll see you Thursday afternoon then?'

They confirmed the time and Andy hung up.

'I'm going to lie on the bed for a while, just feel I need to unwind. That OK?'

'Sure, no problem love. You won't want to eat anything I guess, not yet anyway after the buffet?'

'No, maybe later.' Andy went upstairs to the bedroom and kicked off his shoes and flopped down on the bed. He felt wiped out. His eyes were heavy and his whole body felt kind of numb, like all the energy had been drained out of it. He lay face down and it wasn't long before he was asleep.

He awoke though he had no idea how long he had been asleep, and felt somewhat disorientated. He'd been dreaming, a particularly vivid dream. It was weird, so real. He'd been in the pub with Alan and Steve, Matt was there too. He could remember vividly drinking this pint of lager. It was so real. He realised he could taste it and smell it. It felt like he'd really had a drink, but he knew he hadn't. He blinked to orientate himself and get his head together. He immediately yawned, his mouth felt just like he'd sunk a pint or two. He went to move but realised he felt slightly drunk. Had he been drinking? Had he gone and … no, he knew he hadn't. He could remember coming to sleep. But the dream it was so real. He pushed himself up. He needed some cold water on his face, but he could still taste the alcohol. He staggered off to the bathroom and had a wash and cleaned his teeth as well.

As he left the bathroom Julie appeared. 'Feel better for that?'

'Hmm, oh, yes, I think so, but it was really weird. Just felt like I'd had a drink somehow.'

'What do you mean?' Julie looked and felt drained.

'I had this vivid dream. I really felt like I was drinking and when I woke up I could taste it, smell it, it just felt so real. Even felt a little drunk when I got up. What do you think that was about?'

'Wishful thinking?'

'No, I'm serious, it really did feel real. I really felt like I'd been drinking. I haven't, have I? I mean, it really was that real.'

'No, you didn't have anything today and unless you have something stashed in the bedroom you haven't had anything here either.'

'It would be really easy to think that I had.' Andy shook his head. 'I could do with a coffee.'

'OK, let me just put these towels away, I've just been ironing them. You coming down,' she called over her shoulder as she walked over to the airing cupboard.

'Yeah. I'll go and put the kettle on. Fancy one?'

'Yes, it's been a long day.'

'I could eat something as well now.' Andy went downstairs and hunted around for something sweet. He'd noticed how, over the last few days, he'd been eating more cake, biscuits and chocolate. He found some cake and cut a large slice. He made the coffee and took it all into the lounge. He clicked on the TV and flicked across the channels, nothing really appealed so he left it on some film. Seemed to have plenty of action.

He thought back over the day. 'Well, Terry, that's it.' He was speaking out loud. 'Gonna miss you. Can't imagine how it's going to be without you around.' He hadn't heard Julie come into the room. She heard what he said and came over to him, and put her hand on his shoulder.

'Yes, it'll feel strange, more for you. But he won't be forgotten.'
'No, that's for sure.'

Julie sat down beside him. Andy put his arm around her, drawing her too him and placed his head on her shoulder. It wasn't long before she realised he was crying.

Chapter 14

'So, how is it going Andy, managing to stay dry?' Dr Shira was sitting at her desk, but had turned as Andy had walked in.

Andy explained what had happened over the last few days. It still all seemed very close, which it was. It takes more than a few days to come to terms with a potentially life-threatening event like that, and the stress his body had been put under. 'So, I'm dry but it's not been easy.'

'What in particular?'

'Came close to drinking on a couple of occasions but I've managed to stay dry. Those tablets I think have really helped.'

'Good, but we can't keep you on them forever. We need to start to wean you off them I think.'

'Can't I take them a bit longer, I mean, it feels too soon.'

'We'll take it slowly. No need to rush. Just gradually reduce. You'll be OK. It's normal practice. Otherwise people just switch from alcohol tranquilisers—still end up dependent on a chemical. Some would argue that it is less damaging, and they're probably right but I want you to get free of the chemical crutch, Andy. It may take a while but in the long run you'll be better for it.'

Andy took a deep breath. He really had felt those tablets had helped. 'You wouldn't swap them for anti-depressants?'

'Why, is your mood low?'

'Not really, but I feel very tired.'

'That can be a reaction. And, of course, there's a lot going on for you. Emotion burns up energy. How are you sleeping?'

'Not too good still.'

'Hang in there, it'll settle down.'

'OK, but I really feel unsure about cutting back on what you're giving me.'

'Well, as I say, we take it slowly. Reduce by a tablet and then stay at that reduced level for two or three days, and then reduce again. Gives you time to adjust.'

'OK. I'll give it a go.'

'I'll give you another week's supply but it will only last a week if you reduce like that. Cut out a tablet, say, tomorrow, and than again on Saturday, and down another on Tuesday and I'll see you in the evening. I don't want you back here sooner because you've used them all.'

'Could I have a few extra just in case, you know, I mean, what if it gets bad?'

'If you have the tablets you're more likely to use them and I don't want to encourage that otherwise we'll be sitting here next week, you'll still be on the same dose and you'll be at more risk of having developed an addictive feel for them. That really isn't an option. If you were still in hospital they would probably have cut you back even faster. I know that's a more contained environment, you're more at risk at home, more opportunity to drink, but we've got to wean you off and start you learning to live without the chemical support.'

'I'll try. I'm seeing the alcohol people Friday so they may have some ideas. I'm not looking forward to reducing, though. It hasn't been easy. I feel I need a little longer, I really do.'

Dr Shira nodded, but she knew from experience how easy it was for the tranquillisers to be continued too long and then, well, if the patient began to drink again then there was a greater complication. No, she wanted to see how he could manage coming off them. She knew that if necessary they could review it, but she wanted Andy to try to reduce. Then he would be able to face up to himself and his life without relying on some chemical affecting his perception and experience. She understood his wanting a bit of a safety net—having a few spare tablets—but she also knew from experience that people were likely to take them. She recognised that Andy had experienced some awful things, and trying to obscure them through substance use—illegal, legal or prescribed—was not a final or lasting solution. That was her view. It was tough. She knew it was tough, but she also knew that sometimes that was how it had to be. She didn't want to stereotype Andy. She knew all drinkers were individuals and it was unhelpful to group them all together. Andy was trying, and he had a lot to cope with, emotionally and psychologically, but he had to start doing this without chemicals, or at least, find out if he could.

What she did not fully appreciate was that some people who have had long-term alcohol use, and indeed tranquiliser use, can be left with a damaged central nervous system that is highly reactive and sensitive to stimulation and therefore over stimulation, leading to powerful symptoms of anxiety and of feeling overwhelmed and out of control. Yes, it is important to avoid establishing a tranquiliser addiction, but there is going to be a group of people who are left unable to maintain stability because of the damage done and the symptoms that therefore could continue to arise.

'I appreciate what you say, Andy, but given your situation—you have a supportive girlfriend, a counsellor, and now the alcohol team—and they may be able to offer other forms of support, I think they run a group one evening—let's give that all a go and see if together, along with your own motivation, you can break free of the alcohol habit. You also need to know I have the results of the liver function test they ran at the hospital. Did they mention that to you?'

'They said that there was some damage but that if I keep off the alcohol it would recover. They said it wasn't too bad, though.'

'Yes, it's functioning is a little impaired so there is some damage. You need to keep off the alcohol and it will hopefully repair itself.' Dr Shira went on to describe the various stages of liver damage, mentioning the fatty liver stage which was reversible and then the more serious forming of scar tissue—cirrhosis. She then explained how this damage was then permanent and how it could then lead to developing liver cancer in some people.

Andy heard what the doctor was saying, and he was still anxious about the reduction.

'So I should see you again on Tuesday?'

'Yes.'

'And I'm back at work as of today and that was OK. Taking it steady. I'm not doing much driving, nothing long distance. Doing more work around the warehouse. I need to occupy myself.'

'Sure. But take care. You know what feels best. It's about finding a balance. You need to be occupied but don't overdo it.'

'Yeah, OK. So, I make the appointment when I go out again, yes?'

'Yes. Speak to the receptionist on the way out. Here's your prescription. Now, as I say, try and keep to the reduction regime, drop a tablet every two or three days and we'll see how you are getting on next week.'

'Thanks, doctor, I'll give it a go.'

Andy left holding the prescription in his pocket. This was going to be the real test. He'd had the security of the medication these last few days and it had helped, he felt it was cushioning him. Now he had to begin the process of reducing down. He had a grim expression on his face as he approached the reception area to book in for his next appointment. He actually made it for Tuesday morning. He rationalised that if he did that he'd have a few more tablets in reserve. He felt pleased with that piece of quick thinking. He'd always be able to say he couldn't get an appointment in the evening.

* * * *

Andy had described to Graham what had happened. It had taken him most of the first half of the counselling session. Graham had listened and voiced his shock and concern.

'So, things really were touch and go in hospital?'

'Seems like it. Good job Julie came back. I could have choked. I haven't really thought about that so much what with everything else. But actually, well, it could have all, hmm, could have all ended there on the sofa. Pardon the pun but that is a sobering thought that.'

Graham nodded his head, 'in every sense of the word'.

They both lapsed into silence. Somehow the recognition of the risk of choking demanded it. 'I guess I'm lucky, though I do wonder. Feels like I've got a lot to battle with, and without alcohol or medication.'

'You're not on medication then?'

'Well, yes I am, but having to reduce. Didn't have one today at lunch-time. Feeling a bit more on edge now than usual though the doctor says it will settle down, I just have to adjust, stabilise I think she said.'

'Yes, so more edgy at the moment and hoping it will stabilise a bit as time goes on.'

'And I'm still so tired, and I keep eating sweet things. I'm trying to keep away from sugary, sweet drinks, but it's not easy. I'm getting through so much coffee at the moment. And I'm so hungry, I mean generally hungry. I've always eaten but now I realise that maybe I didn't have as much appetite as I thought I did.'

'It happens. People get their appetite back and they crave sweet things. Some people binge on carbohydrates as well, bread, potatoes, stuff like that.'

'Yeah, that's me. Oh, yes, and I wanted to mention something that happened, when was it, Friday or was it Saturday …, Friday, I think. Anyway, I had this strange dream, but it felt real, felt I was drinking and woke up feeling like I'd been drinking.'

Graham nodded. 'Sounds like a drinking dream—really clear, lucid, hard to believe it didn't happen?'

Andy nodded.

'And, what, it felt like you had the taste in your mouth, maybe even a few physical symptoms of drinking?'

'You got it.'

'They can happen. Some kind of mental process when you are asleep. I don't know what exactly, but drinking is a very intense experience and the memory of that experience is stored somewhere in the brain. I sometimes think it's like the brain reliving the experience but you experience it as a dream, however, the brain seems to also introduce a few symptoms as well, kind of increases the reality.'

'I got up and felt wobbly, like I'd had a few, and I could have been convinced that I had been drinking, though I knew I hadn't. But it was weird. It really did feel real.'

Graham nodded, 'Yes, very clear, very real, quite disorientating. Can trigger people to drink thinking they've started so they'll carry on, or feel so anxious from the experience that they drink on that.'

'I can believe that. Leaves you thinking differently. Hard to define exactly but you know it's different.'

'So, watch out for them. Don't be fooled by them.'

'No, at least I can anticipate what might happen. What is it with alcohol?'

'It's a powerful, mind-altering substance.'

'But not everyone has problems.'

'That's right.'

Andy sat staring into space. His mind had switched off as the tiredness had swept over him again. He closed his eyes but realised he could so easily drift off. He opened them again and looked across at Graham.

'Tired?'

'Yeah.' He paused. He suddenly didn't know what to say. He felt quite blank. He looked towards the window wondering what to do. He yawned and his eyes filled with tears.

'What's tiring you, Andy?'

'Life. Everything. I don't know. Feel stuck again.' He paused to take a deep breath. 'Just, oh I don't know, just feel like I want to just go to sleep and wake up normal.'

'So that sounds like a really attractive idea. Go to sleep, wake up and find all is well.'

Andy nodded, stifling another yawn as he did so. 'Yeah, that sounds good.' He paused and then continued. 'Trouble is, I'm not sure I know what normal is anymore, in fact, I'm not sure that I ever did.' Again a pause. 'That's not fair. When I was with my aunt and uncle I think I kind of felt maybe a little normal, but not completely. They weren't my mother or father, they were kind of substitutes. I suppose I sort of fooled myself into thinking I was normal but, well, reality was that it wasn't normal, was it?'

Graham shook his head slowly, wondering to himself where this was leading and why it had arisen at this time. But he trusted his clients' inner processes. Experience had shown him that if the therapeutic relationship is warm, accepting and trustworthy, then clients will risk exposing a little more of themselves. It always seemed to him that there was a kind of unconscious process at work, enabling people to become more aware of themselves, as if elements within their natures that had previously been in a sense just over the horizon would then emerge into awareness.

'Like the normal you experienced wasn't really normal?'

'Well, so much change and disruption and, well, I guess things settled a bit but they never really did. I was soon into drinking and, well, having problems really. Looking back it's a wonder things didn't go a lot worse. I'm sure they could have done.' As he had begun speaking Andy was very much centred in his own thoughts and experiences. But as he got to the end of his sentence his thoughts had gone back to Terry and the image was there again. He reacted, tears immediately in his eyes. 'I'm sorry, I seem to find it hard not to cry at the moment.'

'Let it out. The tears are coming because they need to come.'

'I just feel like I'm on an emotional knife edge. Just don't seem to be able to contain it. I've burst into tears at home a few times since I came out of hospital. I just feel raw, fragile, like my emotions are so close all the time. Never felt like this before. Just doesn't take much to set me off.'

No, thought Graham, but maybe this is more real. 'Lot to set you off, Andy, and the reaction is right and normal.' He wanted to reassure Andy of the OKness of what was happening—at least, that was how he saw it. Of course, he immediately questioned his response because he really needed to acknowledge Andy's frame of reference and empathise with that. Maybe it wasn't OK for Andy.

'Yeah, I guess so, yet it also doesn't feel right, but I can't help myself.'

'No, like you're powerless to stop it, just can't help it.'

Andy thought for a moment before responding. 'And it doesn't seem to ease. I mean, it does a little, but it builds up.'

'Right, OK, so it can ease a little but then there's a kind of build up?' Graham was aware of not knowing precisely what Andy was alluding to but he felt it important to stay with what he was saying.

Andy nodded. 'And it's Terry. I only have to think of him and it's there, it's happening. I can feel it.'

'It's close, he's close, the thought of Terry and the tears, the emotions, are there.' Graham spoke a little more softly, sensing the sensitivity of the moment and wishing to maintain empathy for the theme that was emerging.

'It's just as if I …, I don't know. The thought of Terry.…' Andy lapsed back into silence.

Graham did not respond, rather allowed the space to remain for Andy to be with what he was feeling. He knew that however painful it might be, these feelings were real and present and part of Andy at this time, and to some degree would continue to be so. Andy had to find his own way of making sense of them, holding them, accepting them—different words with their own emphasis and yet none seemed to quite capture this process.

Andy had closed his eyes and was holding a hand across his eyes. His body shook as the tears flowed. It was the thought of what Terry must have been feeling. 'He must have been so desperate and I wasn't there for him. He was all alone, all alone.'

Graham responded by acknowledging what Andy had said. 'Yes, feeling that he was desperate and alone, and that you weren't there.'

'I know I could have stopped him, but I didn't know. I thought he was OK, but he was lying there, dead. I didn't know.' Another surge of emotion and for Andy it felt like his whole body was racked with pain. He hurt, Oh God how he hurt. Terry, his big brother, whom he had idolised in his life, who had helped him survive the childhood horror in many ways just by being there as much as anything, was now gone. Gone. The thought hit Andy with a new depth. Gone. He was alone now. He'd never hear him speak, see that wicked smile on his face that indicated that trouble was on the way, that attitude to life that was basically one of cynicism and live for the day. Live for the day. There's a thought. Another surge of emotion and hurt made him shudder.

'No, you didn't know.'

Graham had moved over and placed a hand on Andy's shoulder. Funny, it reminded him that Terry used to do that. When he was struggling with something, Terry would put his right hand on his left shoulder, always said, 'it's OK, bruv, we've seen the worst, things can only get better'. But he hadn't said it for quite a while, and he'd never say it again. He screwed his eyes a little tighter once more, taking a deep breath. He held it for a short while, regaining some control before letting it out slowly. He swallowed. The tears began to ease.

'It wasn't to be, was it?'

Graham had moved back into his chair, 'that's how it seems.'

'No. I still feel I should have been there, done something, been able to, I don't know, see it coming, but, well … I just can't get the thought out of my head that I should have been there.'

'Mmm, and that's hard to bear, the thought that you should have been there.' Graham for some reason remembered what Andy had said a few sessions back about wanting to change for his mother's and Terry's sake, and of needed to change for himself so he could help Terry. Now there was no Terry to help. That aspect of his motivation was no longer there. He kept his thoughts to himself as he listened to Terry's response.

'If he'd only hung the phone up. I might have called back or something and got through. I know if I'd called back and it had rang but had not been answered, well, I think I would have been worried enough to go over there.'

'You'd have gone over?'

'I think so. I think so. Oh, I don't know, maybe I wouldn't. Maybe I'd have just thought to leave him to sleep it off. I don't know, I just don't know.'

'No, who knows what you might have done. Part of you feels you would have gone over, but then at the same time you're not sure. You're just not sure.'

Andy was wiping his eyes. 'No.' He breathed out heavily as he spoke. 'No, I don't know.' He shook his head. 'It's that thought of him feeling that desperate, but then maybe he was so affected by the alcohol that it wasn't so … oh I don't know.' Andy looked over towards the window. He was too confused in his own mind. What Terry had been feeling, he didn't know. Was it the past, or was it something else that had happened? Now he would never know. He hadn't left a note or anything, maybe he didn't want to say anything, but maybe it was that the alcohol had put him in a place in himself where he wasn't thinking about anyone else. That thought hurt Andy. He wanted to think that somehow Terry had thought about him. He remembered that last, brief exchange on the phone. He'd felt angry at Terry, phoning him again in the middle of the night. Maybe he shouldn't have been angry, but he had been. He took another deep breath and sighed.

'Last two words he said to me, 'fuck off.' Andy was shaking his head. 'We came through so much together, but when he needed me I rejected him and those are the words I'm left with. I wish …' He stopped because he didn't know what he wished, other than that things had been different.

'You wish …?' Graham sought to help Andy say a little more if he wanted to.

'I … I guess part of me wishes I could have said goodbye, but I know I don't want to say goodbye, I don't want it all to have happened, I want to wake up from this nightmare and know that he's still there, yes, being an arsehole some of the time, he could be that. But he was a sensitive guy, he really was, and I know what happened to mum affected him a great deal, probably more than me, I don't know. What a waste, what a waste of a life. Messed up before he really had a chance. Same with me, but I have things I want to live for. I want to be with Julie, I want a future, I want a family …' As he spoke those last words his concern about struggling to get an erection since Terry's death came back to his mind. It wasn't something he wanted to talk about, though it was on his mind. It seemed to have got worse, seemed to be making him more anxious.

'You look like that's really important to you.' Graham was also aware that there was a look of concern on Andy's face, though he wasn't sure why it was there.

'It is—if it ever happens.'

'If it ever happens?'

'Well, oh, I wasn't going to talk about it, it's kind of difficult.'

'Sometimes the difficult things are important to talk about.'

'Well, it's since, you know, what happened to Terry, I've not, well, I mean, I've struggled to get an erection.'

'That's why talking about starting a family sounded so serious, and you looked concerned.'

'Well, I suppose it'll be OK again, but not at the moment.'

'Maybe we can explore this further, make sense of what may have happened. It sounds like it is something new and it seemed to have started around the time of Terry's death.'

'After.'

'After? You're sure?'

Andy nodded. 'Yes, the last time it was OK was on the night that Terry … oh shit …'

'What's the matter, Andy?'

'We made love the night Terry died. But it was more than that. It happened after Terry had come off the phone. You don't suppose …?'

'Suppose?'

'Oh no,' Andy had closed his eyes, 'we must have been making love when Terry was dying.' Andy opened his eyes again and looked straight into Graham's eyes, it was a deep and searching look, yet it seemed so full of pain and confusion.

'I may have been getting an erection at the same time that he died—it's possible if he died shortly after he called. You don't think …?'

'… that there might be a link?'

Andy nodded.

'Does it feel that way to you?' Graham knew that what mattered was the meaning attached to the event in Andy's mind. If the guilt over what happened, at not having been there for Terry had got itself in some way attached or connected to his own sexual arousal, it was possible that it was contributing to the difficult Andy was now experiencing.

'We were having sex and Terry was dying, and I should have been….' A deep breath and a sigh. 'I should have been there.'

Graham stayed with Andy, wanting to help him explore his own meanings. He communicated his empathy for what Andy was experiencing and communicating. 'You feel that you should have been with Terry and not be having sex with Julie?'

Andy could feel himself going suddenly very quiet. He felt quite limp, all over his body. He took another deep breath and made to say something, but didn't know what to say. He stayed silent.

Graham maintained the silence, allowing his last empathic response to remain—or so it felt to him—very present in the room and in his therapeutic relationship with Andy. Time passed and Graham continued to wait, maintaining his full attention on Andy who had now slumped back in the chair.

'But I didn't know, did I?'

'No, you didn't know.'

'But I should have known.'

'That's how it has left you feeling, that you should have known.'

Andy shook his head and tightened his jaw. His breathing began to get a little faster. He sighed and looked into Graham's eyes. 'What a mess, what a bloody mess.' He felt like he had nothing to say. It was like everything was too much, it was too big, affecting too much of him.

'Feels like a bloody mess.'

Andy sniffed and swallowed. 'I feel absolutely drained. Absolutely wiped out.'

'Drained, wiped out …'

'… yeah. It's like …' Andy tried to find the words but couldn't and actually hadn't really tried, he just didn't have the energy or the real urgency to do so. He just continued to sit back in the chair, like he'd been thrown into it and left, at some level and in some way shocked and shattered. There was a kind of numbness in his body and in his head, as if he'd been anaesthetised, even though he was awake.

'It's like?' Graham sought to enable Andy to describe what was happening for him a little more, to enable him to perhaps connect a little more deeply with what he was experiencing.

Andy shook his head. 'I can't describe it, but it's like I've been flattened by it, all the energy knocked out of me.'

'So in making this connection, in thinking about what happened—having sex at the time that Terry may have been dying—it leaves you feeling flattened and drained of energy.'

Andy stared ahead. He didn't feel he had the energy to even nod his head. It wasn't a tired feeling. He was alert but just, well, numb. He stayed sitting, staring ahead of him, seeing, but not seeing. He wasn't even really thinking any more. Like all the power had been switched off and he'd just been left looking out but with nothing going on inside himself. It was like something had decided he should shut down and he had no control over that decision. But he wasn't thinking that, he wasn't thinking, just staring, just staring into a kind of invisible distance.

Graham could see that Andy was engaged with some inner experience. His eyes were fixed, almost trance-like. His breathing seemed shallow and he looked absolutely shattered by it all. He felt strongly that this was how, for whatever reason, Andy needed to be at this moment and he didn't want to disturb it. There was a process occurring and although he didn't understand it, he felt he could trust it. He believed that everyone did have psychological processes that, in essence, were trustworthy and which worked for the benefit of the individual. For whatever reason Andy looked as though his system had kind of shut down. The thought struck him that perhaps his whole psychological system was, in this moment, manifesting the impotence that had developed out of the events of that fateful night. In a sense, Graham felt that was good, at least it was coming out and maybe would pass if Andy could in some way accept his powerlessness.

Graham wasn't sure quite what to say. He didn't want to introduce anything, or say something that might reinforce what Andy was thinking or the meanings that Andy had and was attaching to those events. He had to accept Andy as he was at this moment, how he needed to be, whether consciously or unconsciously. So he stayed silent and still but continued to put maximum effort into being open to his own inner experience and to his outer experience of Andy, sitting there, still staring blankly ahead of him.

Andy blinked a few times. He was coming out of the experience, out of the numbness. He looked at Graham though he continued to say nothing. What am I doing here, he thought to himself? What is going on? Can you really help me? Can anyone help me? What does help even mean? He didn't know, he had no answers. But he knew that he was glad that there was someone listening, trying to help him make sense of everything. He didn't understand this process, but he didn't want to face all this on his own. On his own. He felt suddenly very much on his own, or rather, it was like the feelings associated with it began to emerge a little more clearly.

Even when his mother had died they'd had each other. His mind had gone back over the years.

Graham noticed that Andy had suddenly taking a deep breath. He anticipated that he might move or say something. But Andy remained quiet. His thoughts now very much with his mother. And yet he felt strangely calm as he re ran in his head the experience of her death. And it was a re-running and it felt like he did have control, it was strange, different. It was like he could watch it but without feeling…., well, just watching it, watching the scene unfold. He frowned though wasn't really aware that he was frowning.

Graham noted the change in Andy's facial expression. He spoke softly, responding to the body language, 'something making you frown …'

Andy took a deep breath and nodded slowly. He didn't known how to describe what he was experiencing, but it was different. It was like he could see it through different eyes. No, that was crazy, it had to be through his eyes, and yet it was different. He couldn't make sense of it and yet it seemed important to try. He knew he had to try and say something about what he was experiencing.

'It's like I'm seeing my mother dying but through a different pair of eyes. They're mine, but they're different.'

'Like she's suddenly being seen but, what, from a different perspective?'

'Sort of, but not quite. It's more like I'm seeing it but not reacting the way I normally do. It's like I'm seeing it but not living out the same reaction.'

'So it looks the same but your reaction is different?'

Andy nodded. He deliberately brought himself out of what was happening for him, stopped the memory tape running. He suddenly realised he'd never really been able to do that before, had never felt he was really in control.

'It's like I can switch it on and off, and I've never been able to do that. It has always simply just been there and stayed with me till it faded—or I had drunk enough to get away from it, I guess.'

Graham nodded. He felt good that something had shifted and, as was so often the case in his experience, he didn't have a clue as to exactly what had enabled this to happen at this time, and in this way. But it was clearly significant for Andy.

'So it's a new experience, feeling able to switch it on but more importantly perhaps switch it off, without using alcohol.'

Andy was nodding. It felt good somehow to hear that because, yes, that was how it was. It felt good to hear your own inner experience being heard, validated and he sensed accepted by someone else, by Graham.

'It's like I feel I've been sort of unburdened, but I really don't understand why, what happened. Why now?'

Graham smiled gently, 'we can't always know why, but we can explore it further. Why now? Why this feeling of being unburdened?'

'It's like …, this will sound weird, but it's like I've kind of given myself permission to put it down, let it go in some way. And yet I know that I can't. The experience is very much part of me, but it's like, what did you say? Yeah, it's like I've got a new perspective. But it's hard to really describe what that is. I just know I'm feeling different somehow.'

'Yeah, hard to describe what it is but a sense of feeling unburdened is very present, very immediate.'

Andy nodded, a little more energetically. 'It really does feel like something has shifted, like I've sort of moved on. Maybe I've laid something to rest.' He paused. 'What a thing to say, but it's like that, and I'm back to thinking about Terry and it's like there's a real contrast between how I feel about that and yet there seems to be a connection, and yet they're separate as well?' He shook his head. 'It's hard to get my head around all of this.'

'So, let me check out I'm hearing you right. It feels like something has shifted, as if you have moved on in some way, and you used the phrase 'laid something to rest'. That sounds really important.' Graham had been struck by a sense of significance as Andy had said that. He hadn't planned to stop at this point in his checking out, but Andy was responding.

'Maybe I've laid her to rest in some way. I was thinking about her at the funeral and in a strange kind of way I think maybe I was finally laying her to rest as well as Terry, although I haven't done that with Terry, not inside myself.'

'So it's like at Terry's funeral you feel like you laid your mother to rest kind of psychologically but for Terry, his body has been laid to rest but your own inner experience of him hasn't. Is that right? Am I catching it right?'

Andy was nodding, 'yes, like I've kind of finally buried mum even though physically we were burying Terry. Well, I mean, not literally because it was at the crematorium, but ..., well, that's how it seems.'

'The psychological process is one of burying, laying to rest, laying your mother to rest and it seems laying something in you to rest that is/was connected to the experience of her death and loss.'

'Hearing you say that, I feel calm and that's unusual, that's new. Could I really have been carrying her—whatever that means—all these years? More to the point, have I now got to carry Terry in the same way?'

'That's quite a thought, will I have to carry Terry in myself for so many years like I did my mother?'

'I actually want to say 'no', and that feels quite strong, and yet I know that I'm not there at the moment.'

'My guess is that you still have a lot of grieving to do for Terry but perhaps the grieving is over for your mother? Would that be fair?'

Andy smiled as he nodded in response. That really did sound fair. 'Hmm, yeah, I think you're right.'

Graham felt himself thinking, and what about your father, but that was his own idea and he was not at all convinced it was appropriate to say it. The thought came to him just as he experienced an uncontrollable urge to cough. He didn't often do that, and immediately wondered what the connection was. Should he voice it? Was it relevant? He decided to trust his own process. 'Sorry about that. I feel I want to say what just happened for me then, I suddenly wondered about your father and where he was in all of this, and promptly found myself unable to resist coughing. And I feel reluctant to say it because it takes your attention away from what you have been saying.'

'He's forgotten. No, he really is forgotten. He's very much in the past. I very occasionally wonder how it might have been if he'd been different or stayed alive, but actually I don't dwell on it. That's gone, he's gone. No. I rather think more of him around blaming him for my mother's death. Yes, but, no, it's gone. I don't need to go there.'

'OK, nothing of him to cough up?' Why am I pushing this, Graham thought to himself, Andy's said it's gone. I'm not hearing him, I'm not accepting him. I need to take this to supervision.

Andy shrugged and pulled a face. 'No. He was a bastard. He deserved to die. He fucked up my life, and he fucked up Terry's.' He felt a surge of anger as he mentioned Terry's name. 'Yes, he was the one to blame for Terry's death. It wouldn't have happened if it hadn't been for what my father did. He's to blame, isn't he? Not me. I was a victim as well. He's the one to blame, he robbed me/us of our mother, and he's robbed me of my brother. Yeah,' he looked into Grahams eyes, 'that's where the blame lies. It isn't my fault, not really, not deep down. I mean, I was powerless when it happened, I couldn't do anything. What could I do? I mean, for fuck's sake, I was a child. Bastard. Honestly, if he was still alive you know, I'd want to kill him, particularly after what happened to Terry. I'd take him out, and I don't think I'd hesitate so I'm glad he's dead. He was never really a father to either of us, just, well, and this'll maybe sound hard, maybe I've lost some memories, but he was just some bloke who gave us crap. He was never a father—don't know why I call him that really. The truth is I never had a father. Maybe that's my problem, no male role model—other than Terry, I guess. And Terry got messed up.'

'So, the man that you call your father, he was the one that caused it all, he's the one to blame?'

'Yes, and you know I hesitate as well because he must have had his reasons to behave like he did, however warped they might have been. I know nothing of his past, his background. Strange that, no grandparents. Don't know what happened. Just don't know. But maybe things had happened to him, for him, but it was what he did that fucked our family up. And I'm the one that's left.' He shook his head.

'Like everything that's happened, the whole chain of events, brings us/you to this point where you're the only one left.'

'No wonder I've been struggling and still do.' He blew out his breath. 'This has been quite a session, Graham, and I do feel a lot calmer. Don't know how long it will last, but something has changed, is different, no doubt about that.'

'I'm pleased. I think you're right. Something has happened and time will tell what effect that is going to have.'

'Yeah. OK. Look, did I mention I'm seeing someone tomorrow from the alcohol team?'

'I think you did, you know I can't remember. As a result of what happened last week?'

'Yes, they referred me for some help and support. I guess I'll go along. I feel different, tempted to say I don't need it, but …'

'See what they can offer. It's early days. That isn't to say that things won't be OK. You're doing great. You're having to face up to so much and you are doing that and slowly moving on. But, yes, maybe they can offer you something more specific around the alcohol use and then we can concentrate on the therapy.'

'That feels good, and it feels right as well. We don't talk so much about the alcohol and this session, well, I don't think it's come up at all. I do need to talk about that and maybe work with them in the way that we started, but there are other things I need to talk about.'

'Do you want me to talk to them, I mean, suppose they wanted to contact me to discuss what I'm offering and how to fit that in with what they can offer. How would that be?'

'I'm OK with that.'

'How much detail?'

'It's OK. Wouldn't have said that when I first came. No, let them know what's happening, what's come up. It's OK. It's really OK.'

'OK, but if you change your mind, please let me know. I want you to feel in control of this process. OK?'

'Sure, thanks. I appreciate it. So, we'll see what's happening next time. Next Monday's a Bank Holiday, isn't it?'

'Yes, so do you want an appointment later in the week, or let it run to the following Monday.'

'The following Monday, that'll be fine. Usual time?'

'Sure, that's no problem.'

The session drew to a close and Andy left, still feeling that calmness. Yes, he was still upset about Terry, but he could see that the chain of events weren't his responsibility, he'd been powerless. He still felt he could have done something more for Terry, but that had eased a little as well. He headed home. Maybe things were going to be OK. He guessed there would still be bad days, bad times, but he was hopeful, yes, hopeful. He realised he hadn't really felt that way for the longest while ...

* * * *

The next day Andy arrived at the Community Alcohol Team for his appointment. He was asked to wait for a few minutes. He'd arrived a little early. He was nervous but not as uncertain as he had been when he had first been to see Graham. After all, he was a bit more experienced now as a client. And he was still dry, and that felt good. He'd had no reaction from the previous days counselling session. He had reduced the tablets, and this was his second day of reducing and so far he was OK. He'd cut out one of the lunch-time ones. He planned to discuss this with the person who was going to assess him. Her name was Cynthia.

'Hello, you must be Andy, is that right?'

'Yes.'

'Hi, I'm Cynthia. Can I get you a tea or a coffee?'

'Er, no thanks.' Andy hadn't expected that.

'Sure?'

'Well, OK, yes, coffee, two sugars.'

'White?'

'Yes please. Thanks.'

'OK, I'll organise that. Come through and I'll take you to the counselling room.'

Andy followed her along the corridor. It was all a bit drab, needed a coat of paint. He went into the room that Cynthia opened the door into. 'Have a seat. Either. I'll go and get your coffee.'

Andy went in and sat down. He looked around. It was more of an office than a counselling room. He guessed it was used for different things. There were books on a shelf, computer on a desk in the corner, posters on the walls including one of a body which had labels on it saying what alcohol damaged. As he looked it over he realised that there didn't seem much that wasn't affected. That felt a bit grim. It was certainly quite different to Graham's counselling room.

He was pulled out of his reading when Cynthia came in and handed him a mug of hot coffee. 'There you are. So, glad you made it. Not every one does!'

'No, I can imagine. I guess I'd have been like that a few weeks or months back but, well, you'll have heard from the hospital no doubt.'

'Yes. Sounds like it was a real difficult time, you must have drunk a great deal.'

Andy nodded.

'OK, well, we need to do an assessment and then we can look at what services will be most helpful for you, assuming you want to use anything that we can offer here. And, of course, we can give you details of other services as well, in case that may be more appropriate.'

'Well yes, I mean, I'm not sure what I want. I'm having counselling and that's really helpful.'

'Specific for alcohol?'

'No, more general really, but we talk about the alcohol as well, though not always. We talk more about the past and how it affected me and things that are going on in the present. I wasn't sure about it at first, but now I can see how it is helping. I mean, I'm dry, have been since I came out, and that's how I want to stay, at least for a while. That's what I've been advised, anyway.'

'OK, that sounds reasonable. Well, I've got a few forms to get through with you. Sorry about that but we do need to complete them.'

'That's OK.'

'Right, well, I've got your name, address, telephone. Got a mobile?'

'Andy nodded and gave her the number.

'Just in case we need to contact you and you're out. So is it OK to phone home?'

'Sure, my girlfriend knows I'm here.'

Cynthia went through their confidentiality policy and showed Andy a sheet indicating who he gave them permission to talk to in order co-ordinate his treatment. 'And we can talk to your counsellor?'

'Sure, we discussed it yesterday.' Andy gave them Graham's full name and phone number. He also said it was OK to talk to his GP. He signed it, not feeling unduly concerned, instead feeling quite good that people would be talking to each other to help him.

'So what is your drinking history. Can you remember when you first started?'

Andy went over his past and how his drinking had developed. How it hadn't seemed a problem but that now he realised that it had become so, hence his trying to do something about it.

'Any other substances?'

'Not much, odd joint now and then, but haven't for a while. Used to but no. Nothing really significant.'

'Not tempted to take it up again?'

'No, to be honest I haven't really thought about it. The alcohol's enough to deal with.'

'Sure. OK.' Cynthia then asked about his family background. Andy felt OK about describing his past—the deaths of his parents, the being brought up by his aunt and uncle and how his life had gone from their. He found it hard talking about Terry and about what had happened to him. He was quite emotional when he mentioned how Terry had died.

'That's a terrible thing to have to cope with. And yet you're managing to stay dry, and that's a real achievement.'

'It doesn't always feel like that. And I'm on medication though the doctor has asked me to start reducing.' Andy described what he was taking and his conversation with Dr Shira.

'Well, we'd advise you to reduce slowly, and take out tablets at the times of day that you feel most confident in being able to cope with. The lunch time tablet is a good place to start. People often need something in the morning to calm themselves down for the day, and in the evening to relax them to sleep. Take it slowly, but try to maintain the momentum of reducing.'

'OK. It's a worry because I'm really not sure how I'll be without them.'

'Yes, especially, as you say, when you haven't really had many days without having alcohol in your system which itself will have had a suppressing effect.'

'What will help me with it?'

'Well, you can keep in touch with us. You can phone through if it's difficult and talk it through with someone. That can help. But I'll come on to what we can offer in a moment. I've got to get the assessment forms completed.'

'OK. What's next?'

'History of mental health problems, or substance misuse problems in the family?'

'Well, I told you about my father his drinking and suicide. Apart from that no, not really, except for Terry, of course. He always drank more than me. But no mental health problems.'

Cynthia had noted down Andy's father's suicide and alcohol use. She knew that where a parent had an alcohol problem then it was more likely that the children would be at greater risk of problems—not necessarily alcohol—later in life. It was so disruptive and generated so much uncertainty and chaos, leaving children struggling a understand boundaries and to really feel secure in themselves. So given what had happened to Andy and Terry she quite understood why there lives had become difficult, and why alcohol had become such a feature for both of them and, in Terry's case, tragically so.

'Working?'

Andy described his job. There were lots of other questions as well, and a whole series that were what she called a *Risk Assessment*. Andy answered as best he could. No, he didn't feel suicidal, though at times he had wondered. No, he had no plans or intention. Yes, his childhood had been abusive, physically and verbally. No, he hadn't been abused sexually.

'OK, well, that's it. Thanks for that. We would normally write to your GP to let her know that you have attended and to let her know what we plan to do. You're OK with that?' Cynthia liked to double check. Some clients could be quite anxious when they arrived and she was never sure exactly how much they took in.

'Sure, and please talk to Graham. He said something about maybe focusing with me on the therapeutic stuff and leave you to focus on the alcohol. Is that possible?'

Cynthia nodded. 'It's not unusual. Some people get a bit precious thinking you should only see one person, but so long as there is a clear differentiation between what is being worked on and, besides, we do focus more on the actual pattern of alcohol use. The longer term, therapeutic interventions we simply don't offer, we are not funded for it. We do have a support group which is for anyone really, we just ask that they do not drink before attending. We also have a relapse prevention group which is for people who are not drinking and trying to remain abstinent. Some people also go to AA.'

'Yes, I think I'd rather stick with what you have to offer. What's relapse prevention?'

'Well, it's a process of helping people understand why they drink and what cues exist that might trigger them back into drinking again. For some people it is quite obvious why they drink, but it can be quite subtle too. From what you've told me, you have clear underlying reasons to drink, but through life experience you may have picked up a few more reasons as well and it is important to identify these.'

'How do you mean?'

'Well, some people might associate drinking with particular feelings, or being with certain people, or going to particular places. One big area is where people try to prove to themselves that they are OK by going into risky and tempting situations. That's rarely a good idea, but it's good to plan how to deal with that kind of temptation. Also to think about what kinds of situation in your life are likely to put you at risk. The friend turning up on the door step with a bottle. The party that you want to go to but you know there will be lots of alcohol freely available. It's important to plan for these things, gives you a better chance and, over time, you slowly adapt more and more to an alcohol-free lifestyle, if that's what you want.'

'Will I have to not drink, well, sort of forever? That's not what I was planning.'

'Not everyone has to never have another drink, but some people do find this necessary. The difficulty for some people is that once they start again it just gradually increases until they are back where they were, at least in terms of the frequency and quantity being consumed.' Cynthia believed in being up front about things. Best for people to know the facts and then they could make more informed choices.

'Hmm. Well I don't want that. If I could have a couple of pints, say, on a Friday and Saturday night, and maybe the odd can in the week, that would be fine. Can I do that?'

'Maybe, but to be perfectly honest I don't know. You are accustomed to heavy drinking. But everyone's unique and individual on this one. It isn't like you have an ingrained habit of continually drinking yourself into oblivion every night, although there may have been occasions when this has happened.'

'Yeah, but doing that consistently was more my brother Terry's style. Though when I was in the pub drinking it was heavy.'

'Pubs you will associate with heavy drinking. You'll need to think through about going into pubs, perhaps, and if you do, certainly plan what it is you'll drink—and how you might handle the reaction of people you know. That's not always easy, however much you might think you'll be OK.'

'Seems like a lot to think about. So when does this group run?'

'We have one on a Wednesday evening and another on a Friday morning. I guess the Wednesday one will be the easiest for you to attend, if that is what you would like.'

'How long for?'

'Two hours. May seem a long time but there are usually twelve to fifteen people there and it doesn't give everyone a great deal of time. I facilitate it with one of my colleagues. There are spaces if you want to join. We do ask that people commit themselves so it isn't a case of people coming and going all the time, though we also know that people may have to address other commitments sometimes. So we try to be flexible and negotiate what will be most helpful.'

'I sometimes work late, if there is a late delivery, but I can probably talk to my boss to avoid Wednesdays. And everyone who attends isn't drinking?'

'Yes. We do occasionally random breathalyse people just to be sure. It's not fair on those who are trying to remain abstinent to be in a room with people who purport the same but actually have alcohol in their blood—and their brains.'

'That sounds good. I'd like that. What else?'

'Well, we'd want you to see someone one-to-one—we call it keyworking. And that person will not only give you regular contact to discuss how things are going, offer support and encouragement, but will also co-ordinate what you are being provided with as far as treatment is concerned. They will also liaise with your GP if that is necessary and with your counsellor.'

'So who would that be?'

'Not sure. We have an allocation meeting once a week where we review the people who have been assessed and then we decide.'

'OK. So it might not be you?'

'Maybe, maybe not.'

'I'd somehow feel comfortable if it was you, I feel I've sort of got to know you even though I know nothing about you.' Andy smiled.

'Yes, it's all a bit one way, isn't it. I guess you've got used to that with the counselling?'

'Yes'.

'There are also some telephone help lines—I can give you a list.' Cynthia picked one off the shelf and handed it to Andy. 'Some are twenty-four hours. Call them anytime—the people are trained and will help to get you through whatever is happening.'

'OK. Thanks for that. I hope I don't need it, but …'

'Yes, keep it close to the phone, or put some of the numbers on your mobile, save you hunting around for the list in a desperate moment. Time can be of the essence, can be the difference between picking up the phone and picking up a drink.'

The session moved on to a more in-depth discussion around the reduction regime for the tranquilisers Andy was taking. They would liaise with Dr Shira. 'We have people in some of the surgeries, but not at hers, unfortunately, although that may change. So we see people on her list here.

'Do you have evening appointments?'

'We have a few but that's going to be difficult. There's a wait at the moment. We'll need to discuss that. There's no way you could get to a late afternoon appointment?'

'What time?'

'Four o-clock. We generally close at five.'

How often?'

'Weekly, fortnightly, depends what you feel will be most helpful.'

'And the group, what time is that?'

'Starts at six-thirty in the evening.'

'What about before the group?'

'Maybe, depends who's available. Let me discuss it with my colleagues and get back to you. I'm sure we can work something out. But we will definitely put you down for the relapse prevention group. And if you can discuss the situation with your boss and let us know if he can be flexible, we'll see what we can do.'

The session drew to a close, the time had gone by quickly. The place, although it was drab, did feel welcoming. He could see the sense of the group. He felt sure he could learn something useful from that. He left feeling a little more positive—not that he had arrived feeling negative. But he was still concerned about reducing the medication, but at least he could phone them for a chat, and there was Dr Shira as well. And Graham, of course, though not to phone. He headed home through the traffic, which was now building up, feeling that he had made some important decisions in his life. He knew he had to put the past behind him, and he knew that he was going to miss Terry terribly for a long while, perhaps for the rest of his life. But he had Julie and he smiled as he thought of her. The smile took on a more serious shape when he thought about his sexual problem. That hadn't come up in the assessment. Maybe, maybe it would be OK next time. He certainly hoped so.

*   *   *   *

'Hello, is that Graham, Andy's counsellor?'
'Hello, it is Graham, who is speaking?'
'Cynthia from the Community Alcohol Team.'
'Oh, hello, how can I help.'
'I gather Andy gave you permission to talk to us?'
'Yes, that's right.'
'He's been over for an assessment and I wanted to touch base with you before we have our allocation meeting next week as I really want to be clear what you are offering so we don't cross-over and Andy ends up getting confused by it all.'
'Sure. What are you planning to offer him?'
'Well, a relapse prevention group and general supportive keyworking sessions, and we'll liaise with his GP over medication and blood tests. We don't offer therapeutic counselling.'
'That's OK. It could have been a problem if you did—having two counsellors working therapeutically would be ethically suspect.'
'I know. We have had similar discussions with other specialist counselling services. People can have multiple issues and, well, we specialise in working with the drinking problem. They don't like to counsel people who are receiving counselling elsewhere. But we are not counsellors—our team is made up of a doctor. social workers, nurses and outreach workers. We are quite clear on our roles, though I have to say that there are times when it would be good to have someone here to do deeper, therapeutic work. But there's not the funding. It's a problem. So many clients need that deeper, longer therapeutic work.'
'No psychologist?'
'No, we have to refer into the Psychological therapies service for that, but they have a long wait and, well, it's not ideal. We'd prefer someone in our team but, again, there's no funding.'
'Hmm, can be a problem.'

'Still, we offer what we can, but so many of our clients need on-going therapeutic work as distinct from the key-working sessions. We aim to make them therapeutic, but sometimes there's that sense of someone needing something more.'

'I can well imagine, Must be frustrating when deep-seated emotional and traumatic issues arise.' Graham was aware that so often, though not always, alcohol problems were linked with other experiences in life. It wasn't just a case of changing the way you think about alcohol, or your life, and changing your drinking behaviour.'

For Graham it was more than addressing cognition and behaviour. There was the emotional element too that needed to be addressed. So much could be locked up inside a person, impacting on their development as a person. Graham was convinced that the relational experience that person had lacked or been starved of was the relational element that they most needed within the therapeutic experience. A person who was never listened to as a child would most need accurate empathy. The person who was rejected, who did not experience love, needed to feel warm, unconditional acceptance and regard from the counsellor—a kind of therapeutic love was how Graham thought of it. And the person who had been lied to, or who had been exposed to people not being open and honest with them, needed to experience genuineness and authenticity. To him it just made sense. Only as the person began to experience what he or she had lacked could they begin to experience adjustment to their sense of self as a result of this new experience. It could go a long way towards offsetting the earlier emotional deprivation. 'Anyway, how can I help?'

'Wondered if I could check a few things out. You've already confirmed that you are working therapeutically, and Andy said that you'd expressed to him the idea of focussing more on resolving his past and present traumatic experiences and let us focus more on his alcohol use and the meanings and motivations associated with that.'

'Yes, does that seem reasonable to you? I've been seeing Andy for some months now and it feels like we have built quite a strong relationship which I am sure is going to prove helpful for a number of reasons—one of which being his not having had much of a father figure and, well, he may be able to live out issues and establish an identity less dominated by his past.'

'I think you're right. So, what model do you work to?'

'Person Centred.'

'I wish more of our clients could access that. So many of them have been messed up by relational difficulties and they need a healthy relational experience.

Yes, cognitive work can help make some changes in behaviour and thinking, but it's the deeper, ingrained emotional issues that really need addressing. That's my view, anyway. I've had a bit of training but not enough to call myself a counsellor.'

'My sentiments entirely, but you'll be offering healthy relationship as well. I think whatever the profession, so much of what is good that is offered is linked to the relational experience that the client gets. It all helps.'

'Yes, but so many of our clients are so needy, so affected and then even more messed up by the years of alcohol use as well.'

'A really demanding client group, I used to work at a non-statutory alcohol team a few years back, so I know it can be rewarding too.'

'Sure—when you feel that someone's got their lives back, maybe returning back into family life before it all falls apart, or back into work when it seemed like they were on a one track route to street drinking.'

'So, anything you need to know about Andy?'

'Just really wanted to make contact. How often do you see him, weekly? I forgot to ask Andy.'

'Yes, Monday evenings although that changed a bit recently with the difficulties he was having and the Bank Holiday. But we try to maintain a regular pattern.'

'That's good. So many people with alcohol problems have internalised chaos as a normal and natural way of being.'

'Yes, well Andy had a lot of trauma to deal with. I think he's moving on from the past but the incident with Terry's death is now the big one and only time will tell how he deals with that.'

'And he's reducing the tranquilisers?'

'Yes, so he tells me. Can you help him with that? He was quite anxious about it.'

'Yes, we've discussed it and we'll keep tabs on it. We've told him he can call us when we're open to talk about it if it becomes difficult. And we've given him a list of helpline numbers as well.'

'I'll reinforce that. He's done so well.'

'Yes, but people don't always change at the first attempt.'

'I know. Let's hope Andy can manage that. He's got support, it's how he uses it and how he adjusts to not relying on alcohol. And how he manages facing his life without the chemical barrier that kept him away from the hurt.'

'OK, well, thanks for talking. Good to know you're involved and let us know if you have any concerns. Obviously, we need to be mindful of confidentiality.'

'Yes, it could only be if something came up that really worried me, or I thought you should know about, and I'd seek Andy's permission before contacting you.'

Do you have spaces, I mean, could we refer other people to you?'

'Yes, but I am private, they would have to pay.'

'Yes, but some people prefer that. We do get some quite professional people who don't want NHS services.'

'Fine.'

'OK, well, thanks for talking. If you ever want to come over we have open mornings where we present what we do.'

'Please send me details. I'd be interested.'

The conversation drew to a close. Good, Graham thought, Andy has made contact. More support and an opportunity for him to gain greater insight into his alcohol use. For Graham it felt liberating, like he could now feel freed up to focus on the therapeutic aspects.

* * * *

It rained throughout the weekend. Andy felt low. He hadn't reduced the tablets, he'd ended up taking extra over the weekend. He'd felt anxious and depressed. He couldn't really settle. Terry was very much on his mind. They had begun clearing out some of his stuff on the Friday evening. It hadn't been easy, in fact Andy had been quite upset by it. They found so many empty bottle around his place. He found some items from the past, things he didn't know Terry had kept. Toys from childhood. One little car he remembered Terry pushing around on the floor. He found a teddy bear as well, a bit battered and moth-eaten, but recognisable. There were comics as well and a toy gun. He could remember Terry getting that for Christmas. It must have been when he was six or seven. He'd kept it. They found a small box of toys that he had somehow hung on to. Andy had sat himself down and taken everything out. Most he remembered, some he wasn't sure about.

It unsettled him and though he didn't say anything to Julie, he did take extra tablets. He realised on the Sunday that he wouldn't have enough and panicked.

'I'm just going out, won't be long, I-er need some fresh air.'

'You OK, Andy, you look kind of strange, on edge.'

'I'm OK, I just need to get out.'

'It's still raining. Where are you going?'

'Out! OK? I'm going out.' He turned and opened the door, slamming it shut behind him. He put his hands in his pockets and realised his car keys weren't there. Shit, he thought, never mind, and set off to walk to the shops. As he walked he kept thinking to himself, 'this is not a good idea', 'turn around, go home, you don't need to do this.' But his legs kept moving, taking him closer and closer to the parade of shops where the local supermarket was located that sold alcohol. He was oblivious to the rain. He was on a mission. The internal dialogue continued all the way.

He passed a number of other shops—they were all closed, it was early Sunday evening, but he didn't really notice them. He knew which shop would be open. He finally paused by the road side across the road from the supermarket. He was still debating in his head the wisdom of his actions. One small bottle of vodka, that was what he had in mind. You couldn't smell that, so they said. He'd slip a small bottle in his pocket, get him through, no-one would know. He'd be fine, wouldn't be a problem. He could handle it. Anyway, it wasn't his fault, she wouldn't give him enough tablets! What was he expected to do?

He turned around to look across the road, he'd heard the sound of a car horn. It had startled him but it wasn't anyone he knew. It had momentarily distracted him, but he returned to his train of thought. He knew what he had to do. He turned back but continued to stand there, his jaw set, his fists clenched tightly by his sides.

The thoughts were racing in his head. This is not a good idea, Andy, you know that. Fight it. You're throwing an opportunity away. You've done so well. You owe it to your mother, to Terry. You owe it to them to be a survivor. But he wasn't sure. He was going to run out of tablets, he had to have something, he'd feel better, he knew he would. Just a small drop, then he'd be OK again. He hesitated. His thoughts were still racing. Think of Julie. Don't put everything at risk. Fight it! You don't have to do this. You're not alone with this. There are people out there helping you. Part of him knew that this voice was the logical one, but … He stood a moment or two longer, the two voices in his head leaving him feeling like he was standing in the middle of a verbal battle-ground. He was oblivious to the sound of the traffic and the wind that had now whipped up as the squally shower moved overhead. The rain continued to fall, intensifying in the wind, the water was running down his face. 'Get the vodka, you'll feel better', 'turn around, go home'. He felt the conflict inside himself. He felt despair, utter despair. It was all too much. But he couldn't give in. He couldn't be like Terry, he needed to live. He needed to be strong. But he felt so wretched, and cold, and wet. The raindrops masked the tears that were pouring from his eyes.

Andy remained standing by the side of the road. He thought of Graham, of his being there to listen, and to reassure him when he had felt so awful. He needed that. He remembered the last session, how he had felt stronger, wanting a future, feeling like, yes, he could let go of his past. He did feel different. He could feel different. But he had to get by without tablets and he could feel the anxiety rising as he thought about it. He felt the mobile phone in his pocket. There were numbers he could call. Cynthia had said some of them were 24 hour helplines. He thought of Julie. He wanted it to work out. Thinking about her caused more tears to flow from his eyes. He sniffed and rubbed his nose with the back of his hand. He stepped back, there was a slight ledge above the shop behind him, he sheltered under it. The rain was less there.

What do I do? The questions echoed in his head. He felt desperate. He wanted that drink, but what would it give him? Relief? Maybe, but it wouldn't be a good feeling. He thought of Julie, of how it felt to be close to her. And then he thought of his difficulties in bed. He just wanted someone to hold him, be there for him, with him. He looked across the road. The light was on in the off-licence. The vodka would be reliable, he knew that. It would work. Would Julie be there for him if he went home? Would she understand? Would she? He closed his eyes. He wanted someone to be there for him. He wanted to feel he could trust them. And he wanted Terry. He knew that they drank together. It wasn't that. He just wanted him, to know he was there. They'd always stood together. He felt the emotions rise up again. But Terry was gone. He had to accept that. He was on his own now. His life, his choice, his future. What did *he* want?

He wanted a drink. He wanted to feel alcohol numbing his brain. He wanted to stop thinking. He wanted to sleep. But what he needed most of all, and it sent another wave of emotion up into his eyes releasing more tears, was to feel love and to feel loved. He wanted to phone Julie but he was scared she'd reject him. He wanted her to say that she loved him, but if she didn't he knew he'd feel ten times …, a hundred time worse. But she was his future. He looked across at the supermarket again. He made his choice and turned away. He needed to hear Julie's voice. He took out the phone and called her.

'Hello, Andy, where are you.'

Andy's emotions were surging through him. 'I love you.' H swallowed.

'I love you too. What's happening, where are you?'

'Outside the supermarket. I'm wet and I'm scared but I haven't had a drink.'

'I'm coming to get you.'

Andy couldn't hold back the next surge of emotion and the tears streamed down his face. 'Thank you.' Julie could hear the emotion in his voice. Andy continued, 'and I'll start walking towards you.' He ended the call. The added meaning to the words that he had spoken were not lost on him, or Julie. Andy began walking. He had systems of support and encouragement. He had people there for him. He was taking his first steps on a new path, and only time would tell where that path would lead.

Some Final Thoughts

The story ends with a choice and yet there remains uncertainty as to where Andy's path will lead him. Life is uncertain, and the outcome of trying to tackle an alcohol problem, particular with the added psychological effects of the traumas that Andy has had to face, will always be unpredictable. So much can hinge on moments of decision. And yet so often the decisions that are taken emerge out of either the traumatised concept of self that the person identifies with, or the chemical impact of the alcohol (or it's withdrawal) on psychological processes.

So what happens next for Andy? Will he maintain his abstinence and, if so, for how long? Will he manage to achieve some degree of controlled, social drinking at some point in his life? Or will the old pattern be re-established, and, if so, to what effect?

Andy has been offered help and has accepted it, but that is no guarantee that a lasting solution has been, or will be, found. And yet we should not be pessimistic. Many people do come through these experiences and do create new lifestyles in line with changes in the way that they think about themselves and process experiences which themselves are the result of engaging in a relational, therapeutic process.

Of course, for Andy, it could all go very wrong. He could go back to drinking heavily and, with his father's suicide and Terry suicidal intent in the family, leaves him at a heightened risk of a suicide attempt himself. A return to heavy drinking might prove the last straw for Julie, and losing her, well, who knows what reaction that would produce. He has come close to drink-driving and therefore losing his job. He could lose his relationship. He could lose his home. If he had to leave Julie—either by agreement or as a result of an injunction—where might he go? Young men are not high priorities on housing lists so it could be a hostel. He would mix with other heavy drinkers and could, so easily, find himself drinking on the street. I have seen this happen for people from all walks of life, and from all levels of the socio-economic continuum. One episode of drinking too much, or a particularly unacceptable set of behaviours that flow out of being alcohol-affected, and a dramatic downward spiral can be triggered.

Unresolved issues remain—further counselling to process the impact of Terry's death will be required and Andy may also have not fully come to terms with the effect of his mother's death either; there is the question of his sexual problem, whether his impotence will prove to be a temporary reaction to recent events or whether it will become more ingrained; and if he manages to avoid alcohol will he then aim for abstinence or controlled social-drinking? What will happen to Andy's mood? Mood often dips following detoxification, a result of the loss and the process of adjustment, but it should then lift once this phase has been negotiated. But for some it will not lift and a depressive state will be revealed independent of the alcohol use, perhaps to be resolved through on-going therapy or perhaps requiring a chemical intervention in the form of medication.

There is a strong likelihood that some form of couples work could be helpful to Andy and Julie as they seek to understand not only themselves, but each other, creating opportunity for them to strengthen their relationship. Both will have developed psychological patterns in response to the impact of a father's alcohol use. These may be similar, they may be different.

*   *   *   *

I do not believe we do enough to help people with alcohol problems in our society and I certainly do not think we provide enough education and alternative non-alcohol social environments to reduce the risk of alcohol use developing to a problematic level. Society has become, it seems, increasingly chemically affected. Substance use (including alcohol) is widespread and growing. Why does society need to have such a love affair with alcohol? Increased availability—longer opening times, more selling points—seems to be likely to increase use and therefore increase the levels of damage to health. Yes, staggered or longer opening times may reduce the intensity of alcohol-related violence and criminal activity associated with closing times being early and at the same time, but is it not reasonable to suppose that greater availability means the likelihood of higher consumption, and quite simply we know that the more you drink, the more your health is put at risk?

So what is the answer? What would help Andy? Perhaps if we could decide what would have helped Andy we will see what could contribute to the necessary changes at a wider, societal level to deal with alcohol and alcohol-related problems.

Andy's drunken and violent father. He needed treatment and clearly the children should have been protected from his violent behaviour. His mother needed protection. They should have been in a place of safety at the earliest opportunity. We need a society that recognises not only the right to a non-threatening domestic life, but that there should be systems in place to encourage the sense of responsibility within people to contribute to this. And services and refuges should be widely available to support and help people, particularly women although we know that men can also be victims of domestic violence.

Drinking from an early age. How and why was it available? Do we need to raise the age at which young people are served alcohol? Do we need much stronger educational messages, not only about the dangers of alcohol use and the need to treat it with respect, but also educational measures to encourage children to value health and well-being?

Traumatised in childhood. Where could Andy and Terry have gone to talk about what had happened? The need for more trained people to be available to work with young people is vital. And it needs to be specialists who can relate to young people who have been so affected, to help them realise that they are still good people with huge potential.

Steady, heavy drinking in the pub. Should pubs be allowed to sell more than the safe drinking limit to any one person in any given drinking session? Sound dramatic? It is. Maybe it's too radical, so what about reducing the strength of alcoholic drinks? If we can reduce the tar in tobacco, can we not reduce the alcohol in drinks? If we can contemplate banning people from smoking in certain public places in order to reduce passive smoking, can we not ban people from drinking in certain public places in order to reduce the risks associated with problematic alcohol use on the community?

Labelling of alcoholic drinks. Units should be printed on bottles and cans, and on pumps in bars, with an indication of how much of that particular drink will take the person over the safe drinking limit. Why not? What's most important in our society—the well-being and the opportunity of informed choice of the drinker, or the profitability of the alcohol industry?

Looking for help. How easy is it for people to access help for drinking problems? Andy found Graham who had experience in this area, but he had not gone straight to his GP or an Alcohol Treatment Service. Stigma and fear of information being held in patient notes is an issue here. Opportunity for low key advice and information for people needs to be available and in ways that ensure it is accessible and confidential.

Opening times and bar layout. Longer hours means more alcohol can be consumed. Standing room only means alcohol will be drunk more quickly and therefore more will be consumed over a given period of time. More seating must be available. Licenses for extended drinking hours must be monitored and statistics kept linking instances of drunkenness to particular outlets for alcohol.

A family member with a drink problem. How do you get help to them? Who will visit someone in response to a relative contacting a service or a GP? Often the only people are the paramedics and by then it may be too late. What support can be offered to family members to also inform and empower them to offer help and credible options to the person drinking problematically?

Drink driving. As a society we seem to want our freedom—and in particular a freedom to drink without interference and a freedom to drive our cars when and where we want to. Most people are able to manage this, but many cannot. At what point must enforced treatment orders be made for alcohol use? Do we ban all drinking and driving, making the limit much lower so that, in effect, one drink would take you over the limit but you would be OK if you had a large portion of sherry trifle?

Treatment—what really works? Do we really know? The *Alcohol Harm Reduction Strategy for England* calls for an audit of alcohol treatment services. I would urge that this be undertaken independently in order to risk it being skewed by prevailing fashions in addiction work. What does work? What research is still required in order to ascertain whether approaches not so widely used may actually have a significant effect? What really does successfully rehabilitate people? What does achieve lasting and sustainable change? For it has to be lasting and sustainable. Yet treatment must be set against the societal and attitudinal changes indicated above. And the judgement as to what constitutes effective treatment must take into account the uniqueness of the individual, and the relational component in the therapeutic and healing process. The truth is that a range of responses is going to be effective, and they will differ from person-to-person. We must avoid only selecting treatment responses that demonstrate effectiveness to the largest number. Any treatment that works must be available as part of the holistic response to alcohol problems.

The debate will continue. As with any addictive substance, the longer alcohol is used, the more it becomes an ingrained habit, the more the system (body and society) adjusts to that use, and more becomes necessary to achieve the same effect. Our society is perhaps at risk of developing—at a collective level—a kind of addictive personality.

I would suggest that we have to begin with two very simple questions:

- Why does a society collectively need to make a mood-altering, addictive and toxic substance like alcohol so widely available?
- What is the real motivation behind individual people feeling the need to experience to extreme the mood-altering effects of alcohol?

Until a society is prepared and able to honestly address these questions, it will remain at risk of spiralling down towards greater addiction to alcohol—society's favourite drug. We owe it to the many Andy's and Terry's at all stages of life to find a response.

Richard Bryant-Jefferies
April 2007

References and Suggested Reading

Addiction and Change. How Addictions Develop ad Addicted People Recover, by Carlo C. Di Clemente. The Guildford Press, New York and London 2003

Alcohol Use, edited by David B Cooper. Radcliffe Medical Press, Abingdon, Oxford. 2000

Counselling for Alcohol Problems, by Richard Velleman. 2nd Ed. Sage Publications Ltd. London. 2001

Counselling the Person Beyond the Alcohol Problem, by Richard Bryant-Jefferies. Jessica Kingsley Publishers, London. 2001

Counselling Young Binge Drinkers. by Richard Bryant-Jefferies. Radcliffe Medical Press, Abingdon, England. 2006

Dying for a Drink: a non-nonsense guide for heavy drinkers, by Dr Tim Cantopher. The Book Guild Ltd., Lewes, England. 1996

Motivational Interviewing, Preparing People to Change Addictive Behaviour. William M Miller and Stephen Rollnick. Guilford Press, New York and London. 1991

Over the Influence: the harm reduction guide for managing drugs and alcohol, by Pat Denning, Jeannie Little and Adina Glickman. The Guilford Press, New York 2004

Problem Drinking: A person centred dialogue, by Richard Bryant-Jefferies. Radcliffe Medical Press, Abingdon, England. 2003

Tackling Alcohol Together: The Evidence Base for a UK Alcohol Policy, edited by Duncan Raistrick, Ray Hodgson and Bruce Ritson. Free Association Books. London and New York. 1999.

The Alcohol Report, edited by Martin Plant and Douglas Cameron. Free Association Books Ltd., London and New York. 2000

978-0-595-44207-2
0-595-44207-2

Printed in the United Kingdom
by Lightning Source UK Ltd.
121789UK00001B/130-177/A